Silverheart

Michael Moorcock

&

Storm Constantine

EARTHLIGHT

LONDON · SYDNEY · NEW YORK · TOKYO · SINGAPORE · TORONTO

www.earthlight.co.uk

First published in Great Britain by Earthlight, 2000
An imprint of Simon & Schuster UK Ltd
A Viacom Company

1 3 5 7 9 10 8 6 4 2

Simon & Schuster UK Ltd
Africa House
64–78 Kingsway
London WC2B 6AH

Simon & Schuster Australia
Sydney

A CIP catalogue record for this book is available
from the British Library.

ISBN Hardback 0–684–86670–6
ISBN Trade Paperback 0–743–20943–5

Typeset by Palimpsest Book Production Limited,
Polmont, Stirlingshire
Printed and bound in the UK by
Selwood Printing Ltd., Burgess Hill, West Sussex

Silverheart

■ Acknowledgements to be supplied ■

CONTENTS

An extract from *Travels in Time* by Cornelius Begg

An extract from *Travels in Time* by Cornelius Begg

There's a city, they say, at the centre of the multiverse. It has been there since the beginning of Time.

The name of this city is Karadur-Shriltasi. Some would have you believe that she is no more than an illusion maintained by illusion; a mirage, that voyagers through the multiverse glimpse once and spend the rest of their lives seeking in vain.

Others say she is the very core of the multiverse, that the fate of the city determines the nature of all ordered matter in myriad worlds and countless realities.

Such disputes are of little consequence to most of us. Few have ever found Karadur-Shriltasi or gazed upon the Shren Diamond, the fabled Jewel of All Time, that came into being long before the city was built. It had been discovered in the distant past by a miner named Shren who had seen it glowing through a wall of solid rock. The Jewel is said to be the crystallized essence of the Original Matter, formed from swirling Chaos when Eternity began, from which all other matter derives.

Mere legend, perhaps? Or commonplace reality for those who live and die in Karadur-Shriltasi and never think to question the bizarre logic upon which their existence depends?

Many will inform you, most forcefully, that Karadur-Shriltasi does not and cannot exist. But I know that it does. I have travelled the moonbeam roads of the multiverse. I have been to the city, seen her splendours, and I can take you there. Words will be our vessel of light to this far-off destination.

We will journey to the centre of the multiverse, from where radiate all other realities, level upon level of universes, each with billions of inhabited worlds.

When I visited Karadur-Shriltasi, I found myself in a paradise of inspiring beauty, but in the taverns and gardens of this place I learned of the city's history. I heard a fabulous tale, one scarcely believable. 'Is this a fiction to gull tourists?' I asked my informants. But with guileless smiles they directed me to the Museum of the Metal and there I saw for myself the ancient evidence: machines from the past, careful chronicles and works of art.

In Karadur, before our tale begins, the city stood in arrogant isolation upon a vast plain of ice. She was known only as Karadur then, and the reason for this is part of the tale. Lacking contact with other realities, perhaps the spirit of the city herself believed she was the only reality – the best of all possible worlds, denying decay, defying destruction. Yet those who knew of her existence, adepts who could gaze into the most hidden areas of the multiverse, predicted she was doomed to collapse beneath the weight of her rulers' extraordinary, all-encompassing self-deception, their own stifling orthodoxy.

Seen from the ice, the city appeared through the chill mist as an asymmetrical mound, its tall, glittering buildings of brick and stone bound about with collars and cuffs of iron, steel, gold and brass. From above, Karadur's four circular quarters could easily be discerned, each a fief of one of the ruling Metal clans. Between the quarters, forming a square of the entire city, were the free zones, traditionally the habitat of lowlifes, criminals and misfits, who either shunned true city life or else had been outcast from it. The zones were surrounded by covered farms, where the city's crops and herds were husbanded, and the entrances to mines, which burrowed beneath the ice.

In the centre of Karadur rose the great Guild Tower, a masterpiece in metal, dedicated to the power of the city's rulers. Each of the Guild Tower's four main girders, or 'legs', was cast in a metal specific to each of the great Lords of the Metal – Iron, Silver, Gold and Copper – whose inviolable authority maintained stability and law within the city. In turn, the girders were bound about with bands of other metals, to symbolize the unity and strength of the Lords of the city.

Far back in its history, Karadur had been divided into its four quarters, each under the jurisdiction of a great Clan of the Metal and named for some ancient, hallowed artisan. Thus Clan Silver controlled Akra Quarter,

Clan Iron controlled Peygron Quarter, Clan Gold ruled in Ihrn, while Clan Copper had responsibility for Shinlech. Each clan had a great dwelling, built in the centre of their circular quarters to represent its power and aspirations, as well as the qualities of its clan metal. Clan Silver inhabited the fabulously structured Moonmetal Manse, while Clan Copper resided within Verdigris House. Clan Iron proudly maintained the simple title of 'The Old Forge' for their massive pile. The Old Forge was a vast foundry complex within which were arranged the living quarters of the Clan. The foundry was worked by the descendants of the ancient Leadworkers Guild: massive foundrymen, who had their own codes and culture.

Only Clan Gold no longer used its traditional seat – the gloomy Gragonatt Fortress, which had been transformed into a prison. Instead, the Golds occupied a smaller and more elegant palace known as New Mint Yard, which was situated close to one of the free zones.

By long tradition, the mechanical militia of the Metal, known as the Roaring Boys and the Blinding Boys, were refused entrance into the free zones. These areas were occupied by the so-called 'free poor', who claimed loyalty to no clan. Generally, the poor supplied labour for all the great factories of the city, except for the foundry of The Old Forge. Their independence had long been guaranteed, for they controlled the city's four great wells, from which came all her fresh water. Each well lay at the heart of a free zone.

It might have seemed as if the noble clans, the regular citizens and the poor of the free zones lived in close harmony, relying upon one another for survival in that hostile territory. But increasingly the citizens had grown impatient with their Lords, who had no real contact with the people and whose justice was abstract and sometimes inappropriate. The city was slowly decaying. Brick and stone were crumbling within their corsets of metal. What had to be done? Couldn't the clans see what was happening? The Lords of the Metal, however, in haughty isolation, believed themselves to be both just and humane, and saw it as their holy duty to maintain the city exactly as she had always been. The concept of change was anathema to them. Perhaps they were indeed blind to the dissolution creeping all about their ancient palaces. If a building sagged, they simply ordered it to be buttressed with more girders of iron or steel. An additional rank of golden gargoyles could hide a listing eave. Metal was both protection and strength. It had always been so.

All the ruling families of Karadur were related to the Clans, often by marriages which created amalgams – thus the marriage of old Lord Septimus Tin and the young Lady Augusta Silver had produced Sir Clovis Pewter. There were hundreds of Brasses and Bronzes, not to mention the powerful Steels, who were closely bound to the Iron family and helped them to control the massive foundries, which continued to pour artefacts out into the shivering, unstable streets of a city beginning to show her age. Death was, of course, an inevitable consequence of old age.

But there were legends in Karadur that predicted a very different fate for the city. Down in the backstreets of the free zones, where ragged savants debated their philosophies over tankards of musty ale, it was said that death would be usurped by change. If Karadur could only rediscover her own salvation, she'd bring salvation to the entire multiverse. The layers of reality, which over the millennia had begun to bend and fracture, would be revitalized, fully prepared once more for the perpetual struggle between Life and Death – what some called Good and Evil.

In keeping with such legends, the outcome was reputed to depend, rather unfairly, upon the shoulders of a single man, a young man with no notion of his fate, who would never willingly accept such a responsibility. Some even dared to conjecture that this man already lived among them, that they knew his name. But such speculations were only whispers, hopeful dreams drowned in puddles of ale. For if the legends were correct, and this man really existed, he would be master of the subtle energies of creation and destruction, what was commonly termed magic.

The Lords of Karadur denied the existence of the occult sciences. Following the dark ages of the Clan Wars, some millennia in the past, the then newly created Council of the Metal had made it a crime to study sorcery, or any related subject. Similarly, the use of electricity had been outlawed, for it was a force that could not be perceived with the naked eye. During the Clan Wars, the subtle powers of the multiverse had been misused to devastating effect. Their manipulation was seen as corrupting, essentially wrong. Thus the great Reformation occurred. Only steam power was permitted, for its breath could be seen and felt by all. It was real before the senses, wholesome, the natural way to power machinery. Electricity was too mysterious to trust and enabled all manner of bizarre devices to threaten the stability of the city. It placed too much power in individual hands. During the Wars, its use had brought the world close to ruin. It had permitted the creation of all kinds of insane devices, such as thinking machines whose ambitions none could control. Thus it was with magic and other false sciences. Those who had courted such delusory powers had always lost control. The students of black, aggressive arts were condemned, punished and disciplined, for they threatened the security and peace of mind of the entire community. The arcane forces of the multiverse were mutable and unstable. They precipitated change.

Magic, said the Lords, did not exist. Those who claimed to practise it were tricksters and liars at best. Charlatans by definition. Therefore, anyone discovered practising the forbidden arts was accused of Public Deception and punished. The worst offenders found themselves in the gloomy Gragonatt Fortress, where they were re-educated but rarely released. None escaped the Fortress. Like magic, said the Lords, escape was impossible.

But statements such as this are fragile, simply made to be disproved. The multiverse, being the essence of change, cannot resist finding cracks in the structure of belief and seeping through with all its perplexing contradictions. After all, if conditions had remained the same in Karadur, until it had merely rusted into the ice and been forgotten, there would be no tale to tell. When great changes occur, they often begin in the gutters, the meanest hovels, the haunts of thieves. And so it was in Karadur.

Book One

Dreams and Disasters

Chapter One

A Thief in Gragonatt

In the dim light of the steam carriage, Lady Melodia Gold looked hungry, but not for food. The gold-pleated tissue of her gown spilled from the front of her red velvet cloak, which was laced tight against the cold. Lord Prometheus Iron, sitting opposite her, observed the extraordinary eagerness in her expression, which she sought to hide beneath a mask of chill disdain. This hunger slightly disgusted him. His own interest in the task ahead was more academic. He wanted to interview the prisoners as much as Melodia did – they'd been caught in the process of stealing some of her jewellery from New Mint Yard – but his motives were more complex, even to himself.

The cold was a predatory beast on the darkened streets that led to the prison building, Gragonatt Fortress, which lay in the centre of Ihrn fief. Night was always a punishing time in Karadur. The chill that had crept in off the ice sought to freeze and still the mechanisms of the carriage, so that the furnace in the forecabin would flicker away. Then the breath of night might investigate the cooling interior and put the blue mark of death upon the passengers within. A cast-iron grille beneath the seats exhaled warm, stuffy breath from the engine up front, but without it the travellers might freeze and die.

The only other passenger was Captain Cornelius Coffin, who sat on the same plush bench as Lord Iron but some distance away from him. Coffin was dressed in a severe steel-studded black uniform and a thick black coat, which hung open. His wide-brimmed beaten-iron hat lay on the seat beside him. His face was strong-featured and square-jawed and always appeared slightly unshaven, whatever the time of day. Coffin looked both eager and gloating, clearly aware he was due praise, if not promotion. So far, Lord Iron had remained purposefully tight-lipped about the reason for their journey that evening. He had made it clear that before he made any assessment he would have to see for himself if the man now incarcerated in the Fortress was indeed the infamous thief Max Silverskin.

Silverskin had been an irritant for years. Bad blood. Something wrong with him. The parentage was dubious, after all. His father had been a nobleman of Clan Silver, who for reasons known only to himself, but which were probably no more than simple lust, had taken up with a distant cousin, a woman of the Silverskin family, who were a minor tributary of the Silver Clan. Maximilian had been the unfortunate fruit of this imprudent union. The Silverskins had always been questionable characters, obviously non-conformists no matter how much they tried to justify themselves as innovators and thinkers. They lived at the edge of Akra fief, as close to the free zones as it was possible to get without being part of them. The Silverskin women had reputations associated with banned or unwholesome arts and the whole family was famous for its heresies. Clan Silver had refused to countenance a marriage between the two. Neither was it known when or where August Silver and Sophelia Silverskin had actually married, though the most fanciful stories suggested their wedding had taken place in one of the legendary Cities of the Rim, which lay far beyond the visible horizon. Other tales declared the eloping couple had escaped to the Ice Caverns below the surface of the plain, where it was rumoured that entire towns existed. These were undoubtedly only fantasies, but there wasn't now a person in Karadur who could or would venture onto the ice in an attempt to see whether any of the stories were true. For a start, the journey would be impossible. Steam carriages could only travel a short distance from the city before they seized up, and no one could survive on the ice without transport. In the distant past, a few reckless souls had set out to explore, but none had ever returned to confirm the accounts of fabulous Cities of the Rim or underground lands.

Lord Iron did not, for a moment, believe the romantic notions that Max's parents had died or disappeared out on the ice or in some mythical landscape. It was ridiculous to think that some strange denizen of the frozen waste had brought the child back to Karadur, where he'd been taken in by kind-hearted people of the zones. Iron knew exactly what had really happened. Silverskins' parents had run into the warrens of the free zones and had there lived with the lowlifes, until becoming ultimately their prey. What happened next was well known. The boy had been fostered by the questionable Menevek Vane, obviously a miscreant of the lowest order. It had only been Vane's persistence that, when Max was nine years old, had eventually persuaded Clan Silver to relent, declare the boy one of their own and take him back into the bosom of his family. No doubt Vane had hoped to ingratiate himself with the Clan, but he'd been proved wrong there. The doors of the Moonmetal Manse had slammed in his face.

Maximilian's acceptance by his family had never worked. Despite the best in education and the guidance of more honourable peers, Max had turned out bad. He baulked at authority, even as a child committing innumerable indiscretions and petty crimes within the confines of the Moonmetal Manse. Lord Iron knew the trouble Silver had had with him. Later, of course, when the boy became more self-aware, his excursions out into the city had led to all sorts of problems. He was attracted to scum, no doubt the legacy of his mother's blood, and clearly felt more at home in the free zones than in the respectable atmosphere of Akra. No amount of discipline and punishment had curbed his criminal urges. He'd actually stolen from the Clan Houses, apparently taking delight in the consternation this caused. What was worse, the lowlifes of the city looked upon him as a kind of folk hero, which had undoubtedly contributed towards his self-important disregard for tradition. Eventually, Silver had had no option but to cast out the embarrassing by-blow. It was hoped that this indignity would chasten him, that once the privileges of palace life were lost to him he'd recognize the error of his ways and reform. Clan Silver had been confident the reprobate son would come crawling back to them, begging for readmittance. Unfortunately, the opposite had proved true.

Among the free zones and the markets of the city proper, Max Silverskin had claimed he'd left his Clan of his own volition and had publicly scorned the long-held orthodoxies of the Metal. He had adopted his mother's name of Silverskin and bore it like a banner in defiance of the Moonmetal Manse, whose protection and disciplines he had rejected and abused. By taking his mother's name, he had declared himself in opposition to all the Lords of the Metal stood for. Now, the scum of the zones viewed him as a herald for their witless causes. With verminous cunning, Silverskin did more than live up to his reputation. He had continued to steal from Clan Houses and revile their names. No more, though. For years, Captain Coffin had hunted the thief, the self-styled Fox of Akra, and now he'd trapped him. Fortunate that there were still lowlifes prepared to accept a bribe for information. One of Silverskin's own tribe of reprobates had betrayed him. This had enabled Coffin to corner and arrest Silverskin and charge him with the loathsome crime of Public Deceit, as well as the lesser violation of Common Larceny. It had been convenient that Silverskin had had no help from his mother's family. The Silverskins might spout heresies, but they were obviously too cowardly to shield a wanted criminal in their midst.

Lost in these aggravating thoughts, Lord Iron arranged his grey robes around him more securely and uttered a tut of disapproval, which conjured curious glances from his fellow passengers. The mere idea of the Silverskins annoyed him. Despite being shunned by respectable society, the family still persisted in their delusions. More than one Silverskin had claimed to possess actual knowledge of the Cities of the Rim and the lands that lay beneath the ice and, in days when they'd possessed more credibility, had sought to initiate exploratory expeditions. Such ideas were not only forbidden but dangerous. They had provoked stringent punishment. During the disruptive early years of the Reformation, Silverskins had died in the Brass Jester and on Old Granny's Skillet, two legendary instruments of torture still exhibited in the great Museum of the Metal in the Shinlech fief of Clan Copper. Now the Law was far more humane. Instead, it sentenced miscreants to Gragonatt Fortress for re-education.

Lord Iron twitched aside the heavy woollen curtain of the observation port. Outside, the cityscape was shrouded in the eternal mist that rose from the ice at night and drifted throughout the city, freezing to a crust upon the roads and buildings as it went. The carriage's metal wheels threw up a vicious spray of glittering shards from the road that tinkled against the sides of the vehicle. And there, ahead, the Fortress itself, rearing up against the indigo sky. It was crafted of a strange fusion of stone and metal, huge and impregnable, an image of human suffering worked in its bulk and severe lines. This was the symbol of law and order in Karadur. It represented the immutable truth that crime would not be tolerated. Criminals, by their very nature, were deceitful and duplicitous.

Now Max Silverskin and Menevek Vane would be sentenced to a lifetime of re-education in the Fortress – from which not so much as a scream had escaped in all the millennia of its existence.

Gragonatt Fortress was a product of the Clan Wars, when the noble families of Karadur had built themselves impregnable cities within cities, wasting generation after generation of workers to realize their architectural dreams. Countless healthy bodies had broken upon the unyielding basalt, so that the rock itself had bloomed with rich young blood. The Fortress was all that remained of that dark period of civil strife, and had been a prison for most of its existence. No place for a person of spirit. It was hard to imagine that once the elegant Clan Gold had lived within it, but that had been uncountable years before and the building had undergone many structural changes since then.

Lord Iron glanced at Melodia, who was also looking out of the port. Did she imagine herself dwelling there, imprisoned by the severe walls, gazing out wistfully at the mist-veiled spires of Karadur?

'Nearly there,' Coffin announced unnecessarily. He shifted in his seat.

Lord Iron both respected and despised the Captain. He was efficient but officious, diligent but often petty. It was also apparent he harboured an affection for Lord Iron's daughter, the Lady Rose. What was he thinking of? True, the man had dragged himself up from the gutters sufficiently to own a modest fortune. Also, if the captive in Gragonatt really was Silverskin, Coffin would soon add to his fortune the substantial reward the Clans had put up for Max's capture. Coffin had revolutionized the security forces of the city. His private army of brutal 'Irregulars' – who were kin to the honest foundrymen but appeared more like monstrous throwbacks to the dawn of humanity – policed the streets with greater and greater impunity. The free-zones were nominally under the jurisdiction of their inhabitants, and the Clans of the Metal were by tradition barred from their streets. This did not stop Coffin and his Irregulars from roaming them at will, behaving with increasing arrogance. The free zoners naturally objected to this and continually sent deputations to the Lords of the Metal, demanding that Coffin's men should be prevented from entering their territory. In view of recent civil unrest, however, the petitions were ignored.

The majority of the Irregulars had been drawn from the ranks of outcast foundrymen who had been banished from their families for worshipping at unwholesome shrines. Religion was seen as a sickness in Karadur, a delusion spawned by fear. Reasonable people were not subject to such fears. Coffin had offered his recruits a re-education of sorts. They were massively muscled men of few words, who were adept with every kind of skinning knife and flensing tool a butcher could dream of owning. When times were slack, many Irregulars worked in the slaughterhouses, where it was supposed they achieved considerable job satisfaction. Coffin insisted they had abandoned the practice of adoring their secret goddess, Sekmet, who was the old pagan deity of the Foundry, scoured from history since the Reformation. When Coffin had first introduced the Irregulars to impress the Lords with their effectiveness, they had been tolerated by the Clans. The Lords' own mechanical guards, the Roaring Boys and the Blinding Boys, had begun to show signs of decrepitude, despite their enormous power. They were likely to lock up suddenly, in a spray of sparks, and emit choking clouds of steam. A familiar sight in Karadur was of teams of mekkaphants – half-organic beasts of burden created in the Foundry – towing away mechanical failures for repair.

Captain Coffin was openly contemptuous of the automated constables. They could no longer keep the peace. The likes of Silverskin were able to run rings round them most of the time. The Captain made plain his view that they were redundant and should be scrapped, replaced by his own efficient force. Reluctantly, the Lords had partly complied and now paid him for his services, while still retaining some control via their ailing Battle Boys.

No doubt Coffin thought that once the million-platinum-mirror reward was safely in his hands, his power and influence would equal that of the

Lords themselves. Lord Iron shrugged contemptuously. *Let him think it.* He had his uses.

The carriage puffed to a halt at the gates of the Fortress. The driver sounded the horn. Guards within the Fortress, who had no doubt been watching the visitors approach and had recognized the crest of Clan Iron fluttering from the carriage's forecabin, began to unseal their domain. First, a great portcullis squealed upwards, followed by the agonized opening scrape of three sets of metal-bound doors. Mist swirled at ground level. The Fortress was mostly dark within, lit by the feverish glow of a few torches. The carriage surged beneath the shadow of the gates and stood panting in a shawl of steam in the great courtyard beyond.

Lord Iron alighted from the vehicle and held out his hand to assist Lady Melodia down to the rusting cobbles. Captain Coffin jumped out nimbly beside them and slapped his hands together, exhaling plumes of smoking breath. 'Ah, here's Mantwick,' he said, nodding his head towards the large man emerging from a lighted doorway.

Mantwick, governor of the Fortress, bowed respectfully to Lord Iron and Lady Gold. 'Welcome, Lords. The prisoners are ready for your inspection.'

Lord Iron made a fastidious gesture. 'Lead on. We have little time. We have to attend the final ceremony of the Jewel in a couple of hours.'

'This way, Lords.' Mantwick gestured for them to enter the building.

Within, the Fortress was haunted by the distant hiss of steam and the churning of great machinery as shifts of prisoners toiled in the workshops. The air was oddly scentless, which always surprised Lord Iron. With so many miscreants packed in together, he expected the rotten effluvia of their corruption to fill the air with foulness. Mantwick led the group down a series of metal-walled passages lined with doors, all of which had closed observation windows at eye level. Halfway down one corridor, Mantwick paused and lifted the keys from his belt. He unlocked the door before him and pushed it open. Lord Iron and Captain Coffin entered the cell together.

The walls of the cell were all of polished metal, reflections from which must have made the eyes ache after a period of incarceration. The prisoners were sitting on the floor, their hands and feet shackled. 'Maximilian Silverskin and Menevek Vane,' announced Mantwick in a toneless voice.

Lord Iron drew in a breath through his nose, conscious of the rustle of Lady Melodia's gown behind him. There was no doubt the prisoners were who Coffin claimed them to be. Max had sunk low. At twenty-six, he had already reached the end of useful life. His pale hair was lank about his shoulders, his eyes deep sunk. Where was his dashing mien now? He looked defeated, dazed, while Vane simply looked old and worn out, his greying dark hair a lunatic mane about his face.

'It was only a matter of time before you found yourself here, Max,' Lord Iron said.

Lady Melodia stalked past him. 'Where is my ring, scum? Where is it?'

Silverskin merely gaped up at her, as if mindless. His face bore the bruises and swellings of an earlier beating.

'My lady,' Captain Coffin murmured, stepping forward. 'Allow me.' He leaned down and struck the prisoner hard across the face, making his head slam against the metal wall behind him. 'Answer the lady, that's a good boy.'

Silverskin shook his head, perhaps trying to gather his senses rather than simply refusing to answer.

'He must have it,' Melodia said coldly. 'It was not recovered from the scene. It was my grandmother's. I want it.'

Lord Iron didn't care about the missing jewellery. He was curious about Max Silverskin. Some part of him felt Max should be disposed of quietly and neatly. There was something dangerous about him, a whiff of chaos. But another part of him wanted Max alive, to understand him somehow. There was something compelling about Silverskin. Perhaps if he was ugly, this would not be so. Was a handsome countenance enough to save a man from execution? He was an enigma, certainly. How could anyone voluntarily give up a life of privilege for one of common criminality? He wasn't a stupid person. As a boy, his mind had outshone those of the majority of his Clan siblings. Max could have had a great future but he'd thrown it away. 'What are we to do with you, Max?' Lord Iron said, shaking his head.

Max smiled crookedly, rather madly. Lord Iron wondered whether the beating he'd received had affected his brain.

'You'll get no sense from him,' Coffin said with a sneer. 'The legend is bigger than the man. Disappointing, really. I'd expected more.'

Lord Iron said nothing. Coffin was a dolt, in that he had no idea what was before him. Still, he'd done his work well. That was all that mattered.

'My ring,' said Lady Melodia.

Coffin raised his hand, clearly relishing the prospect of striking Max again.

'There is no ring,' Menevek Vane said abruptly, in a croaking voice. 'If there was, wouldn't you have found it?'

Coffin bunched his fist, but Lord Iron reached out and stayed his hand. 'There is nothing to be gained from that,' he said coldly.

'They must have it,' said Melodia.

'Max, you know you must remain here, don't you?' Iron said. 'You have brought this upon yourself. I only hope that the hospitality of Mr Mantwick will eventually drum some sense into you. When you are older and wiser, perhaps you may return to life in Karadur. In the meantime, you can help yourself by revealing the names of your confederates in the free zones. I should imagine that one year could be knocked off your sentence for each name you give us.'

Max said nothing, blinking stupidly.

'Insolent wretch!' Coffin snarled, kicking Max's legs.

Lord Iron gritted his teeth. Whatever Max was, or had become, he still carried Clan blood and it galled the Lord to see him being abused by an outclan. 'Max, I'm sure you appreciate that it would be better for you to comply. Neither I nor any of your family can help you here. It grieves me to see a scion of the Silver sink to this state. You owe it to your Clan and yourself to salvage what you can from this sad circumstance.'

'He needs no help from you,' said Vane. 'And why should he care for his so-called Clan? Where are they? They don't give a fish about him.'

Lord Iron ignored the man. He was nothing, even if he did regard himself as Max's surrogate father. 'Think on my words,' Lord Iron said softly. 'I shall return.' He turned to the Captain. 'Come, Coffin, we must leave.'

'But my grandmother's ring,' said Lady Melodia. 'We still know nothing.'

'Perhaps you mislaid it,' said Lord Iron. 'Have your servants search your rooms again.' He marched from the cell and his companions, rather reluctantly, followed.

The door slammed shut and gradually the gaslights dimmed to leave the prisoners in darkness, which was actually preferable to being blinded by harsh reflections from the shining walls. The lights would remain out for six hours. Max expelled a groan and felt Menni's hand grip his shoulder. 'There, lad. There,' the man said gruffly. The only comfort he could offer was human contact.

'They'll kill us,' Max murmured. 'With small abuses every day. With torment. With boredom, with darkness.'

'No, lad, no. We'll work the machines like every other poor sod in this place. We can make it.'

'That is not life,' Max said. 'Even if Coffin doesn't try to kill me, I'll die anyway. I can feel it already. If my body lives, it will be without a soul.'

'Come on, buck up. This isn't like you.'

Max uttered a sorrowful caustic laugh. 'There's nothing left of me. We were careless and stupid.'

'We always danced on the edge of a blade,' Menni said. 'We both knew it. Luck turned away and we tripped. It was a risk we took.'

Many variations on this theme had been played since they'd been brought to Gragonatt a few days before. Menni had suffered less than Max. The guards seemed to take pleasure in abusing a fallen member of the Clans. Max had harboured the hope – ridiculously, as he now realized – that Clan Silver would be so ashamed to have one of their kind incarcerated in Gragonatt that they'd pull strings to get him out. But no Silver had come to visit him and even the head of the Council of Guilds, Lord Iron, lacked the power or desire to help him. Max felt he'd lived a lie, laughing in the face of the Clans, robbing them, teasing them. He'd thought himself invincible. Now, sore and hopeless, he realized that ultimately he'd only been playing, like a child. The adult hand of authority had slapped down and curbed him. He was powerless. Sighing, he lay back and rested his head on Menni's lap, the lap of the man who was the closest to a father he'd ever had. Menni shouldn't be here. He wouldn't live to see the day of release. If it came at all, it would be decades into the future.

'Sleep, lad,' said Menni, laying a rough hand on Max's hair, which was spiky with dried blood.

'Sleep for ever,' Max mumbled. He could feel feathery clouds closing about him, smothering him, pressing him down into a dark place in his mind.

There came to him a strange dream. Thin sheets of brilliantly polished metal clattered and flashed before his eyes and then melted into a shining fluid that poured over him like mercury. He would drown in it.

He heard a mighty roaring voice, the cry of metal itself. His flesh was flayed by flames, as if he was being reforged from white-hot steel. He could almost feel the hammers pounding him into existence.

Blind, he heard voices about him, whispering, cruel and quick. A scream lanced his ears, which he realised was his own. Sight returned in gouts of brilliant light. He was awash in quicksilver, sliding down a helter-skelter of iron.

Max's whole being, his very soul, was filled with a mighty, rhythmic pounding: the spiteful hiss of steam, the crack of sparking furnaces. A flying shadow passed briefly across the all-destroying, all-creating blaze. It seemed to be an immense mechanical owl, fashioned from glowing bronze.

Blackness again. The dolour of bells in his ears.

Max opened his eyes. His head was encased in a pressure that had no visible cause. By dim light that had no source, he saw he was in his cell, lying on the floor. He was aware of someone else being present and could see Menni asleep nearby. But it was not his mentor's presence he could sense. Someone else. An invisible visitor.

Max scrambled to his knees. This must still be a dream. He could see no one but felt as if there was someone very close to him, their face inches from his own.

'Who are you?' Max murmured, and his voice hissed like steam.

Scarlet flames burst before his eyes, a burning brand. He shied away, shielding his face with his hands, but could see what appeared to be a helmet looming before him. It was fashioned of iron and rimmed with gold. At its centre pulsed a circle of copper, pale green and terracotta.

Max shaded his eyes and tried to discern who wore this helmet, but it was impossible. The light of the brand concealed more than it revealed. Now it flared and swooped towards him. Max uttered an instinctive cry of horror and covered his eyes. He was pushed backwards and a heavy pressure fell upon his shoulders, pinning him down. Iron-gloved hands ripped away his shirt. Max was consumed by pain as white heat was thrust against his naked chest. His unseen visitor meant to murder him, burn him with the brand. He could feel the flames eating into his flesh, transforming it to cinders, eating down to his heart. Pain. Confusion. Heat and light. His own screams like the cruel lament of crows that roosted in Gragonatt's lofty eaves.

Then someone was shaking him. 'Max! Max!' It was Menni. Max opened his eyes, blinked. It seemed the cell was filled with blue-white radiance, even though the gas lamps were still dead. How was that possible? Then he realized the source of the light was himself. A blinding effulgence emanated from the centre of his chest. He scrabbled backwards, staring down at his body. A disc of silver blazed over his heart, sending out spiralling rays of light. Was this real? Was he still dreaming? His body was scored by claws of terrible pain. He could not think, focus.

'Max, lie still.' Menni's voice was ragged, edged with fear.

Max couldn't obey. He could see his reflection distorted in the metal walls. His head had turned to metal; iron and gold, with a circle of copper edged in pale green at the centre. His mouth opened and closed, his eyes rolled, but they were made of iron. He tugged at his head, trying to pull it away, sure his real self of flesh and blood still existed beneath it. But it would not come free. The metal had become one with his flesh. And in the centre of his chest burned the disc of silver.

Menni was still speaking urgently, but Max could not hear the words. His head filled with a humming, crackling sound. Menni's face was a mask of disbelief and fear. It was he who was backing away now. His hand shook as he pointed at Max's chest.

Max could hear words now, but they were not Menni's. They existed only inside Max's head. 'You are doomed and blessed, son of silver. Fulfil your destiny – or die. Discover what you are or may be, for you are now truly of silver heart.'

Max uttered a cry and tried to claw the glowing silver disc from his chest. But it had bonded with his flesh. Wrenching at it was like trying to tear out his own heart. He couldn't do it. His senses shrieked in horror.

The dream world engulfed him abruptly once more, but this time with tranquillity. He and Menni drifted on their backs, side by side, in a calm sea of liquid silver. All the colours of the Metal swirled lazily around them. There was nothing else. The ocean was endless limbo.

Then a faint sound, gradually growing louder: the tolling of a monstrous bell.

Out of the ocean, shapes began to form. Max saw a great city rearing upwards. Outlined in metal, a soaring central tower dominated the fantastic roofs and domes, the turrets and chimneys. The structure seemed almost organic, flickering and shifting in the weird light. The stones and bricks of its buildings were bound and buttressed, tied with beams and bands of iron and steel, decorated with gold, silver, bronze, tin and brass. Its stained glass was rimmed with gleaming lead. What was this place? Could it be the legendary Shriltasi, the city of dreams that Max had heard tales of as a child? Menni had always told him the stories weren't true, that there was no magical city hidden beneath the ice, but for some years in his childhood Max had been obsessed with the idea. He had even searched for it. Perhaps Shriltasi existed only beyond life and this was no dream, but death.

Once the city had fully emerged from the ice, the metal ocean began to cool. Its colours faded to misty steel-blue and then, eventually, to blue-white. Ice. It spread outwards in all directions, to every horizon. Nothing but flat, pale ice under a strange, unchanging sky where no sun burned.

The dark city reposed upon a great crag of limestone, perhaps the peak of some buried mountain. It was not Shriltasi, for Max recognized it now. Karadur. She was beautiful and terrible. Fire and smoke constantly curled around her tall towers and massive masonry, filling the surrounding sky and bringing a false, hellish night.

'Max, Max!'

Max was hauled painfully from the dream. He opened his eyes. He was cold, so cold. Menni was shaking him. They were enclosed in chill fog. Another dream? Max moved and winced. His chest burned. Someone had struck him with a flaming brand, that was it. What had happened? Why were they so cold? Had the Fortress been breached to let in the night?

'We're out!' Menni cried. 'Don't ask me how or why – I don't know what happened – but we're out. Must have been an explosion in the workshops. Get to your feet, Max. We may not have much time.'

Dazed, Max peered around himself, unable to obey Menni's frantic command immediately. They were not only outside Gragonatt but the city itself. Karadur was ahead of them, only a hundred yards or so away. 'Someone came,' he said. 'Into the cell . . . Freed us.'

'No,' Menni said. 'Get up, Max.' He began pulling at Max's arms. 'I was dozing. You were still lying across me. Then it happened. I don't know what. It was like being punched by the sky. I fell, or was thrown, then we were here. Lucky to be alive. Our bodies were relaxed.'

Thick mats of fog swirled around them but Max thought he could make out the stark lines of Gragonatt's upper storeys rearing above the city. It looked intact. He tried to point, say something, but Menni wouldn't listen. He had the walls of Karadur in his sight and was clearly determined to reach them, before pursuit came from the Fortress or the cold froze the life from them. Max stumbled forward but was brought to his knees by a sharp, crippling pain in his chest.

'What is it? Are you hurt?' Menni looked almost impatient that that might be the case.

Max touched the fabric of his shirt. Something beneath it. Something hard, retaining heat. 'It's nothing,' he said.

Chapter Two

The Council of the Metal

One year later

High above the Old Forge, in the central tower of his family domain, Lord Prometheus Iron waited in his Camera Obscura for the arrival of the Lords who comprised the Upper Council of the Metal. Iron embodied each and every one of his city's certainties. He prided himself upon being an epitome of unyielding righteousness, possessed of an unquestioning belief in everything Karadur was and ever would be. To the majority of the citizens, he was the supreme symbol of stability and justice, everything that was ancient and good. He was head of the Council, elected every five years. Clan Iron had always enjoyed this position. No one had ever challenged or wanted to change it – until recently.

To pass the time, Lord Iron examined the alleys and plazas of the city through the great lens of the Camera. It was one of the greatest achievements of his inventor ancestors. Through a series of lenses and prisms the Camera could spy into every section of the city and produce upon the floor a moving, living map. By manipulating certain complicated levers, specific areas of Karadur could be magnified up to life size. Details of each of the four quarters could be singled out. The steam-driven hydraulics, which powered the complex clockwork, were almost indestructible monuments to the ancient Metal Masters, when curiosity and creativity had still been valued and cultivated as diligently as rigid orthodoxy was now.

Iron manipulated the levers so that an image of the Grand Central Market was displayed upon the floor. This was the heart of the city, where most of its important business was conducted – from the sale of hardware to exchanges of information concerning the most secret and significant actions of government. Its myriad levels disappeared high into an ill-lit gloom where, in ancient legend, a sleeping she-griffin awaited a particular call.

The Grand Market was one of the oldest, largest and most mysterious buildings in Karadur. It sheltered beneath the central Guild Tower, the soaring monument to the power of the Clans, that loomed over smoky Karadur as if to demonstrate the permanence and strength of the Metal Masters who'd built it.

The market area was a warren of narrow lanes, constructed on many tiers, with long galleries, festooned with sneering gargoyles, stretching into distant gloom. The streets were lined with stalls selling garden produce, kitchen tools, meat, jewellery, beverages, flowers, pets, clothing and shoes. On every level, cafés and food kiosks could be found, as well as lottery booths and shops of a thousand kinds. It was said that anything could be bought or sold at the Grand Market – including souls and consciences. Sparking copper-and-brass cages rode up and down in iron shafts, groaning beneath the weight of passengers being carried from tier to tier.

This vast, bustling area was dominated by the Jewel of All Time, which was set in the main hall upon a tall, slender plinth, crafted elaborately from gold, silver, copper and platinum, shrouded by a globe of translucent glass. At the very beginning of Karadur's history, the miner, Shren, had discovered it. When he'd carried it reverently to the first Masters of the Metal, its power had been recognized and respected. The alchemists of the clans had examined the jewel and learned that its light possessed life-giving qualities. They had installed it at the heart of the nascent city, as a symbol of greatness to come, and since then it had cast its light upon Karadur. In shape, it resembled a faceted pink diamond; in size, a man's head. It was the only legitimate object that still represented the old power that had been shunned during the Reformation. Its light was subtle but powerful. Its energy kept the city alive, or so the superstitious believed. Even when the Lords had destroyed many artefacts forged during the Wars, they had not dared to touch the Jewel. Now it was regarded more as a curio, a symbol of the light of reason.

The Jewel was the chief source of light in the enclosed market. Through the course of a year its energy began to fade but it was replenished annually by the rays of the Ruby Moon, a strange celestial body that appeared only briefly. At present the Jewel was nearing the end of its cycle, which meant the citizens had to supplement its light with their own lamps.

On the night of the Ruby Moon, the Jewel of All Time was taken from the cover of the market square so that it could bathe in the Moon's rays for the course of a single night. On the day before this event, the Upper Council of the Metal would present themselves to the citizens of Karadur to hear complaints and dispense justice not achieved by the Lesser Council of the Metal and its Magistrates. Once night fell, the Ruby Moon would rise and feed the Jewel with her caustic rays.

Karadur was in a celebratory mood in anticipation of the annual Carnival of the Ruby Moon. There would be theatrical displays and masked balls. Ale and wine would flow too copiously. That evening, Lord Iron and his daughter were due to attend a ball at Clan Copper's Verdigris House to celebrate the Jewel's replenishment. Iron held the event in slight distaste. He was not a person for frivolous merriment and over-indulgence in eating and drinking. Still, Rose might enjoy it. She ought to keep more company of her own age. Lord Iron was proud of his daughter's apparent academic leanings. He knew she spent a lot of time in the libraries of the clans – particularly Clan Silver, whose collection was second to none. Rose was well-read, and in his eyes too lovely to be called a bookworm, but she was not disposed to share her knowledge with anyone. While other young women her age went to parties and the theatre, Rose stayed at home. Iron knew this because her behaviour had been commented upon. His daughter did not deign to spend all her free time with him, either. They often ate together and conversed freely, but he knew at heart she was a strange loner. Iron empathized with Rose's disdain of trivial entertainment but he was still concerned that she was too isolated from her peers. One day she would come to govern in his place, and for that she must retain a certain level of communication with her people. The party tonight would do her good. He would suffer it himself for her sake.

The door to the Camera opened and Iron's steward bowed at the threshold. 'The Lords and Ladies are here, your eminence.'

Lord Iron sighed, steeling himself for the meeting ahead. Later, the Council would sit in the Hall of Justice in the Guild Tower and listen to petitions from the common folk, but this morning, they must first meet in private, in order to discuss any governmental problems. Iron was not looking forward to it. 'Good, good,' he said wearily. 'Bid them enter.'

The company meandered in, chattering together. First, Lord Marcus and Lady Melodia Gold, autarchs of their Clan, who were followed by Lady Fabiana Copper and her brother, Lord Reynard. After them came Lord Ulysses Silver and Lady Argentia Silver, then Lord Septimus Tin, his wife, Lady Augusta Silver, and their son, Sir Clovis Pewter. Sir Clovis was not officially a member of the Council but attended every meeting at the insistence of his mother. Not all the seats were taken at present, in any case. Lady Carinthia Steel always came alone since her brother had died. She had yet to take a husband and showed no inclination to do so, being clearly capable of administering her Clan without help. She had many lovers, but had no desire to share her power with any of them.

This group comprised the Upper Council of the Metal. They were the inner cabal of the Council of Guilds and dealt with the most important issues of government. The Lesser Council of the Metal, which comprised elected members of less exalted families, ran the more mundane aspects of the city's administration. They, however, never met in the Camera or the Guild Tower but gathered in a less ostentatious city building off the Grand Market.

Chairs were placed around the central image on the floor, and here the company sat down. According to their fashion, they wore their metallic colours in muted, autumnal shades – the coppers and golds and silvers glowing like an autumn forest. They gathered about the detailed scene reflected onto the tiled floor, barely giving it a glance. As soon as they were seated, they began to talk among themselves in greedy and confidential tones. Gossip. Lord Iron suppressed a shiver of irritation. He alone remained standing, and his voice rang throughout the great chamber. 'May I have your attention, Lords and Ladies.' Heads turned politely towards him as he opened the ancient Book of Laws, which reposed on a cast-iron lectern before him. He put a fist to his mouth and cleared his throat, then gripped the sides of the lectern. He barely had to read the formal words. He knew them by heart. 'Today is the time of our annual ceremony. The Ruby Moon will rise over us to spread her poison light upon our streets while she feeds the Jewel of All Time.

'From our Jewel comes our whole power. And from the Ruby Moon comes all the power of the multiverse to sustain us in our magnificent, eternal stability.

'It is our grave responsibility to ensure this sublime status quo. Since the beginning of Time, the Lords of the Metal have born this burden. In the early centuries of the Reformation, our ancestors, the great Metal Masters, formed their philanthropic guilds and developed the great ethic by which we continue to live. They recreated this city in the image of stability and made it inviolable, closed to all threat of invasion or internal dissent. For eons now, we, the Lords of the Metal, have upheld this responsibility with stern consciences and just administrations, holding together the fabric of society as surely as we hold together the fabric of the city itself.'

Lord Iron leaned forward. The words, and their meaning, were intoxicating to him. A prayer. 'We do not shrink from this duty. Nor do we complain of it. Neither do we challenge its purpose. Millennia have taught us never to change our customs. For only foul chaos follows change!'

After a brief silence, the sound of one pair of hands clapping slowly echoed through the chamber. All heads turned in astonishment towards Lady Steel, a woman in her late thirties, dressed in gauzy grey, her hair of platinum blonde wound up in a severe style from which one sensual tendril dangled. 'I am delighted, as usual, to be reminded of all this.' The voice was as silky and soft as a cat's paw.

'Carinthia?' Lord Iron said coldly. 'Have you something to say?' Lady Carinthia Steel was his greatest rival, and she became ever bolder, to the point where she felt confident enough to challenge him openly.

'Yes, I have,' said Carinthia, her strangely bright grey eyes gazing at him unflinchingly. 'You are head of our Council, so in some measure its character is formed by yours. I applaud your philosophy, Prometheus, and always have, but I feel it is my duty to question your methods.'

'It is not my philosophy,' Iron said grimly, 'but that of the city herself.'

Lady Carinthia shrugged. 'As head of the Council, you certainly embody it.'

'Perhaps you should speak more plainly,' Iron said, with a cynical glance around the chamber at his fellows to indicate she hardly needed a prompt for that.

'With pleasure,' said Carinthia. She turned her head from left to right to address them all. 'Like all of you, I uphold and admire the old virtues. But I think we should apply them more aggressively. We need to employ a more stringent justice. We have become too . . . kind. Karadur is in a state of crisis, which we ignore at our peril. Lowlifes from the zones conduct their criminal activities with greater impunity. A fortune-teller was arrested on the street only three days ago. The hand of justice must take off its glove.'

'For millennia,' said Lord Iron, in ringing tones, 'we, the Lords of the Metal, have ruled Karadur with justice, wisdom and mercy. Tyranny, my lady, is inefficient, as well as immoral.'

'But do we not already practise tyranny, Prometheus?' said Lady Fabiana Copper. Her clear yet husky voice seemed soothing after Carinthia's sharp words. She was an exquisite creature, with fiery red hair falling in shining waves around her slim shoulders. She held out her hands. 'We cleave to orthodoxy as if our lives depended on it. But even what is written in stone is open to personal interpretation. Perhaps, in our desire to maintain the traditional order, we have allowed too much injustice. But we should seek to understand what motivates the criminal element, what has caused their disaffection.'

Lady Steel seized upon these remarks with the zeal of a famished beast. 'Understand?' She snorted contemptuously. 'That is merely a manifestation of weakness – and weakness destroys any system. Some say that, after a thousand centuries, the old blood is too debased, too thin, and serves us ill.'

Lord Iron regarded her stonily. Her remark was a direct affront to the most ancient clans of Iron, Gold, Copper and Silver. 'It is no secret your family has long nursed ambitions to head the Council, Lady Steel. But mere ambition is not a qualification for leadership – good sense and a steady nerve are called for in this present crisis.'

'I see little of that here,' said Lady Steel.

Lord Iron opened his mouth to answer. But the temperate Lady Copper spoke before he could utter a word. 'Why must you quarrel in this way? What good can it do? While the clans squabble among themselves, the honest people of our city suffer! We should not judge one another, or jostle for position, but work together equally to seek a solution.'

Lady Steel spoke with icy politeness. 'Forgive me, Fabiana, but your words are naive. These are hard times and they require hard measures. The only way to progress is through strong debate. You must not be squeamish about it. We must work out a strategy to crack down on these rogues who challenge our authority. And if that takes lively argument, then so be it. It is healthy.'

For the first time, Sir Clovis Pewter spoke up, 'I have to agree with you, Carinthia.' He turned to Lady Fabiana with an unmistakably lascivious smile. 'Believe me, dear lady, we can no longer be liberal-minded in this matter. Ultimately, a little stringency would show our true concern for the people. Sometimes a certain measure of cruelty is necessary. It is kind.'

'Come to order, all of you!' Lord Iron said loudly. 'We have our Law, which is the sum of millennia of wisdom and altruism. Change in this regard is unthinkable.'

'Perhaps change is not the right word, Prometheus,' said Lady Copper, who despite her obvious discomfort with Pewter's attentions had clearly considered his words. 'I personally cannot condone a reversion to savagery, but I feel strongly that we should look for more enlightened ways to rule. The morals of the common people crumble because we have run out of ideas about how to control them. Whether we like it or not, things change, regardless of how many laws we impose. People change.' Languidly, she pointed to the living map and the plaza immediately below them, where a figure could be seen advancing to Lord Iron's door – Cornelius Coffin. 'There's no moral reason, my lord, for employing the likes of that despicable rogue Coffin. Whatever new strategies we might have to devise, we should not allow ourselves to lose our old sense of honour and equity. Cornelius Coffin discomfits me. I feel he is an unpredictable force, and we do nothing but enhance his position within the city.'

'Despite his quirks, Coffin's a loyal servant to the Metal,' Lord Iron said. 'He is most effective.'

'Barking mad, more like!' This remark came from old Lord Septimus Tin, a man worn so thin as to be almost invisible. He sat between his wife and his son, Sir Clovis Pewter, who was whispering in his mother's ear. The woman – Lady Augusta Silver – was far younger than her husband and was the daughter of the Silver autarchs. Iron thought they made an odd trio of conspirators. Lady Augusta's pallid beauty was almost unearthly, to the extent that in some aspects her husband appeared positively beefy beside her. Lord Tin slapped one of his bony knees, their outline clearly visible through his grey robes. 'But I have to admit Coffin's useful to us. He lacks the scruples that our ancestors built into our mechanical militia. The Roaring Boys and Blinding Boys merely defend our property and our constitution. Coffin defends our very existence. There have been too many disruptions to the fabric of our society recently.'

'And why?' Lady Steel inquired. 'Because there is an extremely unpredictable force at work among the people themselves. No matter how much we'd prefer to deny it, we must address this matter.'

There was a moment's silence as all looked at Lord Iron. Here came the moment he'd dreaded. 'You refer to the rumours in the free zones,' he said. 'Rumours only.'

'Indeed?' said Lady Steel. 'I hope you are attempting to delude us, because if not you are only deluding yourself. Max Silverskin is back, Prometheus. We have to accept it.'

Lord Silver uttered an outraged grunt. 'Ah, that's it. Bring out Clan Silver's shame. Blame it for everything.'

Lady Steel turned to him, palms raised in a placatory gesture. 'I cast no aspersions on you, Ulysses. If you feel shame, it is yours alone.'

'We did everything we could for that boy,' Lady Argentia Silver said, her narrow face set in a sorrowful frown. 'We truly did. It is not our fault . . .'

'Enough,' said Lord Iron. 'No one blames you, Argentia, for what happened to Maximilian. He is the master of his own destiny.'

'Indeed he is,' drawled Lady Steel.

'Oh, come now, Carinthia,' Lord Iron said. 'There has been no sign of him since he disappeared from Gragonatt Fortress. Nearly a year has passed and we've heard nothing of him. Then, a few weeks before the Ceremony, his name was suddenly being bandied about the city. Coincidence. Tales. Fictions. If Silverskin still lives, he's hidden himself away in a prison of his own making, that of fear. Other miscreants act in his name because he has become a legend for them. We must not make this problem larger than it really is.'

Lord Tin came unexpectedly to Lord Iron's defence. 'No, we cannot blame every criminal act on Silverskin. Most of his so-called exploits are only folk tales. But I do agree that the level of dissension among the common people is worrying and deserves our serious consideration. We might find that if we suffer many more outrages, with the associated contempt for our traditions, we shall find ourselves with fewer and fewer scruples.'

'Fire must be fought with fire,' suggested Lady Steel, looking Lord Iron in the eye and smiling politely. 'If dissidents have a charismatic figurehead, legend or not, it spells trouble for us.'

Lord Iron shifted uneasily. 'Coffin is familiar with all aspects of the city. If Max Silverskin is indeed out there somewhere, it will not be long before he's back in captivity.'

'You should send Coffin to interrogate those other wretched Silverskins!' exclaimed Lady Argentia. 'I'm sure they know more than they confess.'

'That has already been attended to,' said Lord Iron. 'It was Coffin's first avenue of investigation. The Silverskins want nothing to do with Maximilian. He is as much of an embarrassment to them as he is to you. They can't risk any more scandal.'

'Aha,' said Lady Steel triumphantly. 'These coincidences and fictions mean so little to you, yet now you admit you have already committed your Captain to investigate them!'

'A precaution, that's all,' said Lord Iron stiffly. 'It is Coffin's duty to investigate every untoward happening or rumour in Karadur.'

'We should ensure Silverskin's taken alive,' said Lord Marcus Gold. 'I think, if the rumours are true to any degree, the man possesses a secret useful to us all.' He raised his hands and gazed around the assembly. 'Where is he? How did he escape the Fortress? And what of this peculiar mark he is now reputed to bear?'

'What peculiar mark?' asked Lord Silver. Beside him, his wife had a hand pressed to her throat.

Lord Gold shrugged. 'I heard it from my valet. Apparently, the common folk believe he has some ridiculous hero's mark. I don't know what it is.'

'If he does possess a mark,' said Lord Iron, 'it's nothing more than a common thieves' mark. Coffin would have had him branded when he was captured.'

'Except,' said Lady Steel smoothly, 'that he did not.'

Another silence followed. She was stepping beyond the boundary of propriety now, virtually calling Iron a liar in front of his colleagues. 'You should qualify that remark,' Iron said. 'What do you know that we do not?'

Lady Steel shrugged elegantly. 'I have it on reliable authority that the mark Silverskin bears appeared over his heart shortly before he and his friend vanished from Gragonatt. Such a mark is called a Witch Mark in ancient tradition.'

'Some of you seem to know a great deal about this absurd story,' Lord Iron said sternly, fixing Lord Gold and Lady Steel with a censorious eye.

Lord Gold coughed and lowered his gaze. But Lady Steel stared openly at Lord Iron and smiled coldly. 'As a member of the Council, I feel it is my duty to do so.' She turned to the others. 'When I first heard some servants gossiping about it, a week or so ago, I took it upon myself to research the matter. One of my trusted maids gathered information for me in the markets and it seems the majority of people, even the most sensible, believe the story about Silverskin having a mark to be true. One man claimed to have spoken to Menevek Vane himself about it. But of course, while Vane is still at large, this cannot be fully verified. While my maid busied herself in this direction, I applied myself to a more respectable avenue of investigation. I found an illustration of the mark in an old book, which is kept under lock and key in Clan Silver's library. The book is a collection of very ancient folk tales, from a time when people's beliefs were vastly different from our own.' She paused for effect.

Lord Iron said nothing, taking care to reveal nothing of his feelings through his expression. He knew Lady Steel expected him to react angrily but he would not satisfy her. Even so, a disgusted shudder shook his frame. What kind of perverse mind did this woman have that she would actually wish to read such heretical texts? The answers to the city's problems did not lie in stories of untruth. She could have come to him privately about this matter, before the meeting. But, of course, that was not her style.

Lady Steel was now smiling mildly, as if discussing nothing more serious than the design of a new gown. 'The book was fascinating reading. I learned that anyone who carried the Witch Mark had only a short time to live – which might cheer you up, Prometheus.'

He would not laugh, or even smile.

Lady Steel looked away from him. 'But the mark imparted occult powers. There was a cost, of course – the owner's living heart.'

Lord Tin uttered a mordant chuckle and made an expansive gesture. 'Then it would seem our problems are nearly over! If Max Silverskin carries the Witch Mark, his days are numbered.'

Lady Steel shook her head. 'We should not celebrate yet. The mark does not kill if the bearer performs an act of extraordinary self-sacrifice, an act of monumental courage. You can imagine that this, coupled with the idea of someone having unworldly powers, would appeal to people searching for a hero to lead them. This kind of legend has irresistible allure. It could inspire people to all kinds of unwise and unruly behaviour.'

'Fortunate, then, that it is only a legend,' said Lord Iron. 'I propose we now move on from the frivolous to a more serious debate on our dilemmas.'

His suggestion seemed to be unheard.

Lady Augusta Silver was leaning forward in her seat. 'Tell us, Carinthia, what else did you read in this book?'

Lady Steel made an airy gesture. 'Unfortunately, that was all I could divine. The rest of the text was written in an ancient and forbidden script, which of course I could not read. Who still lives in Karadur who could read it? Perhaps lack of knowledge of these scripts is a sad loss to us. We have thrown something away that might prove useful.'

'Carinthia,' said Lord Iron severely, 'you seek only to divert the seriousness of this meeting with these silly childish tales. I must insist we move on.'

Lady Augusta ignored him. 'Do you think Silverskin knows about this legend?'

'It wouldn't surprise me,' said Lady Steel.

'But what is the history of the mark?' Lord Gold asked.

Lady Steel shrugged. 'It has been lost. I've no doubt our ancestors knew of it. And feared it, I think, if the tone of the book was anything to go by.'

'Dark superstition!' Lord Iron declared. 'Such talk is out of place in Karadur. I would remind you, my lady, that there are sensitive ears here'

Lady Steel stared at him without faltering. 'If I have offended you, I apologize,' she said, inclining her head. But still her eyes were smiling.

'I refuse to allow Max Silverskin to become our problem,' Lord Iron said emphatically. 'Even if the tale of him bearing this mark is true, I have no doubt it was put there by someone like Menevek Vane in order to fulfil some ridiculous common-man's prophecy. As I said before, if Silverskin is still at large Coffin will find him.'

'A year has passed since his escape,' said Lady Copper. 'We still don't know how he managed it.'

'Inside help, of course. There could have been no other way,' said Lord Iron.

'Yet no such help was ever found,' said Lady Copper.

'You risk building Silverskin into the very thing we don't want him to be,' Lord Iron said. 'We must not become conspirators in this silly fiction. How many times must I tell you that Silverskin is not important to us?'

'Yet he manages to dominate our meeting,' said Lady Copper, frowning slightly. 'That is strange.'

Sir Clovis Pewter spoke again. 'Well, in my opinion, for what it's worth, I think it's important Silverskin is recaptured as soon as possible. He has bad blood, even though his father was my own uncle, Augustus.' He turned to Lord Iron. 'I will assist in any way I can, my lord.'

'Your offer is noted and appreciated,' said Lord Iron.

'If Coffin can do the job as he did before,' said Lord Tin, 'then Silverskin can be made a public spectacle. It matters not whether he's a retired rogue, living in a hovel with a slattern and ten children, or whether he is responsible for every crime in Karadur. He is a symbol to the people. His humiliation, I am sure, would do much to restore order. The people must know that the law cannot be transgressed and that retribution will be dire.'

'That is settled, then,' Lady Steel said. 'Our priority is the capture of Max Silverskin. Once we have him, we can investigate the validity of the allegations about him. What else is there to say at present?'

The Lords and Ladies muttered their assent. Lady Steel stood up. 'Then I believe that's all, for now. We should meet regularly to assess Coffin's progress.' She bowed to Lord Iron. 'Forgive me cutting this meeting short, but I have a pressing appointment.'

'I have nothing else to say for now,' said Lord Iron. 'We will meet an hour after midday in the public chamber of the Hall of Justice.'

He turned his back on them as they filed from the Camera Obscura. For some moments he stood still, his head bowed. He'd hoped his daughter Rose would have made an appearance here today. She was not obliged to but he knew she was aware of Carinthia Steel's ambitions and liked to give him her support. Where was she? Abstractedly, he began to work the levers and dials of the Camera, casting his eye over the city. Who knew, he might even catch a glance of Max Silverskin. Iron could not help smiling bitterly to himself. He really had few expectations on that score, being convinced that Silverskin had merely given up one prison for another. He imagined the renegade shuffling out his days in some dank and lightless cellar. Iron experienced a twinge of pity, which he quickly smothered. If a man insisted on breaking the law, he must accept the penalty. Still, it seemed a waste. If a man could command such respect and adulation from the common people, what uses he could turn that talent to as a scion of the Metal.

The Camera's all-seeing eye swept over the hustle and bustle of the Grand Market. Iron focused upon the north quarter, which was filled perpetually with clouds of smoke and steam in which yellow gaslight and naphtha burned with a mellow warmth. This was where all the important daily business of the city was carried out. A few Roaring Boys and Blinding Boys creaked through the streets but Captain Coffin's swaggering 'Irregulars' were everywhere – as were his many spies, no doubt. Iron could see the working mouths of the hawkers and could imagine their coarse cries. He could almost smell the place: perfume, cooking meat, coffee and a faint under-note of rot. But what was that? One person stood out from the crowd, exemplifying a kind of stillness within the chaos. Lord Iron's eyebrows twitched in surprise. His daughter, Lady Rose, in plain, elegant clothing, was sitting at an outside table of the Café Aluminium, chatting and joking with a young man of her own age. The young man wore the fashionable, wide-brimmed headgear of the day and no matter which way the Camera was angled his face was obscured. But he had the bearing of a nobleman and that, at least, was reassuring. Lady Rose and the young man conversed easily. Rose's pale complexion was accentuated by the soft shades of green and brown she wore. Perhaps this assignation was the reason she'd stayed away from the meeting. Since the death of her mother, Laferrine, six years before, Rose had been more than a daughter to Lord Iron, but not in any improper sense. She was his counsellor, his confidant. But Iron had known that one day another man would come into her life, a man for whom she would feel a different kind of love. He had thought about it often and hoped he was prepared for it. But still, a heaviness came over his heart.

Chapter Three

Drama in the Grand Market

Every morning, in defiance of those who would hunt him down, Max Silverskin took his breakfast at the Café Aluminium, accompanied by Menni Vane. Invariably, they would rise late, ambling out from their lodgings at Dame Briskin's in the free zone next to Akra fief, and saunter through the alleys to the central market and the Café, unrecognized by anyone. Today was no exception. Max, dressed in fashionable yet tasteful garments of grey and yellow, was the picture of a citizen at one with himself. He strolled slowly, as if drinking in the steamy sights, the warm, multitudinous scents of the Grand Market and contemplating which of her many pleasures to try next. He could have been taken for a tourist from the far suburbs, or an affluent schoolmaster on his day off.

Only those Max knew well would have recognized him, and these folk he greeted with a sly wink. He was confident that, should danger threaten, he could melt away into the mist and steam of the city. If challenged directly, he could conjure a sword into his hand in an instant. It was said that only Captain Coffin was a superior swordsman and even he was useless with a heavy blade. But since his captivity Max had avoided any further encounters with his arch-enemy. It was only recently that he'd begun to roam the city again. His incarceration in Gragonatt, though brief, had scarred him. The image Max presented to his friends and enemies was often quite at odds with the reality of his character. Only Menni Vane knew the true Max and that the boastful, cocky mien frequently disguised a bewildered despair.

As soon as he'd passed beyond the black gates of the Fortress, Max had lost all hope of ever seeing the city or his friends again. It was as if the thin veneer of his bravado image had been stripped away instantly by the heavy atmosphere of the prison. He had been sure that he was doomed to a shortened life of crushing boredom and deprivation, both of which were hellish prospects to a man who thrived on adventure and sensation. He remembered that alien feeling, the complete absence of hope. It still haunted his dreams. How could he have hoped to achieve all that his heroes had failed to do, those warriors of the Clan Wars who existed now only as distorted memories in legends? For, inevitably, those who defied the Lords of the Metal were always vanquished.

Max recalled little of those clouded days within the fortress. Just impressions. An ice in his stomach, helpless despair, regret, and Captain Coffin's sneering smile as he spat out his questions. The kicks, the beatings. Then the strange dream. The shadowy figure. The pain in his heart. The gradual return of consciousness and the realization that he and Menni had escaped their prison. He still did not know how they had been projected outside the city. They had climbed the cliff to slip through a crack in the wall and make rapidly for their old haunts in the free zone around Akra. Max remembered the terror with which he had privately examined his chest, expecting to see some dreadful wound, but there'd been nothing, just a faint red mark. That must have been part of his dream. It still was. Part of his nightmares, too.

Over the months, he and Menni had often discussed that night. But they could never come to any clear conclusion about it. They had decided the mark must have been inflicted physically, by mundane means, as they'd been flung from their prison. Menni didn't think Max's dream in the cell reflected reality. But what was reality, when the escape could not be explained? Max had wanted to keep the whole thing secret, but Menni, in his cups, had told Dame Briskin the story. She had lost no time in spreading it round the zones. Now Max hid his identity from all but a few and watched his legend grow. It was a lie, he knew that. Some part of him still lay broken in Gragonatt.

On returning to the free zones, Max and Menni had had little choice but to return to their old calling, roaming the groaning alleys and twitterns of Karadur, where the houses leaned towards one another to form tunnels. For some time they'd had to lie low, as Max took some weeks to recover from his experiences. Menni, somewhat less imaginative and therefore less affected, had simply put the memory of that night from his mind. What was the point of worrying about something you could never understand? Just forget it and get on with life, count your blessings. He had dealt with everything, taking a run-down apartment in the notorious Rat-Run Alley, close to the Akra border. During the day, he'd leave Max lying in the darkened rooms and prowl the alleys of the Grand Market, relieving the more affluent citizens of their purses. Each evening, he'd try to cheer Max up with tales of his exploits, but his humour couldn't penetrate his protégé's melancholy. Menni openly confessed to Dame Briskin, even to Max himself, that he feared for the lad's mind.

'What do you think about all day, just lying here?' Menni demanded. 'I risk my skin making us a living, and you just laze about here.'

Max only blinked at him. 'There's something I need to remember,' he said.

Menni huffed in disapproval.

What Max thought about was his own history. He tried to remember his early childhood with Menni, but most of it was cloudy now. Recollections of the Moonmetal Manse were fragmented, mere frozen images. But he could recall his feelings with great clarity: frustration, anger, a need for something he could not name. He remembered haughty, sneering faces, his mother's name like a curse on their lips. And what of her? How had she died? Menni hadn't known her. All Menni could tell him was that he'd been found by an urchin in an empty house, a silver child wrapped in a swaddling of filthy rags. The urchin, unnamed, had sold the child to Menni. Max had asked Menni countless times why he'd decided to bring him up himself. Menni always shrugged. 'At first, I planned to sell you on, but then took a liking to you. I had no son of my own, and you were a bonny babe.'

Max found this explanation somewhat unconvincing. Why would a wandering thief like Menni want to saddle himself with a baby?

There were too many questions unanswered, and they boiled in Max's brain like a poisonous broth. He felt weak and vulnerable, like a newly formed creature that had stepped from a dream. Then, one night, he rediscovered his courage.

Max had dreamed of his incarceration constantly, and the dreams always ended with him being branded across the heart. The pain would bring him to threshing wakefulness. That night, the dream had been no different. He awoke gasping and sweating, his breath steaming in cold air, his hands gripping the soaked sheets. It seemed his small chamber was illumined with an unearthly light and he realized with terror that it emanated from his own body, from his heart. His chest had been filled with a fire at once icy and searing. Uttering a cry, he'd leaped from his bed, tearing his nightshirt from his body. But there was nothing there, and the only light came from the sulphurous street lamps outside. He'd leaned against the chill windowpane, his heart racing. But it was as if he'd been in a stupor, and now had come out of it. Why was he hiding here? Was this any better than imprisonment in Gragonatt? He'd looked out of the window across the twisting streets and it was as if he was seeing them for the first time. The buildings, in their girdles of iron, looked as if they had died in metal arms. As he gazed upon them, he thought he could see them slowly crumbling to dust. The air was filled with it. People devoid of hope lay down to die in the chill night streets. Poverty stalked the streets of Karadur with a death-mask grin. A revelation had hit him. The city was dying. The Lords, who by tradition were supposed to take care of it, were blind and arrogant. They were like golems of metal, unfeeling automata. But once their ancestors had been fierce and passionate warriors. What had happened to them? They needed to be woken from their ignorant sleep. Max stood up straight. He could feel a cold burn in his chest, but now he was no longer afraid of it. He saw it as a symbol. Feel the heart. Just feel. Be aware.

From that day forward, Max had reapplied himself to his calling with enhanced zeal. Menni had been delighted and relieved by the transformation, although slightly suspicious of a new, more altruistic aspect to Max's character. Now there was scarcely a wealthy house in all Karadur that was not intimately familiar to the Fox of Akra. He stole more than enough to keep Menni and himself well fed, and what was left over he redistributed through a network of shadowy contacts among the poor of the free zones. Menni supposed Max's near-death experience must have inspired this generosity. Max let him think that. He decreased his circle of friends, trusting those that remained not to be tempted – as had happened before – by a reward worth an entire city quarter. Miracles, of course, were not permitted in Karadur. So the miracle went unremarked – that not one man or woman trusted by Max Silverskin was tempted by the fortune. Max knew it would not happen again. It was not meant to be. He suspected the Lords of the Metal had concluded he was rotting in some hole, too terrified to emerge lest he be betrayed again. No doubt the only thing that puzzled them was how long it was taking for an informer to come forward. Let them think that. It only made his work easier.

Now, as he strolled along with Menni Vane, he debated whether to confess to his mentor what was on his mind. He'd been having disturbing dreams again. Dreams of the mark – and now, something more. 'Menni,' he said. 'I have a strange compulsion.'

Menni looked at him askance. 'What?'

'What, in your opinion, is the most valuable thing in Karadur?'

Menni stuck out his lower lip to consider. 'I dunno. Everything in the vaults of the Clan palaces, I suppose.'

'Not the answer I'm looking for.'

'Then you tell me.'

Max paused, hands on hips, staring up at the soaring plinth where the Jewel of All Time glowed feebly through its globe with the last of its strength. 'I would say that the most valuable thing in Karadur is the Shren Diamond.'

'Then why ask me?' Menni narrowed his eyes. 'What's the purpose of this conversation, Max?'

'I have decided that I must steal it.'

Menni laughed. 'That's a good one! Steal the Jewel. You crack me up.'

'I mean it, Menni,' Max said, in a low voice.

Menni stared at him, then glanced up at the Jewel. 'You are mad,' he said. 'Come on, I need my breakfast.'

'No, wait,' Max said. 'I dream of it, Menni. Every night now for over a week. I see it in my hands, turning my flesh to fire.'

'You've become a one for dreams,' said Menni, 'whereas I am still a one for my stomach. Leave it, Max. Dreams are for the night.'

Max knew that Menni was extremely uncomfortable when he demonstrated tendencies of being 'fey', as Menni put it. He also knew Menni was afraid the experience of Gragonatt and the escape had permanently damaged his mind. Perhaps it had. 'I must do it,' he said. 'I feel I'm meant to.'

Menni exhaled noisily in frustration. 'Very well. Let's suppose you could manage it. Where would you go once you'd filched the damned thing? You couldn't stay in Karadur, could you!'

'Perhaps I'd go where people say my parents went, to the Rim Cities, beyond the ice on the other side of the horizon.'

'Good choice,' said Menni. 'You'd die out there. Everyone does.'

'There's no real proof of that,' Max said. 'Once we have the Jewel, we can do what we like.'

Menni laughed. 'Who would buy the Shren Diamond from us, you fool? Who in Karadur could afford it, apart from the Lords? Would you sell it back to them?' He rolled his eyes. 'Cursed be the day your father took your mother. He could have chosen a good honest whore, with no crazy blood.'

Max ignored this comment. 'The truth is, I don't care who would buy it. I'm just consumed by the desire to take it. It would the ultimate theft. I want it in my hands. Also, the disappearance of the Jewel might wake the Lords up to reality. If the symbol of their stability and power has gone, what must come in its place? Something would have to change. Will you join me in this venture?'

Menni shook his head. 'Only a fool would join you. There's no way of stealing it. If you try while the Moon is out and the Jewel is feeding, the ruby rays will kill you. And you couldn't nab it while it's inside the Market – and escape. So it's impossible.'

Max laughed. 'Haven't we proved we can perform the impossible?'

Menni visibly flinched at the subtle reference to Gragonatt. 'We've just proved we're uncommonly lucky, that's all. And luck doesn't last for ever, boy. We know that.'

'How can you say that? Hasn't luck proved herself our goddess?'

'Goddess, eh? It's that Silverskin blood again!' Menni shook his head mournfully.

Max began to walk on again. 'Anyway, if fate decrees we must get caught, let's do so in style – or not at all! I am quite prepared to defy Lady Fate.'

Menni grunted. 'If you can come up with a workable plan, I'll eat my own legs.'

'Don't do that,' Max said. 'It would make our task more difficult.' He grinned. 'Come on, then. Breakfast!'

Menni smiled cautiously. 'This is a poor time of day for a joke. I can't laugh on an empty stomach.'

They passed beneath the shadow of one of the Guild Tower's massive legs. Beyond, spilling out into four narrow streets, was Salt Pie Market, named for Salt Pie Alley nearby, location of the fabled Mammy Bappy's Hot Pie Stall. The market rose several levels above the streets, each level crowded with galleries and balconies that housed shops and stalls selling everything the heart could desire. The waning light of the Jewel of All Time illuminated the scene, augmented by sputtering gas jets, yellow oil lamps and naphtha flares. Steam and smog, combining all the waste gases produced by the steam-driven city, drifted heavily at ground level, thick with the aromas of living humans and cooking food. Occasionally, some of the stalls were plunged suddenly into darkness by lamp failures. From every building, hanging banners announced the Carnival of the Ruby Moon.

'By my mother's belly, I'll be glad when tonight's over,' Menni said. 'Makes me uneasy, this gloom.'

'It would be gloomier if the Jewel should disappear after its replenishment,' Max said.

'Now don't start that again,' Menni snapped. 'If the Jewel should disappear, the city would die. You'd have been doing all your charity thieving for nothing, because everyone in the city would die too. Is that what you want?'

'They wouldn't die,' Max said abruptly. 'At least, not because of that. The city's dying anyway. Can't you see that?'

'Looks the same as always to me.'

'That's because you walk around with your eyes shut,' Max said. 'I was lying earlier, by the way.'

'I am relieved to hear it.'

'I wouldn't even consider leaving Karadur if I took the Jewel. It would show me something. It would burn brighter. How can I convey my heart to you? There are no words for what's inside it. I just sense destiny at work.'

Menni expelled a sound of disapproving irritation. 'I've followed you into many dangerous corners, my lad, and led you out of them too, but this seems madness. Utter madness. It must be the rising moon affecting you. I should lock you indoors until it's set.'

Max only laughed.

As they passed the elevator in the tower's leg, a clattering metal cage powered by a groaning steam engine descended from halfway up the tower and came to a clanging halt beside them. Max and Menni were forced to stop as a young woman marched out of the elevator cage in front of them, virtually shoving them aside, with never a thought for her rudeness. In typical Karadurian costume, she wore broad bracelets of various precious metals and a metal corset between her pale green blouse and her russet skirt. Her hair was a rich auburn red, pinned up in a simple yet becoming style. She was stunning to behold, by any standards, but somehow more than that. Menni glanced at Max who raised an eyebrow. The woman possessed an arrogance uncommon among the people here. Could it be that a daughter of the Metal was playing dangerously, in disguise among the common people? It was not unheard of. She would be easy meat. Purse brimming with coin. Without speaking aloud of their decision, and once again allied in purpose, Max and Menni followed her out into the crowd. Perhaps their breakfast might be more sumptuous than usual this morning.

Beyond the tower, where the market sprawled outwards to the edges of the four fiefs, a raucous carnival atmosphere filled the narrow streets. Hundreds of citizens had converged on the area to watch the entertainments held in celebration of the Carnival of the Ruby Moon. Lively music and carnival barkers added to the din of the event. The people were all wearing their finest clothes, rich flowing silks adorned with metallic decorations. Massive Irregulars marched brutally among them, as well as a few of the Lords' Battle Boys, who, puffing and steaming and leaking oil, were clearly long past their prime. However, the mood of the day was too high for anyone to care about these symbols of authority among them.

The mysterious woman meandered through the crowd, apparently oblivious of being pursued. Occasionally she would pause to admire the displays of jugglers, grotesques and acrobats. Eventually she strolled into a narrow side street to watch a puppet show. Max watched in amusement as a teenage girl sidled up behind the lady and dipped her grubby fingers into a silk-lined pocket. This woman must be from one of the Clans: no commoner would be so easily divested of their purse. If you frequented the markets, you had to develop a sense for acquisitive fingers and subtle moves.

The woman, still unaware of the robbery and her pursuers, continued on up the street, turning back towards the looming shadow of the Guild Tower. 'Watch her, Menni,' Max whispered to his companion as he melted into the crowd. 'I have changed my plans and intend to do a little thief-catching.'

Menni raised an eyebrow. 'Looking to make an impression, are you?' he said and shook his head. 'Why waste your time?'

Max grinned and set off in pursuit of the young thief. The girl went directly to Mammy Bappy's Hot Pie Stall where, no doubt with her stomach growling, she pointed insouciantly to one of the proprietress's plump pies and held up two fingers. Max sighed in regret. Poor girl probably hadn't eaten that well in a while, but still he slipped to her side and relieved her of the stolen purse with even more deftness than she'd taken it from the unknown lady. As he moved away, Max heard the sound of portly Mammy Bappy's voice berating the girl: 'No money, no pies! I am not a charity. Be off!'

Swiftly, Max rejoined Menni Vane, who was standing with folded arms at the place where Max had left him. 'So,' said Max, 'where is our mysterious lady?'

Menni shrugged, making it clear that he was not wholly happy about this change of plan. 'What are you up to?'

'I don't really know. It is a whim.'

Menni shook his head. 'Great men are toppled by beauty.'

'Come on, it's more than that. What's the snooty Clan bitch doing here? We could learn things to our advantage from her.'

Menni paused and then, with some reluctance, pointed the way. 'She headed off up there.'

'Let's catch her up, then.'

It was swiftly done. Judging by the way both the crowd and the Irregulars moved instinctively out of the woman's path, she was clearly someone of rank. It was because of the way she moved, her utter confidence. She now approached an area where earlier a stage had been erected. A harlequin troupe, in costumes and masks, was attempting to drum up trade. The woman paused, obviously intrigued, whereupon a grotesque in flamboyant costume leaped to her side and swung his hat beneath her nose. 'None may pass me but those who have paid good coin for their entertainment.'

To Max's surprise, the woman laughed and said, 'How much?'

The grotesque performed a bow. 'Half a bar to you, my pretty.'

The woman nodded and felt for her purse. Max watched as her expression changed. She had realized her loss.

'Half a bar,' said the grotesque, with slight impatience.

At this point, Max stepped forward. With an elaborate bow, he doffed his feathered hat to the woman and presented her with her purse on the point of his sword. 'Yours, I believe,' he said.

'How did you . . . ?' The woman narrowed her eyes. 'Did you steal from me?'

Max shook his head. 'No, but I saw who did and took it upon myself to be a gentleman.'

The woman regarded him angrily for a moment, then snatched the purse from his sword. Before she could open it, Max had given two coins to the grotesque. 'For myself and the lady.'

'Enjoy the show,' said the grotesque, with a wink for Max. He went off to harass potential new customers.

'You do not have to pay for me,' the woman said. 'I have more than enough to pay for myself.'

'I would like to,' said Max. 'Consider it a gift of appreciation.'

'For what?'

He bowed again. 'Your great beauty. It would please me if we could watch the play together.'

He could see the woman was both affronted and flattered by his remarks.

Still, she had to keep up appearances. 'Please leave me be. You are impertinent, sir.'

'I am? This is the Carnival, when all are friends. You talk like a lady of the Metal, for only they are so prim as to find a compliment an insult. Can I expect you to summon a creaking Roaring Boy to carry me off? I hope not, for then the good people here would realize who you were and might not be pleased.'

'Now you flatter me,' said the woman, although Max could tell his remarks had discomfited her. 'Very well, we shall watch the play together, but that is all.'

Max cleared a path to the front of the crowd. The play had already begun, and he was amused to note that the harlequinade was acting out a crude version of his own legend.

A slim young man in a mask and a diamond-patterned costume leaped to the front of the stage. 'Now begins the story of the famous thief and magician Max Silverskin, and how he challenged the power of the Metal. All know the tale of the Silverskins, outlawed kinsmen to the Silver, whose women have the power of magic. When that power is passed to a son of the blood – then shall come a time of change and destruction. Only Max Silverskin can determine if that time is for good or—' he paused and lowered his voice, '—for evil.'

The crowd uttered an appreciative murmur.

Menni leaned towards Max and whispered in his ear. 'We shouldn't be here. This is no ordinary show. These must be rebels who spit in the face of the censors! They're dangerous!'

Max made an airy gesture. 'Don't fret, Menni. We are safe. And besides, look, the lady is intrigued.'

In truth, some vain part of Max was curious to see how he'd be represented on stage. The harlequin stared out at the crowd and, for one breath-stopping moment, Max felt as if he was being personally addressed. But that was impossible. He didn't know these people.

'Thus it is written: when a Silverskin, born of the Silver, shall come as a thief to Karadur and steal all four lost icons of the Clans – then he shall earn a power greater than anyone has ever known before.'

The woman at Max's side uttered a laugh.

'Don't you believe in legends?' Max murmured to her.

She gave him a caustic glance. 'Do you?'

He shrugged.

'Silverskin is only a thief – if he still lives at all. These people are deluded. They have created a religion out of him. To believe otherwise is heresy.'

Max remained silent. In actual fact, he had not heard of this legend concerning lost icons and himself. Perhaps it was new, dreamed up in the hearts of those who needed hope. Now another player had capered onto the stage, while the harlequin had melted into the shadows. Max grinned widely. It was easy to see this new character was a caricature of Cornelius Coffin, huffing about in black armour and waving a sword. He appeared to fight off a horde of invisible attackers. The harlequin, clearly supposed to be Max himself, leapt gracefully back onto the stage. He held up a goblet, made of gold-painted cardboard, as if he'd just stolen it, and slipped it into a sack held over his shoulder. At this point a troupe of comic 'Irregulars' flooded the stage and, under the direction of the blustering 'Coffin', attempted to seize him. 'Max' danced and soared around them, and the crowd roared its appreciation.

'Perhaps that is Silverskin himself up there,' Max said to the lady. 'Now, wouldn't that be a fine trick!'

The woman laughed. 'Nothing short of a miracle!'

On the stage, a 'Roaring Boy' in a costume of creased silver foil and cardboard was beating 'Coffin' about the head an inflated bladder.

'Witness!' cried the 'Roaring Boy'. 'It is our great Lords who have banished false magic. Through us, steam and reason rule the world!'

Dark smoke puffed out onto the stage and scenery cranked down to reveal a rough interpretation of a cell in Gragonatt Fortress. 'Max' was shown curled up in despair. In the audience, the real Max found it uncomfortable to keep his eyes on the stage. Did he really want to see this? Then a blinding flash made the crowd cry out in awe, temporarily blinding everyone present. The harlequin sat up. At this point, 'Coffin' and his Irregulars poured back on the stage, shouting incoherently. In the chaos, the harlequin crept up to 'Coffin' and struck him on the behind with a tasseled slapstick. Then, as 'Coffin' danced about, shrieking and clasping his buttocks, 'Max' raised his arms high and released a stream of glittering motes. At once, 'Captain Coffin' and his blundering Irregulars began to cough and reel about, clutching at their throats, their eyes. The harlequin leapt and spun around them and explosions of purple fire erupted from the back of the stage. The harlequin skidded on his knees to the front of the stage. 'By trickery did Captain Coffin capture brave Max Silverskin. Now, by glorious magic, Max is free!'

The woman at Max's side made a sound of amused annoyance. 'Wishful thinking,' she snapped.

Glorious magic? Max thought. His head whirled in disorientation. For a brief moment, he was back there, the strange lights behind his eyes, the seating of molten metal against his skin. His heart blazed and burned.

Then the crowd began to clap, whistle and shriek their appreciation. Max's vision swayed back to reality, and the only peculiarity inside his ribcage was a heart of flesh and blood that beat too fast. He was aware of a slight ache at his temples, a tightness above his eyes.

The harlequin bowed to his audience. 'So authority maintains itself by lies and strategies. Our lawmakers are suspect. Our law enforcers are more brutal than those who break the law! By deceit alone was Silverskin entrapped. They promised to tell him where his parents could be found. Then left him to rot in Gragonatt, from where no prisoner emerges alive. Yet still brave Silverskin escaped. His freedom gives us hope for our own liberty, for a day when reason and magic are unified once more as in olden times.'

Max made an angry sound and spoke hotly. 'Promised to tell him of his parents? That much is a fiction. Silverskin is not so easily duped. It was simple deceit and greed that trapped him.'

Perhaps he shouldn't have let his feelings erupt in that way. The woman beside him was looking at him with speculation now. She opened her mouth to speak, but at that point a great commotion started up at the back of the crowd. Menni said gruffly, 'This is trouble. We'd better scarper.'

Max caught sight of a troop of tall, implacable Irregulars marching inexorably through the crowd and, with a sick jolt, he realized that

Cornelius Coffin was with them. He heard that hated voice order, 'Take them! Take the seditious rabble. Show no clemency.'

'Time to leave,' said Max. He turned to his female companion. 'It was a pleasure to have met you, but I fear we must . . .'

'If you're leaving, so am I!' she hissed urgently. 'Coffin mustn't catch sight of me here.'

Max paused for only a moment. 'Then we must make haste, madam.'

'You know this place. Get me out of here!'

All around them the players and their audience were hurrying to escape the scene. It was fortunate the Irregulars, and Coffin himself, were too occupied by the fracas to pay much attention to who else might be making a getaway.

At the edge of the square Max looked back. For a brief second he saw the harlequin, poised upon the stage, looking right at him. The rest of the scene faded into a muddled blur. In sharp focus, the player lifted his arm and pointed straight at Max. Max's heart clenched. Then, with a nimble leap, the harlequin disappeared into the shadows at the back of the makeshift stage. Sound and movement surged back, and Menni was pulling on Max's arm. 'Get a move on, boy!'

Presently, Max and Menni were sitting at a table outside the Café Aluminium, as they did every morning. The only change to their routine was their intriguing companion. She had protested at first, apparently being intent on leaving the area as soon as possible, but Max had used his charm to persuade her. Despite a lingering disorientation, he was still intrigued by this mysterious creature. He wanted to play with her mind. 'Brighten our morning,' he said. 'Also, I guarantee you will enjoy the Café's fare. Continue your adventure. Who knows where Coffin might be lurking? We will protect you.'

'Oh, very well,' said the woman, with poor grace. 'But I cannot stay long.'

Menni had ordered breakfast, which a serving girl was now arranging before them. So far the woman had offered no explanation about herself. Max waited until the serving girl had gone back into the café, then said, 'You are a lady of the Clans, aren't you? Don't deny it.'

The woman hesitated. 'What makes you think that?'

'Please don't take us for fools. Why else would you be so anxious to run away from Coffin? Your people would not look upon it kindly if you were found in such a lowly place as this.'

'I could be a criminal fleeing from justice. Surely that's more likely here.'

Max smiled smoothly. 'I really don't think so. We know the sons and daughters of the Clans like to dally in the markets, don't we, Menni?'

Menni made an uneasy sound. 'It's rumoured so.'

'Rumoured!' Max laughed. 'Don't worry about her, Menni. She can't hurt us. She'll be as anxious as we are to keep this meeting quiet.' He leaned forward. 'Will you tell us your name?'

The woman narrowed her eyes. 'Neither am I a fool. You underestimate me, sir. I am not what you assume me to be.'

'You are a lady. I can smell it on you.'

'That's not what I meant! I am not some witless fawning creature, thinking only of gowns and jewels, looking for a bit of reckless entertainment.'

'Then what *are* you looking for?'

The woman waved this question away. 'Not your concern. Anyway, I find you too an enigma. You seem unusually gallant for a native of the markets.'

Max shrugged, confident she would never guess his identity. He found it easy to disguise himself from everyone but his closest friend. He merely willed it so. The only person he feared might pierce this rather flimsy camouflage was Cornelius Coffin. 'As I said, we know the Lords and Ladies like to nose around outside their gilded palaces. Look upon me as the by-blow of such an adventure.'

The Lady snorted. 'You own Clan blood? I think not.' Then she stared at him more closely and, for a fleeting second, Max saw an expression of confusion cross her face. 'Well, perhaps it's possible,' she said, recovering her composure. 'But I find it difficult to believe any Lord would be so careless as to let his seed find fertile ground here.'

'Stranger things have happened during the Carnival of the Ruby Moon.'

The woman shook her head. 'You are all so quick to believe in children's tales. It is this heresy that creates a barrier between you and those who'd help you.'

Suddenly, from somewhere high in the upper galleries of the market, an object fell – or was thrown – to land with a wet, rotten sound on the worn flagstones. The woman made a sound of disgust. An apple had burst at her feet, and now pulpy gouts of it stained her gown. She brushed at them in annoyance. 'Rotten. Everything's going rotten in Karadur.'

Max raised an eyebrow. 'Now who speaks heresy?'

The woman had flushed a little.

'Tell me, madam,' Max said carefully. 'Do you know why our city is falling apart?

The woman looked up at him sharply. 'You should ask Lord Iron, not me.'

'Unfortunately, I am not on intimate terms with him. I'd like your opinion.'

'I come here to see, to observe,' she said. 'I can see what's under my nose.'

'And seeing that, do you intend to do anything about it?'

She paused. 'Somebody has to make an honest report to the Council.'

'I doubt that will be enough, noble though your aim might be.' He gestured up at the Camera Obscura, visible even from this distance looming high above the city. 'Even as we sit here, talking delightfully, we could be observed through the lens of the Camera. No doubt Captain Coffin is already on his way to report to them concerning the incident with the harlequinade.'

The woman glanced up at the Camera nervously, but said nothing.

'Are the Lords of the Metal not meeting this morning, as is the custom?' Max murmured. 'They can see well enough what's what in the city. Unfortunately, they are selectively blind, which is also fortunate for me.'

'How so?'

'A hated enemy of theirs sits drinking tisane and eating toast beneath their noses, in the delectable company of some Lord's daughter. I find that greatly satisfying.'

'Hated enemy, you say?' The woman arched her eyebrows. 'How can you be that? They have no enemies, only irritations.'

'Anyone not of the Clans but with a thinking mind is an enemy of theirs,' Menni Vane broke in, with an admonishing glance at Max. 'That is what he means.'

'Is it?' asked the woman.

Max shrugged. He had a wild urge to tell her who he was – surely unwise, even if she didn't believe him. What was wrong with him? He knew he was in for a severe ticking-off from Menni later. 'It heartens me to discover that at least one daughter of the Metal has a conscience,' he said.

'It seems we both have secrets,' said the woman.

Max smiled. 'How sad we do not trust one another to reveal them – yet.'

'Yet?' Her voice was harsh, but her eyes were not.

Max took a sip of his tisane. 'I feel we should – and shall – meet again.'

'Do you, indeed?'

'Yes. Because we shall arrange it here and now.'

The woman paused. 'You are certainly not a reticent man.'

'Are you agreeable?'

She looked him in the eye. 'I feel I shouldn't be.' She hesitated. 'If we are intended to meet again, then our paths are bound to cross without our organizing it.'

'Here? Tomorrow morning? At the same table?' Max was aghast at his own urgency. Why should he care about this female? If she knew who he was, she'd spit in his face. She was a symbol of all he despised and yet, despite this, he found himself believing his own flattering words.

The woman laughed. 'How fortunate you are, sir, to be able to predict your whereabouts so far ahead. You must have more leisure time than I.'

'I would stop Time herself to accommodate our next meeting, madam.'

'What do you want with me? I can think of the obvious things and can assure you all of them are quite impossible.'

Max shook his head. 'I would not be so gross. I am drawn to you. I must confess my original intention today was to rob you. But now I feel very differently.'

'Only because someone beat you to it.'

'No. It is more than that and I know you sense it. I feel we would both profit from lengthy conversation.'

She regarded him haughtily. 'I have business, sir, that will not wait. I must leave you now.'

She rose from the table, most of her breakfast untouched.

'Do not leave here only to feel regret at leisure,' Max said.

'What you suggest is impossible,' she said. 'You don't know how much so. Thank you for your courtesies, and for breakfast.'

With these words, she walked swiftly away.

Menni kept his silence for a few long, agonizing seconds. Then, clearly having been crafting his rebuke in his mind, he uttered a sound of intense disapproval. 'It's that sort of behaviour that will have you back in Gragonatt quicker than you'd blink. She's a pretty bit of stuff, I agree, but she's one of them. No doubt she'll have her family's militia crawling all over this place tomorrow morning looking for you. Nobody speaks to a Lady of the Metal that way, even if they are playing at slumming it. We've lost our breakfast café now, and all for the sickness of lust.'

'She won't tell,' said Max shortly, still gazing in the direction she'd gone.

'You don't know that.'

'She feels something . . . for the city. She's not asleep. She's awake.'

Menni rolled his eyes. 'Oh, for the Jewel's sake! This is not a time to fall in love, Max. You'll never see her again – if fortune has anything to do with it.' His voice took on a careful, sly tone. 'And what of your plan to steal the Jewel? If you succeed, we'll hardly be able to conduct a relaxed rendezvous outside here tomorrow morning!'

'If we succeed, she'll most definitely be here,' Max said.

Menni put his head briefly into his hands. 'You are a witch like your mother,' he said. 'I should walk away from here now and hide until the Ruby Moon has set.'

Max laughed. 'Magic is certainly in the air today.'

Chapter Four

Dreams in the Eyrie

Built among the smoke stacks and the sharply sloping slate roofs of The Old Forge was a forgotten dwelling, warped with age and heat. It had once been the home of the head foundryman, but a century or so ago a new dwelling had been built for the one who held this position, close to the underground barracks of those he oversaw. The hidden eyrie among the chimneys was now Lady Rose Iron's secret retreat. Not even her father knew of it. She had her own apartments in the family manse amid the chimneys of the Forge but hardly ever used them, preferring the freedom and privacy of the old abandoned cottage in the sky. The wall that faced the main foundry was fashioned almost entirely from glass as if an artist had once lived there, seeking light. Rose liked the way the mood of the day washed its colours through these long windows. She had no shutters there, nor drapes. Beyond the windows was a balcony, and here she would often stand in the evening, sipping cold white wine, gazing out over the cityscape of gouting fire and oily smoke. She had found the place quite by accident a couple of years before. Abandoned buildings had always fascinated her and she had spent many hours exploring the disused areas of her family's property. It was the windows here that had captivated her. She'd walked through the dark hallway and into a room that seemed on fire. Her breath had stilled in her chest. She hadn't seen the blackened walls, the rotting furniture, the holes in the floor. She'd seen the light and merely thought, 'And now I am home.'

She'd refurbished the place herself, taking materials from the foundries and the family manse. Rose was always able to find privacy, because some years ago female relatives her own age had discovered they'd little in common with her and therefore didn't bother her. She had no interest in clothes or perfume or jewellery, and even less in the largely foppish male population of the Clans. Rose had dreams. She had had them for many years and now, as she stumbled upon the iron steps leading to her retreat, they crashed into her waking life so strongly that her chest filled with pain. The realization came with a jolt, like a slap.

Blindly, she unlocked the door – the lock fixed there by her own hand – and felt her way into the main room. 'Why didn't I see! By the Jewel, why didn't I see?' She was close to tears, speaking aloud to the peaceful room where morning light fondled dust motes in the air.

She sat down on a tapestried couch – rather musty, dragged from Clan Iron attics – and rested her chin in her hands. She felt too dazed to function.

'Max,' she whispered to the room.

Rose had been fourteen when it had happened. The onset of womanhood had suddenly made the world much more interesting. At that time she still had close, giggling friends among her peers. There had been a party to celebrate Lord Silver's birthday. The highest-ranking members of the Clans had been invited. For weeks, Rose had been filled with a strange excitement. Every morning, she'd awoken feeling that something momentous was going to happen. And then it did.

At the party, she had spotted the handsome youth of the Silver Clan immediately, and her cousin, Adelia, had whispered to her, 'Look at him: Maximilian, the Silver by-blow. What a novelty he is. Do you suppose he's an evil sorcerer like his mother was?'

This information only made Max more attractive to Rose. He hadn't noticed her, of course. He'd spent the whole party looking bored, which must have taken some effort, for the theatrical and firework displays Silver had put on were amazing. Rose asked questions about him, got the full story. Here was danger and adventure. She'd never seen anyone like him. He was only three years older than she was.

Afterwards, at home, and sick with an unfamiliar longing, she'd fantasized about rehabilitating Max Silver, leading him back to the true path of goodness. She began to pay more attention to the young women of Clan Silver, finding any excuse to visit the Moonmetal Manse. Sometimes, if she was lucky, she'd catch sight of him. He was usually on his own, slouching moodily about or else fending off jibing attacks from his young male relatives. It was peculiar that the sour bitterness of his expression, which turned down his mouth and furrowed his brow, did nothing to eclipse his natural attractiveness. Rose's tongue had turned to glue in her mouth whenever she saw him. She'd wanted to ask a million questions of the Silver women but had been too shy to do so. She'd dreamed of initiating conversations with Max, astounding him with her wit and difference, but she had lacked the courage in reality. Had he ever noticed her? She didn't know. Only a few weeks after she'd begun those painful, delicious visits, Max had been cast out of Moonmetal Manse and Rose had not seen him again. Yet he'd remained in her thoughts. For over a year, she'd suffered in silent agony over his departure. Then the feeling had gradually faded, until he had become no more than a wistful dream.

One thing Rose knew. Max Silverskin had made her the person she was. Unwittingly, he had catalysed something within her. Her fascination with him had led her to wonder about his rebellious tendencies, the reasons for them. And, in so doing, she had begun, slowly, to see Karadur for what it was. He should have shared that revelation with her, but she'd borne it alone.

Over the years, tales of Silverskin's exploits had come to the ears of the Metal. By then, Rose had matured enough to realize that the image she had of him was only a young girl's fantasy. But the fantasy was pleasant enough to indulge in when she was alone. She'd decided she never wanted to meet him again, because she was sure he'd disappoint her. He'd be rough and uncouth, damaged by the years he'd lived with the lowlifes. He was a common thief, after all. When he'd been captured by Coffin a year before, she'd been almost relieved, even though he hadn't entered her thoughts for a long time. Max Silverskin in Gragonatt was a real, unpleasant thing. It proved she could never really have befriended him. Then there'd been the escape and the rumours. She'd deliberately shut her mind to them, curled her lip as her father did to think that anyone would believe them. When certain of her new friends, people that Lord Iron would never have dreamed she'd know, had begun to speak of Max and his legend, she'd still remained sceptical. They needed a hero as much as anyone, and Max was just an icon to them. He could not come back into her life in any form resembling the one she'd believed in as a young girl. That was fantasy, wishful thinking. She'd known this utterly. Until today in the market.

It had been him. She knew it had. Why hadn't she recognized him? Was it because the man who'd spoken to her today was nothing like the ugly image she'd built so carefully? Or was it something else? The face, maybe. The Max she'd known had been turned in on himself, frowning and dark of countenance. The man she'd seen today had been expressive, his mouth always smiling, his brow unfurrowed. Still, she should have recognized him immediately. She remembered the brief moment when she'd thought she knew him, but it hadn't lasted. How had he done that? He'd flirted with her and that was painful too, because he did not know who she was. He'd played with her, driven by despising.

Rose stood up. 'This will not do!' she told the room.

He wanted to see her again. He'd seemed most insistent.

'But you won't let it happen,' Rose admonished herself. She should report what she'd seen to her father, even to Coffin. But she knew she couldn't do it.

The room was quiet, its ambience contemplative. Outside, a siren wailed for midday, summoning the foundrymen to their lunch. She couldn't see him again. It was unthinkable, an action that would doom her in many ways.

Why won't you let it happen? a sly voice hissed in her mind. *Think what you could tell him. The truth, for example. Would he despise you then?*

She sat down again. Truth. She rubbed at her face. Sometimes she didn't feel in control any more. She'd stepped too far beyond the boundaries of what was permitted, had become a stranger in any part of the city, belonging nowhere, yet everywhere.

Rose was destined to take on the mantle of her father's power when he died. It was — at least for now — the most powerful position in Karadur. She intended to fulfil her role totally. She loved her city and feared for it.

If and when she came to power, supposing her father could hold on to Clan Iron's superiority, she wanted to revive Karadur. And to do that, she had to know all that was kept from the people – hidden history, forbidden truths. She had perhaps discovered more than she had bargained for. If her father knew what she'd done, who she'd become, he'd disown her, if not throw her into Gragonatt for eternity.

'What I know is a burden,' she told her room. Truth hung more heavily on her than before.

Gloomily, Rose contemplated the prospect of the forthcoming celebration at Verdigris House. She was in no mood to attend but knew her father would despair if she didn't accompany him there. That was one thing they had in common: a loathing of Clan gatherings. After them, Rose's jaw would ache from the constant forced grinning. She could never remember what she'd said to people, because there was nothing worth remembering. She had no friends, because she spoke a different language to all other Clan females.

Sighing, she decided she'd spend the rest of the day readying herself for the gathering. She could do nothing else with her mind in this state. It was hideous, like a sickness.

'Don't be ridiculous,' she told herself aloud. 'It'll fade. Forget it.'

How pleasant it would be to have someone who could talk back to her. The thought made her smile. 'See, you are nearly mad,' she said. 'Only the mad talk to themselves.'

She wandered into her bedroom and started dragging gowns from her wardrobe. The narrow mirror between the two doors was dark like mercury. In it, the reflection of her face looked yellow and sick. Rose flopped backwards onto her bed. The ancient springs jangled like harness. She lay with her arms spread out, surrounded by swathes of floating fabric and jewels. The gowns smelled of other parties: an aroma of solitude.

Rose rubbed her face. She was exhausted. Her head felt as if it was gripped by metal hands. She wanted to hold her breath. The atmosphere in the room had changed, become watchful.

I should sit up, she told herself. In her mind she could see herself doing it, but her body felt too heavy. Sleep called to her, and the images of sleep.

Rose longed for dreams, because in that other world anything was possible. She could be free. Dreams had led her to knowledge. One night, some years before, she had somehow become awake in her sleep. She'd known she was dreaming, but it had felt so real. She'd found herself in an immense library. Stacks of books rose to the ceiling that was hidden in shadow, too far overhead to see. The books could speak. As she walked through the warren of aisles, Rose had heard them calling to her in dry whispery voices. 'Take me, open me, look into me. What you need to know is here.'

She'd tried to haul one off a shelf, but it had been too big. It had fallen onto her, engulfed her in fluttering pages the size of sails. And she'd been drawn into them, into a world of magic, where there was no ice, no pressing melancholy, no laws.

On waking, she'd been filled with the conviction that the dream had given her an important message. That day, she'd made her first foray in the libraries of the Clans. What she had discovered there over the months that followed had been no less wondrous and startling than the dream that had inspired the search.

Her father would never pay attention to dreams or regard them as important. She doubted he even remembered where his mind roamed at night, free of the constraints of the waking world. But Rose had learned to pay attention to the journeys of the night. Once she began to verify imagery she'd seen only in a dream, it made her think about how perhaps the laws of the Metal were not wholly right. There was another side to life and she could see no evil in it. What had led the Metal to create their rigid empirical world?

Now Rose felt herself drifting slowly down into the darkness where her desires and hopes lay waiting. She would dream of Max Silverskin. Perhaps touch him, hold him. Soft grey feathers seemed to fall around her, carrying her down to slumber. She was weightless, drifting, enclosed in breathing warmth. So safe.

A piercing shriek filled her head. She opened her eyes, expecting to see her bedroom, but she was surrounded only by a grey fog. Dread fell down upon her in a crushing wave. Terror. Stark fear. Something in the fog. The shriek came again, nearer now. 'Wake up!' Rose told herself. 'Wake up!'

She saw a metallic glint in the swirling fronds of mist, heard a clattering, scraping sound. Silence. Her breath ached in her throat. 'Wake up . . .'

Then it was upon her, in a flurry of clashing feathers. An immense owl, but no ordinary bird. This was a creature fashioned entirely from metal, an automaton from ages past when the alchemists of the Metal had birthed monstrous creations in their crucibles. The creature's round eyes were the essence of madness. Its claws were scimitars. Its beak snapped open and closed, razor-edged. Rose flung her arms up before her face, crouched down. 'This is a dream. It can't harm you . . .' She felt the graze of talons upon her back. Physical pain lanced through her, but still she could not wake. The creature would tear her to pieces. She huddled lower to the ground, a ball of fear.

Awareness shifted. All was still. Perhaps it had been for a very long time. Rose raised her head.

There was no bird. The fog swirled lazily around her. She saw a dark blot, which she realized was a figure walking towards her through the haze. It approached at speed and soon she could see it was a woman wrapped entirely in a concealing cloak and hood of dark fabric. The woman halted a few feet from where Rose crouched. All that could be seen of her was a single white hand, which clutched the collar of her cloak. The face was invisible. Perhaps she had no face.

'Who are you?' Rose demanded.

The woman's other hand snaked out of the folds of fabric. She raised it to the darkness where her face should be and lifted one finger, as if asking for silence. A voice came out of the hood. 'Nine things make three things, Three things bring a fourth thing, four things make one thing, one thing makes everything.'

'What?' Rose squinted at the woman. Her image seemed to be breaking up.

'Search,' said the woman, 'as you have always searched. You have seen the owl, who is three.'

'What do you mean? I don't understand . . .'

The woman shook her head and began to retreat into the fog.

'Wait!' Rose called. 'Tell me what you mean!'

But then the fog seemed to gather itself into a great wave and hurled itself at Rose's body. She was flung back, soaked to the skin.

Gasping, Rose opened her eyes and found herself lying stiff and straight on her bed, arms outflung. Her skin was slick with sweat. Her head ached. And the afternoon was silent and still around her.

Chapter Five

Moon Ball at Verdigris House

Cornelius Coffin stood before a full-length mirror in his austere bedroom, adjusting his uniform to best effect. His chin jutted commandingly. His eyes were steely, yet – he hoped – enlivened by a hint of wry humour. Even though he had recently shaved, the skin of his jaw was dark with emerging stubble. Sometimes, when comparing himself to the smooth-cheeked Lords, this characteristic annoyed him. But who among the simpering Lords possessed a jaw as strong as his? He flared his nostrils at the mirror, tugged on the front of his tunic. His boots gleamed like jet and the ornate metallic adornments on his cuffs and breast shone dully in the lamplight. His closely shaven head looked as if it was dusted with iron filings. It accentuated the strength and precision of his facial contours. He reached for his wide-brimmed hat and positioned it carefully. Yes, he looked suitably dashing. Satisfied, he turned away from the mirror and called for his servant.

Coffin knew that the majority of those who would be present at Clan Copper's manse that evening disapproved of him joining the company. Fortunately, he had managed to persuade Lord Iron that, for security reasons, he should be there. Coffin was under no illusion about what the Lords thought of him, but it really didn't matter. Lord Iron was different to all the rest, a relic hanging onto something that was lost. The Lords might speak of honour and nobility, but in reality they were just a gaggle of effete fools. Coffin did not think this of Lord Iron. He respected the man. Just as well. One day, if all went according to plan, Lord Iron would be his father-in-law.

Sitting back in his steam carriage as it chugged towards Shinlech Fief, Cornelius Coffin exhaled a sigh. Lady Rose. She was her father's daughter, all right. Not a silly, simpering creature like most of the Clan ladies. Coffin had loved her secretly for several years. But his attraction to her was prompted by more than love. He knew he was a better man than most of those who governed the city, and was determined to claw his way into their ranks in order to secure a lofty position for himself. Only then would he make an ideal husband for Karadur's future leader. He owed it to both himself and Lady Rose to succeed. After all, no one else was worthy of her hand. He hoped that, one day, Rose would realize this for herself.

The carriage made its way up Sequin Avenue, a wide thoroughfare flanked by soaring buildings, the domain of bankers and merchants, while at ground level high-class shops displayed their wares through lamplit windows. Fantastic bronze sculptures lunged out from the upper parts of the buildings, frozen in flight: griffins, dragonflies, winged lizards. Below them, dwarfed by the size of the imposing edifices, tall copper-leaved trees with sculpted foliage stood to attention tamely at the kerb. At the end of the avenue, the road opened out into Curlicue Court, where the fantastic frontage of the Theatre of the Copper dominated the scene. Bronze caryatids, fully fifty feet high, stood in elegant ranks along the front of the theatre. Tasteful posters for forthcoming events were visible between them.

Coffin rested his head against the quilted cushions behind his seat and watched the city go past. He needed the reward that would follow the capture of Max Silverskin. A million platinum mirrors. A fortune. He could buy one of the old manses in Peygron Fief, close to The Old Forge, and do the place up. There were enough of them listing by the roadside, abandoned and deserted. It would only be a matter of time before Silverskin tripped up. Coffin would search every corner of Karadur. There was nowhere else for the posturing peacock to go.

The carriage had reached the end of the avenue beyond Curlicue Court and now drew up outside the walls to Clan Copper's estate. The great gates, adorned with reliefs of rampant griffins, slid apart. Beyond, the Copper domain stood in its spreading, landscaped grounds, the heart of Shinlech Fief. The turreted house was a blaze of lights and many carriages stood steaming in the curving driveway. Once his own carriage came to a halt, Coffin could hear music. As he got out, he glanced at the sky. Only a short time now until the

Ruby Moon rose. By then, the shutters of the manse would be firmly sealed, so not a single ray could penetrate. And the Lords and their ladies would be celebrating with a fury, as if the end of the world was due. Coffin sighed. He would have too little time to spend admiring Lady Rose. At ten o'clock, he had to leave. On the night of the Ruby Moon, the Irregulars met in their clubhouse near the Guild Tower, close to the temporary plinth where the Jewel lay moonbathing. It was a tradition that had begun among the Foundrymen, which the Irregulars upheld in their own manner. As their overseer, Coffin joined them for a cup of wine or two. He knew where he'd rather be. Still, it should impress Rose that he was prepared to venture out beneath the scarlet rays of the moon. Privately, he thought that people were needlessly terrified. All it took was the proper precautions to provide protection from the poison light. He had made sure his own men had been instilled with this belief. He was not stupid. He wouldn't advocate reckless gallivanting beneath the light of the Moon, but it was well known that certain criminals ran amok when the Ruby Moon was high. It was only right that those who sought to control and expunge them were prepared to take the same risks.

In the hallway, Copper's butler, along with a retinue of staff, were on hand to relieve guests of their coats. The copper-sheathed walls of the hall glowed warmly in the light of a myriad candles. Lords and ladies stood in small groups, their clothes a riot of metallic colours. The coiffures of the ladies defied gravity, many of them decorated with elaborately twisted spines of their family metal.

Coffin made his way to the ballroom, nodding at those who deigned to look up from their conversations and stare at him. No one would greet him, but that only amused him. In the main room, he spotted Lord Iron standing with Lord Gold and Lord Tin by one of the walls and made straight for their group. He knew he was not mistaken in thinking that Iron looked relieved to see him.

'Ah, Coffin!' he said.

Their relationship was strange, Coffin knew. Iron wanted to despise him as much as the other Lords did, because he was a commoner, but, in truth, he probably confided in Coffin far more than in any of his peers. Coffin bowed. 'Good evening, my lord.' He glanced around, looking for Lady Rose, but knew better than to enquire concerning her whereabouts. His heart sank. He hoped she hadn't stayed at home.

'Ha, Captain!' said Septimus Tin, who from the ruddy condition of his normally ashen face had already been sampling the cheer pot. 'Found our elusive ruffian yet?'

'He refers to Silverskin,' said Lord Iron.

Coffin bowed again. 'I can assure you, my lords, that I will have good news for you soon.'

'Any luck with the Silverskins?' Marcus Gold enquired. 'What did they have to say when you paid a visit?'

'Couldn't have been more helpful,' Coffin said, then grimaced. 'However, they're a tricky breed. You get the impression they're laughing up their sleeves all the time.'

'So perhaps they are concealing their wayward relative.'

Coffin shook his head. 'I don't think so. They may be tricksy, but they're not stupid. Many of their Clan are oldsters. They wouldn't want to risk seeing them living out their meagre days in Gragonatt.'

'The Silverskins, for all their peculiarities, are not renowned as thieves,' said Septimus Tin. 'I doubt very much they'd like to add that felony to their list of suspicious traits.'

'They rue the day Augustus ran off with Sophelia as much as Clan Silver does,' said Lord Iron.

'And they never tried to take Maximilian in,' said Tin. He shook his head. 'Given their odd ways, they probably smelled bad blood long before Silver did.'

The men nodded together.

Just then, Lady Rose came sauntering through a doorway behind them, pushing aside the satiny copper-coloured drapes with a languid hand. She was dressed in a simple black gown, whose folds gleamed like mercury in the light. Her long throat was exposed, her hair wound skilfully but not too tightly upon her head. Through her coiffure she wore a single slender iron pin, which was topped by a winking diamond. Her slanting eyes were shaded with a dark silvery powder. Coffin felt his body would melt and run away across the floor.

'Hello, Captain,' she said, smiling.

The smile said everything, but unfortunately its language was complex and Coffin was not arrogant enough to believe he caught all its nuances. She knew how he felt – that much was plain. 'My lady,' he said, clicking his heels together.

Rose's smile widened, then she turned to her father. 'Fabiana wants us all to dance soon. She is most insistent.'

Lord Iron rolled his eyes. 'I am exempt from her commands, owing to my age.'

'Not I!' cackled Septimus Tin. He looked around the room. 'Where's my good woman? I fancy a caper.' He bobbed off into the crowd.

Coffin wondered whether he dared ask Rose to dance. Just as he was mustering the courage, she gave him a sour glance and he changed his mind. She was a beautiful, wild creature who would need careful and patient taming. It was only when Carinthia Steel slid in among their company from behind him that he realized the sour glance had not, in fact, been meant for him.

'Rose,' said Lady Steel. 'How nice to see you. It's been too long. I was beginning to wonder what had happened to you.'

Rose smiled tightly. 'I've been very busy.'

'I know. I visited the Clan Silver library the other day and the librarian told me you'd been quite the constant visitor. Are you studying?'

'Just learning about the city.'

'Cramming for your legacy,' said Lady Steel, with a cruel smile. She was dressed in aching white, her gown speckled with intricate confections of polished steel. Her hair was arranged in a gauzy web upon a spiny net of spikes. Curled locks of it hung down upon her bosom like blind white serpents. Coffin considered her an elemental force, more of a man than most of her male contemporaries yet still divinely feminine. However, he knew she was dangerous, could not be trusted. Rose was, in his opinion, by far the better woman.

Lady Steel ignored Coffin and said to Lord Iron, 'Any news of Silverskin yet?'

'No,' said Lord Iron. He turned away from her to take a goblet of wine from a passing servant who carried a tray of drinks.

'I wonder what he's up to tonight,' said Lady Steel.

'No doubt holed up like the rest of us,' said Marcus Gold. 'Would you care to dance, Carinthia?'

Lady Steel hesitated just long enough to imply insult without actually offering it. 'That would be charming.' She let Gold lead her away.

'Serpent,' muttered Rose.

'Now, now, daughter,' said Lord Iron. 'We don't sink to the level of gossips and shrews, do we?'

Rose uttered a snarl. 'You despise her as much as I do, father.'

'I would not be so foolish as to despise so formidable a creature,' said Lord Iron.

'Now look who minces their merry way towards us to enhance our entertainment,' said Lady Rose glumly.

Clovis Pewter pranced up to their small gathering. He was not an ugly man by any means, but a certain slyness to his features, a tightness of eye, meant he would never be termed handsome. 'Good evening, Clan Iron,' he said. 'Rose, you look radiant.'

'Mmm,' said Rose.

'I saw you standing here and knew I had to ask you to dance.'

'Did you?'

Pewter held out a crooked elbow. 'Well, my lady?'

Iron waggled the fingers of one hand at his daughter. 'Go and dance,' he said. 'It's what you're here for.'

Momentarily, Rose narrowed her eyes at her father and then glanced at Coffin. He knew, as if she'd spoken aloud, that she was wondering whether it would completely breach propriety to claim that he'd already asked her for the first dance. Could it be taken as a compliment that she preferred him to Pewter? Hardly. The man was the ultimate in dolts. Rose should prefer dancing with a rotting corpse in her arms to dancing with Pewter. Coffin inclined his head to her, with a smile to indicate he understood her discomfort. She grinned ruefully as she allowed Pewter to drag her away. Oh, his marvellous Rose!

He came out of his brief reverie to find that Lord Iron was staring at him severely. Coffin put a fist to his mouth and cleared his throat. 'Well, while I'm here, I'll just make a few enquiries.'

Lord Iron raised his eyebrows.

'Clan servants hear much around the markets,' Coffin said. 'Might as well gather the gossip of the day. It doesn't do to stand about wasting time.'

Lord Iron nodded. 'Good man,' he said.

Coffin wandered off into the crowd. Many had gathered at the centre of the room, in formation for the first dance of the evening. It seemed the bulk of Rose's relatives were in attendance. A sour bunch, the Irons. Rose was a beautiful exception. At the hub of the crowd, Fabiana Copper was in her element, her neat body swathed in a hugging gown of what looked like molten bronze. She was held in the arms of a lesser Steel, Sir Rupert, who was clearly aware of his privilege. Fabiana's face was flushed with excitement. Her feet could not keep still. Coffin smiled to himself. She was a fluffy creature: no brains, of course, but still a looker. Nearby, Rose stood holding Pewter at arm's length, her face a composition in ennui.

Coffin went through a wide doorway into a large chamber beyond where the servants were still laying out the buffet. He approached Fabiana's steward, an older man who looked like a giant amphibian walking on its hind legs, owing to the bulk of his torso in comparison with the thinness of his calves. His face, emerging neckless from his impeccable livery, was that of a fractious tortoise.

'Good evening, Truffle,' Coffin said, helping himself to a sweetmeat from the table.

'Hands off, Coffin,' snapped Truffle. 'You'll eat when the rest of them do.'

Coffin licked his fingers. 'What's the talk of the streets today?'

Truffle wagged his head from side to side. 'There's always talk,' he said. 'People can't keep their mouths shut. Just spout rubbish.'

'But any rubbish that might be of interest to me?' Coffin withdrew a coin from the collection he had previously placed in his pocket and held it up so that it winked in the light.

Truffle eyed the coin. 'Might be.'

'My ears are your servants.'

Truffle took the coin with a quick sly movement and slipped it into a pocket of his own. 'I've heard a good one today. Very good. Completely untrue, of course.'

'The best ones always are.'

Truffle sidled closer. 'Mind you, if it *were* true . . .' He sucked in his breath. 'There could be scope in it for a man like you to make a mark.'

'Now my ears are your slaves, grovelling at your feet.'

'Well, I've heard this from more than one source, so you never know. Apparently, an old cult's been revived.'

'What kind of old cult?'

'The worst kind,' said Truffle darkly. 'Came from the foundry originally.'

Coffin moved closer, lowered his voice. 'You're talking of the cult of Sekmet?' He did not want this one to be true, keenly aware that, if it was, some of his own men might be implicated.

Truffle nodded. 'That's what they say.'

'Who is involved in it?'

'How would I know? I'm not anything to do with it. All I heard is – and this is the most unlikely part – that certain Clan people have an interest.'

Coffin frowned. 'In what way?'

Truffle turned back to the table, rearranged a pile of forks. 'The ladies get bored, you know, stuck in their palaces. When they get tired of chasing the pretty servant boys, they look elsewhere for entertainment. That's all I'm saying.'

'You mean ladies are involved?'

'I've said what I'm going to say. Leave me alone. I'm busy.'

'I need to know more,' Coffin said.

Truffle turned on him. 'These are strange times, Captain. Very strange. Things aren't what they were.'

'I need to know exactly what you heard.'

'I've told you. There's nothing more.'

'But what evidence . . . ?'

'There is no evidence. Just talk.' Truffle moved away and began to berate an unfortunate maid nearby.

Coffin pondered what he'd heard. Was it possible? If it was, it could mean a big shake-up for the Clans. And that could certainly be used to his advantage.

Chapter Six

To Steal a Shining Jewel

As the Grand Market closed for the night, the plinth of the Jewel was wheeled out on rumbling steam-trolleys to stand before the great metal gates. A committee of dignitaries from some of the lesser Metal clans was on hand to provide a modicum of ceremony for the occasion. Lord Lead read from an official scroll to a rapidly diminishing crowd. People wanted to get home quickly that night, to ready themselves for the parties that would shake the city until dawn.

The last words were spoken and Lead put away his scroll, perhaps himself thinking of the grand event at Verdigris House that evening. Mechanical guards groaned into position about the plinth, placed there by creaking Roaring Boys and Blinding Boys. They had not even finished their task by the time the first rays of the Ruby Moon fanned out above the horizon. Within only a few minutes, the whole city was stained scarlet by the uncanny light. The streets were empty by then, strangely quiet. No sound came from the hostelries shuttered against the poison rays. The celebrations had yet to commence. Only the Battle Boys were left to police the streets, the strange light lending them a barbaric beauty. Some were designed to appear roughly like men, with stamping mechanical legs and golem faces, while others squealed around on wheels, looking more like giant automated milk churns. All were adorned with multiple limbs armed with weapons, grippers and flame-throwers. As they patrolled, they sometimes emitted whirring sounds and steam-driven shrieks, as if conversing together.

Bells tolled the hour and in the central plaza the metal puppets of a great mechanical clock creaked out from behind their blinds and enacted a gruesome carnival of their own. Time is death, they seemed to say, as carefully crafted skeletons wielding scythes cut the heads from manikins at their feet. Soon, shuttered steam carriages came grumbling through the streets. They paused at the gates to tavern yards, which would grind open to grant them entrance. The yards beyond were covered, so that the passengers could alight without fear of the toxic lunar rays.

By nine o'clock, the Hammer and Anvil tavern in Akra Fief was doing a noisy, appreciative trade; the queue was four deep at the bar. The stage of this hostelry was famous, and tonight top-rank music-hall entertainers sought to caper and sing above the din of the patrons. Steam from the wine vats hung heavily in the air, smelling of spice and fruit. Ruby wine, mulled over open flames.

Max and Menni sat in a window booth, which provided a little seclusion from the hubbub around them. Max fingered the heavy velvet drapes, filled by a compulsion to draw them aside, unlock the wooden shutters and look out. He had his goggles ready in the deep pockets of his capacious coat. They had been purchased from a gentleman of the streets, who – from a dank sub-cellar, deep below a brothel in Ihrn Fief – sold to people of his calling all the tools of the thieving trade. Max and Menni would not be the first to venture out into the venomous light of the Ruby Moon. It was, by tradition, a time when the most courageous of master thieves used the empty streets, and the fact that most citizens would be at public celebrations was to the thieves' advantage. Courageous, but foolhardy, too. Many a thief had been found in the morning after the Moon's brief reign lying blistered and contorted on the street. They seemed to be so safely wrapped, too, in their layers of protective gear, their thick goggles. The Ruby Moon punished those who dared to brave her light. But there had been success stories as well – legends now. Max's heart beat strong and fast beneath his ribs, and he was conscious of a tingling sensation in the flesh above it. He knew he would not die this night, but still he wanted to try the goggles out now, in the relative safety of the tavern. Menni sipped his ale miserably, but Max sensed that the older man's complaining was really part of an act. At one time, in his youth, Menni Vane had been quite a bravo of the streets. The young Menni, who still lived within the older body somewhere, probably bemoaned the fact he hadn't thought of stealing the Jewel himself. They would do it, Max was sure. Some things were just meant to be.

The Moon would set at three o'clock, but then the streets would fill with merrymakers. The job needed to be done now, when the only thing they'd have to worry about would be the cumbersome Battle Boys.

Menni shook his head 'Keep your hand off that curtain, my lad. You'll be seeing the Jewel soon enough.' He frowned. 'It will be burning with new life. How will we be able to hold it? It'll be like trying to steal one of Mammy Bappy's pies straight from the oven with our bare hands.'

'I've done that many times,' Max said carelessly, sipping from a pewter goblet of Vortex Water: a strange, cold-burning liqueur, which left a peculiar metallic film upon his lips. 'It was one of the first things you taught me, remember?'

'Rabid,' grumbled Menni. 'You ought to be hog-tied. And *I* ought to be hog-tied for going along with you.'

That day, during the many conversations and arguments they'd had about stealing the Jewel, Menni had suggested that Max should perhaps work alone. It was the first time he had ever made such a suggestion. They had always worked together. It was inconceivable that they should stop now. 'You are my luck, my talisman,' Max had said, 'as I am yours. I know you don't share the compulsion I have, but please believe I'm doing this for a reason.'

'A reason you do not know,' Menni had said dryly. 'I don't know, boy. I can't see the sense of it. What profit is there to be gained from it?'

Max had shrugged. 'I don't know yet, but one thing I do know is that when we find out, it will be great.'

Eventually, Max had persuaded Menni to accompany him as normal. He hadn't lied or flattered when he'd called the older man 'his luck'. He really meant it.

Max put down his empty goblet and wiped his mouth. 'We must leave now,' he said. 'This job will have to be done fast.' He realized that, at this late moment, he didn't want to give Menni any time to reconsider and back out.

They pushed through the crowd into the covered yard, where revellers yelled and danced among the silent hulks of the steam carriages. Crimson-painted lamp globes emulated the effects of the ruby moon outside, and many partygoers wore scarlet theatre make-up, as if they'd been caught and burned by the toxic rays. The hot wine was red, and even a barrel of ale, which had been tinted with food colouring, came gushing out of the wood topped with a pink foam.

Beside the arch of the main gateway was a small covered corridor that led to a side door, used only by pedestrians. The crowd was too intent on its celebrations to notice two figures slipping into the dark of the short tunnel. At the end, the gate was well locked to prevent any drunken patron accidentally stumbling out into the night, but it took Max only a few seconds to pick it. He and Menni buttoned their coats and secured thick scarves about their heads and faces, leaving only the eyes bare. Then on went the goggles, followed by broad-brimmed hats. Finally, their hands were concealed by silk gloves – close weave, but thin enough to allow dextrous movement of the fingers.

Outside, the streets were eerie. So empty, as if the city had died. Max and Menni rolled a couple of barrels across the side door of the tavern yard so that no one could follow them out. It was difficult to see clearly through the tinted glass of the goggles. The light looked brownish, like that of a dying sun. Max glanced up at the sky and saw the fierce cinnamon globe hanging over him, watching them. They must be quick.

They ran through the back alleys, where the buildings leaned towards one another. Not even a rat scuttled in the rubbish-strewn gutters. From a building came the thin wail of a child, quickly silenced. They passed a house where what sounded like an entire pack of dogs began barking hysterically. It was as if they knew that men out in the moonlight constituted a great wrongness.

They came to the Guild Tower where now the Jewel was displayed outside upon its plinth. Even through the goggles it glowed with an acid light, its strength replenishing rapidly. It cast deep shadows over the buildings and streets: shadow, the friend of thieves. Menni carried a sack containing their equipment: tongs and ropes. Max began to climb the outer struts and buttresses of the Tower so that he could position himself above the Shren

Diamond. Perched on an immense bronze gargoyle that grimaced out over the square, Max took note of the mechanical guards placed at the quarters of the plinth. They seemed lifeless. A group of Roaring Boys marched heavily and conscientiously around them. Occasionally, one of them would halt and bellow into the searing light, for no apparent reason. In contrast, a clutch of Blinding Boys stood motionlessly in a group, clashing their weapon appendages together, their silvery hides flashing in the Jewel's rays. It was as if the automata were bathing in the light. Max wondered then whether the ancient machines had some kind of consciousness, and whether this night was special to them as it was to humankind. He smiled to himself. *What whimsy!*

Menni was now beside him, attaching a rope to the gargoyle's head. When it was secure, Max lowered himself slowly so that he hung above the Jewel. He reached up to Menni, who handed him a pair of scissor pincers. For a moment, Max stared at the Jewel. He was here. He was going to do it. It was too easy. The light of the Jewel seemed to penetrate his heavy clothing, bathing him in a warming glow. He felt almost intoxicated by it, light-headed. How could such healing benevolence be charged by the cruel witch-light of the Ruby Moon?

Menni tugged on the rope, as if to remind Max to get on with the job. Carefully, Max extended the pincers, positioning them around the Jewel. His hand did not shake. He felt full of strength. But the moment the jaws of the pincers closed upon the Jewel, a gout of light burst out of it, accompanied by what sounded like a crash of thunder. At once, the Roaring Boys lifted their great heads and began to emit a loud, bellowing alarm. Max spun crazily on the rope, his head filled with boiling fire. The Jewel was protecting itself, as if outraged by human touch. Max's body banged painfully against the metal struts of the Tower. He wasn't sure whether he still held the pincers, for his hands were numb and the confusing fire obscured his vision. Then Menni was swinging down beside him, no more than a black shadow against the raging light. He reached out for the Jewel with his gloved hands. The Shren Diamond was now glowing scarlet, perceivable even through the goggles. Confusion reigned below. Blinding Boys were emitting furious bolts of light, shrieking and whistling. Then Max and Menni were tumbling backwards down the struts. For a moment, they came to rest on a groaning beam, where both clung in desperation to the metal. Max saw that Menni's goggles had come adrift. He clutched the glowing red Jewel to his chest, but his face above the light was fearsome, demonic. 'I'm blind, Max, blind! Don't look at it.' Max adjusted Menni's protective goggles with one hand, then glanced below. Simultaneously, their precarious perch creaked shrilly and dipped wildly.

'Keep still,' Max hissed. He tried to calm his mind, even though it was filled with the piercing shriek of the Jewel, its whirling colours. *Think. Plan.* The goggles would protect them from the numbing radiance of the Blinding Boys, and the Roaring Boys could not reach them up here. If they remained perfectly still, it was possible the archaic guards would eventually become passive once more. Surely no human would dare to brave the Ruby Moon to come and investigate? It wasn't yet eleven o'clock. They were safe for hours.

Menni uttered a strange whining noise beside him. His body jerked. 'Keep still!' Max said again. But Menni seemed beyond hearing. His shuddering movements reverberated through the rotting beam. With one final metallic scream it broke away, and Max and Menni were falling, helpless. Before they landed heavily beside the plinth, the Jewel fell from Menni's hands and tumbled away into the heaving shadows.

They lay for some moments, engulfed by heatless flame. Max could barely see. He felt that at any moment he would be consumed by the strange fire. They must escape. Now. It would only be a matter of moments before the Battle Boys would be upon them. Max grabbed hold of Menni's coat and hauled him to his feet. The square was totally obscured by whirling colours, which must be an effect of the jewel being dislodged from its setting. But where was it? There was no time to look. Max heard the grind and thump of the mechanical guards approaching through the radiant fog. He drew his sword, thinking that he could dart around the guards, aiming the odd strike at their vulnerable ancient joints.

Then a hated voice, the one he feared above all others, rang out stridently through the square. 'Surround them! Show no clemency!'

Coffin? How was that possible? Max began to retreat, half-carrying Menni who lolled insensibly against him. There must be an avenue of escape. But they were surrounded. A horde of Irregulars was closing in, all of them protected from the Moon's rays by heavy armour and smoked visors. Behind them, silhouetted against the flame, standing erect in a panting steam chariot, was Coffin himself. A pack of snuffers – mechanical hounds – was leashed to the chariot's flank. They moved jerkily in a repulsive mime of canine behaviour. Steam huffed from their angular jaws and their steel claws clipped the cobbles.

Max was filled with a terrible despairing resignation. He had failed. The Jewel was lost and now Coffin had come to claim him. How many times would his vain pride bring him to this? Perhaps this would be the last time. For just a moment, Max remembered the mysterious woman with whom he'd shared breakfast. He would never see her again now. She would come to meet him and the table would be empty. He would be in Gragonatt, helpless before Coffin's smug brutality. *Better to die. Yes. Better to die.*

Menni uttered a groan, perhaps unaware of the direness of their predicament. Mentally, Max prepared to defend himself and his blinded friend. It would be a matter of moments before they were bested by the brute strength of the Irregulars, but at least they might take a few with them. The strange glow in the square was diminishing now and he could see just how many Irregulars were advancing upon them. Behind, lurching back and forth, were distressed Battle Boys, belching steam and sparks, clearly unable to cope with the situation.

The steam chariot chugged forward and Coffin leaned from his perch. 'Is that you, Max Silverskin?' he said, not without a tone of wonder.

Max said nothing, would not look up at the man, gripped his sword with both hands, circling slowly. The Irregulars stood all around him, awaiting orders.

'Take them alive!' said Coffin. 'Take care to do it. Only superficial injuries.'

The Irregulars all took a step forward. But, without warning, another raging fire sprang up again, whirling around Max and Menni, driving the Irregulars back. Was this the work of the Jewel, wanting to claim its own vengeance against those who had dared to violate it? The fire was intense. Its roar drowned out all other sounds. Max expected to be burned alive and fell to his knees, keeping hold of Menni's arm. The older man was still shaking his head and muttering, perhaps hallucinating. 'I'm sorry,' Max said, more to himself than to Menni, who was probably incapable of understanding. He closed his eyes, waiting for the fire to consume him. But instead, he felt only a light touch on his shoulder.

'Get to your feet, Max Silverskin,' said a voice he did not recognize. He turned and saw a vague, uncertain shadow limned against the fire. It was neither tall nor short, but slender. The voice was androgynous. Man or woman? Max couldn't tell. 'Hurry, now,' the stranger urged softly. 'They won't be fooled by this for long.'

'What's this?' Menni said, rubbing at his streaming eyes.

'I don't know,' Max answered.

'No time, no time,' said the stranger. 'Your friend's sight returns. Follow me.'

'The Jewel,' Max gasped. 'The Jewel . . .' He gestured up at the empty plinth. 'We must find it.'

'No time,' the stranger repeated. 'If you value your life, follow me. The Jewel will survive as it's always survived.'

Max felt as if he was walking through a dream. The Irregulars were still there all around him, striking at the air with their weapons, but it was as if he and Menni were invisible. Their strange rescuer led them into an alley that led off the square. Here the labyrinth of streets would make it easier to escape pursuit. The stranger headed off up a narrow alley, which was a dim-lit tunnel between the backs of two rows of buildings. Menni's sight had partially returned and the only other effect he seemed to have suffered from exposure to the Jewel's furious fire was a slight disorientation. They had been lucky the Ruby Moon had been past its zenith. The long shadows in the square, cast by the great buildings, had partially shielded Menni from the poisonous moonlight for the few minutes his goggles had been skewed. Max held onto the older man's arm as they hurried stealthily into the darkness. He cast a few glances behind him, alert for sounds of pursuit, and nearly collided with the stranger who had halted in the middle of the alley to lift up a heavy manhole set into the slick cobbles.

'Down there?' Max asked, gesturing towards the lightless hole revealed beneath.

The stranger nodded. 'Hurry.'

A narrow shaft, into the side of which a metal ladder had been fixed, led downwards. The three climbed down, the stranger leading the way, and as they descended a sound of rushing water became louder and louder. Eventually, they reached the bottom of the shaft and dropped to the ground. Max looked around and discovered they had emerged into the network of sewerage tunnels that lay beneath the city. He removed his goggles and put them into his pocket. The place was lit by an eerie greenish glow, which emanated from lichens that grew along the walls and beneath the water itself. Max and Menni had had occasion to use the sewers as a means of escape before, but never with any great enthusiasm. Neither was an expert on their layout. There were many tales in the city above of people disappearing down here. Predators were rumoured to lurk in the murky tunnels but no one knew what kind. Legends suggested tusked and tentacled monsters but, since no one had ever survived an encounter with one, there was no evidence to support the myths.

Max and Menni stood on a narrow walkway beside a wide, fast-moving canal of pure water that had been processed from the city's waste in plants located elsewhere in the system. The walkway was punctuated by dark access ducts and the vaulted ceiling loomed high overhead, meshed with convoluted pipes and conduits. Sound echoed down here as it would in the immensity of a cathedral.

Max turned to their mysterious guide, asking, 'Who are you? Why did you help us?' But even before he'd finished speaking, he realized the stranger was no longer there. He or she – and he was still not sure which gender their rescuer was – had vanished into the maze of tunnels, perhaps through one of the ducts. Max sighed heavily and his breath steamed in the chill air.

Menni sat down on the damp stone floor, rubbing his eyes. 'So much for our greatest venture.'

'Are you all right?' Max asked.

Menni nodded. 'Vision's still a bit blurred, but otherwise, yes. Close call there, lad. Close call.'

Max ignored the censure implied in Menni's tone and looked up at the shaft they had left, his ears straining for sounds from above. 'We can't linger here. Coffin will have snuffers with him. They'll track us.'

'Then where do we go? We could get lost down here.' Menni got slowly to his feet. 'Where'd our friend go?'

'I don't know,' Max answered.

'Who was it?'

'Same answer. I don't know why they intervened.' Max rubbed at his chest without thinking.

'What is it?' Menni asked.

'What?'

'Your chest. Have you been hurt? Were you burned back there?'

Max took his hand away. 'No, I don't think so. It just itches.' He was aware of a strange sensation beneath his skin, a feeling that was familiar to him. It had felt like this sometimes when he'd awoken from a nightmare of his time in Gragonatt and the escape: an irritation in the strange mark above his heart.

'Let me look,' Menni said.

Max opened his shirt.

'Hmm,' Menni murmured, frowning. 'The skin is hot. Looks a bit inflamed.'

Max drew away and closed his shirt. 'We can worry about it later. First, we need to get moving.' He paused. 'Listen.'

A faint scraping, banging sound could be heard overhead. 'Let's move,' Menni said.

'Well, our mysterious deliverer can't have gone that way,' Max said, indicating to the right, 'otherwise we'd have seen them. So we might as well head off this way.' He began to walk away to the left.

'If they wanted us to follow them, they'd have stayed with us,' Menni said darkly, glancing nervously up a shadowy duct opening.

Max shrugged. 'Whatever their motives, they must at least know a way out of here.'

As they walked, they occasionally heard distant clangs and unsettling wailing sounds but they saw no sign of life. After twenty minutes or so, the canal came to a subterranean precipice, where it poured down into an immense central pool fed by four cascading streams. It had to be Watersmeet. Max had seen pictures of it in history books. At its construction, it had been a marvel of architectural engineering. In the pictures, it had always looked brand new, its massive steel pillars gleaming dully as they reared up from the water to support a vaulted ceiling. But now veins of rust, which had bled through from beneath the pillars' outer casings, and stripes of yellow lichen stained the columns. A narrow walkway ran around the pool at the same level that the canals emptied themselves, and there was a network of intersecting gangways across it. Max went to the barrier and leaned over to gaze down at the water below. For a moment, he was sure that something huge and dark moved beneath the surface, which was turbulent close to the waterfalls but strangely calm at its centre. He sniffed the air. 'I can smell brine. That's strange. This water should be fresh.' There were underground seas beneath the ice, but surely they did not contaminate Watersmeet?

Menni shook his head. 'Can't smell anything.'

Max started. 'What was that? Did you see it? Over there?' He pointed.

Menni peered across the expanse of water. 'What am I looking for?'

'I saw a shadow, a figure maybe, on the walkway opposite. Perhaps it was our kind benefactor. Come, let's follow.'

Max and Menni began to cross the waters towards the opposite tunnel, using a precipitous narrow walkway. Occasionally, Max cast glances over the waist-high barrier. There was nothing in the water now, yet he was sure he had seen something earlier. The dark, sinuous shape did not reappear, but a tension in Max's gut advised him his first impression had not been wrong.

Once they reached the opposite side, they found that the tunnel beyond was not so well lit as Watersmeet itself − or, indeed the tunnel they'd initially followed. The lichen here was perhaps less plentiful. Max led the way, groping along the wall with his hand. He was sure he could hear the sound of soft footfalls ahead. As they progressed, the light became dimmer still, until they were inching along in virtual blackness. Yet still it sounded as if someone walked ahead of them, quite near. Max concentrated on this sound, intent on following its source. As he walked, images of the Jewel kept flashing into his mind. How could they have lost it like that? It had been in their grasp. And where was it now? Had Coffin found it? Max was confused. He'd been sure he was supposed to have the Jewel. And yet, now, he did not feel as if he'd failed in his task. How could that be? Was it perhaps the intention that had been important rather than the act itself? But that didn't make sense, not in the world Max Silverskin was familiar with. Perhaps the Jewel would be found again, at the end of this journey.

After they'd been travelling along the tunnel for half an hour or so, the smooth stone beneath Max's fingers became rougher, almost like natural rock. A few more yards and he found visibility improving, but the new illumination was not the strange glow of lichen. In the dim light, he saw that the canal beside them was narrower, its waters frothing as if it ran over jagged stones. If he straddled the stream, he'd be able to touch both walls with his outstretched hands. He paused and turned to Menni, who bumped into him. 'Did we take a turning? This doesn't make sense. The water can't just peter out like this. It was a cascade rushing down to Watersmeet.'

'We kept close to the left hand wall,' Menni said. 'We couldn't see. It's possible we followed a tributary somewhere back there.'

'If we did, then we were led,' Max said. 'There was someone ahead of us, I'm sure of it.'

'I heard footsteps, too,' Menni replied. He gestured with a nod of his head. 'Look, there's light ahead. Let's keep moving. If a person takes it upon themselves to save us from danger, we can only assume they're leading us to safety.'

Max began to walk forward once more. The tunnel was lit now by a soft blue-white radiance, like dusk or dawn, but it was impossible to discern where it came from. He could see that the walls and ceiling were indeed of natural rock. No human hands had carved them. Stalactites hung down, encrusted with pale crystals. Max increased his pace, Menni following. By this time, the path had disappeared and they were forced to wade through the water. Then Max came to a standstill with a cry of frustration. A few feet ahead of them, a curtain of water ran down from the ceiling to supply the stream they'd followed. This was a dead end. They were trapped.

'What is this?' Menni said angrily. 'Someone was ahead of us and now they've disappeared into solid rock. We can't go back. Coffin will be on our trail by now!'

'Wait!' Max said. 'Perhaps this isn't what it seems.' He put one hand to the water and pushed through it. As he thought, there was cold air on the other side. He took a deep breath, then walked through it. Beyond, he dropped to one knee and called. 'This isn't the end of the trail, Menni. Come and look.'

Menni splashed through the water and came to crouch beside him. They were on the edge of another shaft where, as before, a metal ladder was set into the wall. Max picked up a pebble from the stream bed and cast it down. After what seemed a long time, they heard a distant splash.

'Flooded,' said Menni.

Max looked up and saw the shaft continuing above them. Cascading water seemed to surround him. He felt disorientated, no longer sure which way was up and which down. 'We can't stay here,' he said. 'Come on.' He swung himself into the shaft and began to descend.

'Max, we could be trapped down there. We should climb up, not down.'

'No, this is the way. I can sense it.'

'But if we go up, we'll most likely be able to climb out into a different area of the city. We could go to ground easily there. We know that territory.'

Max paused and looked up at his friend. 'I know that, but I feel strongly we have to carry on. We were led here, Menni. We can't go back to the city without finding out why and by whom. Come on. Who knows, perhaps we'll find the legendary Shriltasi down here!'

'You want to believe in legends too much.' Sighing, Menni heaved himself over the lip of the shaft and followed Max's descent. 'I'm not as young as I was, lad. What are you doing to me, having me climb and clamber about the sewers like this? I should be at home with my feet on the fender, a good cup of ale by my side, thinking about how fortunate I am to have survived another of your escapades.'

Max laughed. 'We are learning something new,' he said. 'And it will be of use, I know it.'

Slowly, they made their way down the shaft. Its sides were covered in greenish slime, amid which small iridescent beetles scuttled. But the ladder was strong and true, suggesting it was maintained regularly. Presently, Max saw what looked like natural yet greenish light below. Only a few rungs more and he found that they had come to a metal grille set into the wall of the shaft. It was overgrown with ferny vegetation, which explained the greenish cast to the light. Another wave of disorientation swept over him. They'd climbed down, not up. How could they have come to a place lit by the sun and where plant life grew? Anyway, it should still be dark outside. Had they lost their sense of time as well?

'We didn't climb *up*, did we?' he said to Menni, only half joking.

Menni shook his head, frowning. 'Perhaps it's difficult to tell when the floor's sloping in that darkness. We could have been travelling upwards for a while back there.' He shrugged. It was an unfeasible explanation.

Max gripped the ladder with his legs and one arm, and leaned out to peer through the grille, pushing the greenery aside as best he could between the rusting bars. 'Menni, this is . . . this is unbelievable. There's daylight here, foliage . . .'

'Are we up top again?'

'Must be. But . . . I'm not sure. I've never seen anything like it.'

'Can we get in? We have to suppose the person we were following did so.'

Max examined the bars of the grille, ran his fingers round its edge. 'As far as I can make out, this hasn't moved in a millennium. But the bars are rusted. I think we can break through.'

'Then make haste, lad. I don't enjoy clinging precariously to ladders for any length of time.'

Max began to tug at the bars. Rust came away in his hands, in great flakes. He could see now that an old stream bed lay beyond the grille, its waters trickling out into the shaft. The light was so strange in the place beyond. Like daylight, yet not. It had a bluish cast to it. The ferns that clustered around the grille looked thick and lush, overgrown, untended. They were rustling and moving as if in a breeze, but Max could not feel it. He had an eerie feeling the vegetation outside was sentient somehow, rustling because it was alert to their presence and considered them intruders. But he knew his was nonsense. Max pushed the thought from his mind. He and Menni must somehow have come up in one of the covered farm areas that skirted the city, where all produce was grown. They could ponder how they'd got there later, once they had broken through the grille.

'Hurry, Max,' Menni urged in a whisper. 'I hear something overhead. The scratch of snuffer claws.'

Max shuddered. The mechanical snuffers were relentless trackers, and formidable foes once they'd hunted a man down. He kicked at the grille with one foot and to his satisfaction a couple of the bars gave way, providing just enough room for he and Menni to squeeze through. Max went first, scrambling through a riotous mass of fern. He splashed through the water, which ran over mossy stones, then he pushed through a short tunnel of greenery. When he saw what lay beyond, he stood up straight, silenced.

Menni came to stand behind him and peer over his shoulder soon after. 'By all that ever lived and breathed!' he exclaimed. 'What *is* this place?'

Chapter Seven

The Garden of the World

At the sound of Menni's voice, a herd of startled deer bounded away into the dark green shadows, followed by several rabbits, their white tails bobbing. Birds clattered upwards, squawking. Max and Menni were in a forest, where vast ancient trees created a ceiling of foliage overhead. Wan light came down between their thickly woven branches. The ground was carpeted with a mass of blue and purple flowers, which grew amid a lawn of soft grass. There were dense clumps of unkempt shrubbery and wanton spills of wild rose. Butterflies swarmed among the flowers. Yet, for all this unexpected vitality, there was a slightly faded quality about the scenery, as if the sun had shone on it all for far too long.

'This can't be real,' Max said, venturing forward and turning in a circle to examine his surroundings. 'We've walked into a dream.' He had only ever seen sights such as this in study books or museum reconstructions of how the world had once been. Before the ice. Before the steam. He remembered the old stories of legendary Shriltasi. Was it possible . . . ?

'Now, let's think rationally,' Menni said. 'We've clearly been splashing about the sewers for longer than we thought. This must be the private garden of one of the Lords. The farm areas are heavily guarded. Who knows what lies hidden there among the crops and herds?' He shook his head. 'But this is an uncommonly well-guarded secret. I thought I knew everything there was to know about Karadur.'

'Whatever it is, it's amazing,' Max said. 'This must be what we were led to discover.'

Menni nodded. 'Yes, and I wonder who by? Why should they hide themselves?'

'The same reason we do most of the time, I expect,' Max said. 'Our benefactor must be someone outside the law.'

'Rebels, dissenters,' Menni grumbled. 'If they seek to press us to their cause, they can forget it. I want none of that. It leads only to Gragonatt.'

'Well, let's see where this path leads us,' Max said and headed up a narrow track that snaked through the trees.

Eventually they reached a hedge wall, with a ragged opening before them. It looked like the entrance to a formal garden. Max glanced at Menni, who shrugged. 'Go ahead. We've come this far.'

They stepped through into the strangest garden imaginable. It was surrounded on all sides by tall dark green hedges, which had tiny glossy leaves. Waxy flowers of purplish blue nestled amid the foliage. There was no other cultivation but for an overgrown lawn. This was not a flower garden but something far more eerie. It was filled with statues, a great crowd of them, fashioned from what appeared to be pale green marble. Most of them were smothered with hanks of desiccated vine, while a few others were decked in garlands of flowering fresh growth. The statues represented a host of mythological beings, which again Max had only seen in books: dryads, sylphs and satyrs. They were human-looking, but also inhuman. Many of the grotesque faces resembled the masked figures of the harlequinade they'd seen earlier. It was almost as if they'd flitted away from their makeshift stage in Karadur and returned to their places here, where they'd turned to stone. The detail on the carvings was magnificent. Despite their coverings of foliage, they looked as if they had only frozen into place the moment before Max and Menni had entered the garden.

Menni walked forward, shaking his head in wonderment. 'This is a treasure trove. How can its owner keep it such a secret, and leave it so untended?'

'It looks forgotten,' Max said. He became aware that the mark on his chest had become hot once more. It seemed like a warning. The atmosphere in the garden was close and watchful. It was as if they were intruding into some kind of sacred cemetery.

'Look at her!' Menni said. One statue, near the centre of the group, was unadorned in vines. It was of a young elfin-looking woman, with attenuated features and pointed ears. Her expression was surprised. The stone lips were open a little, revealing perfectly formed teeth. 'This must be the newest,' Menni said. 'Such craftsmanship.' He put his hand upon the statue's shoulder. 'It feels warm, strange.'

'Menni, be careful,' Max said. 'I don't think we should touch . . .'

But Menni seemed bewitched. Even as Max spoke he leaned down and kissed the statue on the lips. The moment was strangely still. To Max's horror, he saw the statue move. The fingers flexed upon the air.

'Menni, get away!' Max cried.

But the woman lifted her arms and curled them around Menni's neck. She stood on tiptoe to kiss him on the mouth once more. Then she stepped gracefully away, a small green-skinned creature, clad in close-fitting garments of what looked like a patchwork of leaves. Her long ragged hair was the russet of autumn foliage.

'Menni, get back here!' Max called, backing towards the trees.

But Menni did not move. The woman fixed her attention on Max, her wide mouth stretched into a feral grin. His first urge was to flee – all his human instincts advised him to do it – but he could not leave Menni behind. He ran forward and grabbed his friend's arm, only to be met by an unnatural resistance. Max's stomach clenched. He could not turn his friend to face him. Dreading what he would find, he stepped around to look Menni in the face. Max uttered a cry of revulsion and averted his eyes. His comrade had become cold stone, his face caught in an expression of unutterable surprise.

Max wheeled round and found the green-skinned woman standing behind him. He drew his sword. 'Whatever you have done, you must undo it, now.'

The woman drew herself taller, her face still wreathed in a mischievous smile. 'But, sir, I did nothing. Your friend took it upon himself to embrace me.' Hands on hips, she took a few sauntering steps towards Max who could not help but back away, his sword still held before him. The woman reached out and took hold of the tip of the weapon. 'Put your blade away, sir. I can explain this situation. Your loss is my gain, and for this I am grateful.'

Reluctantly, Max lowered his blade. 'What kind of creature are you?'

The woman put her head on one side. 'Me? I am a native of this place. My name is Jenniver Ash. Jenny. I am of the Ashen. I do not wish you harm.'

Max eyed the peculiar greenish skin, her slyly slanting eyes. 'You're not . . . you're not human.'

Jenny Ash raised her hands expressively. 'I'm not. Why does that surprise you?' She laughed, as if knowing full well how shocked he was. Surprise was an understatement.

Max swallowed with difficulty, trying to remain calm. His first instinct was to flee the scene. His skin crawled with revulsion for the inhuman creature before him. But flight would not help Menni. 'If you don't wish me harm, explain what you've done to Menni, and how it can be undone.'

Jenny Ash folded her arms. 'Ah, it is a long story. Suffice to say I found myself in the unfortunate condition you discovered me in. Few things can reverse its effects, but one that can is the kiss of a human creature. Your friend did not know what he was doing. Once he touched me, the effects were transferred to him.'

'That's not possible. It's a trick. How did you do it?'

Jenny Ash indicated Menni with one hand. 'Is not the evidence before you? How can this be a trick? I wish it was.'

'Then you made it happen somehow. You called him to you.'

Jenny Ash shrugged. 'I don't deny it. Wouldn't you have done the same?'

Max shook his head. 'This is insane. A living person cannot be turned to stone.'

'Or what looks like stone,' said Jenny Ash. 'My friend, you know too little. But now you are here and you may learn. It is not before time.'

Max narrowed his eyes. 'What do you mean?'

She came a step closer. 'We have long awaited the advent of the Fox of Akra onto our soil.'

Max backed away. 'You know of me? How? What is this place?'

'Your first two questions will be answered shortly, but I'll gladly furnish you with the third explanation.' She indicated a narrow opening in the hedge behind her. 'Will you come with me, noble Fox? All the answers to your questions lie this way.'

Max hesitated, giving Menni a quick glance. He found it difficult to look upon his friend in that state. 'How do I know I won't end up like him?'

'You won't. I know it's pointless to give you my word, so I won't waste my breath. But I trust your natural curiosity will conquer your fear. Come. You must not worry about Master Vane. He is quite safe where he is.'

'Undo what you did!'

'It will be undone, I promise you. But first, we must speak.'

With one last glance at Menni, Max shuddered before following Jenny Ash into the thick foliage. Beyond was a narrow pathway where the evergreen shrubbery met overhead. The path was strewn with thick petals. There was just enough room for Max and Jenny to walk side by side. 'This place is Shriltasi, the underside of Karadur,' Jenny said. 'The underworld, if you like.'

Max could not suppress a shiver, which was due to awe and wonderment as much as to dread. 'Shriltasi is a myth. It does not exist.' Yet hadn't he been looking for it, secretly hoping it might be real?

Jenny shook her head. 'You are wrong.'

Max squinted up through the thick leaves above them. He could perceive a wan soft glow. 'But the light . . . How is that possible underground?'

'I will explain, but first things first. Shriltasi is everything the Lords of the Metal refuse to accept in their narrow reality. I will tell you of it.'

Jenny explained that, at one time, Shriltasi had been known as the Garden of the City and was where all the foodstuffs for Karadur had been produced, where its meat and dairy herds had been husbanded. It had been constructed to preserve the beauty of the natural world and to provide a farming area, back when the ice had been only an advancing creeping threat. In those days, Max's people had been more open to ideas and concepts beyond their limited perception. They had invited the inhuman creatures of the wildlands to help construct a safe haven for both races. The Ashen and their subjects were a race quite apart from humanity. They had for ever lived among the shadows of the forest green. Traditionally, they had had little contact with human folk, but even the Ashen recognized they were facing perilous times. The two races had to work together to survive. The contract between them stipulated that the Ashen would farm the garden in return for being allowed to live in it. No one had any idea how long the ice would endure or, indeed, if it would ever disappear. The Ashen Elders decided they had no choice but to comply. The lands above would freeze and die, but in Shriltasi the Ashen could live on, in an acceptable approximation of the world they'd known. The Karadurians, adept at both engineering and alchemy, constructed vast and complicated mechanisms that gathered the meagre light of the sun above, amplified it and refracted it throughout the hidden realm.

'If you could glimpse our sky,' Jenny said, 'you would see only a golden haze, but behind that there are mirrors and machines, keeping all in order. It is to our great advantage that the ancients built well, for I doubt any Lord above would take care to service the mechanisms now. I fear they no longer have the knowledge and ability.'

'How are they cared for, though?' Max asked. 'Why don't they just wear out?'

'They are serviced by creatures created in the crucible of the foundry,' Jenny said. 'Metallic yet alchemical beings. We never see them, but they are eternal.'

'I find it hard to believe people such as yourself had any dealings with our ancestors,' Max said.

'But it was all so different then,' Jenny replied. 'Your people were different. They were prepared to accept that the Ashen followed different laws to themselves. We had different notions concerning the birth and death of living creatures, the cycle of the seasons. But we fulfilled our part of the bargain and the humans were content with that. Then things changed.'

Jenny spoke of the terrible Clan Wars, when brother had fought against brother. Nobody really knew how they had begun, other than that the alchemists of the clans had somehow come into competition with one another. What might have started as a quest for excellence had descended into resentful power struggles. The alchemists had used their knowledge and abilities to devastating effect, turning Karadur-Shriltasi into a pandemonium of conflicting magicks. The Lords of the Metal had eventually realized that the wars were destroying what was left of their civilization and that the alchemists, mad in their single-minded desire for power and now acting independently of their masters who no longer wanted war, must be curbed. Iron, Gold, Copper and Silver formed an historic alliance to combat the alchemists. The Battle Boys had been created in the Old Forge because, lacking minds and therefore imagination, they were less prey to the effects of magical combat than human warriors. To the alchemists, fear was their greatest weapon and, finding themselves disarmed, they soon fell before the inexorable might of the mechanical militia.

Victorious, the Lords had vowed to create order from chaos. They had formed the Council of the Metal, full of restrictive dogma and fear. A constitution had been drawn up, the heart of a movement termed the Reformation. No longer would human beings utilize the subtle forces of the multiverse, for they were ill-equipped to deal with them. Alchemy and other occult sciences were outlawed. It was decreed that the Ashen were abominations against nature, their ways tainted with dark magic.

'The Lords had closed minds,' Jenny said. 'Their clans had suffered terribly during the wars, and they were determined to make lasting changes so nothing like that could ever happen again. They were afraid of the subtle forces of the multiverse, which we call *barishi*.'

Max nodded thoughtfully, partly aghast that he was giving this story any credence. 'It's true that one way of dealing with something you fear is to deny it exists.'

'Quite so,' Jenny said. 'The Lords decreed that *barishi* was evil and dangerous, the product of deluded minds who wanted to believe in it so they could control others. But when it officially no longer existed, then neither could we, for we were living proof of what *barishi* really was.'

'So how did they manage to separate the two realms so successfully?'

Jenny explained how, in secret, the Lords had constructed the great farms around the city. Then, when they were ready, the link between the upper and lower world had been officially severed. Every misery, hurt and destructive act was blamed upon the corrupting beliefs of the Ashen. The alchemists had gained most of their knowledge from the underworld people.

To survive and remain pure, humanity must turn from them, shun them, deny them. All mention and consideration of Shriltasi had been wiped from the official records and the minds of the human populace. The thoroughfares between the worlds had been bricked up and blocked. It had been ordained forbidden even to speak of Shriltasi, so children grew up ignorant of what lay beneath their feet. People were afraid. They obeyed the will of the Lords, thinking them their saviours. Only the name of Shriltasi lived on in certain history books, annexed to that of the upper city. Karadur-Shriltasi: a splendid name for an entity only half what it once was.

Max shook his head. 'Despite what you have told me, and the evidence of my eyes, I cannot bring myself to believe in magic. I can see why the Lords distanced themselves from your people. Ideas such as that lead only to madness.'

Jenny smiled sadly. 'Ah, you are so much a son of Karadur, despite your mother's blood. It is a great shame. But whether you choose to believe it or not, we have a little *barishi* here, which helps us to survive. Magic, as you call it, is nothing more than the instinctive manipulation of natural energy inherent in living things. It permeates the multiverse with its song of life. There is nothing strange about it, if you can only accept what it is.'

Max stared at her grimly.

Jenny only shrugged. 'Think of it this way. In some respects, steam is but a diminished reflection of what true magic is. But the natural life-force has become stagnant, because of fear and ignorance. How can *barishi* flow freely and healthily through such dark, twisted energy? It is why your city is crumbling. Even here, we are affected by it. Our *barishi* is withering and because we, as a people, are so enlivened by the life force, once it recedes, we lose animation. We turn to stone, as you saw back there.'

Max uttered an incredulous sound. 'This is too improbable for words. I cannot believe it.'

'I understand your confusion,' Jenny said, 'and it will take time for you to accept this new knowledge. I stole some of your friend's life-force, which enabled me to escape my fate.'

'Then you are a thief of the worst kind – in fact, a murderer.'

'Your friend is not dead, Fox. And we are both thieves.' She sighed heavily.

'Above us, Karadur crumbles and dies, while down here, all is turning to stone, to dust. I will show you.' She reached up and plucked one of the blooms from the canopy just over their heads. To Max's astonishment, it powdered to dust in Jenny's fist. 'Both our worlds are in trouble, Sir Fox. They'll be destroyed by superstition and fear. Overground, they already seek victims to blame among their own kind. That's how they justify employing the likes of Captain Coffin and his predatory militia.'

'You seem to know a lot about Karadur,' Max said.

Jenny nodded. 'We make it our business to do so. We move in the upper world without people realizing it, utilizing the secret thoroughfares like the one you used today.'

'How much longer will they be secret? Coffin was tracking us.'

Jenny smiled, an expression touched with cold. 'Fear not. His snuffers are already rusting in the deep well you climbed down and the few Irregulars who accompanied them have vanished. Their sacrifice of life will help my people. Anyone who dares to venture into the tunnels is fair game to us. All trace has been expunged of your passage. Coffin will never find you here.'

'You killed them,' Max said.

'Are you complaining? You're alive and free, aren't you?'

'How do you know these things? You were stone when we arrived here.'

'My brother knows,' Jenny said. 'And what he knows, so do I. All the time I was frozen there, Jack fed me with his thoughts. He is waiting to meet you.'

'You are amoral creatures,' Max said. 'I myself have stolen and – in extremis – killed to save myself. But what I do seems clean to me. What you do does not.'

Jenny pulled a bitter face. 'In Shriltasi, my people have become like vampires. Even though we are not greedy, we are sometimes forced to take morsels of human life-force in order to survive. This was not always the case. Once we worked with and for you without thought. We provided all you needed, while we took nothing. *Barishi* sustained us. Now we need a little of what you took from us.'

'You still had no right to take Menni's life-force against his will. It is the worst form of violation.'

'No, Fox, I did not. But neither did your people have the right to the bread my ancestors provided for them. They did not have the right to banish us and try to disempower my people through starvation of energy.'

'Surely, if they'd wanted to do that, they'd have destroyed the mechanisms that provide your light and heat.'

Jenny shook her head. 'You don't understand. Karadur and Shriltasi are intimately linked. If this realm was destroyed completely, it would affect the overworld. The mechanisms that run them are one. Also, I'm sure you know it is not the Lords' way to kill overtly. They prefer to inflict slow suffering and keep their lofty morals intact.'

They had come to a place where the tunnel of foliage ended. Beyond, tall stately trees ringed a wide glade. In its centre was a large building, artfully fashioned from woven branches and leaves. Banners of ragged green silk hung down from it. The building was surrounded by humbler dwellings, livestock pens, and what appeared to be workshops. Other Ashen went gracefully about their business there, casting curious glances at the newcomer. 'Welcome to my home,' said Jenny. 'This is our palace, Asholm, seat of the exiled royal family of Shriltasi. Here you will meet my brother, Jack.' She smiled. 'He knows already that I am free, and is grateful for it.'

Max shuddered. It was discomfiting to think this creature could communicate with her own kind through thought. 'Did one of your people lead us here to Shriltasi?' he asked.

Jenny hesitated, then said, 'It was time. Don't worry. You will be told everything. Enter our domain of your own free will.'

Max could not suppress a shudder at those words. They had a sinister ring. His mind was reeling with everything that Jenny had said to him. He wanted to deny it, but how could he ignore the evidence of what had happened to Menni, of Jenny's bizarre appearance and of the very existence of this strange realm? He had stumbled upon something momentous, and he was expected here. The mark on his chest seemed to thrum with a peculiar vibration. But it did not feel threatening, rather anticipatory.

Jenny led Max beneath a high-arched doorway and along a series of dim-lit corridors into a room that looked like a miniature forest. The twining branches and swags of foliage might be furniture, or just natural growths. Jenny summoned what must have been a servant, although she looked far from subservient. 'Linni, fetch King Jaxinther. Tell him the Fox of Akra is here at last.'

The Ashen girl bowed and departed, but it seemed that Jack Ash must have been anticipating his guest. After only a few moments, a curtain of shivering willowy leaves drew apart at the back of the hall to reveal the form of a man, a male version of Jenny, as weirdly beautiful as she was. He was dressed in a costume of russet and dark green that appeared to have been fashioned from leaves. His long nut-brown hair was decorated with sweeping black-and-white feathers, and at his side hung a sword that looked like a giant thorn. A billowing silvery cloak of snakeskin adorned his shoulders, thrown back to reveal his body. He bowed. 'Welcome, Max Silverskin. I am Jack Ash. I thank you for releasing my sister from stasis.'

'I had little to do with it,' Max said. 'It was my friend Menni who fell victim, not I.'

Jack Ash smiled. 'You are angry. I understand that. But I hope that once we have conversed your attitude will change. There is much that you should know.'

A black imp came scuttling into the chamber, bearing a wooden tray upon which stood three goblets and a flagon. Jack indicated that Max should seat himself on what looked like a bench covered with a blanket of woven leaves. 'Partake of our hospitality. We shall talk together.'

Max remained standing. 'We shall only talk if you will guarantee that Menni can be restored.'

Jack sighed through his nose impatiently. 'That is a minor matter. You will soon see this for yourself. Now sit. There is little time.'

Cautiously, Max did so. The imp came bobbing and ducking towards him: a disturbing creature that appeared to be made of burned sticks. Max took a goblet from its twiggy fingers. Jack took another seat, while Jenny curled up at her brother's feet on the leaf-strewn floor.

Max sipped the drink in his goblet. It tasted like the purest water, with a woody undertaste. After he'd swallowed it, he realized it was also extremely alcoholic. He must be careful, guard his senses. Discreetly, he put the goblet down on the floor beside him.

'Do you know who you are?' Jack said.

Max smiled grimly. 'I think I am aware of that, despite having taken a mouthful of your sorcerous draught!'

Jack shook his head. 'Perhaps we should examine the basics first. Only a few of the Lords who rule in Karadur are aware of our existence, and they guard the secret carefully. The rest think it's impossible for us to exist. You consider yourself superior to them, but that is a self-delusion. You dream the same mindless, unquestioning dream they do, Max Silverskin. All of you overworlders are profoundly, wilfully ignorant. Your whole existence is based on lies and deceit. Despite their lofty morals, I could show you members of your own estranged clan behaving in a manner so bestial and depraved that you wouldn't believe it – yet they call us less than human! When humans become too powerful, they forget that words merely describe reality, they don't create it. Shriltasi exists, and *barishi*, the force you call magic, exists. The Silverskins, alone of all citizens in Karadur, have always known this. They refused to forget like everyone else, and kept the knowledge alive as a secret tradition. That's why the other Clans despise them, without exactly knowing the reason. How did you escape Gragonatt last year, Fox? Can you remember? Do you ever think about it?'

Max shifted uncomfortably on his seat. 'I suspect you know more about that than I. Of course, I have thought about it, but answers and conclusion elude me. If you know, tell me.'

'You haven't thought about it as much as you should. You are afraid, and rightly so. What might have seemed like salvation has doomed you, Fox, but it was necessary.'

Max frowned. 'What do you mean?'

'Open your shirt,' Jack said.

Max bridled. 'Why?'

'Just do as I say.' Jack touched his sister lightly on the shoulder. 'Jenny, go to him.'

Jenny uncurled from the floor and sauntered to Max's side. Warily, he unlaced the front of his shirt and Jenny leaned down to pull the fabric aside. Max could feel a great heat in his chest. The brand was reacting violently to Jenny's presence.

'Look at it,' Jack said. 'Now you must learn its nature.'

Jenny reached out and placed her cool dry palm flat against the brand. Immediately, Max was consumed by a wave of white-hot pain. He cried out and drew back, nearly falling from his seat.

'Look,' said Jack. 'See the truth of it.'

Max looked down and saw that the brand had changed into a disc of glowing metal that was somehow melded with his flesh. It was how it had appeared in his dreams. But this was no dream.

'That is the silverheart,' Jenny said. 'Your destiny.'

'What is it?' Max said. The pain had receded, but his flesh still burned as if he was sitting too close to a furnace.

'It is known as the witch mark,' Jack said. 'It was given to you on the night of your escape a year ago, by the person who liberated you.'

'Who was it? You? Jenny?'

Jack shook his head. 'It does not matter for the moment. When you were given that mark, you were set on a path of great responsibility. There is a legend, which I doubt you know but which my people are already instilling into the minds of the populace of Karadur. When a male of the Silverskin clan is born with the power of a Silverskin woman, the time has come for a great change that will not only affect Karadur and Shriltasi but the many layers of the multiverse itself.'

'I have no powers, female or otherwise,' Max said. 'This is ridiculous.'

'Yet you have the mark.'

'Someone gave it to me – you said so.'

Jack rolled his eyes, caught the glance of his sister and shared with her a conspiratorial smile. 'How did they give it to you? In your narrow reality, how is it possible for a hunk of metal to be part of your flesh, to burn you, to chill you, to fill you with fear? Pluck it out, if you can.'

Max felt nauseated at the very idea of touching the unearthly disc, but gingerly poked it with his fingers. It seemed to be sunk deep into him, so deep that if he attempted to remove it he'd pull out his own beating heart beneath.

'For most of the time, it is hidden,' Jack said. 'For your own protection more than anything, but Jenny used *barishi* to awaken it. *Barishi* is in you, too, Max, but dormant. Your mother made it so to keep you safe until the appointed time. Now is that time. You have to bring harmony back to Karadur-Shriltasi. You have to reawaken the *barishi*, cast out stagnation. But you must do it quickly. That silverheart, which will enhance your abilities, will also destroy you. Even as we speak, it is eating into your body. When the Ruby Moon rose last night, the silverheart awoke. When it meets with your heart of flesh, your human form will be no more. Hard though it is for me to tell you and for you to accept, you have only six days left to you. It is eating down towards your heart, Fox. And when it eats your heart, you will belong to it forever.'

Max uttered a stunned laugh, then fell silent. He glanced down at the silverheart, remembering all the nightmares of pain and destruction. Could it be true? Even as he looked at it, it was fading, waves of burning chill ebbing away. Soon it was only a puckered red mark once more.

Jenny, who had sat down beside him, put a slim hand on his knee. 'You know in that silver heart of yours that we speak the truth, Fox.'

Max swallowed with difficulty. He felt as if reality was slipping away from him. 'If I am to die, why should I do anything? It won't matter once I'm dead.'

'It depends on what you think death is,' Jack said. 'All we know is that in six days' time the form you know will be changed. Whether you retain any conscious memory of your previous state is unknown to us. You won't know until it happens. But I'll tell you this: unless you fulfil your destiny, neither you nor your city will have a future. You have no choice but accept your fate. Haven't you noticed what's happening to Karadur? Your buildings petrify in their death throes. We're all turning to stone.' Jack turned a fond gaze upon Jenny. 'I and my sister have done all that we can to try and do something, even to the point where our own people cast us out. We ruled them once, but now we live in exile. Yes, even down here, where the last of the *barishi* glows in the landscape, ignorance holds sway. Our people are afraid too and have reverted to primitive ways in order to feel safe. They have created gods and worship them. They have surrendered all responsibility, many of them living like savages. Some days ago, a group of them came across us as we attempted to use our own life-force to enliven an area that has almost been destroyed. Thinking we were making things worse, these people attacked us. They took Jenny's *barishi* from her, reducing her to the state you found her in. I managed to fight them off, but it was too late. All I could do was carry my sister to the Stone Grove, where you found her.'

'Menni said you were rebels or dissidents. He was right.'

'Sir Fox, we know you have tried to make a difference in your own way, ignorant of where the trouble really lay. We have established a few important contacts in Karadur. Together, we can all make a difference.'

'How? If what you say is true, six days will not be enough.'

'We know only that the four clan icons must be found and brought together.'

'The play,' Max said slowly. 'Yesterday, in the Grand Market. A harlequin spoke of these clan icons.'

Jack smiled. 'I saw you there. The harlequin was me, Fox. That is one way we reach the people of Karadur, feed their belief in you.'

'What about Menni?' Max said. 'I care more for his well-being than I do for my own. If you want my cooperation, you must restore him. Or can't you do that?'

'There are several ways it can be done,' Jenny said. 'You could kiss him yourself, of course, but that would only turn you to stone, which is hardly desirable. One of the artefacts we spoke of is reputed to reverse the affliction. It is the icon of Clan Copper known as the War Owl. Its stare allegedly has great powers. Seeing as you have to acquire this artefact anyway, it makes sense that this is the method you should use to bring warmth and life back to your friend's body.'

'How convenient for you,' Max said. 'Why have you never sought out these artefacts yourself?'

'You can venture where we cannot, because you bear the witch mark,'

Jenny said. 'The War Owl is very important to you as well as to ourselves. You should know that there are four symbols of great power. In time, you will learn them. They were known as the Four Signs of the Metal, given to humanity by the multiverse in a vision to an ancient seer, when *barishi* was still an accepted fact of life in Karadur. They represent the blazons of the founding clans and were given concrete form by the ancient craftsman. Now they are known to only a few as the four lost icons. They were banished from Karadur because of their associations with the forbidden sciences.'

'The icons,' said Jack Ash, 'were originally created to display the skills of the Clan artisans and the beauty of their particular Clan metal. Each artefact possessed powers of its own. The War Owl, for instance, embodied wisdom, vision and skill – as well as ferocity. These attributes could by owned by whoever possessed the Owl and mastered it.'

Max shook his head. 'This is all too incredible. How am I to find these objects – supposing I want to?'

Jack shrugged elegantly. 'You have already begun your search. Your intention is of prime importance. Once you have committed yourself to the task, synchronicity will work in your favour. Events have to proceed in the proper order. First, you will need the Talon. It will help counter-attack the debilitating effects of the silverheart.'

'What's that?' Max demanded. 'And why do I need it? There's nothing wrong with me. I feel fine.' Unconsciously, he touched himself on the chest.

Jack shook his head. 'The witch mark imparts great powers of sorcery but, as we have told you, it exacts a price, which you will soon feel for yourself. The Talon is represented by a jade bird's foot. A small, deceptively inconsequential thing. However, it contains an elixir that can kill almost all living things – save the one who carries the witch mark. The pain will very soon begin to take its toll upon you. The essence of the Jade Talon will help control it, so that you can fulfil your destiny and restore your friend.'

'And how do I acquire this particular object?' Max said.

'I can help you find it,' Jenny said without hesitation. 'But first, you must help me. It is part of the contract.' She sighed. 'I know already you will protest about it, but you must find for me my amber bead.'

'Amber bead,' said Max stonily. 'Another artefact. We shall have a veritable museum between us. What is this thing and why do you need it?'

'The bead protected me from the stone plague,' Jenny said. 'If I am to go into hostile territory with you, I must have it with me. I lost it in Karadur.'

'How?'

Jenny looked away. 'For some time, we have been keeping an eye on you. I visit the city often. Unfortunately, a short time ago, I was careless. I had infiltrated the Moonmetal Manse of Clan Silver, intent on investigating their library. But Clovis Pewter happened to be visiting his relatives there and discovered me – the lust-enfeebled fool! He caught me and tried to hold me. I was in disguise, a glamour thrown around me. He thought I was just a little human thief, mere flotsam of the city, and decided he would have some fun with me. I used *barishi* to get away – although he would not know that – but in the process he took my bead. Tore it from my throat. He has it still. You can get it back, Sir Fox. We know you can.'

Max considered. 'A cynical man might say this is the sole reason for you bringing me here. You are prey to this peculiar plague and your protection is lost. No doubt you'd use any means to regain it.'

Jenny's skin flushed a strange deep green. 'We have not lied to you, Fox, not once. But it would mean much to us if you would help us in this matter.'

Max suspected that both Jack and Jenny were extremely clever and calculating individuals who seemed more innocent than they were. But he could see it would not help to alienate them. They could be the only means of bringing Menni Vane back to life. 'So, is this bead on Pewter's person?' he asked. At these words, he noticed that both Jack and Jenny relaxed visibly in relief. They thought they had him.

'He wears it sometimes,' Jenny said. 'I've heard reports of this. He can't possibly know what it is, but the power within it has attracted him. If it's not about his neck, it's kept in the family strongroom of Clan Silver. The vaults are impossible to break into. I know – I've tried.'

Max observed wryly how his senses pricked up at these words and guessed Jenny Ash was well aware of their effect. Nowhere was inaccessible to the

Fox of Akra. He also knew the Moonmetal Manse intimately, having spent many years there. 'Very well. It seems I have little choice and, to be honest, the prospect of thieving from Pewter is pleasing.'

Jenny leaned over and kissed his cheek, which made Max wince away. 'Don't fear!' she said, laughing. 'My kiss won't turn you to stone. Thank you, Fox. I appreciate your help.'

'Even though it was rather press-ganged,' Max said. He stood up and spoke cynically. 'Well, if I only have six days left to me, I'd better leave here at once.' He still didn't believe that part of the story, thinking the Ashen sought to frighten him in order to make him compliant.

'Before you leave, I want to give you something,' Jenny said. 'Come.'

She led him out of the main hall into another chamber, where a wicker basket of fist-sized crystal stones lay on a gnarled table. Jenny picked up one of the stones. It was carved into the shape of a four-leafed clover, with a hole in its centre through which a leather thong was strung. The centre of each section was concave, as if meant to hold further ornament. 'This is a spellstone,' Jenny said. 'Do not lose it. It gives you control over certain frequencies of *barishi*, and will also protect you from malign *barishic* attacks. It might take you a little practice to use it well, but you have the ability within you. Watch the symbol I make.'

'Are you asking me to use magic?' Max asked, raising one eyebrow.

Jenny ignored this remark and began to draw upon the air with flowing strokes. Her actions left a scintillating green trail in their wake. She drew the symbol several times, so that it hung for some moments in the air around them. 'Remember this sign,' she said. 'It conjures a particular frequency of *barishi* into being. Can you do it? Show me.'

Hesitantly, Max copied what she had shown him – although *his* fingers did not leave a glowing trail in the air.

She pursed her lips. 'Well, that will suffice. Drawing the symbol correctly is the most important thing. If you're in danger, take out the stone and use the sign. This will awaken the energy within the stone and give you power over what we call the autonotype of any species you direct the *barishi* towards.'

Max turned the stone in his hands. 'What's an autonotype?'

'They were forms devised by the ancient alchemists of Karadur, augmented by their spiritual beliefs in the Metal. I know you will not believe
in it at first, but that doesn't matter. The symbol and the energy will work,
regardless of your belief. *Barishi* knows when it is needed and will flow to
that place in the right form. It has intelligence, far more than you or I.
You must respect this, Fox Silverskin. No human has been given one of
our stones before.' She placed the artefact in Max's right hand, closing his
fingers over it. 'Find my amber bead.'

'I will do my best.' He hesitated. 'Jenny Ash, are you deceiving me? Can
what you and your brother told me be true? I find it all hard to believe.
You are asking me to change my whole view of the world.'

Jenny was silent for a moment and did not let go of his hands. 'It is true,
Fox. I wish it wasn't.' She looked up into his eyes. 'I have watched you
grow, become a man. I was conscious always of your destiny. I will protect
you as much as I can. I am the bane of your enemies. And I recognize
them better than you do. Whatever you think of my morals, I know how
to destroy in subtle ways, with the poisoner's arts and with the power of
barishi that can make a man do anything. These are the old ways, which
the people of Karadur deny. I'm your greatest ally. And if it is meant that
you must give your life, I would gladly give mine to save it.'

Max studied her for a moment, surprised by the heat of her words.
Then he bowed his head. 'You embarrass me, madam. Until today I was
in ignorance of you and your world, yet now you make this pledge. I hope
I am worthy of it.'

Jenny smiled, withdrew her hands. 'I am confident you are.' She turned
away from him and drew aside a curtain of leaves to reveal a tier of shelves.
From this she picked up a scroll, tied with a strand of vine. 'To return
here, you'll need a map of the Garden.' She unrolled the scroll and bade
him help her keep it straight. 'This reveals the location of the four main
entrances, which are a much quicker way to get to us than the route you
took today.' She pointed at four points on the map. 'These are the wells that
serve Karadur: the Well of the Dragon, the Well of the Gibbold, the Well
of the Owl and, lastly, the Well of the Heart. Some of them are guarded,
so you will need to take care when you use them. The map will guide

you through the great tangled forest our world has become. It shows the old paths, which in many places have become hidden by undergrowth.' Jenny pulled the map from Max's hands and rolled it up once more. 'This time, I shall show you the way out myself. But there will be other times, when I am not around to help. It would be best if you could familiarize yourself with this territory as soon as possible. When you return with my bead, make your way to the Stone Grove. We will meet you there. You can be sure we'll know when you set foot in Shriltasi once more.'

Max rubbed his face, found stubble beneath his fingers. 'I'm losing track of time here. Something tells me I should have been asleep for hours.' He smiled wryly. 'Perhaps I have been.'

Jenny laughed. 'You are in need of sleep, perhaps. Our daylight hours are sometimes different to those of the upper world. Time is a fluid thing here, perhaps because we elect not to regard it as linear. But before you seek your bed, Sir Fox, go directly to Clan Silver. It is the best time of day for your task – early morning.'

'You do not need to advise me on my trade,' Max said. 'I shall return, with your bead, when I have rested.'

'Then let's make haste. If you follow my route, you can be back in the upper city very shortly.'

Max realized then how Jenny – and probably her brother – believed they had won him over entirely. But what was their real agenda? He could not be sure. Neither was he wholly convinced by what he'd been told of the silver heart. If he was to help Menni, he should go along with them for now. But he vowed he would do a little investigating of his own before he put himself at their mercy completely.

Chapter Eight

Silverskin Legacy

Lord Iron had mixed feelings about being called away from Fabiana's party. Part of him was relieved to escape the tedious conversation he'd been having with his cousin, Fedric Iron, while another part of him sensed great trouble. Coffin hadn't come back into the party himself. One of Copper's servants had been sent to summon the head of the Council. Rose, standing nearby, had hurried out after him. He was grateful for her presence.

They found Coffin standing in the entrance hall of the manse. His expression was at once grim and wild. Lord Iron's heart sank. Coffin was a man of few aspects. This could only be bad news.

'What is it, Captain?' he demanded.

Coffin glanced at the knots of lords and ladies who had made no secret of edging closer, clearly curious about what he had to say.

'I would speak to you in private, my lord.'

Lord Iron nodded. 'Very well.' He turned to Fabiana's steward, Truffle, who was lurking nearby. 'Conduct us to a secluded room, if you please.'

Truffle bowed. 'Follow me, my lord.'

He took them to the chamber that Fabiana and her brother used as an office. Lord Iron knew it would not be long before their hosts barged in, demanding to know what was going on. The moment Truffle closed the door, he said 'Speak quickly, man. What has happened?'

'The Jewel has gone,' Coffin said.

Rose uttered a cry, pressed her fingers to her mouth.

Lord Iron blinked. 'What?'

'It's true. This is dire news, my lord.'

'How can it be gone?' Lord Iron snapped. 'What are you talking about?'

'Max Silverskin . . .' Coffin began.

Lord Iron groaned, turned briefly away. 'This is not something I wish to hear.'

'Well, I do,' said Rose. 'Explain yourself, Captain.'

'It was fortunate I was with my men at the time, in their clubhouse. There was a commotion in the square and the Battle Boys made a terrible racket. Useless in all other respects.' Coffin shook his head. 'We lost no time in going forth, at considerable risk to ourselves, and found Max Silverskin crouching on a beam of the tower with his confederate, Vane. They had the Jewel in their possession. Ropes were dangling everywhere.'

Rose had to suppress a laugh at the image this conjured in her mind. 'Go on,' she said, with difficulty.

Coffin frowned. 'Something very strange occurred. We'd got the wretch cornered, but then one of his comrades came to help him. They managed to create a wall of fire that enabled the criminals to escape.'

'And the Jewel?' Lord Iron said. 'He took it?'

Coffin shrugged uneasily. 'I cannot say. We know the miscreants had taken the Shren from its plinth, but then we saw it fall. After the commotion had died down, and Silverskin had fled, we searched the area to no avail.'

'He took the Jewel,' said Rose, careful to keep her voice neutral.

'That man has unspeakable gall,' said Lord Iron. He paced the chamber. 'This is terrible. It will cause anarchy.' He took out his watch and examined its face. 'In a scant few hours, the taverns will disgorge their patrons and everyone will behold what has happened. I dread to think what might occur.' He turned on Coffin. 'Did you pursue Silverskin?'

Coffin nodded. 'To the best of our ability. He went down into the sewers.'

'The sewers, you say?' Lord Iron snapped. There was an urgency in his tone that alerted his daughter immediately. She felt her skin flush and wondered whether she shared the same suspicions as her father as to where Max might have fled. It concerned a subject she never dared address with him. Did Max know of this place? If so, how? It was Karadur's most closely guarded secret.

'Yes,' Coffin said. 'I sent snuffers and some of my men after him. I have the greatest confidence they'll hunt him down before morning.'

Lord Iron uttered a snort of contempt. 'Let's hope so! I can't believe you let him get away from the scene. What were you thinking of?'

'We did everything in our power . . .'

Iron waved away the excuses. 'Oh, we have no time for that. A substitute Jewel must be placed upon the plinth without delay. This will buy us time.'

'A substitute?' said Rose. 'How will we manage that?'

Lord Iron fixed his daughter with a stern stare. 'Our Clan is famed for its precaution and preparation,' he said. 'We have, in our vaults, a stone that was grown in the foundry. It is not the Shren Diamond, by any means, but it should fool people for at least a while.'

'But the Shren is unique,' Rose said. 'What about its light? What about Karadur?' She was already thinking of a certain assignation she had told herself she wouldn't keep in the morning. Would he show up now? What would she say? It was clearly up to her to recover the Jewel. Max Silverskin must have gone insane to take it.

'The Shren is a symbol, nothing more,' said Iron coldly. 'I doubt anyone ever looks at it with any great attention. But it's easy to see why Silverskin decided to steal it. An act bound to cause chaos. It's what he wants, poor deluded fool.' He pulled himself up straight. 'We must go to The Old Forge at once. I trust you have secure and protective transport, Captain?'

Coffin bowed. 'Of course.'

The door opened and Fabiana and Rufus came into the room. 'What's afoot?' Fabiana enquired. 'You all look most grim.'

'An accident,' Iron said. 'Some drunken fools went out into the night and attempted to touch the Shren Diamond. It became dislodged from its plinth during the fracas. I have to go at once to supervise its reinstallation.'

Fabiana frowned. 'Has it been damaged?'

Lord Iron shook his head. 'Not to our knowledge, no.'

Fabiana sighed. 'This is just another sad symptom of all that's wrong in our city. I can't believe people are becoming so wild, so uncontrollable. Is nothing safe any more?'

'It means we must re-evaluate the Ceremony of the Jewel,' said her brother. 'If louts are going to do things like this, perhaps the time has come for more security. Because of the perversity of a few, the majority of Karadurians will no longer be able to view the Jewel. It's obvious.'

'We can discuss this later,' Lord Iron said, 'at an official meeting of the Council. For now, our prime concern is the safety of the Jewel.'

'Of course,' said Fabiana. 'You must go at once. Will you be safe from the Moon rays?'

'We will take every precaution,' Iron said. He went to the door with Coffin. Rose followed him, but he turned to her and put his hands on her shoulders. 'Not you, my daughter. I cannot countenance you risking your own safety out there.'

'But father,' Rose said. 'I am not afraid. I must go with you.'

Iron shook his head. 'No. That is my final word. Stay here and try to enjoy the party. I will send word when all is well.'

Once he'd left, Fabiana hooked an arm through one of Rose's elbows. 'You must not worry about him, my dear. I'm sure he will be quite safe.'

Rose smiled weakly, her mind in turmoil. Something was happening, building up fast, like a storm. She could feel the prickly power of its approach.

Fabiana patted Rose's hand. 'You should visit me some time, my dear. I feel you are too much alone. One day, you will take your father's place as head of the Council. You will need friends then.'

'You are kind,' Rose muttered, thinking she could not possibly endure a meeting with Fabiana alone. What would they talk about?

'You are still young,' said Fabiana in a silky voice. 'Perhaps you should learn not to make judgements upon people so hastily.'

Rose stiffened. 'What do you mean?'

Fabiana laughed lightly. 'Let's just say we should be friends. I'd like you to see me as I really am. I am not merely a fabulous hostess and socialite, but a woman of conscience and thought. We are all actors, my dear. It is part of our condition.'

Rose smiled ruefully. 'Perhaps I have lost the art of socializing. I do not wish to appear arrogant.'

'Never that,' Fabiana said. 'I admire you greatly, and believe we may have things in common. Come now, let's return to the party.'

In a hidden corner of Akra fief stood Filigree House, the domain of the Silverskin family. At the top of the building, a skylight was thrown open to the night. Beneath it, in a bare attic room, Dame Serenia Silverskin stood bathing in the ruby light. She held up her arms, felt the Moon beams push through her skin, blend with her blood. She did not fear this night. For those who were wise, who knew the true ways of being, the Ruby Moon held no threat. It replenished Serenia as it replenished the Shren Diamond. It could not grant immortality, nor hold back the tide of the years, but even at the age of seventy-two Serenia was still a spry and energetic creature. Ruby Moon-bathing was not for everyone. What she did now was a secret tradition that had been cherished by her family for millennia. Even in the days before the Reformation, this knowledge had been closely guarded. It required years of dedicated training to be able to face the Moon. In the early days, it had made Serenia sick, driven her insane for weeks at a time. But she had persisted, as had others of her Clan. Not all of them had survived the process.

Now Serenia lowered her arms and sighed deeply. She felt tired, which was unusual. Not even the Ruby Moon could lift the weight of responsibility that hung so heavily upon her. She had hoped this moment would not come in her lifetime, because there would only be one chance. If it went awry, all was lost. There were so many secret influences at work, some conflicting, some dangerous, some merely unwise. At this point, it was difficult to discern who was friend and who was foe, for roles became muddled and many major players acted in ignorance. Serenia knew she might find herself seeking allies in places that normally she would shun. In some ways, she had already done so. Part of her wondered whether she was doing the right thing. Perhaps it was wrong to interfere. Perhaps Karadur should be left to die. All things come to an end. Was it unnatural to influence that process?

We are vain creatures, Serenia thought. *We hold ourselves in such high esteem.*

We believe the multiverse to be ours, but perhaps we are simply parasites upon its back. Perhaps the multiverse wants rid of humanity, and this is the only way. We are too clever. We can fight back. But should we?

She closed her eyes, saw in her mind the face of Rose Iron. Poor Rose, so easily led, so eager for life, so hungry. She would make a good leader for Karadur, but she was not indispensable. No one was. The only important thing was the Transformation, a new age. Sacrifices would have to be made.

'And none greater than yours, Maximilian,' Serenia murmured aloud. His was a tragic beauty.

Chapter Nine

Feet Upon the Path

Just before three o'clock, the Ruby Moon slipped below the horizon to begin her annual slumber after her brief and hectic dance across the sky. At Verdigris House, the party-goers spilled out into the chill night, muffled in their fur-rimmed spangled coats. Some of Fabiana's servants set off fireworks in the grounds, so that the sky was once more filled with red flares of light. The sparks wept down, sizzling among the frost-rimed ornamental trees of the Copper garden. Ladies shrieked in delight, lords guffawed and filled their wine glasses from slopping flagons, and a troupe of musicians began to move among the crowd, playing a merry jig on drums and fiddles, the sound of hope restored.

Beyond the garden walls, firecracker displays throughout the city splashed against the sky, eclipsing the stars. Music filled the air, and wild shouting. People ran past the distant gates, trailing streamers, blowing upon party horns, throwing red paper petals around them. On this night of bonhomie and festivity, Lady Copper had sent servants down to the gates to dispense mulled wine to any passers-by.

Standing on the terrace at the back of the manse, her coat of black fur held tight against her throat, Lady Rose felt removed from everyone present. These were her people, yet they did not know her. Was she wrong to suppose there was nothing to know in them? They did not inspire her, none of them, yet she knew that essentially they were not bad folk. Fabiana was right. She did judge people – and that was wrong, for one day she hoped to lead them. But, at that moment, she wanted more than they could offer.

Her father had sent word that the Jewel had been successfully replaced upon its plinth, which she took to mean that the substitute had been made. Why had Max taken the Jewel? What had he to gain from such a reckless feat? He threatened everyone. Rose was not superstitious, but she still wondered how the Jewel's loss would affect Karadur. She did not share her father's view. The Shren Diamond was more than a symbol.

In her furs, she shuddered. Fabiana intended for her guests to celebrate until dawn, when they would shuffle, bedraggled and yawning, back to their carriages, no doubt to spend the rest of the day in bed. It all seemed so empty, pointless and wasteful.

Rose slipped away from the other guests – no one was paying her particular attention anyway – and requested one of Fabiana's servants to summon her father's carriage. It was in her mind to return home and speak to Lord Iron, but what could she say? All that she knew? Impossible. He would be aghast, disgusted. Ultimately, she feared hurting him. Yet Rose could not just go home and sleep. Her mind was wide awake, dizzy with thoughts. Memories of her strange dream in the afternoon kept coming back to her, like a sour taste in her throat. So, instead of taking the long broad street to the Forge, Rose asked her driver to take her to the Moonmetal Manse. She yearned for the peace of the great library there. She would look for something that might explain her dream. Her hands would lead her, and her heart.

The gem in the heart of Akra fief, the Manse reared like a fairy-tale castle towards the sky. Atoms of Max Silverskin might still conceivably float in its temperate air. Rose alighted in the courtyard and sent her driver to join the Silver servants in their Carnival celebrations. Alone, she passed the great tower that housed the family vaults and approached the main doors. The guards let her proceed, for they knew her well.

Where the Forge and its family manse were massive, imposing and perhaps slightly suffocating, the home of Clan Silver was a light and airy place. Now the light was muted but even in the middle of the night the main areas were not in darkness. Many of the decorations were of spun glass, twinkling with polished silver motes. In courtyards, scented fountains plumed and mercurial fish mouthed the water lilies. Music played faintly in every corner, just a suggestion of sound, designed to lull the senses. Max had been an irritant in these serene surroundings. And they, in turn, had made him itch, as if with a black plague.

Lost in melancholy thoughts, Rose made her way to the library. It was getting on for four o'clock, so the librarian, Madam Pergo, would be absent, perhaps celebrating with the other staff. She and Rose had got to be on quite good terms. Pergo considered Rose to be a dutiful, studious creature, and forcefully declaimed how she admired that in a woman. No Silver girl would ever come to pore over the priceless books. To Pergo, the heretical texts were archaeological treasures. Their very antiquity was what made them precious. She would handle them wearing silk gloves, turning the fragile pages with reverent hands.

'You must not believe everything you read in these texts,' she had said to Rose, 'but despite that they have value, in that they allow us ingress into the minds of people long dead. If anything, they serve to make us realize how enlightened we are now.'

Because Pergo had come to like and trust Rose, she had eventually revealed to her the hiding place of the key that opened the locked and shuttered doors of the forbidden bookcases. It was to this place that Rose went now. She stood behind Pergo's desk and pressed a series of carved panels just beneath its top. A drawer slid open and there was the key. Rose took it out and held its silver filigree up to the meagre light. The library was silent, almost watchful. She fancied she could hear it breathe. So much knowledge resided here. It was like a vast brain, full of secrets.

Before she went to take out a book, Rose glanced through the register of visitors, which lay closed on Pergo's desk. She had been intrigued earlier by Carinthia Steel's mention of visiting this place. What interest had that woman in books, ancient or otherwise? Sure enough, Carinthia's name appeared several times over the past month or so. It was lucky that Rose hadn't run into her here. Or perhaps the opposite was true. It might have been informative to see what Lady Steel was reading nowadays. She had taken nothing away with her, which in itself told a story. The only books Madam Pergo would not lend out to someone of Carinthia's status were those of extreme value, or of sensitive content. In the libraries of the Metal, those two aspects often went hand in hand. So, who else had been using the library recently? Fabiana Copper had withdrawn a few classical romantic novels, members of Lead, Platinum and God had borrowed other books of a mundane nature. Only Carinthia had taken nothing.

Rose went to the locked bookcases and selected a volume on ancient folklore, one specifically about the fantastic realm Shriltasi. She wanted to find out if there was any mention of a Silverskin in relation to that subject. The family was often thought of as a fairly recent branch of the Silver breed, but their name cropped up so regularly in so many of the old texts that Rose had had to revise her opinion. The Silverskins were a very old family, and at one time had been greatly respected by their Silver relatives. Naturally, a Silverskin hand had penned every remark of this nature, so perhaps they weren't that reliable. But, even so, the Silverskins had been around, smelling faintly of magic, for a very long time. Perhaps she should approach them soon. Only caution had prevented her from doing so already. Lady Steel, for example, was a constant worry. She was an observant, sharp-eyed creature, hungry for any morsel, however small, to use as ammunition against the Irons, whom she hoped to usurp on the Council. Rose did not want to risk embarrassing her father by being accused of fraternizing with the Silverskins. Also, Rose felt the Silverskins would close ranks tightly against any possible interrogation. No doubt they had already had to endure visits from Captain Coffin and his charming retinue. Yet they intrigued Rose greatly.

She sat down at a table in a secluded corner and turned up the white-globed gas lamp on the wall. She sat in a pool of light in an otherwise shadowy environment, her head bent down towards the pages, peering at the cramped script. What had the owl represented in her dream? It was a symbol of wisdom but, in ancient tradition, also a symbol of magic. That made sense, she supposed. Magic had claws. She had opened herself up to the impossible dangerous idea of it. She shuddered. There was another meaning to the owl. The memory surfaced in her head. Part of the Silverskin legend involved the lost icons of the Clans. The icon of Clan Copper was an owl, she was sure of it. And when she'd had the dream, she'd been just about to visit the Copper domain. Coincidence? But what was the true meaning?

She did not hear footsteps approaching, and there was no other sound, but presently her neck began to prickle and she turned in her seat abruptly. He was standing right behind her, smiling a feral smile.

'What are you doing here?' she hissed, glancing instinctively at the door.

'Tracking you down, Lady Rose,' he answered, and sat on the edge of the desk before her.

'It's too dangerous. If we're caught . . .'

'We won't be caught,' he said. 'Have I ever been?' He laughed. 'You should learn to trust me more.'

'Only a fool would do that, Jack Ash,' she said.

He could slip between the worlds like a ghost, and he had taught her some of his magic. Not the kind she was really interested in, but that of perplexing a slow human mind. She knew how to be invisible when she wanted to be. She knew that Jack Ash had very recently sauntered into the Manse and past the guards. If they'd noticed him at all, they'd have believed he had official business there. It worked on very small groups – no bigger than three individuals – or large crowds, but could be problematical if there were more than three and less than a multitude. At this time of night, and this night in particular, Jack Ash wouldn't have had much difficulty.

'What are you reading?' he asked, twisting round to see.

She fought an instinct to close the book. 'About Shriltasi,' she said.

'You'll learn nothing up here,' he answered. 'You should know that by now.'

'You can learn just as much from supposition and lies as you can from fact,' Rose said. 'You learn from what people believed, how they felt. Don't you know that?' And now she did close the book.

He laughed. 'What are you looking for? Ask me anything.'

She did not want to tell him. 'Killing time,' she said, 'that's all. I'm in no mood for parties.' She paused.

He frowned comically. 'At this hour? What about your beauty sleep?'

She ignored the question. 'Anyway, why are you here? Why are you looking for me?'

'Jenny thought you should know something,' he said. 'We shall be needing you soon.'

Rose stared at him with a hard expression. 'You will be needing me? I think you forget the terms of our alliance.'

He shrugged. 'You know what I mean. The Fox of Akra came to us today, the infamous Max Silverskin. We have set him on the path.'

Rose felt herself go slowly numb, as if a cold drug had been injected into her. It was not a shock. She'd known this was coming. Perhaps the dream of the owl had foretold it. Jack and Jenny had talked about the legendary Silverskin since she'd first known them. They believed he could save their world, save Karadur. It had, to Rose, been as silly a fantasy as her own girlish yearnings of romance. 'When?' she murmured.

'Very recently. I had to save him from certain incarceration.'

'You took him to Shriltasi? You were there when he stole the jewel?'

'Obviously you have heard gossip already,' Jack said, 'but not enough fact.' He eyed the closed book contemptuously. 'The Fox tried to steal the Jewel, as I knew he would. He is drawn to it, but now is not the time. It was too soon. He lost the Jewel.'

'Then where is it?'

Jack smiled slyly. 'How should I know? I was there only to save the Fox from himself.'

Rose put her hands flat upon the desk. 'Jack, the Jewel has to be found. How will its disappearance affect Karadur? I'm extremely concerned about it. Help me find it.'

'You shouldn't worry,' Jack said. 'The Jewel isn't lost, Lady Rose. I'm quite sure of it. Events have been set in motion, that's all. Fate is at work.'

'That's no comfort. Now, we need facts. Who has the Jewel? Do you know?' She suspected it might be the Ashen themselves.

Jack shrugged. 'It is safe. And, before you accuse, no, I don't have it. It will reappear at the proper time.'

Rose sighed. 'This is all too bizarre.'

'Aren't you interested in what happened with Master Silverskin?'

Rose gave him a hard glance. 'So what happened with Master Silverskin?'

'I lured him to Shriltasi.'

Rose shook her head, briefly closed her eyes. 'It gets worse.' She looked up. 'How did he react?'

'With a certain amount of incredulity, as you can imagine. We have told him about the silverheart.' He put his head to one side. 'Remember the prophecy we told you?'

Rose frowned. 'I do.'

'Did you look for information about it here?' Jack spread his arms and gazed about the hushed room.

'No. You told me enough.' She hadn't been able to look for it. She'd shied away from anything connected with Max. She hadn't wanted to find that kind of truth hidden here. Until tonight.

'You are foolish,' said Jack Ash. 'You should trust us in this matter. Put aside your Clan ideals and morals. The Fox of Akra is not just a simple criminal, as you all believe. You would benefit from having an open mind in this regard.'

'And what of his mind?' Rose asked. 'How open is it? What did he say when you told him of the legend?'

'He doesn't believe it, of course.' Jack narrowed his eyes. 'Neither do you, I can see that. I wish you could overcome your rigid prejudices. I know it's difficult for you humans to accept anything beyond the limits of your weak senses, or to go against centuries of bigoted conditioning concerning certain families, but you should at least try.' He sighed. 'Poor Lady Rose. You belong in neither world, do you? You are hungry for knowledge, and part of you yearns to feel the thrill of *barishi* through your flesh, as your ancient ancestors once did. But another part of you is still your father's daughter, principles, fears and all.'

'Some aspects of my father's beliefs are erroneous,' Rose answered with dignity. 'But accepting something without any empirical evidence is just as wrong. I aim to find the middle path. Neither am I prejudiced about the Silverskins.'

'Applaudable, my dear lady. Which is why we're friends, of course.'

'Oh, are we that, Jack Ash?' She couldn't help smiling. Sometimes, the Ashen disturbed her greatly, but she was drawn to them too. They were like cats, friendly when it suited them, but capable of supreme acts of indifference and cruelty. And like cats, they were beautiful to behold. She still found it difficult to believe she knew these people.

When she wasn't faced with the reality, she wondered whether it was all a dream.

A year or so before, she had come across a reference in one of the old texts to hidden thoroughfares between the worlds. Until that point, Shriltasi had been a fairy tale for her, as it was for everyone in Karadur – or so she'd believed then. But the details given about how to negotiate the tunnels of the sewers to find these hidden entrances had intrigued her. They'd seemed so real. So she'd resolved to try and find them herself. In fact, she'd become lost and panic had begun to mount within her. Then, to make matters worse, she had been attacked.

A slight figure had materialized swiftly out of the eerie gloom, brandishing a knife and hissing imprecations. Luckily for Rose, her assailant had underestimated her ability to defend herself. Once she'd disarmed him and had him helpless at her feet, she'd pulled his concealing cloak from his head. At the time, she had half expected a girl to be revealed, because his body had been so slender. But once she'd examined him, the truth had hit her. He wasn't human. She should have felt terrified, repulsed, but the only emotion she could remember feeling was excitement. 'Shriltasi,' she'd said to him, just that word.

His black eyes had stared back at her, without fear, full of fury.

'Does it exist?' she'd asked him, taking the collar of his tunic in her hands, shaking him.

'Human filth!' he'd snarled, which was confirmation of sorts.

She'd ordered him to take her to his realm and, after she'd made a variety of threats, he had done so. He'd taken her to Asholm, to the surprised and delighted Jack and Jenny Ash. They'd tried to seduce Rose with words, fox her and trick her, but she'd held her own and earned their grudging respect. They weren't stupid, after all. An alliance with potentially the most powerful woman in Karadur, who was clearly sympathetic to their dilemmas, was not to be scorned or abused.

'We will have our time,' they'd said. 'All of us.'

For over a year, Rose had visited Shriltasi regularly, learning the history of the realm and the ways of its people. If her father ever found out, she feared it would kill him. But, as Jack Ash had rightly said, she was hungry for knowledge, starved of it, prepared to take risks. Very recently, the Ashen had spoken of the silverheart legend on several occasions. They wanted a hero so badly. They wanted him to be Max Silverskin. And now, perhaps, with Max's complicity, they'd recreate him in this mould. Rose did not know Max any better now than when she'd first seen him. She couldn't predict how he'd react. But, despite her feelings for him, she had no doubt that, should Max Silverskin lead any kind of revolt in Karadur, it would mean the end of the Clans of the Metal. Barbarity would hold sway. The old order of justice would be overturned. Jack Ash and his people were bitter and resentful. So was Max. The Clans might be selectively blind about reality but they were not cruel people. Ultimately, they strove to do their best, in their own limited way. Rose was not sure the same could be said for the Ashen if they acquired power. This whole situation was worrying. For this reason alone, she had to remain part of it.

'What do you want me to do?' she asked, staring Jack in the eye.

'Watch him,' Jack replied. 'Look out for him. He's fragile.'

Rose smiled grimly. 'Well, that's an interesting observation. Can't see it myself.'

'Perhaps that is because you look at him with the eyes of a young girl full of dreams.' Jack smiled at her with disturbing awareness. How much had he guessed or intuited?

Rose fought the blush that strove to express itself. 'Actually, my assessment comes from a more recent encounter. Only today – well, yesterday now – I met him in the market. He did not know me, of course.'

Jack nodded. 'I know. I saw you with him.'

'Where?' Rose shuddered. It unnerved her, the way Jack and his people seemed to know so much.

'I was the harlequin you enjoyed watching so much. I saw what happened with the purse, and the Fox's little flirtation. It was amusing.'

'You take dangerous risks.'

'Hardly. No one ever truly sees me in Karadur – except, perhaps, for you.'

She would not be flattered. 'Well, whatever you think, the man I met in the market did not seem fragile. He was cocksure and insolent.'

'That is an image he presents,' Jack said. His expression became distant. 'You met by coincidence, but I'm quite sure it was meant to be.'

'That's what he said.' Rose shook her head. 'I won't believe it.'

Jack grinned. 'Don't underestimate the power of the Ruby Moon. All manner of strange things can occur around this time.'

Rose sighed through her nose, unwilling to enter into an argument about magic. She was intrigued by it, but refused to believe in it fully without proof. Jack was coy. He wouldn't give her any proof. 'How do you expect me to watch out for Silverskin?'

Jack leaned towards her. She could smell his body, a scent of cut flowers and loam. She wanted to draw closer and inhale. She also wanted to shy back.

'Very shortly,' Jack said, 'he will be here at Clan Silver, attempting to steal an artefact from the vaults. Can you be on hand to assist him, if necessary?'

Rose swallowed, her throat full of the scent of flowers. 'Assist a thief? Do you really think I would do that?' She rubbed her face, shook her hair.

Jack drew back, as if aware of how he was affecting her. 'He comes here only to retrieve an object that was stolen from us. Oh, come now, Rose. I know you yearn to save the Fox from himself.' He grinned more widely, extended his hands. 'This is your chance. He can be what we want him to be. He just needs guidance. And who better to guide him than the Heir-in-Waiting of Clan Iron?'

Rose hesitated, torn by conflicting emotions. 'I can't assist him openly. That would be stupid. You know that.'

'I don't mean openly,' Jack replied.

Rose sighed. 'I can't see the point. He won't need me.'

'He will. I know so.'

'Then you should tell me what you know and how.'

Jack shook his head. 'How can I express an instinct? The Fox works in a team. Circumstances prevail that mean he has to change his methods.'

'What are you saying? Has something happened to Vane?'

'The Fox is alone now. It is a necessary part of his education, but he will find it hard.'

'What have you done?'

Jack jumped up. 'There is nothing more to say. Be on hand for your fellow human, my lady. Be alert.'

'That might be difficult. I haven't slept.'

'Then sleep here. Lay your head down on the desk and doze. I guarantee you will not sleep for long. He will be here soon after dawn.'

Rose folded her arms. 'I do not have to do this, Jack.'

'No,' he agreed, 'but you will.' With these words, he bowed and swept his shimmering grey cloak around him. She watched him leave, slowly, without a care. A creature of intrigue and schemes. As he moved into the shadows beyond her meagre light he seemed to disappear completely. It was as if he'd not been there at all. An illusion. A fetch. Rose could never be quite sure if Jack's appearances were accompanied by a physical body. She shook her head. How had she become involved in this? It was too dangerous, foolish even.

You are doing it for Karadur, she reminded herself. *You are doing it for truth.*

Sighing, she idly turned the pages of the book on the desk before her. There was nothing here she hadn't already read. But then, at the turn of a page, an image seemed to fly out of the book towards her. She uttered a cry and drew away, found herself standing over the desk. The owl. There it was. Rose extended a hand and touched the picture. It was just a drawing, and not very skilful at that, but that initial impression had brought back the terror of her dream. She sat down again. The section she had turned to discussed the lost icons of the Clans. As she'd thought, the owl was the icon of Clan Copper. Rose rested her elbows on the table, her chin in her hands. She began to read.

Chapter Ten

Master of Tricks

Sawhollow House, the family residence of Clan Tin, was situated in another part of Akra fief, some distance from the imposing Moonmetal Manse. Its estates were not so grand, and the house itself sagged comfortably. Unadorned buttresses supported groaning eaves. The peaked roofs were tufted with grass and seethed with starling nests. The manse was old, but sound. Fripperies were inconsequential to it. Sawhollow simply endured. It seemed the house had taken on the character of its patriarch, Lord Septimus, but perhaps the opposite was true.

Clovis Pewter had come home from the party at Verdigris House. His blood ran wildly in his veins, encouraged by the liquor he'd consumed and the continual dancing. His feet ached slightly. He felt enervated yet alert. Now, in his locked rooms, he kneeled before a secret shrine. It was normally hidden in a cupboard but now the cupboard's doors were wide and the cult statue was revealed, three feet tall. Candlelight softened Pewter's face, shone kindly upon his sweat-lank hair. His hands were clasped white-knuckled in his lap, his arms straight and stiff. His head was bowed. Beneath his breath, he muttered a prayer. 'Oh Great Lady, mistress of the flame, thy fire is in my blood. I am thy priest . . .'

He looked up into the scowling countenance of his statue. Lady Sekmet, goddess of the foundry. Sometimes, alone here in the night, he was afraid of her. Yet a braver part of him craved her power. She had never died but had lain waiting, slumbering in the fabric of Karadur. Her breath was the oily smoke that rose from the chimneys. Her glance was the gout of fire in the night. Her sinew was the fabric of the buildings, veined with every metal.

And she prowled, growling softly, through the sleeping streets. Waiting, always waiting.

Pewter raised himself towards the statue and breathed into its face. 'I open thy mouth that thou might breathe.'

He dabbed his fingers into a bowl of anointing oil, spiced with cinnamon, that lay on the altar, and wiped the eyes of the image. 'I open thy eyes that thou might see.'

The candle flames flickered in a breeze he could not feel. Was that the wind outside the window, or the low snarl of a stalking gibbold? The only ones he had ever seen were contained and tamed, living in the zoo that was part of the covered farmland that girdled the city to the north. Since he had found his new calling, he visited the gibbold compound often, gazing at the lazy sleek beasts that dozed amid the humid foliage. They seemed to have no fire, no rage, not like that which emanated from the inscrutable countenance of his goddess.

I am not afraid, he told himself and composed himself more comfortably upon the floor. 'Lady, I give praise unto thee. Look upon me with gentleness. Grant to me the power of thy eternal fire. I work in thy name, oh Sekmet, to rekindle thy presence in this, thy holy city.'

He was tired now, in need of sleep, but superstitiously felt he could not go to his bed until his nightly prayers were complete. Yawning, he cast incense on the charcoal that smouldered in a metal crucible before the statue. He closed his eyes. 'Oh, great Sekmet, Lady of Life and of Death, come unto me. Mine are the sinews of the goddess. Mine the blood. I am thy priest . . .' He stiffened, his back prickling. The atmosphere in the dim-lit room had changed, become charged. Did he dare look round? Pewter held his breath, and for some moments sat motionlessly. Then he glanced over his shoulder, saw the figure standing there. He uttered a cry, fell to the side, then backed up, scrabbling, against the front of the shrine.

'Be not afraid, my priest,' said Jack Ash softly, 'for am I not with you?' His smile was a sickle, sharp and curved.

'How did you get in here?' Pewter gabbled, glancing wildly round the room. The door was still closed, the key protruding from the lock. The windows were shuttered against the night.

'No place is locked to me,' said Jack Ash. 'Get up. You look foolish down there. It will displease the goddess.'

Pewter recovered his composure. He made the final sacred signs before the statue and cast some more incense onto the coals. 'You have no right to come creeping in here.'

Jack was still chuckling. 'I thought we were allies, Clovis. Why should you take offence?'

Pewter blinked. 'What do you want? It's nearly dawn. Why come here now?'

'I'm making my social calls,' Jack said. 'I like the peace of the night.'

Pewter got up. 'This is not a social hour. What's your business?'

Jack leaned against the bedpost. 'I have news for you. It can't wait, and you can stop glancing longingly at your pillows. Very soon, Max Silverskin will come to steal from you.'

Pewter frowned. 'What do you mean?'

'I mean he will go into the vaults of the Moonmetal Manse, where it is rumoured you keep a certain bauble you filched from a young thief some months back.'

Pewter's frown did not ease. 'Bauble?'

'An amber bead. I'm sure you remember.'

Pewter nervously covered his left hand with his right, aware at once of how he'd betrayed the hiding place of the bead. 'I'm not sure,' he said lamely.

'You are,' said Jack. 'It's set into that ring upon your finger. You found the setting, empty of a jewel, in a carelessly unlocked drawer, in the desk of Lady Copper's office when you were visiting three weeks ago. It was so fortunate. It might have seemed like an inconsequential broken relic to the Coppers – they won't have even missed it – but you recognized it for what it was, didn't you? You just knew the bead and the setting were meant to go together.' Jack winked at him. 'You knew this, because I put the thought into your head. I imagine you rarely take the ring off now.'

Pewter was silent for a moment. He was never sure how much of Jack's apparent arcane knowledge was simple psychology, an attempt to play with his mind. He decided not to question the remark. 'Well, the bead is safe, then, isn't it? Or do you expect Silverskin to come looking for it here?'

'No, he will not come here. But *you* will go to the Moonmetal Manse.'

Pewter uttered a choked laugh. 'I most certainly will not! I'll send word to Coffin. He can arrest the vermin if he shows up.'

'You should, of course, notify the Captain,' said Jack. 'But you should also be there yourself. Let Silverskin see the bead.'

Pewter hesitated. 'Why? What's going on? Why are you taking an interest in it?'

'Let's just say it's part of the great tapestry of history. A strand is being woven. And you, my friend, are part of it.'

Pewter nodded, then looked up sharply. 'You promised us the gibbold artefacts. Where are they?'

'You will have them at the right time. Guard against impatience, Clovis.'

'You know where they are, though.'

'I have never said that. Have a little faith. First, you must face Silverskin.'

Pewter shook his head. 'I must go to the temple again. I need guidance.'

'I understand,' said Jack. 'But this is part of the great work, too. You knew when you made the oath that the cost would be high. Are you courageous enough to pay it?'

'Of course,' Pewter snapped.

'Good, then ready yourself. You should leave for the Moonmetal Manse at once.'

Pewter would have asked more questions but, in the space of blinking his eyes, Jack Ash had vanished. Pewter shivered and hurriedly closed the doors to his shrine, turning the key in the lock. His heart was beating fast. Had he gone in too deep?

He remembered the day when he'd met Jack Ash. It seemed only moments ago, but in fact it was about eight months. Pewter had been in the markets, eyeing up the common talent, when he'd paused to watch a play. It had made him shiver. Not the words so much, nor even the zeal of the players, but something between the words, the movements. It seemed a secret oozed out from the stage, like light seeping from the seal of a closed box. He could no longer remember what the performance had been about, but he did recall the moment when the lead player had met his gaze. The man had been masked, but a black glitter at the eye slits seemed to fix itself right on Pewter's face. *Would you like to know what I know?* the eyes had suggested.

After the production had finished, Pewter had hung around the stage and managed to attract the attention of the lead player. He had invited the actor for a meal, saying he wished to discuss the play. The actor had agreed at once. It had been Jack Ash, the greenish cast to his skin disguised by thick white make-up. That whiteness had only made him seem more inhuman. When he'd finally taken off the mask, it seemed he'd worn another one beneath.

In the dimness of an exclusive restaurant in Akra fief, Pewter had opened up his heart to the actor, telling him of his frustrations, his desire for change. 'Something is wrong in Karadur,' he'd said. 'I think everyone feels it, but no one wants to talk about it. I feel it's time for people to do something.'

'Perhaps *you* can do something,' Jack Ash had said.

Pewter had shrugged. 'I'd like to, but my voice is barely heard.'

'What would you like to do, if you could?' The actor had rested his chin in his hands.

'Well, I'd crack down on the criminal element in the city for a start. Gragonatt is all very well, but it's not enough of a deterrent. Some of the old methods need to be revived.'

'Execution?' Jack had said sweetly.

Pewter had hesitated. Should he admit to that? 'Well, certainly some flogging.'

Jack had laughed. 'My lord, what if I said to you that you could make a difference? And that I could show you how?'

'I don't know,' Pewter had replied. 'Explain.'

Jack had conjured an image of Sekmet then, not before the eyes – which Pewter was convinced the Ashen was quite capable of doing – but in the mind. Ancient power had seemed to drip from the softly spoken words. Pewter's spine had tingled. He'd felt Sekmet's presence round him.

'If gods are forgotten, they die,' said Jack. 'But Sekmet isn't dead. She's asleep. She's waiting for you, my lord. Wake her up once more and see Karadur begin to thrive.'

'But why gods?' Pewter had asked. 'Religion isn't the answer to our problems.'

'Indeed not,' Jack had agreed. 'But, strangely enough, gods and religion are quite separate. The powers of the multiverse exist, but that does not mean you have to bow down and worship them like a blind fool. Respect them. Give them attention and they will help you.'

Pewter had frowned. 'I'm not sure I understand.'

'Let us look at the way things are,' Jack had said airily. 'Imagine I am Lord Iron, perhaps the epitome of what Karadur represents. I am quite convinced that accepting gods, archetypes and spirits as real leads only to illusion. The mind should not waste time thinking about things that cannot be seen. If you live in illusion, it leads to chaos and anarchy. We should live out our purpose as human beings. And what is that purpose?'

'Reason, of course,' Pewter had said. 'It's drummed into us since birth. It's the only thing that sets us apart from the beasts.'

'Indeed,' Jack had said. 'If humans don't conform to their purpose, they cannot be happy. An axe is made to cut. If it cuts well, it is a good axe. A human is made to reason. If it reasons well, it will be a good human and therefore happy.' Jack had curled his hands into fists. 'Is not virtue in Karadur seen as fulfilling your purpose to its greatest degree? Instincts, emotions, intuition are regarded as lower than reason. They have to conform to what reason says is right.' He had leaned back in his seat. 'Lord Iron doesn't want to deny emotion exists. He knows that it does. He just believes that when it is expressed, it should conform to rational principles.' He had leaned across the table again, spoken lower. 'But rational principles aren't the self. They are not the soul. Reason is no food for the soul. And that is part of what is wrong in Karadur.'

Pewter's skin had tingled as he'd listened to these words. 'Then what must we do? How will this goddess help us? Is she real?'

Jack had smiled. 'Real? That's a good question. But, ultimately, it is irrelevant. What is happening here is that the people's needs aren't being attended to. Intuition and instinct, the feelings and faculties beyond the senses, are denied. But these things find a way of coming out. You lords may be trapped in your rigid thinking and believe yourselves happy there, but the common people of the streets are intrinsically more instinctive than you are. Therefore they are drawn, without their realizing it, back to the old ways. Their instincts have been forcefully directed towards what they can perceive in the world, but the human spirit always desires to go above and beyond mere objects. Instinct can be suppressed, in order to find the truth of objects, but this does not encompass the truth of the self, of existence. For that, you need intuition and awareness, which is beyond reason. The old gods and their archetypes will give humanity a way to discover the multiplicity of their existence. It will give faces to their instincts and emotions, so that they can explore and understand what's within themselves, rather than just what's outside. They will no longer have to suppress their instincts, which has led only to lawlessness and discontent. They will be free-thinking, aware people. Truly happy.'

Pewter had felt breathless, dizzy, as if he'd been given the secret of life. 'Who are you?' he'd asked.

'If you really want to know the answer to that,' Jack had replied, 'you must be brave enough to step off the precipice into the dark.'

Once he got home, Pewter wondered whether the whole encounter with Jack Ash had been an illusion. The words the actor had spoken were dangerously heretical, insane even. Yet they had seemed so right. It was simple. Karadur was heading towards chaos and anarchy because the people had estranged themselves from the higher powers of the multiverse. In casting out all that had been bad about their society, the Lords had cast out many good things as well. It had been a mistake, and now it should be rectified.

The following day, a box had arrived at Sawhollow House. Pewter had seen his name on the address label and had dragged the package up to his private rooms. In his heart, he'd known something amazing was about to be revealed. His skin had tingled, his eyes smarted. Inside the box had been a mass of sawdust, the fragrant bed for a remarkable artefact: the cult statue of Sekmet. Pewter had known at once that the package had come from Jack Ash. At that stage, he'd had no idea who or what Jack really was, nor about Shriltasi. All he'd known was that the gibbold-headed woman staring out at him through the sawdust possessed immense power. It had filled his room, dripped hot and smoking from the walls. And it was his.

Jack had trained Pewter carefully, eventually allowing him ingress to Shriltasi. By that time Pewter was accepting anything that Jack told him, so the incredible reality of the underworld realm wasn't quite as shocking as it might have been before. The cult statue had come from one of the old Shriltasian shrines to the goddess, which were now overgrown with weeds and vines and hidden by rambling shrubs. Initially at Jack's direction but then increasingly under his own volition, Pewter had begun to restore a large temple to Sekmet in Shriltasi. Jack had been able to direct him towards certain of the foundrymen who needed very little persuasion to revive their old beliefs. These massive taciturn men worked stoically under Pewter's command. Eventually, they had begun tentatively to practise old rituals together. But more recently recruits had been sought from other areas of the populace.

Only a few weeks ago, Jack had brought a masked woman to one of the temple gatherings and had told Pewter she was to be his high priestess. Pewter had felt uneasy about this at first. It was clear from the woman's bearing and manner that she was a Lady of the Metal, but she kept her identity disguised, even from him. Surely, if she were part of the great work, as Jack called it, she should trust her fellow believers enough to reveal herself. Pewter had tried to penetrate her camouflage, and sometimes felt he recognized her, but she was too clever for him. The masks she wore, fashioned into the semblance of the face of the goddess herself, distorted her voice and covered her hair and face entirely. Her robes were bulky and ornate, widening her shoulders and hiding her true shape. The priestess had initiated other ladies of the Clans into the sect, and Pewter had to admit the women's presence and commitment had brought a new and colourful dimension to the old rituals. Despite the priestess's secretive nature, she did her work well. But how did Jack know her, and what was his ultimate plan in this matter? Events were building up to some kind of climax and Pewter was fairly sure Jack Ash knew what form that would take but, for the time being, he had to trust the Ashen.

Now Jack Ash clearly had an interest in Max Silverskin. But why? The man was a strutting, empty-headed rooster, who measured his own worth in terms of how much he could thieve from good, honest people. Jack had told Pewter to notify Cornelius Coffin, but why did he need Silverskin to see the bead? Pewter shook his head. It was baffling. He stood up straight, yawned, and reached for his boots. So far, everything Jack had predicted had come true. Pewter had no reason to doubt him now.

Chapter Eleven

Old Haunts, Old Habits

Max Silverskin crept through Akra fief, every nerve alert. He should be exhausted but, if anything, his senses felt more honed and aware. Around him, the city was starting to wake up and stretch, to begin its daily business. On the steps of the houses, cans stood waiting to be filled by the milk vendors who drove carts laden with churns from the outlying farms. Already, people were beginning to venture from their houses, heading in the direction of the market, perhaps to buy breakfast bread. Later, children would be collected by mentors to be taken to school, and the merchants and businessmen would emerge from their homes, checking their timepieces, frowning as they waited for public steam carriages, or else, in the case of the more affluent, chugged off to work in their own.

As Max moved through the streets, keeping to the shadows, the city seemed more vivid to him than ever before. He could see the bustle, the industry, but every peeling wall, every cracked paving stone, every half-hidden alley full of rubbish and misery seemed to cry out to his senses. The Karadurians, he decided, were united in a common hallucination and found comfort in it. No wonder. Those who dared to see through it were punished as heretics.

It was so clear to him now. The Lords of the Metal didn't just rule Karadur, they controlled reality. The powers of communication and authority were theirs. They wrote the history books, determining what was true and false. They castigated any innovative thought, so that even the most intelligent citizens were almost incapable of thinking for themselves. This, thought Max, was what all the great dreams of liberty and stability had come to. It could not continue. It was insane. But how could circumstances change when the very word 'change' was anathema to the Lords?

Max felt uneasy now that Menni was not by his side. He was conscious of something missing, something that gave him security. He had taken Menni's presence for granted, the only true family Max had ever known. He must be restored soon. Max could not help feeling that everyone in and below the city was seeking him, each with a slightly different motive. Jack Ash and his colleagues, with their sly theatrics, had brought the legend of Silverskin to life in the city. Max was uncomfortable with the exposure. Those who craved change were seeking a figurehead, and were making one of him – but was that right? He was sure the plan had begun when he'd been sprung from Gragonatt. The Ashen, or someone known to them, had branded him to help fulfil the prophecy. But was it more than that or not? He had been foolish to believe he could steal the Jewel of All Time. And where, in fact, was the Shren Diamond now? He couldn't help feeling as if he'd been an unwitting player in a carefully contrived drama. The Ashen knew something, but they would not speak. No doubt Coffin had intensified the search for him too. Was his only sanctuary in the hidden world of Shriltasi, subject to the unstable whim of its peculiar denizens? No. He had hidden himself successfully in Karadur for a year. There was no reason for that not to continue. He'd sort this mess out, get Menni restored to his former self, and then quietly disappear for a while. People were crazy. They wanted to believe in magic.

But you've seen Shriltasi, a voice murmured in his mind. *Is that not evidence enough that something out of the ordinary is going on, and has always been going on?*

Perhaps so, but he still thought he should guard against being seduced by Jenny's skilful flattery and story-telling. Could he really only have a few more days to live? He felt completely healthy. As if to refute that thought, the mark over his heart suddenly burned hot. Suggestion. Magic. They had made him feel this way.

At least he could console himself with the fact that the job ahead should not be too difficult. He knew the Clan Silver vaults better than anyone. However much he despised his relatives, he'd never wanted to steal from them before. Perhaps that was because it would have been too easy. This situation was different. Pewter had stolen Jenny's bead from her, and there would be no dishonour in stealing it back.

The Moonmetal Manse dominated the Akra fief. It was a filigree celebration of the silversmith's art, a confection of metallic flourishes and curlicues. Unlike some of the other Clan manses, which were situated in the centre of landscaped grounds, the Silver domain was built flush against the northern walls. The gardens swept away behind it to the south. Max made his way to a secluded area of the complex, moving like a shadow himself against the walls. At a side entrance, where servants had stationed an army of refuse barrels, he began to climb, gliding like a ghost between flying buttresses and winged roof peaks, heading always for the central keep, below which lay the vaults.

Some thirty feet up, he dropped over a balcony. Here, long window doors led to a room beyond. Max deftly picked the lock. The chamber was empty, its high walls covered in tapestries of metallic thread that depicted various Silver ancestors, their weddings, elections and funerals. Max stole to the door and looked outside. All seemed clear. Now he would have to make his way to the central tower and the entrance to the vaults.

In these upper reaches of the manse, the haunt mainly of servants, the place was not as well lit as below. The gas lamps upon the walls were turned low, making a stooped monster of Max's shadow. Occasionally, Silver staff would pass him, talking among themselves or on lone errands. Guards patrolled the corridors and passages with nonchalant ease. Max avoided them all, slipping into niches, darting into doorways, hiding behind them.

The tower was situated in the central courtyard, connected to the main building by a network of gangways high overhead. At ground level, it was approached by a long flight of steps to the only door, which was set into the silver-clad walls halfway up its height. Max walked up the steps without urgency, hoping that if anyone was around, they would take his confident manner to mean he was entitled to be there. At the entrance to the tower, he grew more cautious. Sometimes, the vault beyond was guarded by more than men. He needed to work quickly.

The first lock succumbed to his attentions with an almost sensual ease.

He passed through the gate and entered a curving passageway that encircled the chamber within. Max padded round the corridor until he reached the opposite side of the tower. Here was the second door. The locks proved slightly more resistant, but eventually their mechanisms tumbled obligingly beneath Max's fingers. He opened the gate and found himself in a high-ceilinged chamber, which was circled by a gallery some twenty feet overhead. The walls were again covered in immense tapestries of metallic thread. Here, generations of Silver lords sat amid their treasures, their long dead features captured in incorruptible metal, to scowl forever over those who dared to live after them.

At the centre of the chamber, a lift shaft led down to the vaults. Max approached it cautiously. All was silent. He had almost reached the gate to the shaft, one hand extended to touch it, when the chamber shook to the resounding clamour of the main gates slamming shut. Max turned quickly, dropped into a predatory crouch and drew his sword. The chamber was empty behind him. For a moment he remained motionless, but it seemed the gates had closed of their own accord. Max straightened, and it was then he heard a sneering laugh above his head. Looking up, he saw his cousin, Clovis Pewter, standing on the gallery.

A pet snake was coiled around Pewter's left forearm, and now he held it close to his face. 'Look now, Persimmon, my sweet. We thought we'd catch the little thief who's plagued us these past months, but now it seems we've caught a big thief instead.' He lowered his arm and grinned at Max. 'Good day to you, cousin. It is too long since we last met.'

'Good day to you, cousin,' Max replied. 'It's fortunate we meet today. You might be able to help me, because I'm here not as a thief but as a gentleman. You took something that was not yours and I am here to reclaim it.'

Pewter laughed. 'Now there's a mishmash of morals! I have taken nothing. Thieving is not my proclivity, cousin. It is yours.'

He began to descend a spiral staircase that led down from the gallery. Max was uneasy. Pewter was a lily-liver, certainly no bravo. Why was he behaving with such easy confidence? There had to be others on their way. He flicked a glance towards the main gates.

'Give me the amber bead,' Max said, 'and I'll be away. You know what I'm talking about.'

Pewter pulled a mournful face. 'The little trinket I snatched from the thief I caught? It was only fair recompense. What's your interest in it? Was the girl a creature of yours?' He held up his left hand to inspect a ring on his middle finger. It was a large amber stone fixed into an oddly shaped setting. That must be the bead, larger than Max had imagined it. He could not discern any further details before Pewter lowered his hand.

'You don't want to fight me, Clovis,' he said. 'You wouldn't last a minute. See sense.'

Pewter shrugged. 'But why spoil the party, cousin? There are friends waiting to meet you again. It will be a touching reunion, I'm sure.'

He must have set off an alarm on the gallery. There could be no other explanation for his careless manner. 'I'm harder to keep than to catch,' Max said. 'You should know that.' He moved forward menacingly, sword raised, intending to snatch the ring and make a swift escape before reinforcements arrived. His ears strained to detect any warning sounds.

Pewter laughed and took a step backwards. 'Will you kill me, cousin, and add murder to robbery?'

Max knew Pewter was only trying to delay him. Without further words, he lunged forward. Pewter skipped nimbly away and the doors behind him burst open, to slam back against the metallic walls with a resounding clang. A troop of armoured men came clattering into the chamber – Irregulars. Max's flesh went cold, while at the same time, he experienced a stabbing, burning pain over his heart. Behind the Irregulars, his face set into an arrogant sneer of triumph, was Cornelius Coffin. Why was he always on hand to interfere with Max's plans? The man seemed to have an almost preternatural sense for sniffing him out, but was perhaps aided more by an efficient intelligence network.

'Ah, Sir Silverskin,' Coffin said silkily. 'We meet like this too often'. The ranks of Irregulars parted and Coffin came striding forward. A mechanical snuffer strained at the leash ahead of him. 'It's over for you now, Silverskin. It was only a matter of time. You seem intent on delivering yourself into my hands.'

Max said nothing, his mind juggling possibilities of escape. He had to concentrate, focus himself.

'See to him, Captain,' Clovis Pewter cried. 'Let the snuffer slip. My cousin's a wily fox.'

'And like a fox, no more than vermin,' Coffin said smoothly. He released the snuffer, which began to prowl forward, its eyes blazing red. Steam and acidic liquor dripped from its fanged jaws. 'Contain!' Coffin ordered the snuffer.

For a moment, Max considered whether he could make it to the gallery and try to find an escape route from there. The odds were unlikely. But then he remembered the spellstone Jenny Ash had given to him. He couldn't believe it might help him — but hadn't Jenny said his belief in its powers was irrelevant to its efficiency? He had nothing to lose. The snuffer was approaching slowly, crouched down, its multi-segmented limbs moving with a slippery grace. Max lifted the spellstone out of his shirt, half sure he would die a fool. Holding the stone in his free hand, he pointed it towards the snuffer and described in the air the symbol he'd been taught. The snuffer, oblivious to his intentions, now stood before him, clashing its teeth.

Coffin began to laugh. 'What is this? The cur resorts to market-place charms when all else fails?' He turned to his sergeant, Rawkis. 'He was never a worthy enemy. Merely a lucky gutter rat. This is poor sport. I expected more of a challenge.'

Max ignored these jibes and concentrated on completing the symbol. Despite his earlier doubts, he felt that he could see the magical sign himself this time, hanging upon the air as an emerald-green mist. His spine tingled. He could feel something humming in the air, perhaps the power of *barishi*. The group of Irregulars looked on in a mixture of bewilderment and scorn. It was clear they could neither see nor feel anything unusual. Nor was anything magical occurring. Jenny had lied. The stone meant nothing. The sign was an illusion.

'Bring him down,' Coffin said coldly to the snuffer.

But would a mechanical dog have an autonotype? It was not a living creature. Swiftly, with a flare of hope, Max turned to point the stone at

Clovis Pewter, specifically towards the snake curled about his arm. Max willed the influence of *barishi* to touch the little creature.

The effect was immediate. Before the entire company's startled gaze, the snake transformed into a scintillating bronze serpent, unrolling like a bolt of magical bronze cloth. Hissing, it reared up and out towards Max, seven times as long as it had been. Vestigial wings sprouted from its flanks, like those of the legendary firedrake.

Coffin uttered a low curse, half disbelief, half involuntary fear, while the Irregulars grunted in surprise. Max instinctively grabbed hold of the serpent's waving head. It curled around his arm, compliant as a faithful weapon. Without conscious thought, Max flicked the serpent at the snuffer like a whip. The shining coils entangled with the beast's limbs, bringing it crashing to the floor, where it lay gnashing its jaws, its mechanical eyes whirring and rolling. Without pause, Max cracked the serpent whip again. The tail sliced upwards, finding purchase on the gallery rail, curling around it like a rope.

Coffin collected himself and ordered his Irregulars to advance. He had clearly worked out Max's immediate plans, therefore Max had to work fast. He released his hold on the serpent, which still hung from the gallery rail, its head flashing round the chamber. He resheathed his sword and stuffed the spellstone back inside his shirt. Then, with both hands free, he flew at Clovis Pewter and sent him staggering backwards. There was a short struggle, during which Pewter uttered a string of profanities, but then Max had torn the ring from his cousin's hand and slipped it over one of his own fingers. The bronze snake still writhed and hissed around him, spitting a fiery venom. Max could barely dare to look at it. Everything about the creature was unnatural. It could not and should not exist. Coffin would no doubt think it was only an illusion.

Coffin's sergeant, Rawkis, jumped forward, the only Irregular apparently not still wary of the snake. He lashed out at it with a monstrous cleaver. The serpent turned on him, hissing and striking. To Max's delighted surprise, Rawkis recoiled. This would be easy now. He backed away from his retreating enemies, towards the stairs to the gallery. The snake's head seemed to be everywhere at once, it moved so quickly. The men stumbled back behind it. Then the creature lunged towards Coffin, who raised a hand to protect his face. The snake's tongue touched the iron bands about the Captain's glove. At once, to Max's utter horror, it turned to stone, fell to the floor and broke into a thousand pieces. Max froze.

Coffin rediscovered his composure. 'Whether that's a conjuror's trick or a clever mechanical device, it's clearly vulnerable,' he said. 'Didn't expect that, did you, Silverskin?'

Max didn't wait to reply. With all his strength, he leaped towards the staircase, knocking Pewter aside. Coffin came forward, roaring, his blade ready. Max ascended the stairs, feeling the wind of Coffin's blade at his heels. He was forced to turn and fight, but at least there was no room for anyone else to attack him. It was fortunate none of them had crossbows. Coffin's blade sliced superficially across his shin, but he was so fired by adrenalin he barely felt the wound. Max had the advantage of position. He glanced upwards. The gallery was only a few steps away, but once there, he'd be more vulnerable. Fighting was a waste of energy and time. He ran up the final few stairs and lunged towards the wall of the tower. Seizing hold of one of the tapestries, he began to haul himself upwards at great speed. There was a window some fifteen feet or so above him. When he reached the sill, he kicked out the glass, then turned once to salute Coffin with his sword. Below him, he saw Coffin's furious face. 'I enjoyed our tryst,' he said. 'Until next time, Captain.'

Max climbed through the window. His whole being was intent on escape. He almost flew across the convoluted surface of the tower. Service walkways attached it to the main building high above, and Max reached them in what seemed like only moments. Already there was a commotion in the square below. Not even bothering to look down, Max ran across a metal walkway and plunged back into the labyrinth of the main building. He knew this place intimately, all its secret byways, for he'd haunted them as a child. His head had begun to swim and he felt slightly feverish. His heart was beating too hard and it seemed to him that he heard an echo of it, resounding from the silver walls of the manse.

Minutes later, he'd reached the outer wall and was clambering down it towards the streets. Now his limbs were shaking severely. It would be touch and go. No doubt a swarm of Irregulars was already pouring from the building.

When he hit the floor, Max's legs buckled beneath him. He looked down and saw that the wound he'd received across the shin was deeper than he'd thought. Coffin's blade had sliced round into his calf muscle. Blood soaked his trousers from the knee down. It would not help his escape. Wildly, he looked around himself, sure he could already hear the clatter of booted feet approaching from both sides. Then a voice cried, 'Silverskin, here!'

He looked up and saw a hooded figure standing at the entrance to a narrow alley that led off into the city. It was beckoning to him urgently. Max limped over to the shadows, his heart pounding. Light specks boiled before his eyes. He was on the verge of losing consciousness and well nigh collapsed against the dark figure, which close to was revealed to be a woman wearing a long dark hooded cloak. Max, his senses reeling, felt a shimmer of recognition, but was unable to think clearly enough to remember who she was.

'You are a fool, master thief,' the woman said. 'Are you set on suicide?'

Max could not answer. Leaning against the woman, he allowed her to just about drag him off into the labyrinth of alleys. She was strong. Strong as iron.

Chapter Twelve

A Rose Pricked by Thorns

Rose stared at the man lying on her couch, a cup of wine held to her lips. Why was she doing this? She could not divine her own motives. Complying with Jack Ash's suggestions was only part of the reason. It would be a disaster if she was found out by her Clan. Max Silverskin groaned and raised an arm to his face. Rose had cleaned and stitched his wound, and had also given him what she hoped was an effective antidote to the poison with which Coffin coated his weapons. It was not a life-threatening toxin but it could addle the brain for days. She needed Max Silverskin lucid. Impulse had led her to bringing him here – and something more, perhaps. She put down her cup and marched towards the couch. 'Wake up,' she said. 'I wish to talk with you.'

Max Silverskin lowered his arm and stared at her with inscrutable pale grey eyes. He'd clearly been conscious for some minutes, perhaps pondering how he could escape. Rose could not help but admire what she saw before her.

'Who are you?' he said. 'I remember our last meeting.'

She smiled. 'Didn't we have an assignation? You stood me up.'

'Who are you?'

She sighed and turned away, suddenly embarrassed about confessing her identity, sure she would invoke only anger. ' You were not wrong in your assumption yesterday,' she said. 'I am a daughter of the Clans.'

'Which?'

'Clan Iron.'

Silverskin snorted in contempt. 'Dear friends of mine.'

Rose turned back to him. 'We have met before – when we were children. Don't you remember?'

He stared at her, frowning. He wouldn't remember. Why should he? When Max had come to Clan Silver he'd had no time for his own kind. In some way, he'd inspired her to become the person she was, but she knew she should now guard against being influenced by her teenage infatuation. This was not a sulky youth but a dangerous man, who by his own confession had no love for the Clans. Still, she knew he was interested in her, which might afford some protection. 'You don't remember,' she said, pulling a rueful face.

He shook his head. 'I'm sorry.'

'I am Lady Rose Iron, daughter of Prometheus.' She watched his face change, before he masked it with a blank expression.

'And what do you want of me, Lady Rose? How did you come to be by Moonmetal Manse just as I was taking a fond leave of my relatives? Where have you brought me – and why?'

'You are an ungrateful fox, it seems. Coffin had poisoned you and within minutes you'd have been senseless. If I hadn't taken you out of there, you would be in Gragonatt by now.'

'Thank you,' he said stonily. 'But I would still like you to answer my questions.'

She sighed again. 'Perhaps I helped you because you helped me yesterday. Is that not reason enough?'

'It is a good reason, but not the real one. Clan Iron wants to see me in chains. Why should you be different?'

'I did not lie to you yesterday morning. I care about what is happening in the city. We are actually confederates in many respects. I was only helping a comrade.'

'If this were true, surely I'd know about this intimacy?'

She did not react to his sneering tone. 'You know very little, Max. I'm sure you've realized that by now.' She paused. 'I know also about the mark on your chest and what it means.'

'Perhaps I do know little, but that does not mean I'll eagerly believe every incredible fairy tale I'm told. Some faction, or factions, want to use me as a figurehead. They need one, and I fit the bill. My history is conveniently fitting. I find it difficult to believe you are associated with such people.'

His tone – pompous and condescending – angered her now. 'You have ignorant preconceptions, Silverskin. You know nothing about me or the people you arrogantly profess need you so badly.'

'You are the Heir-in-Waiting to the greatest fortune in Karadur,' he said. 'Why should I believe or trust you? Your father is my sworn enemy. I'm sure that if the law permitted it he'd have me executed. This is the man who encourages the contemptible Coffin to run roughshod through the city. He tolerates tyranny and oppression, and perhaps more than that. You share his blood, you are his heir. You must surely appreciate how unlikely your claims to be a rebel are?'

She shook her head vehemently. 'You are blind. Consider this. Perhaps, as the heir to the Seat, Fate has decreed I must be aware of what's happening around me. If anyone can do anything, I can. But I have no allies among the Clans. I must look to the common people, befriend those who would be my enemies. We must make plans for the future.'

Max narrowed his eyes at her. 'You should be careful. They might not be your enemies, but I doubt they are your friends. You might outlive your usefulness.'

'I am not stupid and neither are they.'

'Who are your confederates then?'

'I think you know – at least some of them. Jack and Jenny Ash, for example.'

Max laughed. 'What an unlikely conspiracy! If your father knew that, you'd probably be in Gragonatt yourself!'

'I know that,' she said. 'Can't you see how serious I am? I would not take such risks otherwise. My father knows of Shriltasi – he is one of the few that does, and considers that knowledge to be a terrible burden. He has to be aware of a mythological place that officially doesn't exist. He has to believe in it and disbelieve in it at the same time.'

'And how did you discover it?'

'I have a curious mind, and delved into ancient scripts that are forbidden to others. I learned about Shriltasi by piecing together very vague bits of information. Eventually I had to test my theories and so I went into the tunnels beneath the city. One of their people found me there.'

'You could have been killed.'

She shrugged. 'I was prepared to take the risk. I had to know. You can't imagine how I felt back then, having stumbled upon the most important secret. I felt it was my duty as my father's heir to know the truth. If the day comes that I take the Seat, I want to do so with full awareness of Karadur, its history and its secrets.'

'Presumably the underworlder who found you was impressed by your zeal.'

She smiled grimly. 'Not at first, no. Fortunately, I'd taken the precaution of learning self-defence. I made the creature take me to Shriltasi, at the point of my blade.'

Max laughed. 'I would like to have seen that.'

'Jack and Jenny were more astute. They realized the usefulness of allying with me.'

'And who suggested hunting me down? You or them?'

'You have not been hunted down. I believe that if it wasn't for these people, you'd still be in Gragonatt, or dead. I had nothing to do with your release. They didn't even inform me of what you represent until quite recently. It was not their decision, Max, but that of Fate itself.'

'Fate did not brand me. Who did?'

'I don't know and that is the truth. All I've been told is that something was given to you. I don't think that Jack and Jenny themselves were responsible.'

'But they must know who was.'

She nodded, frowning. 'Yes, maybe.'

'They told me it was killing me, that a silver heart was eating into my own. They told me my days are numbered. You can imagine I find this difficult to credit.'

Rose hesitated, noticing that, despite Max's apparent scepticism, his left hand was now pressed against his chest. 'I know the legend of the silver heart,' she said. 'But how can I tell whether it's true or not? Will you show the mark to me?'

'It is only a rather ugly burn scar. It isn't silver.' Still, he opened his shirt.

Rose leaned over him, swallowing with difficulty. It was as if a delicious scent rose from his body, a scent that her nostrils couldn't perceive but that intoxicated her mind. This wasn't like the redolence of Jack Ash but something completely different. Human. She blinked to clear her sight and saw the mark, red and puckered, beneath his left nipple. 'May I touch it?'

He grinned crookedly. 'Go ahead.'

Carefully, she pressed the mark, trying to discern whether any foreign body lay beneath it. Impossible to tell. All she could feel was ribs. No doubt Max himself had made the same exploration many times. She straightened up. 'I can't feel anything. Have you ever done so?'

'Sometimes it burns,' he said. 'Increasingly of late. I was told that the Ruby Moon had activated it in some way.'

'Perhaps we should assume the story is correct,' she said, straightening up. 'Then we cannot be taken by surprise.'

'Death, if it comes in this form, can hardly be anything but a surprise,' Max said dryly, covering his chest once more. 'Anyway, why the "we"? I haven't agreed to anything. I'm still puzzled as to how you were conveniently in place to rescue me from Coffin in Akra. A cynical man might assume you and he were confederates, involved in an elaborate plan to foil the dissidents.'

Rose shook her head. 'I realize I cannot convince you easily, but you are completely wrong about me. I despise Coffin as much as you do. Jack Ash informed me you would be at Clan Silver looking for the bead. I'd waited many hours in that alley. I saw you climb the Manse. I had only to wait. I did not anticipate that you'd be injured. I did not intend to reveal myself to you. I just wanted to make sure you got away safely. I think Coffin knew you'd be coming. Why else would he be stationed at the Manse? It's too much of a coincidence.'

'Implying he has informers in Shriltasi?'

Rose frowned. 'That seems likely. The Ashen have many enemies there. I think there is more interaction between certain people in Karadur and denizens of Shriltasi than my father knows. A lot of people have an interest in what is happening in Karadur and see it as an opportunity to seize control.'

'And you feel you can do something about the situation?' Max did not bother to hide his scorn.

Rose again made an effort to ignore his tone. 'The Ashen will have told you about the lost icons,' she said. 'I feel strongly that if these artefacts could only be rediscovered, they would in some way help initiate the changes Karadur needs. It would make sense for us to team up and find them. I can help you move around the city, and you can help me with your criminal skills.'

Max uttered a choked laugh. 'You flatter me! Criminal skills, indeed!'

'You know what I mean.'

Max sighed, shaking his head. 'Madam, you have partially convinced me your aims are noble, but I cannot see how artefacts can make a difference – only people can. Forget hunting for lost treasures, appealing though the venture may be, and think more about how you can influence the Council of Guilds.'

'I disagree. I'm sure that if the icons are restored to the Clans, old values, our old sense of honour and justice, will be restored. The icons are no ordinary artefacts. When they were forged, they were imbued with what the Ashen call *barishi* – magic. Oh, don't pull that face at me! I too have doubts, but I also feel we have to maintain an open mind. The Ashen believe that if we can't accept the existence of *barishi* we are doomed.'

'I don't totally disbelieve, I assure you.' He pulled an object on a thin cord out of his shirt and held it over his head. 'Look at this. It's a spellstone. I used it to quite dramatic effect against our beloved Coffin.'

Rose took it gingerly, and turned it in her hands. It was warm from the heat of his body. 'I've heard of these. Did the Ashen give it to you?'

He nodded. 'Jenny did.'

'She holds you in high regard. For all her and her brother's willingness to work towards a mutual goal, they are reluctant to share their knowledge of *barishi* with humankind.'

'Such was impressed upon me.'

'What did it do?'

Max described what had happened in the Moonmetal Manse, including the full reason for his being there. When he'd finished speaking, he held up his hand. 'The ring! I'd forgotten it.'

'Let me see.'

Max removed it from his finger and handed it to Rose. 'The setting's made of copper,' she said, holding it up to the light. 'Looks like a twisted feather. Why would Pewter have had the bead set into a ring?'

'He probably just thought it was a pretty bauble.'

Rose returned the ring to Max, who slipped it back onto his finger. 'Don't underestimate Clovis Pewter. That would be a grave mistake. There are those among the Clans who, like me, are aware of *barishi*, but they seek to use it for selfish ends. I wouldn't be surprised if Pewter knows of the bead's significance.'

'But what use is it to him? Jenny said it was a talisman that protected her from the stone plague.'

Rose twisted her mouth to the side. 'I think it is rather more than that. We shall see when you take it back to her.'

Max covered the ring with one hand. 'I'm tempted not to, but I made a deal with her. I have to help Menni.'

'So what will you do after that? Will you work with me or not? You don't have much time, Max. You need help.'

'I've never shared my business with the Metal,' Max replied, clearly uneasy. 'I see no reason to change my habits.'

Yet Rose could tell he was very tempted. She knew that, like her, he had a great sense of curiosity. She had intrigued him. 'Put aside your pride,' she said. 'Do not be governed by it.'

He did not answer for a while. Then he said, 'I must return to Shriltasi. Menni's restoration to his normal state is my only consideration at the moment.'

'Rightly so. First, refresh yourself here. I have another pair of trousers for you. I had to cut the leg of the ones you're wearing when I was attending to your wound. When you leave you must take care with that leg. I've sewn you up, but it won't take much punishment.'

'You have many unexpected talents,' Max said.

Rose shrugged. 'I'm no physician, but I do believe in being prepared for any eventuality. When I chose the life I lead, I realized I should know how to treat injuries. I suggest you ask Jenny to look at the wound for you. She can use *barishi* to heal it.' She knew there was a certain mordant tone to her voice and recognized the prickings of jealousy in her heart. Unearthly Jenny was a bewitching creature and certainly not shy of being forward. She'd made no secret of the fact the Fox of Akra fascinated her. Rose had had to keep her own feelings private but had winced inwardly whenever Jenny had boasted insouciantly of how she was intent on seducing Silverskin before he died. She did not really care about him, though — not like Rose did. Jenny's concern for his welfare was inspired only by his usefulness to her cause.

Rose brought Max a plate of food and a hot beverage. She watched him while he ate, carefully and neatly like a cat. After he'd finished, he lay back down again, one hand over his heart, staring at the ceiling. Rose picked up the empty plate.

'I'm not ungrateful for what you've done,' Max said, 'but it will take some time for me to get used to this. I've never had a friend among the Clans.'

'They are blind,' Rose said, 'but I hope that will change. Like the Ashen, I have great faith in you. I know you're finding it hard to accept all you've learned, but I trust you will soon.'

Max grimaced and sat up. He winced, both hands flying to his chest.

'What is it?' Rose asked.

He shook his head. 'A burn,' he said. 'Pain. Jenny said there was something called the Jade Talon that would help me with that.'

'Then you must make haste to Shriltasi,' Rose said. 'We will meet again soon — I am sure of it, as you were yesterday.'

Slowly Max got to his feet. 'I wish that none of this had happened. How idyllic it would have been if we could have met this morning at the Café, simply to enjoy each other's company.'

'I wish it too,' Rose said, 'but it was just a dream. Now, go into my bedroom and dress yourself.'

As he limped towards the door, Rose's heart contracted. Despite her words, she was afraid that, once he left her, she would never see him again.

Chapter Thirteen

Tea With Dame Serenia

Filgree House, domain of the Silverskins, was situated in a corner of Akra fief so secluded that it seemed as if the family sought to make themselves invisible in Karadur. The house itself lacked any ostentation, being square and solid, its windows obscured by diaphanous drapes. A small overgrown garden surrounded it. Cornelius Coffin stood at the front door, accompanied by half a dozen Irregulars. He'd rung the bell twice and still no one came to respond to the summons. Coffin sighed, tapping his foot against the worn step. He could not believe the house was empty. He could almost feel the nervous eyes peering through the drapes. Surely they must know he would not simply go away? Now he pounded upon the door with his fist and called, 'Open up! Don't force me to break down your door.'

He leaned closer to the ancient wood and heard the echo of footsteps that seemed to come from very far away. Presently, and before it sounded as if the footsteps had actually reached the door, it swung open before his face. Coffin jumped involuntarily. A tall mature woman stood at the threshold, wrapped in a long woollen coat of shimmering grey. Her white hair was wound severely upon her head and her eyes were like shards of polished silver. 'Captain Coffin,' she said politely. 'Have you been waiting long?'

Coffin ducked his head. 'Good day to you, Dame Serenia. It seems to me you need the service of a butler. Have you no one to open the door to visitors?'

Dame Serenia smiled tightly. 'We have no servants. What is the purpose of this visit?'

'I am hoping you will invite me in. I would like to talk with you.'

Dame Serenia cast a disapproving eye over the Irregulars, who stood silent and motionless behind their master. 'You may enter,' she said.

Coffin nodded to his men and stepped into the gloom of Filgree House. It was cold in there and, even though the hallway was tidy, evidence of decay was everywhere. The carpet was a mere mat of faded threads beneath his feet, the walls were peeling and there were lighter spaces where once pictures or tapestries had hung. It was clear the Silverskins were gripped by declining fortune. Coffin almost felt sorry for them.

Serenia closed the door. 'What is it you wish to say to me?'

'It is about Maximilian.'

Serenia frowned, her lips a bloodless line. 'I believe we have discussed all there is to discuss concerning that matter. I have nothing else to say.'

Coffin nodded affably. 'Hm, hm, I realiZe this. But sometimes a person knows things they aren't aware that they know.' He extended his hands. 'Max is a puzzle to us, my lady. I need help.'

He knew Serenia would not be fooled by this appeal but he trusted she would go along with the game for a while. 'Perhaps we should retire to my sitting room,' she said. 'One of my granddaughters can make us tea.'

'That would be splendid.'

The sitting room was more cheerful than the draughty hall. Here the chairs were plump, their rents disguised by colourful throws. A fire burned high in the hearth. Serenia spoke to a girl who sat sewing beneath the window. She must have observed Coffin waiting at the door. 'Lorany, a pot of tea for us, please.' The girl nodded and stood up, avoiding Coffin's eyes. For all their penury, Coffin had to admit the Silverskins were a handsome breed. He stood aside to let the girl flinch past him.

'Now,' said Serenia, sitting down and indicating that Coffin should take a seat opposite her. 'Tell me what you think I know.'

She was confident, unafraid. This alone suggested she had no knowledge of her renegade younger relative, yet Coffin couldn't help coming back here. His instincts dragged him to Filgree. There was something here for him. He didn't yet know what. Patting his lips with a closed fist, he cleared his throat. 'The Silverskins have knowledge of forbidden things,' he said.

Serenia raised her eyebrows. 'Do you listen to gossip, Captain?'

He smiled. 'Of course. No investigator worth his salt would ignore it.' He leaned forward. 'I think you may be able to help me in a certain matter. It may be connected with Maximilian, it may be not.'

Serenia smiled. 'Next you will be telling me you have come here for a potion of love, for a spell to be cast against your enemies.'

He held her gaze. 'Do people come here for such things?'

'It has been known. None of them have made it to my sitting room, however. How do you think I can help you?'

'It has come to my attention that certain misguided individuals are delving into practices best left untouched. I speak of the revival of an ancient cult. The cult of Sekmet. Do you know anything about this?'

Serenia threw back her head, laughed silently for a few moments. Then she shook her head and smiled. 'Ah, Captain, you think I lead it, don't you? Admit it. Isn't this why you're here?'

'No. I do not take you for a fool, my lady. No Silverskin could risk associating themselves with such a cult. More to the point, I think that if you *were* involved in anything of a forbidden nature it would certainly not be found out, nor gossiped about in the markets.'

'Then why ask me about it?'

'Call it intuition.'

Serenia put her head to one side. 'Does Lord Iron know you employ such questionable devices in your work?'

'Ultimately, if I produce results, he does not question my methods. Tell me what you know, my lady. If you can offer me anything at all, I will see to it that you are rewarded.'

Serenia's gaze flicked towards the ceiling, where a lump of plaster was missing. 'If the cult of Sekmet has been revived, it should be stopped,' she said. 'The ignorant should not delve into what they don't understand.'

'Then you do know of it? Where does it meet?'

'I have heard rumours, like you have, but nothing more. Perhaps it is only a fantasy.'

Coffin nodded. 'Perhaps it is.' He looked directly into Serenia's face. 'Have you heard from Max?'

Her expression did not falter. 'No. You have had men stationed around our property for weeks. He would hardly come here and I would not grant him entrance if he did. I have my family to think of.'

'He broke into the Moonmetal Manse early this morning. Fortunately, one of the Lords had been warned this would happen and made sure I was on hand. Despite this preparation, Maximilian still managed to escape. Someone helped him.'

'He must know a host of thieves, any of whom would eagerly act as accomplices. No Silverskin would help him, Captain.'

Coffin nodded again. 'I know this, my lady. My common sense tells me you would not jeopardize your people.' He paused, then shook his head briefly. 'But, for some reason, I am drawn back here to Filgree House. I am like a hound with a scent. It is quite beyond my control.'

Serenia drew back in her chair, her spine straight. 'You watch the house, you no doubt watch me, and the movements of all my family. You have searched our home twice and found nothing incriminating. I cannot help you, Captain. I think your intuition is merely clutching at straws.'

'You know the legend concerning Maximilian, of course?'

She nodded. 'I know of it, yes.'

'Is it true?'

'A man of reason would know that it cannot be.'

'Hm, yes. He would, wouldn't he?'

Lorany came back in, carrying a tray. Serenia and Coffin each took a cup from it and the girl left the room once more. Coffin curled his hands around ancient, delicate china, inhaling the fragrant steam that rose from it. 'You serve the best tea in Karadur, my lady.'

'You find excuses to come here, then. Perhaps I should serve you something less tasteful, then you won't bother me again.'

'Who helped Maximilian escape from Gragonatt?'

'I have no idea, as I've told you countless times. You know the criminal element far more intimately than I do, Captain. Would you like sugar in that?'

'No, I would not pollute so rare a blend. I don't think it was a criminal. Someone more . . . powerful. I'm convinced your instincts are more acute than mine. If I feel something unusual is afoot in Karadur,

I'm sure you do too. I would be flattered if you'd share your thoughts with me.'

Serenia inhaled slowly through her nose. 'Some things are inevitable. Nothing ever remains the same, no matter how much effort is put into maintaining the status quo. People are restless, discontent. Perhaps they feel trapped here in Karadur and yearn for freedom. That might be why the ancient legends of lost cities and heroes hold such appeal. We are prisoners of the ice, tunnelling away beneath it, scouring limited resources. Eventually, we will die. Perhaps, from the chaos that encroaches now, some men or women will emerge who may challenge our imprisonment. The Lords will not address the matter. They are fools.'

'You speak bluntly.'

'You asked me to. Will you arrest me now for heresy?'

He smiled. 'And lose my favourite tea-house? I think not.' He put down his empty cup. 'You have given me something to think about. For this, I thank you.'

'I have given you nothing, Captain. In some ways, I wish I could do otherwise.' She sighed. 'Cults, Max Silverskin, restless people, rising crime. They are linked, but even though I may speculate as to how and why, I cannot give you the answers you seek.'

'I want Maximilian back in Gragonatt. He holds the key to every mystery, I'm sure of it.'

'Karadur is no more than one big prison. Max cannot escape. He is out there somewhere.'

Coffin nodded thoughtfully. 'That is true, yet he's like a ghost.' He held out a hand before him, slowly closed it into a fist. 'Even when you hold him in your hands, he is of a subtle substance that simply drifts away.' He opened his hand, let it fall. 'I will tell Lord Iron of your cooperation. You may expect recompense. If you hear anything at all that may be of use to me, please send word.' He stood up.

Dame Serenia inclined her head. 'You are kind to think of us. I know nothing, of course, but I believe you should question your own men concerning the matter of Sekmet.' Her eyes were away from him, gazing at her white hand, which plucked at a thread on the arm of her chair.

Coffin stared at her. 'What do you mean?'

She looked up. 'They are kin of the foundrymen who were the original worshippers of the goddess. They might know something of use.' She smiled. 'But I'm sure you've thought of that already.'

'My Irregulars are above reproach,' Coffin said stiffly.

'I was not suggesting otherwise. Still . . .'

'Good day to you, Dame Serenia,' Coffin said, and marched from the room.

Dame Serenia waited until she heard the door close and the crunch of the men's footsteps as they walked away down the short gravel path to the street. Then she called for Lorany. The girl came softly into the room, her eyes narrow. 'Bring me my keys,' Serenia said.

Chapter Fourteen

Ashen Hands

Max's skin crawled as he made his way swiftly to the Well of the Gibbold, in the heart of the free zone between Peygron and Shinlech fiefs. This was the nearest route to Shriltasi. He felt vulnerable, exposed, which was not a natural condition for him. The fact that Coffin seemed to materialize at unexpected moments was a matter of concern. Someone was informing on Max – but who? And was it wise to trust the daughter of Prometheus Iron?

Max entered the well-house, which looked like an ornate mausoleum, almost pyramidal but with a truncated top. Metal sculptures of gibbolds adorned its outer walls. Over the main entrance, the head of a gibboldess snarled down in contempt. Inside, men and women supervised the great pumping equipment that dispensed clean water throughout the fief. Max knew he should proceed with extreme caution here, but impatience raged within him. He hurried past the workers, occasionally nodding at those who looked up from their tasks, as if he had legitimate business there. Jenny had explained to him about a network of service shafts around the main well. Her map indicated the way to a point where he would have to use the spellstone and open up a hidden doorway, an entrance sealed by *barishi*.

Max reached the entrance to the shafts without incident. But as he made to climb down the first ladder, a foreman called out to him. 'Hoi, you! What you doing there?'

Max paused but did not look up. After a moment, he continued to descend.

He heard the man utter a low curse and then the scrape of his boots on the rungs above. 'Halt! This is private property. Halt! Or I'll call out the Boys.'

Max knew he couldn't lead the foreman to Shriltasi and that it might be difficult to shake him off in territory unknown to Max but familiar to the water-workers. He glanced up and saw the man had taken out a hand-held warning siren from his utility belt. Max halted. 'I have important business here. Business of the Metal.'

The foreman was just above him now, hanging onto the ladder with one hand. 'And what business might that be, then?'

Max looked down. Dim gas lamps set into the walls showed him that a side tunnel branched off the shaft a few feet below. 'I'll tell you in a moment,' Max said, injecting as much charm into his voice as he could muster. He ducked his head towards the tunnel. 'Let's talk there.'

The foreman would not think that such a courteous, handsome gentleman could be up to no good. Shrugging, the man gestured for Max to continue. Max entered the tunnel and, moments later, the foreman joined him. 'Well? What's your game?'

Max did not reply, but floored the foreman with a single, well-aimed punch. Menni had taught him long ago how to disable an enemy as quickly as possible. The foreman would wake up in a few minutes, wondering what had happened to him.

Wasting no more time, Max climbed back into the shaft and continued to descend. After only ten minutes or so, and having taken the side tunnels indicated on the map, he reached the bucket lift that Jenny told him he could use to make a swift final descent. He had to look out for a sign scratched on the damp lichened walls of the shaft. Occasionally, as he lowered himself using the rope pulleys in the lift, he heard distant voices. Workmen in other tunnels. The foreman would no doubt be conscious again now. People would be searching for the intruder. Max shook his head. Perhaps this was not the best way to enter Shriltasi. It was too public. The way he and Menni had used initially was safer.

Eventually, after peering through the gloom until his eyes ached, he saw a large glyph scratched into the wall as Jenny had described. He came to a halt. There was no doorway here. The wall was seamless. Drawing out the spellstone, he described in the air the same symbol that appeared on the wall. Nothing seemed to happen. Cursing, Max repeated the process. Still nothing. He leaned out of the bucket, reaching to touch the wall. It gave at once beneath his fingers and he nearly fell out of the bucket. A doorway had appeared in the stonework. Max climbed out of the lift and pushed through the portal swiftly.

Using Jenny's map, Max returned to the Stone Grove. The forlorn sight of Menni, appearing as if he was a freshly carved statue, tugged at Max's heart. He wondered what would happen should a limb be broken off. Would the restored Menni suffer the same disability? Carefully, Max inspected the stone to assure himself that Menni was intact. 'I don't know if you can hear me,' he said softly, 'but I pledge to restore you. I've heard outlandish things in this place, old friend. They've put me under a sentence of death. All you need to know, if you're capable of knowing, is that I refuse to die until you stand before me once again, in flesh and blood.' A twinge of pain twisted in his chest. He gasped and leaned against the statue. He felt close to tears, like a child. He wanted Menni's reassuring arms around him, the bear hug of sanctuary that had sheltered and sustained him throughout his infancy. How fleeting that time had been. His life seemed to be a chaotic blur, leading always to this point. He did not want the responsibility. He wanted to deny it, yet how could he deny the reality of the sensations that clenched and burned within him? Who had done this to him? 'I don't want to die,' he murmured against the stone. Resentment churned within him for the way others had apparently taken control of his life. They had cursed him.

Lost in disconsolate thoughts, Max didn't notice at first that he had company. Then his neck prickled and he drew away from the statue to find Jack and Jenny Ash standing behind him – too close. Jack was grinning, while Jenny looked more sombre. Was that sympathy in her eyes – or simply disappointment that the hero they wanted was so distressingly human?

She seemed to sense his thoughts, for she stepped forward and flung her arms around him. She felt small-boned and delicate against him, like a bird, which was not altogether pleasant. Her body smelled of wet leaves and loam. Max was unsure whether he wanted to pull away or return the embrace. She could take offence if he rejected her, which might not bode well for Menni. Hesitantly, Max patted her shoulder.

She gave him a final squeeze, then released him. 'You have it?'

Max nodded. 'I have. Now, we have business, do we not? You said you would help me restore Menni.'

Jenny hesitated, glancing at her brother. 'Certain artefacts need to be recovered first.'

Max narrowed his eyes. It might be that, with Menni by his side, he'd be more difficult for the Ashen to control. He sensed they wanted to delay that happening. He must play the situation carefully. Perhaps these strange people were capable of destroying Menni, as well as bringing him back to life.

'Give me the bead,' Jenny said.

'You can have it when Menni is restored to me.'

Jenny was silent for a moment, then said, 'I cannot help you if I'm at risk from the stone plague. I've already told you that you need the Jade Talon. You won't be able to restore your friend if you are crippled by pain. Can't you remember what we told you? At least show me you have the bead.'

Max eyed her stonily, holding up his hand.

Jenny peered at the ring, and her face lit up with pleasure. 'This is better than I thought! Look, Jack, the setting.'

Jack stepped forward and Max lowered his hand. 'First things first. What must I do to acquire this talon?'

In response, Jenny smiled, and began to sing, 'Nine things make three things, three things bring a fourth thing, four things make one thing, one thing makes everything.'

Max frowned. 'Excuse me?'

'That was the Silverskin Verse,' Jenny said. 'Your family have sung it for hundreds of years – and once they even knew what it meant.'

'What *does* it mean?'

'It refers to the lost icons. In effect, each of the great artefacts is composed of different parts. They were sundered at the time of the Reformation in Karadur, disguised and hidden by the discredited alchemists of the clans, or rather by their novices, for the majority of the magi were incarcerated. If you can recreate the War Owl, you can use it to help your friend, and happily it seems you already have two parts of it.'

Max frowned. 'What do you mean, two parts?'

Jenny's smile widened. 'The bead is part of the owl – its eye, if you like – and so is the setting. It is fashioned into the representation of feathers, and symbolizes the body of the owl. It is fortunate for us that Pewter has already recovered it. He only required – as you do – the third artefact to summon the Owl: its claw.'

'You knew this, didn't you?' Max said. 'Why didn't you tell me what the bead was? Why all that nonsense about me stealing it back for you?'

Jenny frowned. 'You misunderstand. It was not nonsense. You took risks to find the bead for me. It was a selfless act. That was important.'

'The less you know the better,' Jack said. 'Look on it as a magical education.'

'I won't play games,' Max said.

'Oh, but you should,' Jack replied. 'It is all a game. That is the irony of it.'

'The jade talon is the third part, isn't it?' Max said. 'At least admit that.'

'You have guessed right,' Jenny said. 'That's good.'

Max nodded grimly. 'Yes, it's very good. You need it and, to persuade me to find it for you, you told me that ridiculous story about how it can help me.'

Jenny frowned. 'But we did not lie to you, Fox. The talon *will* help you. This I swear.'

Max folded his arms. 'So where is it? I presume you know. Do I have to pay another visit to Pewter?'

Jack shook his head. 'That will not be necessary. The talon is here, in Shriltasi.'

Max uttered a growl. 'This is absurd! I get the feeling that once I've found your third object, there will be a fourth, then a fifth. You are deceiving me. Restore my friend at once. I'll not help you any further until this is done.'

'But it can't be done without the owl,' Jenny said lightly. 'You already know that. We are not deceiving you. I felt you use my spellstone, Fox, felt its *barishi* stir in my blood. Did I fail you then? The spell will work for you again – as will the next I'll teach you. You're an adept, with more *barishi* in you than the rest of us put together. But you must learn how to use it.'

'Your scepticism is a great weakness,' Jack said.

Max turned on him. 'I see it as a strength. If I'm sceptical, I'm not gullible. Why should I do what you want of me? This legend of my family is new to me and, if it's true, it's hardly a welcome discovery. I've never felt this thing called *barishi* within me. I have no proof it's there.'

'The spellstone worked, didn't it?' Jenny said and then clawed the air in exasperation. 'Oh, what will it take to convince you? This petty debate is a waste of time. Give me the spellstone.'

Max hesitated, then took it from his neck and gave it to her. Jenny held it in her hand and fashioned a new symbol in the air with it. 'This sign conjures another frequency of *barishi*. It will shrink or enlarge any object you touch with the energy, and place it temporarily in your power. However, use it wisely, for the effect does not last long.' She handed the stone back to him. 'Show me you can do it.'

The symbol had been simple, just five strokes upon the air. Max found he could remember it easily. As he drew it, he felt a tingle course up his arm. Something was happening: it was undeniable.

Jenny nodded in satisfaction. 'You are progressing. Now go and retrieve the talon.'

Max put the spellstone back around his neck, unable to repress a feeling of excitement at what he'd just felt. 'I thought you were going to assist me.'

Jenny remained expressionless. 'I have, with the stone.'

'Excuse me, you did imply . . .'

'Listen,' Jenny interrupted. 'Jack and I cannot go into the territory where the talon lies. I would be more of a hindrance than a help, because my presence would be felt by my enemies. Alone, you have more chance of success. We have given you the map and knowledge of *barishi*. Put together with your own skills, this is more than enough to help you.'

'I presume the artefact is guarded,' Max said. 'By what?'

'Forest dwellers called Porporrum,' Jenny said. 'They have installed the talon in the centre of a graffy run.'

'Graffies,' Max said, deadpan. The creatures were large predators and, as far as he'd known, only a few of them remained alive, in the Karadurian zoo. He had no doubt that any that still resided in Shriltasi would be rather more fearsome than their captive counterparts. He gave Jenny a pointed look that conveyed all his feelings on the matter.

'You must do this, Fox,' Jack said. 'Not just for us or Karadur, but for yourself. You've been given a great opportunity, blessed with a mighty power that has yet to fully manifest. But you are already paying for that power. Unless you learn about your gift, and use it correctly, it will obliterate you so surely that it will be as if you never existed at all.'

'More threats,' Max said sourly.

Jenny shook her head. 'No threat, Fox, just advice. The spells I have taught you, and your own agility will be protection enough against the graffies.'

Max sighed in resignation and took out the scroll-map. 'Where is this place, then?

Jack pointed to a certain point. 'Here. The run is a kind of maze.'

Max took note of the location and rolled the scroll up.

'Will you leave the ring with us?' Jenny said. 'I feel it will be safer here.'

Max shook his head. 'Oh no, I don't think so.'

'It will,' Jenny insisted. 'You must trust us, Fox. When will you realize this?'

Max hesitated, then drew the ring from his finger and placed it in Jenny's waiting hands.

She smiled. 'I will keep it safe for you.'

'For me?' Max shook his head. He made to leave the garden but found himself staggering. His wound hadn't troubled him greatly on the journey to Shriltasi, probably because he'd ignored it, intent on avoiding capture. But now, since he'd rested the leg a little, it had begun to throb with pain.

'Wait,' Jenny said. 'What ails you?'

Max turned back to her. 'Just a small token of esteem I collected from Coffin while liberating your bead.' He glanced down and saw that blood had seeped through his trouser leg. Perhaps one of Rose's stitches had burst.

'You were wounded,' Jenny said. She turned to her brother. 'Jack?'

Jack nodded. He beckoned to Max. 'Come back here.'

Max did so. Rose had told him Jenny might be able to heal him.

'Sit,' Jack ordered and crouched down beside Max on the grass. Jenny stood to one side. Her face was creased in concern, which perhaps indicated the wound was more serious than Max had thought.

Jack peeled Max's trouser leg up to the knee, wrinkling his nose in aversion when he saw the wound. A couple of stitches had indeed come loose. 'Who patched you up?' he demanded.

'A friend,' Max answered, reluctant to reveal his association with Rose.

Jack shook his head. 'Poor job, but the best you could achieve in your community, I suppose.' He placed one hand over the wound, about an inch above the broken skin. Almost at once, Max felt an immense heat pour from Jack's open palm, enough to make him cry out and jerk his leg away.

Jack yanked it back into position, conjuring a yelp of pain from Max. 'Stay still. I have to work quickly. It will hurt, but you're no good to yourself or to us in this condition. How can you run from a graffy with your leg split open?'

Max steeled himself, gasping at he spoke, 'I hope I don't have to run. You told me I have *barishi* on my side.'

'You still have to reach the graffy run,' Jenny said. 'Without healing, that leg would be bleeding badly by the time you got there.'

Max couldn't help feeling weirdly invaded by the energy that poured from Jack Ash's hand. It conjured nausea in his gut and set the mark above his heart prickling painfully. After what seemed like an eternity of agony, but which was probably only a minute or so, Jack withdrew his hand. Max glanced down at his leg. The wound had not healed completely but the flesh had knitted together somewhat. 'That will have to do,' Jack said. 'I can give it more attention when you return.'

Max hoped that would not be necessary.

Chapter Fifteen

Taming of Wild Beasts

In Shriltasi's overgrown beauty, the ghost of formal planning still remained. Max emerged from beneath the forest canopy to find himself at the edge of spreading fields where once crops had grown, now run wild. Above this expanse, where large herds of cattle browsed knee-deep in seeding grasses, the sky was a hazy gold, as if the sun shone through a sheer blanket of cloud. Was Shriltrasi the same size as Karadur, or even larger? The horizon seemed impossibly far way.

Max passed abandoned farms, where strange, scuttling, semi-humanoid creatures fled at his approach. In the distance, nestling against the arms of immense copper-leaved trees, he saw a grand mansion. Only as he drew closer to it could he see the vines crawling out of its shattered windows, the missing roof, the purple-plumaged birds roosting in the naked rafters. Was that a face at one of the upper windows? It ducked from view as he walked by. From sights such as these, it was clear that, whatever the Shriltasians had become, they had once lived very much as the Karadurians did, with order and industry. At one time these neglected fields would have provided all the food for the city above. How sad to see them in decline, fading and plagued by weeds.

Gradually, the wilderness took over completely once more. Max found himself walking through a forest of thorn trees. Brittle foliage hung desiccated upon the cruel branches. He consulted the map and realized he must be very close to his destination. A furtive rustling among the bushes nearby made him tense up, but nothing showed itself. Moving forward with more care and alertness, Max came to an opening in the scrub, its flaming arch fashioned of woven withes. A huge skull was nailed at the arch's apex. Its yellowed fangs and hollow eye sockets oozed menace. It appeared peculiarly sentient. Beyond this strange portal the branches curved in, black and ancient, barbed with thorns, to form an almost perfectly circular tunnel.

Max drew his sword and, treading lightly, passed beneath the portal. The only sounds were a soft crackling hiss, as if the branches were gently rubbing together, and the droning mumble of insects that hovered among the thorns. As he progressed, the tunnel became narrower and darker, pervaded by a stench of mildew, like rotten hay. The air was humid and close.

Max heard a new sound and paused, straining to determine what it might be. Then it came again: a throaty snuffling, as of a great beast tasting the air. Whatever had made the sound was behind him. He glanced upwards, wondering whether it was possible to claw his way through the branches to safety, but the roof was a thick tangle of limbs. Graffies might even be able to climb. He could only assume that more of the animals waited ahead. There was no sign yet of the creature behind him but its soft growls were becoming louder. It must have smelled or sensed his presence. Cautiously, Max continued to advance. This was madness. At any moment, he could turn a corner and be face to face with a predator. How could he escape when there was clearly another behind him? Yet he was driven to continue, almost as if something ahead called to him.

Max smelled the graffy before he saw it. A thick, overpowering stench of animal musk filled his nose and he turned quickly. The creature slunk into view in the curving tunnel behind him. It was immense, its huge shoulders higher than its haunches. The pelt was dusty black and the great head, whose jaws were armed with scimitar-like canine fangs, swung gently from side to side. Its eyes were yellow, filled with a weird intelligence, and its claws were incredibly long, protruding over an inch from its paws. The creature seemed a strange mixture of feline and canine. When it caught sight of Max, it halted, and for long, agonizing seconds the two appraised each other. Max experienced a jolt of recognition, which, bizarrely, he was sure the grafenak felt too. He knew he'd have to fight the creature, as if the whole situation had been preordained. He had assumed an archetypal role:

the beast-slayer. In legends, heroes vanquished the beasts. He had to believe in that now.

The grafenak approached slowly, totally without fear, as if confident it could kill this pathetic human morsel with one swipe of its paw. Max feinted at it with his sword, which the creature ignored. Its massive bulk filled the run. Max felt his own confidence dip alarmingly. His meagre weapon could do no more than prick this great beast. He was a dwarf in comparison with it.

The grafenak halted some feet before him and expelled a great roar, which was followed by a foul gust of carrion breath. With one lazy swipe of its paw, it knocked Max's sword from his grasp. The weapon skidded across the dirt floor of the run, twisted and ruined. Softly growling, almost purring, the grafenak crouched low, triangular ears flat against its gigantic skull. At any moment, it would pounce.

Without thinking, Max reached for the spellstone. The new spell Jenny had taught him could enlarge or diminish any creature – but how was the choice made? If he cast the spell upon the grafenak and it grew in size, he'd be finished. The only other creatures in the run were insects: butterflies, bees and beetles.

Swiftly, Max drew the symbol he had used in the Moonmetal Manse and pointed the stone at the thorns, praying the *barishic* influence would touch something that could help him. At once, the air seemed to writhe and twist and, from this aching confusion, a swarm of brass bees puffed up before the grafenak in a coruscating buzzing cloud. The great beast growled and batted at them with its front paws. Instinctively, Max ran further into the run. Behind him, he heard maddened coughing howls. He did not turn back to see what had happened.

The din had clearly aroused other beasts in the maze, for he could hear them snuffling and snarling around him. The warm stink of musk was overwhelming.

The path ahead of him divided into three. Max plunged down the central tunnel. The maze seemed endless. He was conscious of being pursued by invisible grafenaks that must be tagging him in tunnels that ran parallel to the one he had taken. Once he heard a mighty roar overhead, which suggested the maze was constructed on more than one level.

Then, turning a corner, he found himself at the entrance to what appeared to be a central roofless arena. Staggering he came to a halt. High tangled thorn hedges formed a circular wall, broken only by the entrances to other dark tunnels. A few lethargic adult grafenaks, smaller than the animal Max had encountered in the run and hence presumably female, supervised a clutch of sleepy cubs. The grafenaks raised their heads in curiosity, but did not appear immediately hostile. Perhaps they did not have to be. The sound of approaching male grafenaks was louder than before.

Max scanned the high thorny walls around him. He could tell it wouldn't be too difficult to scale them, but he hadn't come this far simply to try and escape. Where was the talon? As if aware of his thoughts, a couple of the female grafenaks rose slowly to their feet, revealing an iron plinth some five feet high. Its sides were scored as if the animals had sharpened their claws upon it. A small dome of glass rested upon its summit, and beneath this, Max saw a glimmer of greenish stone.

Simultaneously, a fiery pain ignited in Max's chest. He cried out, forced to sink to his knees, his head reeling. He was surrounded by the sound of the grafenaks, their tapping claws and threatening roars. Their heavy smell filled his head. Maybe they wouldn't have to kill him. It seemed that in the presence of the artefact, which was supposed to assuage his pain, the unknown thing within him raged and resisted. How could he deny the truth of what Jenny and Jack had told him about the silverheart? He could feel it now, hard and relentless against his ribs.

Uttering a cry of defiance, Max ripped open his shirt, clawed hooked fingers over his flesh. At once, a blaze of silver light erupted around him. For long seconds, he was held frozen in its insubstantial embrace, then his body began to jerk uncontrollably. He felt as if he was being raised from the ground. Abruptly, the sensation ceased and he realized the pain had abated. His first instinct was to leap towards the nearest hedge and start scrambling. His flesh was tensed for the onslaught of cruel claws and powerful jaws. But something was wrong with this image.

Max shook his head, disorientated. It took him some moments to realize that all was quiet around him. He blinked, clearing his sight, and found that the grafenaks were motionless, their great heads hanging down, their eyes filled with dim fire. Max glanced down and saw, through his torn shirt, that the mark on his breast was glowing faintly with a weird blue-white light. Had this calmed the beasts?

Without pausing for further analysis, Max leaped forward and knocked the glass dome from the plinth. It fell to the ground and shattered, but still the grafenaks did not move. The artefact upon the plinth was small, a mere curl of jade shaped like a bird of prey's claw. Max grabbed it and, as he did so, the female grafenaks uttered a strange sigh in unison. Behind him, the males growled and scraped their claws against the packed dirt of the arena, while the cubs threw back their heads and emitted chittering cries. Max was filled with the conviction that the creatures somehow approved his desire to take the artefact. Was it possible the grafeneks protected the talon only from those who were not fit to wield it?

Conflicting emotions boiled within him: a sense of brute power and divine compassion. He was inspired to approach the strangely quiescent, even reverent beasts, and lay his hands upon their shaggy heads. They would bow down to him, let him command them. Max fought this compulsion. Common sense told him not to test the idea, and his ingrained instinct for survival prevailed. He loped across the arena and began to scale the walls.

Once he reached the roof of the run, he glanced down and saw the grafenak tribe all staring up at him with inscrutable eyes. They knew him, understood what he was. Without further pause, Max hurried across the uneven roof of the run. The grafenaks might have accepted his theft, but he had no doubt their masters would think otherwise.

As he scrambled over the withes, his feet occasionally slipped between the woven branches and once his leg went right through. He winced and bit back a cry as his wound was scored by the hard thorns. He crouched on hands and knees, breathing hard, trying to dispel the pain. A sense of urgency coursed through him. Perhaps the grafenaks were about to awake from their trance and had decided to pursue and attack him after all. Perhaps their masters had appeared. Max knew he could be overtaken easily, because of the wound. He summoned the last of his strength and pressed on, determined to ignore the throbbing pain. His trouser leg was warm and wet against his flesh.

After what seemed like an eternity, he reached the edge of the run, close to where he had entered it below. His limbs were shaking badly now. He managed to slither down the front wall and stumbled in the direction of the open fields. The air seemed to hiss around him and his sight was dim, as if a veil had been cast across the source of light in this strange world. His strength was draining away with the steady seep of blood that ran from his leg.

Trembling, almost delirious, Max came to a stream. He collapsed to the ground and plunged his head beneath the icy water, which brought a jolt of clarity to his mind. Lapping like a wild beast, he drank deeply of the refreshing flow, which gave him enough strength to sit up and examine his wound. The thorns had opened it up again but most of Rose's stitches still held, no doubt strengthened by Jack Ash's healing energy. His head pulsed to the rhythm of his blood. He hadn't the strength left to take a single further step. Perhaps some dreg of Coffin's poison still coursed through his veins. He needed to rest for a while and was surely far enough from the grafenak run by now to do so. The idea of sleep seemed irresistible.

Max lay down in the long grass, serenaded by the chuckle of the water and the comforting drone of insects. He closed his aching eyes. Sleep. Yes. His body filled with peaceful languor. He could no longer feel his limbs.

A silvery hiss jolted him awake. He opened his eyes, unsure of whether he'd been dozing or not. Something had flown swiftly over his face. An insect? His instincts clamoured for him to become alert, fight off the lethargy that gripped him. He knew intimately the feeling that pervaded his body. A sense of surveillance, impending attack.

Max raised his head cautiously above the grass and peered around him. The insects had gone silent, or had been scared away. The air was full of tension. The hiss came again, and this time Max uttered a smothered cry, for something had grazed his cheek. A small thornlike dart had fallen into his lap. Then another came, plunging into his hair, and another that pierced the fabric of his shirt. There was no doubt: he was under attack, weaponless and debilitated. His only course of action was to flee, and that seemed nigh on impossible. He dragged himself to his knees and, as he did so, found himself looking into the distorted face of a small humanoid creature. Its skin was green and covered in strange thorny protuberances and it was gibbering at him in what appeared to be rage. Its face was like an immense nut carved into the semblance of a gargoyle, although its eyebrows were weirdly mobile. It held a wooden club in one twiggy hand and a wooden spear, with which it now poked at Max's torso, in the other.

Max raised his hands in a gesture of what he hoped would be interpreted as submission. 'I mean no harm,' he said, which seemed ridiculous under the circumstances. He saw that twenty or so of the small creatures had surrounded him, all gesturing with their weapons and uttering hooting calls. Many of them carried dart tubes, which they held to their lipless mouths, their eyebrows jiggling like frenzied caterpillars.

'Porporrom,' said the first creature, who was presumably the troop's leader.

Max remembered what Jenny had told him about the forest dwellers. Had the name been offered as an introduction? Max decided he could only try to pacify the troop and rose slowly to his feet, hands held palms up. 'I am Max Silverskin,' he said.

The creatures all began to jump up and down at what they clearly perceived as his effrontery, emitting ear-splitting shrieks.

The lead creature said, 'Porporrum,' once more, then threw its club at Max's chest.

The weapon caught him precisely on the witch mark, which clenched in pain and sent him collapsing to his knees. At once, the gibbering creatures capered forward with an absurd high-stepping gait. They poked him with their spears, breaking his skin, peppering him with tiny wounds. 'Ashen stink!' they cried and spat malodorous green spittle in Max's face.

Max groped for the spellstone in his pocket, the only thing in his possession resembling a weapon. What he could do with it, he had no idea, but before these bizarre little people cut him to pieces he would have to try both spells and hope one worked in his favour. But before he could even draw the stone from his pocket, a loud melodious cry rang out across the fields and groves. The Porporrum all froze simultaneously and then began to shriek in greater rage. Max heard the unmistakable hiss of an arrow being released and one of the creatures fell backwards with a surprised squeak, a feathered shaft protruding from its chest. A swift shadowy figure leapt over Max's body, yodelling a battle cry. The only impressions he received were those of grace and litheness, a flying cloak, a banner of flying hair. The Porporrum's eyebrows all shot up and, with excited shrieks, they began to leap away through the grass, some of them urinating indiscriminately in fear. Max inhaled deeply and bowed his head, trying to collect his thoughts.

A small hand curled around his shoulder, burning hot. Involuntarily, he shivered and looked up into the elfin face of Jenny Ash, who was slinging a bow over her shoulder. 'It was as well I decided to wait for you near here,' she said.

'I am gratified beyond measure to see you,' he said. 'As you can see, I met the Porporrum.'

'Mmm,' Jenny replied, hunkering down beside him. 'They created the graffy run. I can only presume you robbed them of their treasure.'

Max nodded wearily. 'I have it, yes.' He frowned. 'A strange thing happened there . . .'

'Tell me later,' Jenny said. 'I must get you to safety. I surprised the Porporrum, which is why they ran off, but they'll soon find their courage. It'll take them a while to work it out, but eventually, when they've stopped pissing themselves in terror and leaping about, they'll remember I was alone. Come. Get to your feet. I'll help you.'

Max leaned on Jenny for support as they made their way slowly back to the Stone Grove. For so small and slender a creature, she was surprisingly strong. As they went, she explained that the Porporrum had once been her family's subjects. 'At the time when the Ashen ruled in Shriltasi, the Porporrum were the guardians of the wild beasts, the grafenaks and the gibbolds. They trained these creatures for the hunt and as domestic guards.' She sighed. 'But now they do not recognize our sovereignty. They turn our own sacred beasts against us and it's only the Porporrum's innate cowardice that prevents them from attacking Asholm outright.'

Max was silent for a moment. 'Perhaps the beasts are not as stupid as those who claim to be their masters.'

'What do you mean?'

'When I was in the run, something happened to the witch mark. It . . . came alive somehow. Flashed silver. The graffies became quiescent at once. I was sure they allowed me to take the talon. It was as if they recognized something within me.'

'Yes,' Jenny said excitedly. 'That makes perfect sense. It is a good sign, Sir Fox. You should be heartened by it.'

Max laughed wearily. 'I will only be heartened by more of your brother's strange medicine,' he said. 'I'm useless like this.'

'I can work similar medicine,' Jenny said coquettishly, 'and many other magics besides! I could amaze you.'

'I'm sure,' Max said. He was holding onto consciousness only by a supreme effort of will. The pain in his leg was severe and the burn over his heart made it difficult to draw breath. Jenny appeared to notice this, for she encouraged him to talk. 'Tell me all that happened in the run,' she said.

Max did so, then said, 'When I wanted to use the spell you showed me – to enlarge or shrink objects – I didn't know how. The symbol was not enough. How do you direct the spell to attain the desired effect?'

Jenny looked surprised. 'Isn't it obvious? It's the intention you put into it when you describe the symbol. Forgive me, I thought you'd realize that.'

'It would have been more useful if you'd mentioned it before.'

Jenny shook her head. 'I disagree. If you'd shrunk all the graffies, then how would you have known they'd react to you in the way they did? Everything proceeds as it's meant to do. Fate works with you.'

When they reached their destination, there was no sign of Jack Ash. Menni's statue seemed to stare at Max with accusation. 'We must do it now,' Max said. 'We must bring Menni back to life.'

'You are so impatient,' Jenny said, smiling. 'Let me fetch Jack. He is asleep in Asholm, dreaming of a fishtailed siren. He won't heed my call unless I shake him in person, because he's having far too much fun.' She shook her head in amused vexation. 'Anyway, you need that leg looking at and I think we should all examine the artefacts together. We have the pieces of the Owl, but none of us know how to unite them.' She made Max sit down in the grass, his back resting on the legs of one of the statues.

'There's no point you staggering all the way to Asholm with me. Wait here and rest. You'll be perfectly safe. I'll be back very soon, then Jack and I can work on you.'

Max perceived a slightly lascivious tone to this remark, but felt so weak and sick that he was beyond protesting. 'Hurry,' he said.

Left alone, Max did not feel comfortable resting against stone that was once, presumably, living flesh. He shuffled away a little to lie back in the grass, supporting himself on his elbows. A single bird sang a haunting song somewhere high in the branches above him. Once again, a languor stole over him. It was difficult to keep his eyes open. 'Menni, I need you here beside me,' he said to the statue in front of him. 'I need your guidance.' The statue peered back at him, its face caught in an expression of surprise. It was doubtful Menni could hear him.

Max shook his head, and perceived a spark of amber light at the corner of his vision. It appeared to have flashed from the statue. He blinked to clear his sight and saw that the ring he had taken from Pewter had been placed on one of Menni's stone fingers. Why would Jack leave it out in the open like that? Puzzled, Max hauled himself slowly to his feet. Specks of light boiling before his eyes, he groped to take the ring from Menni's finger, half-suspecting a trick. But nothing untoward happened. Swaying slightly on his feet, Max held the ring with one hand and took the jade talon from his pocket with the other. How could they be combined? He felt a slight movement in the talon. Had he imagined that? No. The tiny jade claw was flexing between his fingers, as if grasping for something, desiring something.

Instinctively, Max placed the ring and the talon close together so that they were touching. At once, the jade talon leapt from his grasp to seize the ring. He was so surprised that he dropped both objects into the grass. To his astonishment, the claw crawled towards the ring at his feet. Then, somehow, it began to merge with the copper feather and the amber bead. For some moments, the whole arrangement was strangely blurred and emitted smoke that smelled of acrid verdigris. A sharp orange light flashed out from it. Then, just as abruptly, it solidified back into an amber stone set into a ring. It rolled and trembled upon the grass as if something moved within it. Max didn't want to touch it. He wasn't sure what he'd done, or whether it had been the right thing to do. Something was moving within the stone. He could see it. Something was trying to escape.

Max took a step backwards. At the same time, a tiny creature emerged from the ring. An owl. Its feathers were metallic as if it was made of copper. With a high-pitched whirring sound, it flew upwards, the size of a large bumble-bee. Max held out his hands, expecting the little bird to go for his eyes. But instead it perched on one of his outstretched fingers, where it dug in sharp copper claws. Max brought his hand close to his face to examine the little creature. It was utterly perfect in every detail, glaring at him with round amber eyes. The owl rustled its wings in apparent agitation, as if trying to communicate.

'What do I do with you, little thing?' Max murmured. 'How will you work for me?'

The owl merely turned its head to the side and blinked.

'Revive my friend,' he said. 'Over there.'

The owl did not move. Max sensed that something wasn't quite right. The owl should be larger. Instinctively, he drew the spellstone from his pocket. 'Where intention goes . . .' he said, and described the symbol of the sizing spell in the air before pointing the stone at the owl. 'Become your true form,' he said. The little creature uttered a low cry and lifted into the air.

Before Max's eyes, the owl enlarged. It was as if it drew substance from the air itself, gathering motes of being. Its wings beat the air, its eyes stared at him, full of ancient wisdom. It whirred and clattered in all its marvellous mechanical beauty – exactly like a living owl save for being fashioned entirely from metal. Max was filled with such awe that he had to fight an urge to drop back to his knees, from respect rather than from pain. The owl hovered before him, its great body hanging upon the air with unnatural ease.

Max felt something quiver in his hand and realized the spellstone had begun to pulse. When he examined it, he saw a symbol burning in one of its quarters – the symbol of the War Owl, ancient totem of Clan Copper. The owl hovered closer to him, its wings a slow blur upon the air. He could smell verdigris strongly. The creature extended one foot and placed its fierce claws upon Max's chest. He felt a constriction within him, but then came a flooding sensation of soothing coolness. He had not been aware of the faint persistent pain within him until it was removed. When had he learned to live with it? Looking up at the War Owl, he said, 'Revive my friend. Gaze upon him. Fly!'

The owl reacted at once. It flew to one of the statues and landed upon its shoulder, gazing at Menni with its glowing amber eyes. Max's skin prickled. He felt an unseen force radiating out from the owl's unblinking stare. It was clear the creature was trying to interpret his will, but at first nothing happened. Max began to suspect that Jack and Jenny had lied to him about the artefact's properties. But, just as this doubt was beginning to take proper shape, he saw Menni blink.

Max felt a surge of relief and laughed aloud. Once Menni was beside him again, no danger would be too great, no challenge too difficult, as long as they met them together.

Colour was slowly seeping back into Menni's form. Again, he blinked. His face was greyish green, but already it had mobility. He smiled in recognition at Max and opened his mouth as if to speak. But then his eyes widened in what looked like fear. He was looking beyond Max, behind him.

'Menni?' Max cried. 'What . . .?' He made to turn round. But before he could do so, a heavy blow to the head sent him crashing to the ground.

Book Two

Mysteries and Curiosities

Chapter One

Dream Journey of the Rose

At midnight the great clock in the market square enacted its gruesome play. There was no one to witness it. The third midnight since the Ruby Moon had risen.

In her bed in the eyrie, Rose Iron writhed in restless sleep. She dreamed she was a young girl again, dazzlingly elegant in a dress made of silver chain mail and dancing beneath the great tinkling chandeliers of the Moonmetal Manse. Shadowy figures waltzed around her. Max Silverskin was there, the only vivid presence. He was dressed in black, his hair like a banner of gold. He wore a mask but, beneath it, his mouth was set into a cynical smile. He bowed to her and she moved to dance with him, but could not reach him. Perspective dipped and swayed. Max swept another bow, walked away. Rose twirled helplessly, as if directed by an invisible partner. She danced in a hall of mirrors and countless images of her reflection paraded around her. Her gown glittered and flashed, blinding her. Then it seemed she was surrounded by a court of metal dragons, who danced within the mirrors. They breathed against the glass from the inside, misting it, melting it. Soon they would break through. Terrified, Rose spun round and round, seeking a way out. She was caught in a whirling kaleidoscope of metallic colours. There was a core of blackness above her, bearing down. She was pressed against the ground, still spinning, her body out of control, contorted in agony. Staring up, she saw a form began to take shape within the boiling darkness. It was as if she were peering into an endless tunnel, and something, someone was approaching her. She saw the strange female figure who had appeared to her in dreams before. The woman held a finger to her invisible lips. 'Gold has it,' she murmured.

Rose felt her spine would break. Her head was bent back towards her toes in an impossible arc. She retched and spluttered on bile. Then her head filled with a deafening clang, as of a thousand metal doors slamming shut. Darkness was absolute. She could hear her own tortured breath wheezing around her. Her arms ached. She was sitting up, her face resting against a hard surface. Her eyes were closed.

Clarity came back in an instant. Rose jerked upright, opening her eyes. For a moment she was totally disorientated. She was in the library of Clan Silver, sitting at a desk, her arms outstretched upon it. Between them lay an open book. She must still be dreaming. It was all right. The hideous sensations had gone.

Learn, she told herself. *Quickly, before this fades.*

She tried to focus on the pages before her but her vision was blurred. Images swam before her eyes. She shook her head, dragged her hands over her face. The sensations felt so real. The book was clearer now. She looked upon the image of a dragon, which was curled about a mirror. No – the dragon was part of the mirror, its frame, a carving in metal. She tried to read the text beside the picture, but it was written in a language she could not understand. Her head was aching, the pain condensed behind her eyes. She turned the page and found the next one blank. Hurriedly, she leafed backwards and on the page before the picture of the dragon saw an image of the copper owl. Before that, the pages were again blank. The dragon mirror was one of the artefacts: that must be the message here. What had the strange woman said? *Gold has it.* Rose flicked through the pages of the book, but there was nothing more to learn there.

'Wake up now,' she told herself.

She couldn't. Groaning, she put her face into her hands, ground the heels of her palms into her eyes. What was happening to her? She almost wished Jack Ash would appear, drag her from this strange state. She hated the way she had no control over it.

'Wake up!' she cried, and her voice echoed round the stacks of the library.

At once, lights were turned up further down the room. Rose turned her head and saw Madam Pergo approaching, her face set into an expression of surprise and concern.

'Rose,' she said, 'what are you doing here?'

Rose looked about herself, unsure. She glanced up at the window by the desk and saw the grey light of early morning in the sky outside. 'I . . . I don't know.'

'Have you been here all night?' Pergo put a hand on her shoulder. 'You study too hard. You must have fallen asleep at the desk.' She shook her head. 'This won't do. You'll make yourself ill.'

'Am I . . . am I really here?' Rose looked up at the woman in appeal.

Pergo frowned. 'What do you mean?'

Rose shook her head. 'A dream,' she said. 'I'm dreaming.'

Pergo hesitated, then said. 'I'll fetch you a nice hot drink, then have someone drive you home.'

Rose pressed her fingers to her lips, then said resignedly, 'I'm not dreaming, am I . . .'

Pergo sighed. 'Too many late nights.'

'I don't know how I got here,' Rose said. 'I was at home . . . The book . . .' She looked down at the desk, found it empty. Tears pricking her eyes, she began to laugh.

Pergo made a worried sound. 'You spend too much time here, reading things that upset the mind. Perhaps you should stop for a while.'

Rose nodded, still laughing. 'Perhaps I should.'

'You sit there, and I'll get you that drink,' Pergo said. She walked back up the library, occasionally glancing behind her, as if to make sure that Rose was still there.

Left alone, Rose felt numb. She put her face in her hands again. Was she going mad? She must have sleepwalked here. She could not bear to contemplate any other explanation.

Presently Pergo returned with the promised hot drink, a tall glass of aromatic coffee held in a silver cage. Rose sipped from it, scalding her lips.

Pergo sat down on a chair beside her. 'Now, Rose, what is all this about?

I'd expect some silly behaviour from the Silver girls who get in such states at their parties that they can't remember *who* they are, never mind *where* they are. This is not like you.'

Rose nodded, rubbed her eyes. 'I know. I have been studying too hard.' She smiled weakly. 'The trouble is, I want to know millennia's worth of history and knowledge in such a short time.'

Pergo reached out and patted her hand. 'You already know more than enough.'

Rose took another sip of coffee. 'You must know about the legend of the lost icons of the clans.'

Pergo studied her for a moment. 'Of course. It is hardly obscure. And, in all fairness, it's not really a legend. The artefacts genuinely were created during the Clan wars, there's no doubt of that. They were designed as ultimate objects of the metal-masters' arts, but in fact they were little more than weapons.'

'What happened to them?'

'They were supposed to have been dismantled at the time of the Reformation.'

'*Supposed* to have been. So the old stories might hold some truth, then – that the artefacts were merely hidden.'

'It's not beyond the realms of possibility. But, if they were, the Council of Guilds would have made sure they were safely stowed.'

'What of the dragon mirror? Was there such a thing?'

'Yes. It was allegedly part of the totem of Clan Iron, although there are stories to suggest there was some dispute over its ownership.'

'Can you tell me about it?'

'According to the histories, Clan Iron used the dragon mirror to great effect as a weapon during the wars. But at some point, warriors of Clan Gold stole the mirror from them. Gold had been used in its construction, so both clans felt an affinity for the artefact.'

'Gold has it,' Rose murmured. 'That makes sense.'

Pergo stared at her beadily. 'Why are you so interested in this, all of a sudden? The artefacts were dismantled because they were engines of destruction. They were part of the dark times. They should stay lost.'

Rose glanced at the librarian. She was not a stupid woman. 'You are quite right. The trouble is, if someone else thinks otherwise, then surely the Council should be prepared.'

Pergo's gaze was steady. 'There are strange things afoot in Karadur.'

Rose nodded.

'Be careful, that's my advice. You are not in your father's seat yet.'

Rose smiled wanly.

Sometimes it seemed that the library was able to hide its secrets from prying human eyes. On certain occasions, Rose couldn't find information she was looking for. That morning was such a time. After assuring Pergo she really didn't need driving home, Rose perused the locked stacks, searching for anything on the Clan icons. Theoretically, there should have been a wealth of material, but Rose could find none of it. Eventually, with some reluctance, she asked Pergo for assistance, causing the librarian to tut and sigh because she couldn't find anything either.

'I'm sure there used to be a little book that was devoted entirely to the icons,' Pergo said, shaking her head. 'But I haven't seen it for a long time. It's possible Lord Silver has it. He, of course, does not have to account to me for his reading matter.'

'Who has keys to the locked stacks?' Rose asked, intrigued.

'Only Lord Silver and myself,' Pergo replied. 'It's not that we want to keep people away from the old books, you know. The library is open to anyone of the Clans, but the reality is that few are interested.'

'Lady Steel is, though, isn't she?' Rose asked.

Pergo looked away, clearly embarrassed. 'She visits sometimes.'

'And what are her reading preferences?'

Pergo looked back to Rose. 'The situation between Lady Steel and your father is no secret,' she said hurriedly, her cheeks blooming with colour. 'You could say the lady is interested in the same material as you, and undoubtedly for the same reason. I do not want to say more.'

'I understand,' Rose said gently, thinking *But you don't, Pergo.* It was obvious the librarian believed Carinthia was applying herself to an earnest study of Karadur in order to be worthy of leading the Council one day. Rose could not help feeling this was not her only motivation. Could Carinthia Steel have stolen the book on the icons?

At midday, Rose left the library and made her way to the Foundry, where she knew her father would be working in his office. She meant to question him but did not harbour any great hopes of gaining information.

The Iron Tower, stronghold of her Clan and heart of the Forge, reared above the foundries that surrounded it. The foundries worked night and day to produce the materials that helped maintain the city. Virtually every building in Karadur was either bound or braced by iron and steel. The foundry chimneys ringed the Iron Tower, puffing out clouds of vivid cinders. Black smoke billowed around the scarlet sparks, and tendrils of it investigated every street below.

Rose made for the Great Foundry itself, which housed the vast main crucible as well as the administrative offices. Stepping through the mighty portal of the foundry was like entering an ancient vision of hell. As a child, Rose had been frightened by it while at the same time held fascinated. Within the vast chambers, fire-bronzed foundrymen shovelled fuel into the furnaces or worked the great steam-winches and presses. Around them, enormous steam-hammers pounded amid the boiling crimson rivers of molten metal, which flowed through a network of stone canals. The foundrymen jumped nimbly back and forth across these smoking channels. Sometimes their clothes might begin to singe, but they hardly seemed to notice.

A strange crew, the foundrymen, Rose thought. Some of them seemed barely human with their oversized muscles and crude facial features. They were the perfect human incarnation of the Clan that had once spawned them: Lead. Now they were a separate breed: men of few words, enigmatic and powerful. None of them raised their heads from their labours as Rose walked among them. They too had once frightened her, and even now her flesh shrank against her bones. It was like walking through a pack of tamed gibbolds, who might suddenly remember their wildness and attack.

Rose ran up the iron staircase that led to her father's office. She found him hunched over his ledgers, but his pen lay idle between his fingers. He was deep in thought. Rose went up behind his chair and put her hands upon his shoulders. He gave a start, then turned to smile at her. She bent to kiss his cheek. 'You were in another world,' she said.

He smiled. 'Too much in this one, my dear.'

Rose went to sit on the edge of his desk and folded her arms. 'Any news of the Jewel yet?'

He shook his head. 'No.'

She hesitated, then said, 'What if it's never found? The replica will eventually be recognized for a fake.'

Lord Iron rubbed his hands over his face. 'We will do as Lord Copper suggested – have it removed to a private place. We have justification enough.'

Rose shrugged. 'Fair enough, but what of the effect on the city? We still don't know about that, do we?'

Iron frowned sadly. 'Rose, Rose, don't irk me with these questions I cannot answer. Don't you think I ponder them over and over every day?'

'We need help,' Rose said.

'Help?' Lord Iron laughed caustically. 'We can only help ourselves and it seems we lack the power or wit to do so.'

She could have told him then her thoughts about Max Silverskin and the prophecy. Perhaps that was the only hope Karadur had. But looking at the sad desperation in her father's eyes, she could not speak. However, she could risk a partial honesty. 'Father, what do you know of the lost icons of the Clans?'

He peered at her in apparent astonishment for a moment. 'What did you say?'

'The lost icons. They were created during the Clan Wars. You must know about them.'

Iron's voice assumed a slightly pompous tone. 'I sincerely hope this is not the "help" you were referring to.'

Rose said nothing.

Iron shook his head. 'The icons could do nothing for us, in any case. They were weapons, nothing more.'

'How lost are they, father?'

'Rose!'

'Please, indulge me. I'd like to know about the Dragon Mirror. It used to belong to our Clan, didn't it? Madam Pergo told me it was stolen by Gold warriors during the wars.'

Lord Iron sighed. 'I know what you're thinking. The old icons might be a kind of replacement for the Jewel, something for people to honour, to find strength in. The idea is not without merit, but we have no parts of the icons in our strongholds and Gold has never actually admitted they took the mirror. As for the other artefacts . . .' He shrugged. 'They are lost, Rose. Nobody really knows what happened to them.'

'But the mirror,' Rose said. 'At least we know the whereabouts of that.'

'Perhaps, but Gold would never surrender it. At the time of the theft, they probably thought they were doing the right thing, but now Marcus and Melodia would consider it a great dishonour to own up to it. This is a subject never mentioned. It would only open up old wounds, and the Council is in dispute enough as it is. Carinthia would no doubt take great delight in using the opportunity against us.'

'Perhaps we should steal it back ourselves.'

'Don't be ridiculous. We might as well hand over the Council to Carinthia now and save ourselves the trouble.'

'I know. I was joking. Still, it would be intriguing to discover for sure whether Gold has the mirror or not, and where they hide it.'

'If they have, it will be in their vaults. Rumours surfaced in the early years after the wars. The stories may be apocryphal, of course.'

'Stories?' Rose was surprised her father was being so open about what she would normally expect to be a fairly uncomfortable subject. She didn't want to push him too hard, in case he backtracked and assumed his habitual scorn of anything to do with pre-Reformation topics.

Lord Iron drew a picture in the air to illustrate his words. 'The story goes that the mirror is kept in the Gold vaults, within a golden cage, chased with silver and platinum, roofed and floored with brass, decorated fancifully, in the elaborate style of Clan Gold. It is said the artefact is guarded by a strange beast that was created by Gold alchemists in their hidden workshops.'

'What kind of beast?'

'It's called the nomonon, a dragonlike creature.' Lord Iron laughed. 'Such is the story.'

Rose frowned. 'But surely not entirely unlikely. Such things *were* created during the wars, weren't they?'

Lord Iron nodded grimly. 'Unfortunately.' He studied his daughter for a moment. 'Rose, don't make the mistake of looking into the past for answers to current problems. We have learned all there is possible to learn from our history. The major lesson being: avoid repetition.'

Rose smiled. 'You needn't worry. I have no desire to repeat past mistakes.'

'I trust you,' Lord Iron said, and for a moment held her eyes.

Rose's heart contracted within her chest. So much lay unsaid between them.

Lord Iron shuffled some papers before him. 'Anyway, I hope you will come to dinner tonight, Rose.'

'Of course, if you wish it.'

'With all my heart. Fabiana Copper has elected to invite herself to dine at the Tower.'

'Fabiana?' Rose grimaced. 'Why? She's never done so before.'

'She claims that you are the reason. Apparently you don't mix with other people enough. I think Fabiana fears you will mature into a bore.'

Rose laughed. 'Ah, as much was mentioned on the night of the Carnival.'

'It really would do you no harm to make a friend of Clan Copper. I know you feel the same way as I do about intimate clan soirées, but there is a difference between polite approachability and intimacy.'

'Father, really!' Rose said. 'Would you describe yourself as approachable?'

'I can't be that much of a fearsome creature if Fabiana feels she can invite herself into my home.'

'She wants something,' Rose said.

'Probably, but it might be of use to you in the future.'

Rose sighed. 'I'll come. I'm sure I can grimace and grin my way through the evening.' She went to kiss her father's cheek. 'For your sake, at least,

I'll be there. I couldn't leave you to the predations of the delightful Lady Copper. Perhaps she's looking for a husband.'

'Your humour is poor,' said Lord Iron.

After Rose had left, Lord Iron resumed his blind contemplation of the objects on his desk. So many thoughts churned through his mind. The Council was supposed to lead Karadur, to maintain the status quo, but now it seemed as if control was slipping away. As Head of the Council, he should be clear in his mind about what was happening and devise solutions to the problems. But the problems seemed to concern an intrinsic corruption of the Karadurian heart. The people themselves were becoming resentful and petulant, as if ignorance was a disease sweeping through the streets. Whatever he'd said to Rose, he suspected that the true reason Fabiana Copper was coming to dinner was because she was anxious about the situation and sought reassurance. What could he say to her? Even Rose was beginning to walk down some dark avenues in search of answers.

For a moment, Iron was paralysed by a spasm of black fear. What if the past had never really gone away and, deep in their being, the people were as superstitious, barbaric and ignorant as they'd been during the Clan Wars? What if the Reformation had been nothing more than a fragile veneer over a writhing chaos of unenlightened thoughts and actions? The reason the Lords had originally outlawed magic was not, as was popularly supposed, because they disbelieved in it. The secret was that they had believed wholeheartedly in the unseen. They had simply examined the evidence before them and come to the conclusion that humanity was too primitive to work with the subtle forces of the multiverse.

Like schoolchildren, the people needed discipline and education. Until they had matured, they had to live their lives by what was, not by what might be. The unknown, in whatever form, was subject to fallible human interpretation. Lord Iron was not arrogant enough to suppose he was any more enlightened than the next man, but he had been given the responsibility of guardianship. He had to fulfil that duty to his best ability.

Perhaps a day would come when the people of Karadur could step forth from the academy of life and gaze with awe and expectation upon the mysteries beyond. But that day was far away. What was happening now was truancy of the worst kind.

Chapter Two

Thief after Thief

Max opened his eyes to find Jenny Ash gazing down at him in concern, her hands hot and dry upon his face. 'Can I not leave you for a moment?' she said.

Max tried to haul himself upright but was assailed by nauseous dizziness. He flopped back into the grass, blinded by pain.

'Lie still.' Jack's voice.

'Heal him, Jack,' Jenny said. 'Heal him quickly. Oh, why weren't you here when we first got back? This is your fault!'

'Quiet, sister,' Jack hissed. 'Let me concentrate.'

Half swooning, Max could feel an unnatural heat moving over his body, which he presumed emanated from the hands of Jack Ash. The burning sensation intensified so much that for some moments Max lost consciousness. When he came to once more he felt drugged, but his body was free of pain. Jenny and Jack were kneeling on either side of him. Jack's face was drawn, his colour strangely grey, as if it had taken a great deal of effort and energy to perform the healing. Max sat up with a start. The first thing he saw was Menni Vane, his body still frozen into place. Had he imagined Menni beginning to wake? Before, his old friend's expression had been that of shock, but now his immobile face registered warning and fear. He must have seen the person or persons who had attacked Max from behind. 'The Owl,' Max cried. 'Where is it?'

Jenny shook her head. 'There is no owl. The parts are gone. Whoever felled you took them.'

'It was whole,' Max said. 'Real, a living thing. I saw it happen. How could someone steal that?'

Jack and Jenny exchanged a glance.

'It's true,' Max said. 'Menni was beginning to wake. He blinked at me, smiled. The Owl obeyed my will. It touched me with its claws and soothed my pain.'

'We are beset by enemies,' Jenny said. 'I was foolish to leave you.'

'Your brother left the ring here,' Max said. 'All in all you seem encompassed by foolishness.'

Jack said nothing, his expression inscrutable.

'But who would come to this place?' Jenny said. 'The Porporrum fear it, and our own people would be alert to any renegade Ashen on the approach route. Who could creep here past our guards?'

'An upworlder?' Jack said

Jenny shuddered visibly.

An image of Rose Iron flashed across Max's mind. Would she do such a thing? She'd already confessed she was searching for the artefacts herself, yet at the same time she'd professed to be an ally of the Ashen. Perhaps Jenny and Jack had taken it themselves to deprive Max of the Owl's healing properties. They wanted him malleable, without Menni as support.

'Someone knew what I was doing,' Max said. 'They let me do the hard work, then took the fruit of it.' He glanced at Jenny critically. 'It's too convenient you weren't here. I'm not sure I believe your story of Jack being asleep. You've already said you communicate by mind. You could have left me here deliberately, or else sneaked up on me yourself so I wouldn't realize who attacked me.'

'Max, your words are hurtful,' Jenny said. 'How could you suspect such a thing? Haven't we helped and healed you?'

'From my perspective, it appears I've helped you and incurred injury along the way.' He stood up shakily, experiencing a slight twinge of guilt at the sight of Jack Ash looking so diminutive and drained upon the grass. 'Anyway, whoever stole the Owl, it still amounts to the same thing. Everything I've done has been for nothing. Menni is still a statue, Jenny has no protection from the plague, and I have no means to keep pain at bay. What do you suggest we do now?'

Jack leaned on his sister's shoulder to rise to his feet. 'We always knew forces would work against us,' he said. 'We must not give up.'

'That is not an answer,' Max said.

'We will do all that we can, using our spies in Karadur to discover the thief,' Jack said.

'But time is running out,' Jenny reminded him. 'The Fox needs help.'

Jack regarded his sister without expression, but Max felt sure they were communicating without words. 'No,' Jack said at last. 'We cannot risk that. We are still not sure of where alliances lie.'

Jenny turned to Max. 'There are people in Karadur . . .' she began.

'No!' Jack said.

Max shook his head. 'You need say nothing more.' He glanced at Jenny meaningfully. 'I will return to Karadur. May I keep the spellstone with me?'

She nodded. 'Of course. I gave it to you. Do you understand what you must do?' She didn't look sure.

'Lady Rose Iron, I presume,' he answered.

Jenny's shoulders slumped a little, but whether in relief or disappointment he could not tell. 'You know of her alliance with us,' she said.

'Yes.'

'Iron is Silverskin's sworn enemy,' Jack said. 'We should not place our trust so hastily.'

'You've trusted her enough in the past,' Jenny snapped. She addressed Max once more. 'Go to her. She will help you, I know. You must recover the Owl. You know I did not lie to you. It will assuage your pain and reawaken your friend as I promised.'

'I saw Menni blink,' Max said. 'I felt the claw's soothing properties. I know you did not lie.'

Jenny's face relaxed into a smile. 'I will walk with you to the edge of Shriltasi.'

As they strolled beneath the spreading canopy of the forest, Max thought about how hidden Ashen must have observed his and Menni's approach from the very first moment they set foot in Shriltasi. They had been carefully manipulated, guided. Now this strange and alarming creature walked lightly at his side, her forest-coloured hand slipped through his elbow. Who to trust? What to trust? Max felt as if he was swimming in the spuming tides of Watersmeet, deafened by the crash of cascades, blinded by foam. 'Will Jack be all right?' he asked. 'He looked bled half to death back there.'

Jenny nodded. 'He will rest and recover. Jack is not like any of us. The stone plague cannot take him. He is the king of this land, exiled or not. His life-energy is Shriltasi and vice versa.'

'And you are its queen?'

'No. I am its princess, perhaps. Jack did have a queen. Her name was Mag. The renegades took her when we fled Ash Haven, our ancestral domain. She fell behind us. We believed they'd keep her for bargaining purposes, but we were wrong. They were filled with hate for our dynasty. Mag died upon a bed of thorns.'

Max frowned. 'It cannot be a pleasant memory to live with.'

'It isn't,' Jenny said quietly. 'A part of Jack died when she did. We felt it happen, hiding in caves deep in the forest. I heard Jack cry out in his sleep, and I woke him. His body was running with blood. Our life-blood is green. He looked streaked with moss and lichen. His eyes were bleeding. He could see every moment of her death, and his body writhed in torment for every thorn that entered her flesh. I held onto him tightly so I could feel it too. I couldn't let him live it alone.'

Max could think of nothing appropriate to say to that. After a while he said, 'And was there ever a prince for you?'

Jenny smiled, but sadly. 'Many died,' she said. 'Many of us.'

'I'm sorry,' Max said, feeling acutely the inadequacy of those words.

Jenny squeezed his elbow. 'It was a long time ago,' she said. 'There is nothing to be gained from living in the past.'

Before going to the dining hall of the Iron Tower, Rose went to her own rooms in the manse. They felt dusty and abandoned, even though Rose visited them regularly enough to keep them clean. As a young teenager, she had made it clear she wanted no servants tidying or poking about her room while she wasn't there, so consequently her absences from her chambers now were barely noticed. In these rooms, she'd fantasized about Max Silverskin. She'd wallowed in the isolation only a young adult can feel, sure that she alone knew the answers to everything. A feeling of melancholy pervaded the air.

Rose felt quite affronted that Fabiana Copper seemed insistent on deepening their friendship. It seemed intrusive and a little patronizing. Part of her was suspicious. Why should Fabiana take an interest in her now? Had she made such an impression on the night of the ball?

Idly, Rose looked through the gowns hanging in the wardrobe. Most of them were too small for her now. She should perhaps get rid of them, offer the best to some of her younger Iron relatives. But Rose didn't like discarding the past. Her history resided in the memories conjured by each garment. Through her involvement with Max and the Ashen, her forays into forbidden territory, she was trying to reclaim the past of Karadur. Her gowns seemed like a symbol of that. Rose walked right into the wardrobe and enveloped herself in the hanging fabric. Satin, brocade, silk and taffeta rustled around her. Jewels winked in the dim light and the ghosts of old perfumes blended with the must of neglect. It was a moment of pure joy and pure sadness.

Fabiana had already arrived when Rose presented herself downstairs. The Copper matriarch was with Prometheus in the library, arranged gracefully in a chair next to the hearth, where a hungry fire chewed logs of fragrant pine. The term 'matriarch', which conjured images of imposing formidable females, seemed a misnomer for someone of Fabiana's elegance and charm. Rose noticed that her father did not seem in the slightest discomfited by his guest's presence. In fact, when Rose walked between the great double doors, he was laughing. Rose dismissed a smirk from her face. Perhaps her earlier joke about husbands had not been as far off the mark as she'd imagined. Despite his mature years, her father was still a handsome man.

Lady Copper made a great display of appearing delighted to see Rose, who in turn bent with as little stiffness as she could muster for the traditional kiss of greeting. 'You look lovely,' said Fabiana. 'A jewel hidden in the Forge.'

Rose glanced at her father, whose smiled faded a little. He turned his eyes towards the fire.

'Thank you,' Rose said. 'It's a surprise to see you here, Fabiana, but a pleasure too.' She sat down on a sofa next to their guest's chair.

'Please, call me Fay,' said Lady Copper. '"Fabiana" is such a mouthful.' She turned to Lord Iron. 'You don't entertain enough, Prometheus.' She raised her hands. 'The Tower needs to ring with merriment, to drive shadows from the corners.' She laughed, a free, ringing sound.

Lord Iron cleared his throat. 'Well, since Laferrine died, we've not had many visitors to our chambers. At first, it was because we were in mourning, but I suppose it has become a habit.'

'Laferrine was a great hostess,' Fabiana said. She reached out and patted Rose's hands, which were clasped in her lap. 'But you will make a great hostess too, my dear.'

Rose blanched at the thought, then considered. 'I suppose I ought to think about becoming one. I'm aware that one day, hopefully far in the future, the world will come banging upon my door, demanding I take part in it.'

'Exactly. The Head of the Council should not hide away behind closed doors.'

'Have you made a mission of us, Fabiana?' Lord Iron enquired. Clearly, the prospect did not distress him too much.

Fabiana's light, airy laugh rang out again through the room. Rose could easily imagine it dispelling shadows. 'Oh dear, am I so transparent? I must admit that when I saw you both – especially Rose – at my little party the other night, it struck me that it is a great shame the Irons are so reclusive. It is not just your fault.' Her fine brow puckered into a becoming frown. 'The truth is that people recognized the strength of your grief when Laferrine died, and respected it. They kept their distance and a gulf opened up. Like you said, it has become a habit. But, Prometheus,' and here she wagged a finger at the Iron lord, 'it is time Rose took her place in society.'

'I am not a social animal, particularly,' Rose said.

'I know,' Fabiana agreed. 'I understand you have a serious mind. But surely you can see the sense of achieving balance? After all, isn't that what the Council of the Metal is all about?'

'Well . . .'

Before Rose could formulate a full reply, her father's gaunt steward, Sword, presented himself at the door to announce that dinner was ready to be served.

Fabiana rose to her feet. 'Good, I am famished.' She looked at Lord Iron meaningfully. He dutifully took her arm to lead her to the meal.

For the next couple of hours, the sombre dining room rang with Fabiana's laughter, which seemed to conjure more gleams than usual in the crystal glasses and the pendants of the chandelier. It was not necessary for Rose to speak a lot because Lady Copper filled any silence more than adequately. Her conversation was quick and witty. Rose began to wonder whether she'd misjudged the woman. She was aware she was adept at making condemning judgements. *This night is as much a part of your life as any other*, a quiet inner voice informed her. *As matriarch of Clan Iron, you should aspire to some of what Fabiana embodies. Such behaviour encourages loyalty and trust.* No one among the Metal disliked Fabiana or felt uneasy in her company. And she was far from empty-headed. Was it possible to achieve that balance? Rose found herself wishing she could be as open as this woman, who seemed to love life and experience every moment to the full. *I am dour*, thought Rose and sipped moodily from her wine.

Fabiana seemed to intuit her thoughts. 'Rose, you are scowling,' she said. 'Is it because you can't get a word in? You should tell me to be quiet. Rufus is always telling me I never give other people room to speak.' She smiled at Lord Iron. 'I know you might find this hard to credit, as I'm never a strident voice at Council meetings.'

'Stridency is hardly a worthy quality,' said Lord Iron. 'When you do speak, you are generally the voice of quiet reason.'

Fabiana smiled delightedly. 'I am a woman of many faces, but if you saw more of me, you'd realize I'm a chatterbox most of the time.'

'Not at all,' Rose said. 'I was enjoying listening to you.'

'But I would like to hear some of *your* thoughts,' said Fabiana.

'On what?'

'Well, your opinions concerning what is happening in Karadur would be interesting.'

Rose sensed her father's body stiffen and guessed he had been waiting for this moment. She took a breath. 'Well, I'm sure my thoughts are no different to anyone else's. We are facing a crisis and need to work together to overcome it.'

'You have your father's knack for temporization,' said Lady Copper. She made an airy gesture with one hand. 'Speak frankly, Rose. Our conversation will not go beyond these walls.'

Rose noticed Fabiana did not look at Lord Iron as she spoke. Iron's expression had become bleak. Rose glanced into his eyes, sought to reassure him. She must answer to please him now. She had no intention of sharing her secrets. 'I'm sure the Council are doing all that they can. Your thoughts will no doubt be more interesting than mine, since you are better informed.'

'Fabiana is a liberal,' said Lord Iron. 'She thinks we should understand the criminal element rather than punish them.'

'You simplify my words,' said Fabiana. 'Or perhaps I am economical with them during Council meetings. Carinthia Steel has no regard for sensitivities, because that is the nature of her Metal. I am more malleable and aware of others' feelings. Our responsibilities can be a burden sometimes, Prometheus. You know to what I refer.'

'Do you seek to make this a private unofficial meeting of the Council?' asked Lord Iron in a cold voice.

Fabiana shrugged, her shoulders rising gently in a smooth movement. 'I do not view it as such. Consider it a discussion between friends.'

'If you have come to make a suggestion, please do so,' said Lord Iron.

Fabiana frowned wistfully. 'Don't be angry with me. I know it is merely a defence mechanism on your part, but it still smarts.'

Rose could not suppress a laugh. 'What are you talking about, Fay? You told me to speak plainly. I think you should do so yourself.'

'Very well. I think a time has come for us to reassess decisions made in the past. We are losing control because we have lost contact with the people. Why are they turning to myth and magic for comfort? Because something is lacking in their lives. We cannot provide it with laws and discipline. As we continue to apply old traditions, with ever greater severity, we contrive only to increase resentment and mistrust. Our ancestors bound a wound, Prometheus. But it has not healed. It suppurates beneath its dressing. "Beneath" being the most important word.'

'A colourful analogy,' said Lord Iron, his face pinched in distaste. He shook his head, sighing deeply. 'Fabiana, I will be honest with you. I am not stupid and have for many days considered the subject to which you allude. In my mind, I have dared to look beneath. But I found no answers there.'

'What subject is this?' Rose asked lightly. Her heart was beating fast now. Could Fabiana be referring to the burden of knowledge, that of Shriltasi and *barishi*? Her instincts advised her this was so. Some of the Lords must still be aware of the hidden realm. She was shocked the woman dared to speak of it to Lord Iron, even in the vague terms Fabian had used, but Rose wanted to hear more – especially what her father might confess or reveal.

Fabiana clearly realized it would overstep propriety to answer Rose's question. She stared at Lord Iron, who eventually spoke to his daughter. 'You came to me earlier to discuss a subject, which I dismissed. It seems evident that Fabiana, to some degree, shares your opinions.'

Fabiana drew in her breath and turned to Rose. 'Do you, my dear? What exactly did you say?'

Rose now felt extremely uncomfortable, unsure of how much she should reveal. 'It was just a rather wild idea. I've been reading a lot recently, and came across a brief reference to some lost ancient artefacts. I just thought that if they were recovered, and perhaps instated in a museum or something, the people would realize the Lords are not as hidebound as they appear. It's nothing, really. My father explained why it wouldn't work.'

Fabiana's eyes were enormous in her delicately boned face. 'There is really so much more to you than appearances suggest,' she breathed. 'But I am delighted by your mystery.'

Rose was embarrassed. 'I don't deserve the flattery. The idea was impractical.'

'I disagree,' said Fabiana. 'There are some aspects of the past we need to reassimilate.'

'No, there aren't,' said Lord Iron. 'We risk opening a door through which all manner of monsters might pour.'

'Literally?' said Fabiana sweetly.

'People can be monsters,' said Lord Iron. 'I don't believe there exists anything worse than that.'

'How widespread throughout the Metal are your opinions, Fay?' Rose asked.

Fabiana glanced at her empty plate. 'Many people are thinking about our problems deeply. They are forced to examine disconcerting subjects. But whether their thoughts are the same as mine, I do not know. People speak in allusions, afraid of revealing their true opinions.'

'What of Carinthia Steel?' Lord Iron snapped. 'Have you discussed this with her?'

'No. I have not spoken to anyone else about this, not even Rufus. I wanted to come to you first. Obviously, Carinthia has her own ambitions. Her Clan do not share our . . . responsibility. Therefore I have concluded she knows nothing of it. Her desires are for temporal power.'

'I wouldn't be so sure of that,' Rose said, regretting the words the moment she'd spoken.

'What do you mean?' Fabiana asked.

'Just that she has been visiting the library of Clan Silver quite regularly, in order to examine the historical texts kept under lock and key.'

'Ah,' murmured Fabiana, her expression becoming thoughtful. 'Perhaps through instinct Steel seeks evidence and information her female intuition already senses.'

Lord Iron uttered an exasperated groan. 'You and she should pack your bags and move in with the Silverskins,' he said. 'Really, Fabiana! Listen to yourself. Such statements belong to the people of the markets and the free zones.'

'Indeed they do,' said Fabiana. 'Perhaps we can learn from them.'

'In some ways, I wish you were right,' said Lord Iron. 'But I know you are not. We are in danger of being seduced by these ridiculous ideas that infect the city like a disease. Can't you see this for yourself? You are an intelligent person.'

'I am intelligent,' agreed Fabiana smoothly. 'neither am I afraid to face unsettling issues.' She smiled. 'Oh, Prometheus, I am not gullible nor deluded. Don't fluff up your feathers in alarm at my words. I must speak strongly and say that I think you should be prepared to discuss this subject openly, at least between ourselves. The answer might well not lie there, but until we have examined it thoroughly, how can we tell?'

'You're speaking on more than one level,' said Rose. 'Will you share this information with me? I'm getting only half the sense of it.'

'Not now, Rose,' said Lord Iron. 'There will come a time when you must know, but I will preserve your innocence for as long as possible.'

'Then let us hope you do not die unexpectedly,' said Fabiana.

'If that should occur, then I entrust you with my daughter's education,' said Lord Iron.

'What conspirators you are!' said Rose. 'You realize you have pricked my curiosity beyond endurance?'

'Curiosity can be dangerous,' said Lord Iron. 'I wish to finish this conversation. Shall we move back to the library for liqueurs?'

As they left the dining room, Fabiana linked her arm through one of Rose's and held her back while Lord Iron strode ahead. 'You father exhibits the natural inhibited tendencies of a man,' she murmured. 'I feel you are more open to certain ideas than he is. Perhaps we should speak in private about them.'

Rose felt her hackles rise. Why? Did she want to keep her secrets to herself to maintain their special nature? 'I would be interested to hear more of your thoughts,' she said carefully.

'Good. Come to visit me soon. Very soon.' Fabiana squeezed Rose's arm, then led her forward. 'Your father is afraid. You should be aware of the nature of his fear. I recognized something in you the other night, my dear. The light of the future. I have great faith in you.'

'I hope that faith is not misplaced,' said Rose. She wondered what Fabiana would think if she learned the truth about her. Was it possible she might find an ally among the Clans? Despite this, Rose knew she would not visit Verdigris House before Max's fate was revealed. After that, many things might change and it could be the time for honesty. But, for now, she sensed she must walk her path only with the Ashen and Max himself, until the matter of the silverheart was resolved.

★   ★   ★

Later, Rose climbed the iron staircase to her retreat with heavy steps. The amber late-evening light seemed to swirl around her in a depressing cloud. Fabiana's overtures, though intriguing at the time, now seemed somehow threatening. Rose resolved she would not mention the conversation she'd had tonight with Lady Copper to Max or the Ashen. She could, after all, be misinterpreting Fabiana's words, reading a desired meaning into them that was not there in reality. Rose knew the way she'd perceived the evening's events had been coloured entirely by her awareness of Shriltasi and *barishi*. She should guard against assuming her father, or Lady Copper, knew as much as she did. Gripped by uncertainty, Rose couldn't help wondering why she believed she had to power to make change. Whatever she – and clearly anyone else – said to her father, the words would be like drops of moisture running down metal. They couldn't penetrate. Iron would rust, of course, but slowly. Ridiculous thoughts! She needed better analogies than that to aid her.

Shaking her head, Rose moved to unlock her door and found it already open. A shiver coursed through her flesh. Stealthily, she entered the retreat, which lay in darkness. A figure stood silhouetted against the windows at the far end of the room. Her first reaction was fear, for she was unarmed, but it was brief. Affecting nonchalance, she took off her velvet cloak. 'I was not expecting visitors,' she said, with barely a tremor in her voice.

Max Silverskin stepped forward and bowed with formal reverence. 'I sought to surprise you.'

'"Shock" might be a better word,' Rose said. She turned away from him to light the gas lamps around the room. 'Seeing as you're here, I can only presume you've decided to trust me,' she said.

'I'm sure you knew I'd come here again.'

'Indeed not. I wouldn't be so presumptuous. Did you find your artefact?'

He shrugged. 'In a manner. Things went slightly wrong, however, which is why I'm here now. Was your offer of assistance genuine?'

'No, a complete lie. I intend to arrest you.' She couldn't help smiling at his shocked expression. 'Max, please! Of course my offer was genuine. I appreciate you were brave to come here.'

'Hardly brave. I know all the Clan strongholds quite intimately and can negotiate them with the ease of a shadow.'

'Except when you run into Captain Coffin,' Rose said.

Max ignored this comment. 'I have to ask you something. Do you have in your possession the War Owl of Clan Copper?'

Rose frowned. 'No, what makes you think I have?'

'The artefact was recovered in Shriltasi, but I was – shall we say – relieved of it there.'

'You believe I can steal from you, the self-styled master thief? You flatter me.'

'Will you answer me?'

'I do not have it,' she said. 'Perhaps you should tell me what happened. Would you care for wine to lubricate the story?'

Max nodded and sat down. While Rose busied herself with pouring the wine, he began the story of what had happened in Shriltasi. She offered him a metal cup and sat down opposite him, watching his long mobile fingers curled around the drinking vessel. He did not drink until he'd finished speaking. Then he drained the entire cup.

'You think the Ashen might have taken it?' Rose said.

Max shrugged. 'I don't know. I feel I have to trust them until it's proved misguided. Same for you.' He held out his wine cup, which Rose refilled.

'Such a silver tongue you have, never mind a heart,' she muttered.

'I wouldn't have survived long in this world if I'd made a habit of trusting everyone I met. Neither would you, I suspect.'

She detected an attempt at flattery. 'That is true. But I'd like you to believe I'm well disposed towards you. You've nothing to fear from me that you would not fear from any friend.'

He raised an eyebrow. 'You play with words.'

'It's the truth – no more and no less. I believe in your curse and your destiny, but that it is your responsibility alone to ensure they do not engulf you. As the Heir-in-Waiting, I want you on my side. Together we can restore the Clan totems to their original eminence.'

Max stared at her stonily. 'I find myself wary of aiding your ascent to power. You are still of the Iron.'

Rose returned his stare without flinching. 'I am not hungry for power. I am merely aware of my duty. I was born to a privileged position and therefore have the means to make a difference. I want justice for all.' She leaned forward earnestly. 'I believe that you and I are among the few whose sight is unclouded, who are prepared to accept both truths – harsh realities of mundane existence as well as the reality of *barishi*, the unseen, the unknown. I feel we have a duty to unite the two and thereby ensure the security of our world and the endurance of her noblest ideals.'

Silverskin seemed almost buffeted by her passionate words. His smile was without its usual mockery. 'We will make an unlikely partnership.'

'You are of Clan blood, Max. Is it really so unlikely? You chose your path, but you cannot deny your roots.'

'Why not? Haven't they denied me?'

'For your parents, then. Do it for them.'

Max averted his eyes and Rose guessed she had probed a weak spot. 'I am told my differences are the legacy of my mother's blood, yet even the Silverskins turned their backs to me. If they knew of what lay in store for me, why didn't they advise and support me?'

'Fear,' said Rose. 'The Silverskins have lost their courage over the years. It has been beaten from them. I doubt they even believe *barishi* still resides in them.'

Max shook his head. 'No, you shouldn't argue their cause. They despised my father and, to them, I was his get, responsible for my mother's demise.'

'I'm sure it's not that simple,' Rose said.

Max nodded glumly, then visibly cast off his melancholy thoughts. 'I need a sword,' he said. 'Mine was lost in the graffy run. Can you can find me one in this iron-master's eyrie?'

Rose nodded. 'I have an excellent selection, gifts from Clan Steel. They are of the rarest type, blades of the finest pedigree. You may take your pick of those I do not use. I already have my favourites.'

Max smiled wryly. 'How fitting to use one of the Clan's special editions against them.'

Rose took him into a chamber off her bedroom, where a strongly locked cupboard on the wall housed her collection. Once she opened the double doors, the weapons gleamed in the lamplight. Max whistled through his teeth when he saw them. 'This is a master's hoard! How can I possibly make a choice?'

'Take the one that speaks to you,' Rose said. 'Don't you have a feeling for a good blade?' She waited, holding her breath, to see which sword would draw Max's attention.

Max examined them all for a few moments, tapping his chin with the fingers of one hand, and then carefully pulled a weapon from its setting. It had a hilt fashioned into the shape of a glove. 'This is unusual.'

Rose released her breath. 'Indeed. And very old. You like it?'

Max slipped his hand into the metal glove. 'Strange, it feels almost familiar.' He made a few passes in the air with the blade.

'It's yours,' Rose said. 'I'm not surprised you chose it.'

'Why?'

'It was fashioned for a great-great-uncle of yours – on your mother's side – who supplied the design. Unfortunately, he died before he could collect it. You see, it is a Silverskin blade.'

'You wanted me to choose this one, didn't you.'

'I hoped you would.'

He shook his head. 'I think you are a romantic, my lady.'

'A smattering of romanticism helps dispel dourness, I feel.'

'So what romantic suggestions do you have for recovering the War Owl? I need it for several reasons, but mainly to help Menni Vane.'

'I appreciate that the recovery of the artefact is important, but I have unearthed equally vital information about another icon.'

'Meaning?'

'I have not been idle. Come to the Camera Obscura with me. There are things I wish to show you. Would you mind affecting a disguise?'

'Not at all. It is my natural habit.'

Rose provided a costume of a gentleman of Clan Iron, such as would have been worn to the Copper masque she had attended two nights before. Rarely an evening passed that one of the Clans did not hold a party of some kind. While Max dressed in her bathroom, Rose changed her own gown for the clothes of a man. Once they were both dressed, she produced elaborate half-masks of jewels and feathers, as well as enveloping dark cloaks. With her own hands she bound up Max's pale hair and covered it with a skull cap decorated with a forest of carefully wrought iron spikes.

'Now we will look like a couple of gallants returning from a clan ball,' she said. 'We shouldn't excite too much attention. Also, the hour is late, so there will be few people about.'

Rose led Max out of the eyrie and made her way to one of the entrances to her father's private thoroughfare to the Camera. As she'd predicted, there were few people around, although the foundries were clearly still fully operational. Rose possessed a set of keys to Lord Iron's sanctuary and retreat. The only guards were a couple of Battle Boys that Rose knew how to pass. Once in the Camera, she locked the doors behind them. If necessary, they could make an escape through one of the passages concealed behind the walls but she had little fear anyone would come there. Her father had gone to bed directly after dinner.

'This is an amazing sight,' Max said in a low voice, walking around the great image on the floor. 'But why have you brought me here?'

'Patience,' Rose said. 'Just watch.' She manipulated the controls expertly to show him the four quarters and the main buildings in each, eventually focusing the image on New Mint Yard, the stronghold of Clan Gold. 'Remember I said I've found something out about another icon?'

Max nodded, frowning.

'It's called the Dragon Mirror. Have you heard of it?'

Max shook his head. 'I don't think so.'

'It was an artefact constructed by my Clan before the Reformation, and was used as a weapon during the wars. At some point, warriors of the Clan Gold stole it. Since then, no one has admitted its existence, so there has been no quarrel over it. It seems it formed part of one of the icons – in much the same way as the ring you acquired was part of the War Owl. I believe we must get hold of this artefact without delay.'

Max stared at her inscrutably for a moment. 'You've discovered its hiding place?'

She inclined her head slowly. 'I believe so. I think it resides in the Gold vaults.'

'And does this mirror possess *barishic* qualities?'

Again, Rose nodded, but with more vehemence this time. 'I am certain of it.' She could tell him about her strange experiences now but shrank from doing so. It would sound too incredible, as if she was making it up, or else just trying to impress. 'I doubt Marcus and Melodia are aware of its potential. It will just be a curio to them, with embarrassing associations. My father made clear they would deny they had it in their possession now. So it seems to me that if we steal it they are hardly likely to make a fuss.'

'That is a major assumption. Also, the Golds will undoubtedly have taken many precautions to safeguard their property. We could do with more information. It will no doubt be well protected by a host of fanciful traps and tricks. This is Clan Gold we're talking about, after all. I don't suppose you've discovered any details of its protection?'

'Some.' Rose described all that her father had told her about the mirror and its legendary guardian, the nomonon. 'So now you know. Do you think you can do it?'

Max examined the image of New Mint Yard. 'Maybe. How far would you be able to get into Clan Gold without arousing suspicion?'

Rose indicated her costume. 'Like this – not very far. But I daren't risk going there openly.'

Max cupped his jaw with one hand, his expression becoming thoughtful. 'We'll need to spring the traps ahead of us, which will no doubt be connected to alarms of some kind. If we succeed, we'll have the problem of getting the mirror out of the place. How big is it?'

'I don't know. I've seen an illustration of it, but there was no indication of its size.'

'And what of this nomonon? Can you tell me anything that might help us vanquish it?'

Rose shrugged. 'I haven't been able to research it. All I've learned is that the nomonon was developed when biometallic experiments were still conducted in Metal workshops. Perhaps the beast is energized by *barishi*. Obviously, it's illegal to attempt that sort of alchemical horror nowadays.'

'I would say it's even illegal to own one – if it exists,' Max added.

Rose nodded. 'Undoubtedly. It will be flawed, however. All those creatures were. Their production was abandoned even before the Reformation. What we need to do is discover those flaws.'

'It seems we've set ourselves a difficult project.'

Rose nodded. 'But the challenge is stimulating, isn't it?'

He grinned. 'There's nothing I can't steal from the Clans. Of this I'm sure.'

Rose smiled back, wondering whether Max was over-confident. 'What equipment will we need?'

'A few items that shouldn't be too hard to come by in the Foundry,' Max said. 'I presume you want us to attempt this theft tonight?'

'Why wait?' Rose said lightly. Already her mouth was dry, her heart beating fast.

Chapter Three

Ghosts in the Vaults

Unlike the vault of Clan Silver, which lay deep underground, the Gold treasures were stored in a high narrow tower at the centre of New Mint Yard. Rose and Max made their way to the alleys that bordered the Gold estate. Splendid gilded walls encircled the manse and its grounds, as well as the renowned workshops of the master metal-workers of the clan. Guards patrolled the sheer walls, which were devoid of entrances other than the grand main gateway. The guards were accompanied by lantern-bearers and in the wan light their breath could be seen smoking on the chill air. Clearly, security had been stepped up since Max had last paid a visit to the place. Gold were known for their love of ornament, but on these walls there were no elaborate carvings to use as handholds and footholds. The only buttresses were sheathed in nets of razored steel. Max knew that, in contrast to entering the Moonmetal Manse, finding a way in would be extremely difficult. 'We could do with making ourselves invisible,' he said dryly.

'Like Jack Ash does,' Rose remarked.

Max glanced at her. 'What do you mean?'

Rose explained Jack's technique, or what she knew of it. 'Perhaps you could use *barishi* to similar effect,' she said. 'What do you think?'

'I've never attempted such a thing,' Max replied. He considered. 'It seems that for *barishi* to create an effect, it only has to be directed towards something with intention, so I suppose it is feasible. But even if I was successful, I could't guarantee that protection would extend to you.'

'We have to try.'

'You shouldn't be placing yourself in this danger. I should proceed alone.'

Rose unhooked a rope from her belt, a thin silken cord that was immensely strong. 'I'm coming with you. My welfare is not your concern.'

Max sighed and shook his head, taking up the rope that was coiled upon his own belt. At the end of the rope was a grappling hook. 'If you become an impediment, I might have to abandon you.'

'And I you. Use *barishi*, Max.'

Max closed his eyes, and for some moments a host of strange symbols pulsed before his mind's eye. It was almost as if the moment he thought of *barishi* it awoke within him. His fingers were tingling, and also the mark over his heart. Should he use any of the symbols that Jenny had already taught him? They didn't seem appropriate. Yet Jenny had told him how strongly *barishi* flowed within him.

Imagine that streaming current now, a golden light flowing through the veins and arteries of your body . . .

He had to believe it. He had to will himself to be invisible to the guards and he had to attempt to extend that influence over Rose. His whole body tingled, his heart burning icy cold. In his mind, he was surrounded by a caul of golden light that shimmered against the sky. *Is this belief? Is this enough?*

He opened his eyes to find Rose staring at him through her mask, in curiosity and not a little fear. He knew that fear. It was the primal instinct when faced with the 'other', those things beyond normal human experience. He saw her throat move as she swallowed.

'Take my hands,' he said.

She stared at his extended fingers for some moments before hesitantly putting her own into their grasp. At once, Max felt energy flow from his hands into Rose. She flinched away, uttering a soft cry, but he tightened his grip on her. 'You wanted this,' he hissed. 'Remember that.'

'Too hot,' she gasped.

He felt the power of it, power over her. Where did it come from, this limitless energy? He could do anything with it, anything. As if in response, his heart clenched within his breast. He let go of Rose's hands with a grunt, pressing his fingers against his chest.

Rose expelled a shaky laugh, which petered out into silence. Max drew in long, painful breaths.

'I can feel it,' Rose murmured at last. Max raised his head and found her gazing at her hands, which she held before her face. She looked beyond them, into his eyes. 'Now,' she said.

The wall rose above them, shining dully beneath the light of the stars. They heard a guard cough as he made his way along the high walkway. Max threw his grappling hook into the air. They saw it arc, glint in the starlight, then fall behind the parapet with a metallic chink. Rose and Max tensed. From their position at the base of the wall, they could not see whether any of the guards had heard or seen the hook fall. No sound came. No shout of alarm, no running feet. No faces appeared looking down over the wall.

Max pulled the rope taut. He began to climb, swiftly, without looking down. He felt as if he was held in a strange etheric bubble that was beyond space and time. Why fear detection? It was not part of what was meant to happen that night.

Once at the top of the wall, he peered over it and then quickly pulled himself over the low parapet. He could see a pair of guards strolling away from him in both directions, followed by their attendants. It was clear they had heard nothing unusual. Max looked over the wall and beckoned for Rose to climb. This would be the test. He was confident that the guards would never see him, but Rose was an unknown quantity. What if she could not believe wholeheartedly in the power of *barishi*? That was beyond Max's control, but he felt sure that any weakness in her will would mean she would still be visible to all.

Rose climbed swiftly and Max helped her up the final stretch. Even in the starlight, she appeared slightly flushed. Her eyes looked enormous through the eyeholes of her mask and her breath came in steamy clouds. Max took hold of her hand and began to run up the walkway, following a pair of guards in the direction of the main gate. From previous visits, when the Gold guards had not been so plentiful or vigilant, he knew that he would soon come to a flight of steps that led down to the grounds below. There it was, ahead. Almost dragging Rose behind him, Max hurried to the top of the steps and began to descend. Halfway down he came face to face with a guard.

Both froze. The guard simply stopped climbing the steps, staring up at the walkway above, a slight frown on his face. He called, 'Bufred, are you there?'

Max realized at once that the guard really could not see him. The man was aware of some kind of obstruction, because he'd stopped moving, but there was confusion in his face, perplexity. Still holding onto Rose, Max edged round the guard. His flesh felt tight against his bones, but he dared not give in to fear. He might have to have enough belief and conviction for both Rose and himself. Once they'd passed him, the guard continued to climb.

At the bottom of the steps, Max and Rose ran as fast as they could to a grove of yews, where a circle of benches stood. Here, no doubt, members of the Gold clan would sit on warmer days. Max drew Rose into the shadow of the trees and held her against his body. He felt dizzy now, light-headed, and his limbs had begun to shake. Perhaps this approximated what Jack Ash had felt like after healing Max's wound. Max could feel Rose's heart beating wildly in her chest. She too was shuddering. In that shared moment, Max knew they were both stunned and silenced by what they'd just done. They had invested their actions with an unrestrained, almost childish, belief in magic. And it had worked. *Barishi* as an idea was acceptable, but its reality was something else. It was shocking.

Rose was the first to pull away. 'I have never experienced anything like that,' she said softly, clearly trying to make her voice sound steady and calm. 'There was a feeling . . . like fire . . .' She screwed up her face. 'Like what? I don't know. It came into me from you. I felt I could have flown down those steps, flown right through the guard like a wisp of smoke.'

'The Ashen say that *barishi* is in everything,' Max said. 'Perhaps I awoke it within you too.'

Rose looked grave. 'This is the start of everything, Max. Don't you see? Everything.' She shook her head. 'It's all different now.'

'We can't stay here,' Max said. 'We must keep moving.'

'It's still working,' Rose murmured. 'Can't you feel it? Can't you?'

'Yes,' Max replied shortly, 'but we don't know for how long. The guards will eventually come across our rope on the wall. They'll realize they've got intruders on their hands and will raise an alarm. We have to move fast.'

They hurried through the silent gardens and across a square of darkened workshops. Beyond stood the Gold manse, encircled by another wall. Rose took her rope in her hand and was about to throw the hook over the wall. But luck was with them, for several guards came out of the gate as they approached. Rose and Max were able to slip through the portal undetected before it was closed upon them.

'We are ghosts,' Rose whispered. 'We really are.'

Max said nothing but led the way to the main building. The Gilden Tower, home to the treasure vaults of Clan Gold, reared high against the sky. Its barred windows were in darkness.

Although Max had made several forays into New Mint Yard before, he had never attempted to enter the vaults, mainly because they were too closely guarded and there had been enough booty available in the family rooms in any case. But he did know the way to the tower. As a boy, he'd made sure he was familiar with the layout of all the Clan manses he'd visited with his Silver relatives. The entrance to the tower was locked and two guards were on duty outside it. Hesitantly, Max and Rose approached them. But the guards gave no sign of being able to see them. However, Max sensed that if he directed his concentration upon breaking the locks, it might have detrimental effects on their state of invisibility. They needed to create a diversion. The idea came quickly. Almost without thinking, he projected his mind and imagined that two ragamuffin street-urchins were creeping along the wall nearby. After only a moment, one of the guards cried 'Hoi!' and began to move purposefully towards the illusion. Max imagined the urchins scampering back into the main building. Both guards ran off in pursuit, calling out threats.

'What did you do?' Rose asked.

Max shook his head for silence and began to apply himself to the lock on the tower gate. This was the easy part. As he worked, Max wondered whether, in fact, he had used *barishi* unconsciously all his life. When he inserted one of his skeleton keys into the lock, he became aware of somehow making that key become the proper shape to move the mechanisms within. Surely Menni hadn't taught him *this*?

The door swung open on silent hinges and Max and Rose hurried inside the tower. Rose closed the door behind them, unlocked now. But perhaps the guards wouldn't notice.

Before them was a winding golden staircase. Occasionally they would come to landings where there were barred doors to central rooms, but Max felt instinctively they did not have to investigate them. The real treasure, the most secret and forbidden, would be at the top of the tower, farthest from the ground, from the manse itself. He hoped that if the guards on the wall had found his rope they would eventually meet up with the tower guards and, between them, come to the conclusion that the two illusory urchins were the intruders. This would give Rose and him some time.

The top of the tower was larger than its stem, like the cap of an immense gilded mushroom. They came to a door that presumably led to the final climb. As Max worked upon the lock, he sensed that it was bound by more than physical means, but this seemed only to encourage the energy in his hands. If anything, it was easier to trip this lock than any of the previous ones. Beyond the door a staircase led upwards to a curving corridor, which presumably circled the high chamber. Its roof sloped in towards the centre of the building. They came to the main door of the chamber fairly quickly. It was carved with the image of a dragon. 'Is this a representation of the nomonon?' Rose wondered aloud.

'Probably,' Max replied. 'Which is why we're not going to take the obvious route inside.'

Rose frowned. 'Meaning?'

Max jerked his head upwards. 'We'll climb one of those service ladders that no doubt lead into the roof of the chamber. Let's take a look around from above.'

'Sounds good to me.'

They began to climb a golden ladder, set into the wall, whose rungs led up to a hinged grille high above their heads. Once they were both inside the duct beyond, they were forced to crawl on hands and knees. Max felt his skin prickle. He had no doubt that he was picking up on some *barishic* frequency but he said nothing to Rose. Eventually they came to another grille, from where they could drop down with comparative ease onto a railed catwalk. The chamber was brightly lit, but there was no obvious light source. Perhaps the radiance came from the artefact stowed within the room.

They could see it below, within a complicated net of fine gold and silver wires, which were vibrating gently. Max cautioned Rose to silence by holding a finger to his lips, indicating that the wires below might be sensitive to movement and sound, designed to bring attention to any disturbance. The Mirror lay at the centre of the web, resting in a nest of brass and copper spars. It was, without doubt, a fabulous artefact, intricately crafted. Half the size of a man, its surface did not appear to be glass but a highly polished metal alloy, glinting with oily colours. It could have been a single scale from the hide of a legendary dragon. The frame was gold and covered with detailed representations of coiling serpentine beasts, whose claws splayed out over the shining surface of the mirror. The eyes of the beasts were jewels and their scales glistened with gemstones. It was a thief's dream. And there was no sign of a guardian, human or otherwise. The whole chamber hummed gently.

Max took a few moments to examine their surroundings. He had an idea, but needed a living creature to work on.

'What are you looking for?' Rose whispered, close to his ear.

'Something to work *barishi* on,' he whispered back. 'An insect. Can you see anything in here? It looks like a sterile environment.'

Rose smiled at him and extended her hand. Max thought she was going to stroke his face and for a moment wondered what had taken hold of her. Then he realized she had plucked something from his coat. 'Will this do?' she murmured. In her hand lay a small sleepy moth.

Max smiled back at her and nodded. He took out the spellstone from his shirt, described the symbol of the autonotype spell and directed it towards the moth in Rose's hand. At once, the air around them shimmered and convulsed. Before their eyes, a spiralling ball of light rose up from Rose's palm. Her eyes registered fear, but she did not move, keeping her hand held out rigidly in front of her. The ball was a mass of metallic moths whose wings shed golden dust. They hung in the air, their shimmering wings emitting a soft, sighing sound.

'Amazing,' Rose breathed.

Max felt more confident with the spell now. He formed a clear thought of what he wanted the moths to do and sent it to them. Without pause, the swarm flew down and threaded their way through the intricate wires around the mirror, without once disturbing them. Their tiny bodies slipped between the invisible defences, down to the cage, through the bars and out again. Max formed a second command in his mind. Now the swarm began to alight upon the delicate web of wires, agitating it, deliberately setting off the alarms.

Rose glanced round nervously. 'What are you doing?' she hissed. 'We'll have the guards upon us.'

Max did not reply, but crouched down upon the catwalk. In the chamber below, a golden door slid to the side, revealing an ochre-dark corridor beyond. A serpentine hiss echoed out of it, followed by the unmistakable click of claws upon metal.

'Is that the nomonon?' Rose murmured. 'Can it reach us here?'

Max raised a hand. 'Say nothing,' he said.

A sinuous beast came slinking from the dark corridor. It was a beautiful creature, a sculpture come to life. Max considered that it could almost be an autonotype of a dragon, if such legendary creatures had ever existed, although it did not have wings. The nomonon was serpentine in appearance, with a handsome equine head above an attenuated neck, a long, elegant snout and neatly curved teeth. Its jaw was hung with chinking tassels of gold and its eyes were sparking gems, slit-pupilled as a cat's or a snake's, and shining with a cold passion. It was the image of grace and beauty, but also of ferocity.

The nomonon appeared to assess the situation before it, lifting its elegant snout to scent the air. Then, expelling a strange grating whine, it shot forward on swift feet. Reaching the web, it began to snap at the moths, swallowing them up. Max directed one last thought at the swarm, almost with regret. He ordered them to fly deep into the nomonon's body, find the core of its being and destroy it. So beautiful a thing should not be so casually ruined, but if he was to acquire the mirror he had no choice. Below, the nomonon continued to snap and hiss, but now its body twisted and writhed, as if in agony, as the moths penetrated its core.

Max rubbed his face. The manipulation of *barishi* was becoming increasingly easy for him. It really was as if he'd worked with the hidden force all his life. 'Rose, the vial,' he said, and Rose handed to him the item she'd picked up from the Foundry along the way: a substance that could corrode metal.

Max carefully dripped the corrosive fluid onto the wires below them. An acrid steam, which brought tears to Max's eyes, rose into the air. Rose covered her mouth and backed away, coughing. The wires snapped and sprang back, wrapping around the flailing limbs of the nomonon. Max gestured for Rose to hand him her rope, which he tied to the rail of the catwalk. Then he climbed down the rope towards the broken wires of the web. He was surrounded by a cacophony of buzzing alarms and shrieking steam-whistles, a din so loud he could barely think. Glancing up, he saw Rose's mouth moving urgently, an expression of dismay upon her face. She gestured wildly towards the door. Yes, he could hear it now, if he concentrated hard enough. Someone or something was pounding upon the doors to the vault – presumably the guards of Clan Gold. Fortunately, the bulk of the fallen nomonon, its tail still lashing in dying fury, effectively blocked the entrance.

The moths, working furiously, had opened up a cavity in the nomonon's thorax. Inside, the complexities of its animating mechanisms could be seen whirring and turning. Oily viscous fluid leaked from it. Max noticed something flashing deep inside the creature's gut: a throbbing, pulsing thing. Its heart? Ignoring Rose's warning cry from above, he jumped down from the rope and, in a vibrating haze of moths, reached out and plunged his hand deep into the nomonon's body. There was a slight resistance but then something came away in his fingers, slimy, slippery, somehow alive. It was just small enough to be grasped in one hand. Without even pausing to examine it, he secreted into one of his capacious coat pockets and, with greasy fingers, grabbed hold of the rope once more. He saw Rose's concerned eyes above him, peering through the fripperies of her mask. The moment was oddly still, as if he'd lived it before.

He gestured for her to join him. Rose dropped down among the shattered fronds of the web and began to prize the spars away from the mirror with dark gloved fingers. The pounding against the doors had become heavier, more insistent, clearly audible above the scream of the alarms. The twitching remains of the nomonon were gradually being forced away from the entrance.

Max was filled with a sense of silent urgency, and knew Rose felt the same. They worked with precision, deftly, the great chamber ringing all around them like a bell as the guards battered the door. Max could hear the low, furious mutters of the men denied entrance. Rose leaned forward and stared into the mirror, her breath clouding it. Max took hold of the frame and it lurched in their grip. Rose had provided a strong leather sling, stolen from the Foundry, clearly used for hoisting heavy objects. Between them, they manoeuvred the mirror into it. Rose swarmed up the rope onto the catwalk, moving quickly, economically. Max, steadying the mirror below, could not help but admire her concentrated effort. She made a good accomplice, just getting on with what had to be done, almost as if she'd lived on her wits in the free zones all her life.

The mirror swayed alarmingly as Rose began to haul it upwards. Max followed it, gripping the rope with his thighs, guiding the precious thing on its journey. Once they'd positioned it between them on the catwalk, it became clear that every alarm in New Mint Yard was shrilling around them. Below, armed guards had begun to pour through the door, clambering over the motionless bulk of the nomonon. Max knew that the gold in their armour made them far less vulnerable to the spells at his disposal. He and Rose had no choice but to rely on their wits and agility to escape.

The grille through which they'd entered was above them, a short distance away, but a group of guards was already moving along the catwalk in front of it. Others were dropping down from the roof through hidden entrances. Rose swore beneath her breath, her body curved into a crouch. Max, oddly serene, took out the mechanism he'd pulled from the nomonon. It was more or less spherical, still throbbing, a heart of glass and gold. Max could see that many of the tiny moths had clustered in its centre, as if drawn to it.

'We've got to reach the grille!' Rose hissed desperately. She had drawn her sword. 'Max, are you ready to fight?' Receiving no response, she turned and growled, 'Max! Wake up!'

Smiling quizzically, Max showed her the heart. She shook her head, as if it meant nothing to her, and her eyes looked fierce. Max shrugged and tossed the heart at the guards who stood between them and their avenue of escape. It hit the leader of the troupe in the chest. He staggered backwards and at once the moths swarmed out of their oily nest. They poured over the men, tiny flashing darts of brightness. The guards raised their arms to protect their faces, some uttering shocked cries. The moths made to smother the men, fill their shouting mouths, blind their eyes. As soon as the winged insects touched the gold of the men's armour they fell lifeless to the floor, but the distraction gave Rose and Max enough time to reach the grille, carrying the mirror between them. It wasn't too big to fit into the duct.

Max felt as if he was in a daze. All that had happened was right and preordained. He had no doubt they would escape. Once in the duct, Rose gripped Max's arm. 'They mustn't see us now, Max. Do you understand? This is the most important time for you to make us invisible to their eyes. Can you do it?'

Max shook his head to clear it. 'I don't know.'

'You must try. We'll be surrounded.'

Max nodded and summoned every last shred of strength and stamina he had. The power of *barishi* seemed to howl in his ears. His chest was on fire. Rose held onto his shoulders, her eyes wild. Her mouth moved silently, almost as if she was praying under her breath.

Max swallowed with difficulty. Specks of light boiled and danced before his vision. His mouth was dry and filled with an acrid taste. He began to crawl along the duct, Rose following. Somehow, they manoeuvred the mirror between them. Max prayed they wouldn't meet any resistance in the cramped confines of the duct. They wouldn't be able to slip past anyone in there. They'd be trapped, invisible or not.

It wasn't until they reached the outer grille that they met any Gold guards.

Max saw a face peering into the duct up ahead. He uttered a soft curse. Rose pushed past him, scrambling towards the open grille. She thrust her clenched fists out wildly so that the guard fell backwards with a cry. 'Come on!' she hissed.

Max showed the mirror towards the end of the duct. Rose was standing beneath him, at her feet a dazed guard who appeared to be wondering what had just happened to him. Rose virtually yanked the mirror from Max's hands and began to drag it up the corridor. Other guards were approaching. What was she doing? She shouldn't leave Max's side. Surely, the *barishi* wouldn't work if they were separated?

Max fell out of the duct and staggered to his feet. Almost blind, he ran after Rose. Men pounded past him, yelling at one another. Sometimes they buffeted his body, sent him crashing towards the walls, but it was clear they could not see him.

Rose was like a bright flame ahead of him, seemingly possessed of an inhuman strength as she hauled the mirror along the corridor. Max felt as if he were dreaming. Were his feet touching the floor? He was gliding down the stairs of the tower, a disembodied thought, a memory, a phantom.

The whole estate of Clan Gold had been thrown into turmoil. Guards and servants ran everywhere chaotically. Alarms shrilled and men bellowed orders at one another. Rose did not falter. Max caught up with her to help her with the mirror and together they walked out of the manse into the grounds, panting deeply, unable to run any further. But no one accosted them.

By the time they reached the walls, Max was close to collapse. He felt as if his life-energy was draining away. His head pounded and his vision was blurred. He knew he had to use every last resource to keep them safely unseen. At the top of the wall he fell to his knees.

'Max, keep going,' Rose said in a panicked voice. 'We've nearly done it. Come on!'

'Get the mirror to safety,' Max gasped. 'Remember what we said. I can't go on. You have to leave me.'

Rose kicked him. 'Shut up. Get to your feet, you idiot. I can't do this alone.'

Max almost crawled along behind her to where their rope still hung from the wall. Perhaps it too had been affected by the invisibility spell Max had worked. Rose busied herself with the sling so that the mirror could be lowered to the ground. Max lay with his face against the cold metal of the walkway, feeling he was about to die. Rose was a tormentor, cruel beyond words. She slapped him to get him to his feet. He could barely breathe. His chest was a cauldron of fire. But Rose had a will of iron. She *was* iron – steadfast, invincible, a dark goddess on the winds of night, driving him home.

In her retreat, Rose let Max rest for an hour or two on the couch, then woke him with a hot drink. She didn't feel tired or exhausted at all. Quite the opposite. As she'd fled the Gold manse, she'd felt like a leviathan, a hundred feet tall. Barishi. Power. It was heady, perhaps corrupting. But how could the Metal ignore it as they did? She was convinced the power of *barishi* could save Karadur. It seemed clear to her that its absence in the lives of the people had instigated the decay.

As Max sipped from the cup Rose had given him, she said, 'We worked well together, didn't we?'

He nodded. 'I know I couldn't have done it without you.'

'So, you trust me now?'

He smiled, rather grimly. 'You wanted the mirror.'

She sighed, but didn't bother to argue, hoping he was just too proud to admit a member of the Metal might be a staunch ally.

Rose positioned the Dragon Mirror against the great window of the eyrie and, in the wan light of night rising from the sulphurous lamps below, she and Max inspected their prize. 'It really is remarkable,' Rose said, running her hands reverently over the frame. 'What does it make you feel, Max?'

He shrugged. 'I feel nothing. I'm no adept, Rose. Sometimes I feel at ease with the concept of *barishi* and its uses, at other times totally ignorant.'

'I think we should take it to Shriltasi.' She went to stare out at the smoking towers of the city, one hand splayed against the pane. 'By now Clan Gold will have realized an insider broke into their vault,' she said. 'The entire city will be in a state of alert. I've no doubt my father will have been woken up and informed.'

'We should keep a distance between us for a while,' Max said. 'My presence here puts you in danger. The Lady Rose Iron is quite above suspicion, I'm sure!'

She turned to stare at him, silent for a moment, then said, 'I find the prospect of estrangement oddly unsettling.'

Max's expression was bland. 'Why? We barely know each other.'

Rose felt as if he'd slapped her. She knew rather more of him than he guessed. His words were cold, suggesting she had not reached him in any way. She'd helped him, at some risk to herself, on more than one occasion, and when they'd first met – before he'd known who she was – she knew he'd found her attractive. It was clear they worked well together, so why hadn't he warmed towards her? Did his hatred for the Metal run so deep? Rose collected herself. She must not behave like a silly child. Max Silverskin was of use to her. He must be her ally, if nothing else. 'Perhaps you are right, it will be safer if you don't come here. However, I will help you transfer the mirror to Shriltasi. It's too big and cumbersome for one person to carry alone.'

Max smiled. 'Actually, it might not be.'

Rose frowned. 'I don't understand.'

Max took the spellstone from his shirt, turning it in his hands. 'Jenny taught me a spell to affect an object's size. I can reduce the mirror and therefore carry it with ease.'

'Convenient,' Rose said.

'I haven't tried the spell before, but this seems an ideal opportunity to attempt it.' He looked into her eyes. 'You don't have to risk coming to Shriltasi with me. Now I've learned that little technique of invisibility, I feel far more confident about moving round the city.'

Rose hesitated. He looked too exhausted to climb a stair, never mind use *barishi*. 'Stay here for the rest of tonight at least. You need to rest. Working with *barishi* clearly diminishes your strength. Tomorrow morning I will go to my father and see how the land lies, what was reported. I think you should know that.'

Max nodded. 'Very well.' He lay down on the couch again, closed his eyes. His face looked so grey. Time was running out. Just three more days to go, and the only artefact they had in their possession was the Dragon Mirror.

Rose felt swamped with despair. All the lingering effects of Max's *barishi* flowed away from her on a tide of emotion. She went to the window again. A yellow light hung around the dome of the great Camera like a halo.

Chapter Four

The Hardness of Iron

Prometheus Iron stood in his Camera Obscura, gazing at the morning bustle of the city. The day was uncommonly dull, almost like twilight, and lamps were lit around the chamber, so that Iron's shadow was cast on the domed wall behind him. Was this dimness an effect of the Jewel's absence? He shuddered to think that all light might fade from Karadur. Superstitious nonsense. He was just tired.

The previous evening had been eventful, to say the least. First, the astounding meal with Fabiana Copper. She had surprised him considerably, but perhaps 'shocked' would be a better word. She had burst into the Iron Tower like a cascade of fireworks and had forced him to think about many things. He could not argue that life at the family manse had changed immensely since Laferrine had died. Perhaps he had infected Rose with his melancholy, making her the antisocial creature she appeared to be. He knew he had certainly influenced her rather condescending view of her peers. Fabiana was right: Rose should take her place in society. She could not rule effectively as a reclusive aesthete. Her enemies would always use that against her.

He had also surprised himself with the unplanned remark about placing the responsibility for Rose's education in Fabiana's hands, should he be unable to pass on the knowledge guarded by the inner cabal of the Council. He had meant it at the time, which was unusual for he was not given to placing trust in someone so spontaneously. Fabiana had affected him and whether this was positive or not he was unable to decide. Her views were certainly unorthodox, which was worrying, and yet Fabiana had spoken with such calm conviction that he found himself more tolerant of her words than if they'd come from the mouth of someone like Carinthia Steel. Was he simply blinded by her beauty, warmth and charisma? Perhaps he should speak with her further on the delicate issues they had tentatively broached. He could not concur with her opinions, but perhaps he could explain frankly why the Council must continue to uphold the old traditions. He was aware the prospect of this discussion invoked a feeling of pleasurable anticipation within him.

Following the revelatory events of the evening, Iron had been called from his bed in the middle of the night to a less pleasant situation. A bevy of indignant messengers from New Mint Yard had come to the Tower to inform him that Max Silverskin had delivered yet another affront to the Metal. Clan Gold claimed he had broken into their vaults and stolen some valuable jewellery. Silverskin had been identified by some of the guards. Gold's forcefully worded complaints seemed to indicate they held Lord Iron personally responsible for Silverskin still being at large. How could Max slip around the city as he did, without being seen? It was almost unnatural, but Lord Iron could not really admit that, even to himself. He would not, could not, surrender to the feeling of losing control. There were always mishaps, mistakes − it was part of life. He would pay no heed to the apocryphal rumours sizzling through the Metal, engendered and embellished, no doubt, by Carinthia Steel. He wouldn't put it past her to have Max Silverskin on her payroll in order to embarrass Clan Iron. He would not let her win.

It seemed that everyone in Karadur believed Silverskin had access to occult powers. This could not be so, despite the blood of his mother's family that ran in his veins. Lord Iron was sure that the ancestors of the Metal had closed all portals to the world of the unseen, dark and dangerous. He had to believe that, for if the opposite was true what defence would the Council have? He had not lied when he'd told Fabiana he'd considered what lay beneath. It had pained him to face the idea, but he'd forced himself to do it. Ultimately, he did not think the answers to Karadur's dilemmas lay there. Opening up old thoroughfares would only compound the city's problems, not solve them. But clearly some members of the Council were beginning to have doubts. It was his duty to reassure them, to lead them back to the comfort and certainty of the ancient traditions. They were the only weapons Karadur possessed against encroaching chaos.

Only one thing still kindled uneasiness within Iron. Clan Gold had been strangely reticent to give a full description of exactly what jewellery had been stolen from them. Normally he would just conclude they were items of a personal nature, perhaps with erotic overtones, for in the past Gold had been known for its hedonistic excesses. But because of the conversation he'd had with Rose the day before, the thought crossed his mind that Silverskin might actually have taken the Dragon Mirror from New Mint Yard. It was a ridiculous thought, yet Iron found it hard to dispel. He did not believe the lost artefacts possessed supernatural powers – they were simply weapons that had been operated by using the outlawed subtle forces – but, as Rose had pointed out, they might have immense significance for the common people. Symbols had power, because the easily led invested meaning into them. It would not do for Silverskin to get his hands on such artefacts.

There were footsteps on the cold stairs outside the door: precise, heavy footsteps. Until last night, Iron had felt that Cornelius Coffin was his only ally. Now he dared to think this might not be so. He looked up as Coffin came into the room. 'Good morning, Captain. You were no doubt called from your bed last night, as was I, by the shrill, angry voice of Clan Gold.'

Coffin nodded, his face dark. 'Indeed. I am only saddened I was not called more promptly. The Gold guards wasted a lot of time, which helped the miscreants escape.'

'Miscreants? More than one?'

'Silverskin has a new sidekick. It wasn't Vane with him.'

Lord Iron fixed Coffin with a stern gaze. 'By the Jewel, man, this can't go on! You must take Silverskin into custody. He's causing havoc, laughing in our faces, and no doubt has the Shren Diamond. I'm disappointed in you, Captain, I really am. I know you are far more use than the Battle Boys, but why can't you catch this thief? He's just one man!'

Coffin bowed. 'You are right to be disappointed, my lord, but the wretch has unusual assistance at his disposal. As you know, he wielded some arcane weapon at Clan Silver, and last night he employed similar devices. Difficult as it may be to accept, I think we should consider that these weapons have an unnatural origin.'

'Enough!' Lord Iron raised a hand, and Coffin visibly flinched. 'I will not hear this nonsense. You, of all people, I expect to remain level-headed, Captain. Max Silverskin is a trickster, who for most of his life has lived among tricksters. He wants you to think he has unnatural powers, and I'm surprised you indulge him so willingly. There's a mood in the city that Silverskin seeks to exploit. It is no more than that.'

'My lord, forgive me, but you weren't there, on either occasion. I know what I saw at the Moonmetal Manse, and the captain of Gold's guard is no fool. I interviewed him personally, and he had astounding things to report.'

Lord Iron stared at Coffin until the other man dropped his gaze. 'No, I was not present at these events,' he said. 'I wish I had been, for I would not have been dazzled by theatrical displays. You can see trickery like that every day, on makeshift amateur stages in the markets. It seems a rational mind is sorely needed in this case.'

'I can only report what I see, my lord, and what I have seen has been unusual. That's all I'll say. At New Mint Yard last night, Silverskin literally vanished into thin air. We still don't know how he got in.'

Lord Iron sighed haughtily through his nose. 'Assistance, obviously. You should interrogate all of Gold's staff. Why haven't you found Silverskin's bolt-hole yet? He has to be in Karadur somewhere – or do you suppose he's living in a cave out on the ice?'

Coffin cleared his throat. 'The city has been searched thoroughly, my lord. We located his rooms in the free zones and they are under surveillance, although it's doubtful he'll return to them now. Even our usual informers don't know his whereabouts.'

'And you are quite sure the other Silverskins are not involved?'

'As sure as I can be, my lord. I have searched their manse personally and have stationed two dozen Irregulars on duty there. The family is watched continually. If Max Silverskin is hiding in some secret hole, he will starve to death. But I don't think he is with the other Silverskins.'

'Meaning?'

Coffin paused. 'When Silverskin tried to steal the Jewel, we chased him and Vane into the sewers. I wouldn't be surprised if they don't have a hideaway down there.'

Lord Iron felt a chill course up his spine. The sewers. Was it really possible Silverskin had found some secret portal to what lay beneath? If he'd stolen the Mirror as well . . . Forcefully, Iron dispelled the rising unease within him. He must not become a conspirator in Silverskin's carefully scripted drama. He must remain the voice of reason. 'Draft in extra men to search that warren again,' he said. 'More thoroughly. Immediately. Drag people off the street if necessary.'

'It'll only be a matter of time before we sniff him out. I don't believe we need extra men.'

'But it is urgent, Captain,' Lord Iron said. 'If Silverskin is scurrying through the sewers, he must be found at once. At once, do you hear, before . . .'

Coffin frowned. 'Before . . . what?'

Lord Iron turned away. 'He could damage our water supply, foul the canals, poison us all.'

Coffin looked perplexed. 'Poison? I despise Silverskin utterly and want nothing more than to end his career. Yet I have to say that his criminal acts have never included terrorism of a murderous nature. In his delusion, he believes himself to be a champion of the people. Killing them would hardly help his cause.'

Lord Iron ignored these remarks, aware that his accusation had been desperate and therefore incredible. He began to operate the levers of the Camera. 'There are few places in this city into which I cannot look.' He gestured for Coffin to examine the image on the floor. 'Here is Watersmeet, where the purified water pours towards the four wells of the free zones. I believe you should begin your search here and spread outwards. Fill every tunnel, however small, with men. Use children to gain access to the tighter access ducts. I'm sure there are plenty of urchins in the free zones who'd welcome a little extra income.'

His expression still unsure, Coffin said, 'If that is your wish, I'll get Rawkis onto it this very morning.'

Lord Iron waved a hand towards the captain. 'Never mind him. Lead the party yourself. Sweep in from all quarters, arresting anyone you find and bring them to the surface. Even if you do not net Silverskin, I have no doubt you'll catch someone who knows him.'

Coffin frowned more deeply. 'My men are quite capable of conducting the search themselves, my lord, but if you insist I must be present, then I will of course do as you command.'

A light female laugh rang out and both men turned away from the image on the floor. Lady Rose had come into the Camera. 'Father, I fear Captain Coffin has no stomach for such gross work as searching the sewers.' She grinned at Coffin. 'You look positively pale at the prospect, sir!' She went to her father's side and stood on tiptoe to kiss his gaunt cheek. 'Good morning, father. Why so grave?'

Lord Iron stroked his daughter's face. She was the light to banish his darkness. 'The self-styled Fox of Akra was active again last night, my dear.'

Rose laughed again. 'Oh? What did he steal this time?'

'This is a serious matter,' Lord Iron said reprovingly, though without any real censure in his voice. 'This time he stole some very valuable items of jewellery from the vaults of Clan Gold. Melodia and Marcus, as you can imagine, are outraged. They had me hauled from my bed last night, although what they expected me personally to do at that hour eludes me.'

'As does the self-styled Fox of Akra, it seems,' Rose said sweetly. She glanced coquettishly at Coffin. 'Are you neglecting your duties, sir? Is no maid safe in her bed in Karadur now?'

Captain Coffin flushed. 'My lady, think no such thing. I swear on my life that nothing in this city can harm you. I would die to protect you.'

'How charming of you,' Rose said. 'Please don't die on my account.'

Lord Iron winced inside. From arrogant lawman, Coffin had transformed in moments into a stammering, red-faced boy. Iron thought the man was all but trembling with passion. Thank the Metal Rose clearly found him a buffoon.

'So, the elusive Max Silverskin is hiding out in the sewers, is he?' Rose said. 'It seems appropriate somehow. He is, of course, far too cunning to remain at large on the surface, and must therefore sink into the shadows, haunt the dark places, some mysterious underworld.'

Lord Iron eyed Rose sternly, disturbed by her humorous words, even though he was sure she hadn't intended to imply anything by them. 'He's just been lucky so far. The truth is that Silverskin has become yet another stick for Carinthia to beat me with – and you, of course.' He nodded towards Coffin.

Coffin inclined his head. 'I've long been aware of Lady Steel's feelings for me and my loyal force.'

Lord Iron noticed that his daughter was staring at him meaningfully. He knew what she was trying to convey. He should not be so open in front of Coffin. But it was difficult. In these trying times, Coffin was the closest he had to a friend outside his own family, even if that friendship was self-serving on Coffin's part. Carinthia Steel was delighted about, if not instrumental in, Silverskin's exploits. The situation provided her with a means of gathering fresh support among the Council. 'I have no fear that our good captain won't soon remedy the situation,' he said. 'Silverskin is young, vain and proud. He becomes too bold and that will be his downfall.'

'He has acquired a new accomplice,' Coffin said to Rose. 'Perhaps old Vane is too stout for the job nowadays.'

'A new accomplice?' said Rose icily.

Coffin nodded. 'A youth. I have studied Silverskin carefully, and it seems clear he's averse to working alone. That might be a weakness to exploit.'

'Then by all means begin exploiting it,' Lord Iron said, in a tone of dismissal.

Coffin bowed smartly to him, executed a more leisurely obeisance to Rose and then marched out.

Rose shook her head. 'That man!'

'That man,' said Lord Iron, 'is important to us.'

'He regards me with great importunity,' Rose said. 'I find it offensive.'

'I do not blame him for admiring you,' Iron said. 'Let him dream, my dear. His fixation on you only strengthens his loyalty to our Clan. He needs all our encouragement now. Silverskin must be found.'

Rose cocked her head to one side. 'Why is capturing this thief so important to you, father? Has it occurred to you that Silverskin might make a strong ally rather than a foe?'

Lord Iron's eyebrows shot up. '*What* did you say?'

Rose shrugged. 'Well, it just seems to make sense, that's all. He is a very charismatic figure, surely useful.'

Iron grimaced. 'He makes light of our authority. At such times as these, authority should be respected more, not less. He would never ally with us. He despises everything we stand for. He seeks to undermine our ordered structure. That to me speaks only of a foe.'

'Perhaps he is misunderstood,' Rose said. 'After all, it cannot be denied he has Clan blood. Also, there is something different about him. Perhaps the rumours about him are partly true.'

'Such ideas should never spill from Iron lips,' Lord Iron said. 'Contempt for tradition weakens us all.'

'Authority is respected when it is worthy of respect,' Rose said. 'When it is seen to achieve what it claims to achieve. Remember what Fabiana said last night. I know you can't have been that offended by her ideas because you didn't order her from the manse. We should be seeking new solutions to our problems. None of the traditional methods seem effective now. You say Silverskin is vain and proud. Don't you think the Clans are also riddled with these qualities?'

Lord Iron stared at his daughter expressionlessly for some moments, then said, 'What point are you trying to make?'

'I feel you are being sidetracked by the issue of Max Silverskin. The city is ailing, and Silverskin is but a symptom of it, not the cause. There are those in the Council who want to see you flounder, you know that. What you need is the support of the common people. Iron needs to make a difference out there, do something positive. Silverskin is seen as a voice of the people. That is why I think you should meet with him across a table, to discuss Karadur's future, rather than through the bars of a cell to gloat upon his capture. That would be a pointless victory. It would change nothing.'

'Rose, I know you mean well, but you have no real grasp yet of how the Council operates.'

'Maybe I don't, but I do spend time in the city, father. I walk among the people, trying to see into their minds, to understand them.'

'I have watched you doing so in the Camera,' Iron said. 'It is hardly fitting behaviour for a young woman of your status. You put yourself in danger out there.'

Rose made a sound of exasperation. 'I had hoped you'd be proud I took my future role seriously. I don't want to see our city die. I want to rejuvenate it.'

'Then spend more time studying our traditions and laws,' Iron said. 'Learn the pattern. Attempts to change it will only cause disintegration.'

'You don't believe that. You can't. I think you're afraid. Of the past. Of the secrets. Trust me, father. Let me in. We must vanquish the fear.'

Lord Iron gazed upon his daughter. He wished he could tell her everything, for then she would understand why the past must never come back. But no Iron heir had ever been burdened with the knowledge before the appointed time. He wanted to shield her, protect her. 'I am not afraid,' he said. 'Neither should you be.'

'You never really listen to me, do you?' Rose said wistfully.

Lord Iron smiled sadly. 'You are young and filled with the zeal of youth. The ideas you have derive from that. I appreciate your noble aims but you must see they are unrealistic. Our city has existed for countless generations in this form. It is the perfect form, decided upon by the most learned men and women of the Reformation, who wanted only to create a safe society. It cannot be improved upon.'

Rose opened her mouth to speak.

'And that is my last word on the matter,' said Lord Iron, silencing her before she began. He shook his head, smiling. 'Sit round a table with Max Silverskin! Really, my dear, the idea is preposterous.' He turned to manipulate the levers of the Camera.

'What do you see?' Rose said. 'What do you really see down there?'

Lord Iron did not reply, scanning, scanning for he knew not what.

'It saddens me that your hearing hasn't improved,' said Rose.

'What?' said Lord Iron.

'Goodbye, father,' said Rose.

★   ★   ★

Max Silverskin was not happy to receive Rose's news about Coffin's investigation of the sewers. 'This might put Shriltasi in jeopardy,' he said. 'If the search is too thorough some of the hidden entrances might be discovered. While I skulk here in a lady's boudoir, Menni remains trapped and frozen in the Ashen's domain, and at any moment Coffin might discover it.'

'There are more forces at work here than you know, or than either of us understand,' Rose said. She leaned back on her couch, staring up at one of her overstuffed bookcases. 'But there's also more knowledge available than you can guess. People in the past preserved everything about our city and its environs and hid it somewhere. We have only to find it. It's human nature to store and record, and no law, however stringently applied, ever outlawed human nature successfully. Or human wisdom, for that matter.'

Max shook his head. 'You've spent too much time poring over dusty old books.'

'Never too much time, Max.' She sighed. 'However, the really important grimoires are hard to find. It makes me angry to think how many were burned in the days of the Reformation. Just imagine if we possessed such knowledge.'

Max winced and rubbed his chest.

Rose sat up straight. 'Are you all right?'

He nodded. 'I can bear it.' He looked bleak. 'I have to say I don't think I have the strength to use *barishi* to any great effect at the moment.' He uttered a frustrated cry. 'Great Jewel, Rose, why are we sitting here indulging in meaningless conversation? I need to be doing something. I could die before Menni is restored.'

'You are obsessed with that,' Rose snapped, regretting the words even before she'd finished speaking.

Max stood up, wobbled, leaned against her table. 'Now the Rose shows her thorns.'

'I'm sorry. I didn't mean to offend you. It's just that I can't help thinking of the greater implications of your condition.'

'I have to reach Shriltasi, Coffin or no Coffin.'

'It would be suicide. If you can't hide yourself, you'll never be able to enter the sewers.'

'Then what other suggestions do you have? The War Owl is lost to us and we have another artefact we don't even know how to use. If the Ashen are correct about me, time is running out, and we're doing nothing.'

Rose scraped her fingers through her hair. 'Let me think,' she said. 'Let me think.'

'You can't think. There's only one course of action. Take the Mirror to Shriltasi. The Ashen must help us more. I'm sure they're capable of it. They're playing with us. I must go to them.'

'Not yet. There must be . . .'

Max raised his hand. 'What was that?' He went towards the window, his hand pressed to his side.

Rose turned in her seat. 'What?'

'Open the window,' Max said, his fingers running over the frame as if seeking a locking mechanism.

Rose frowned. 'Why?'

'Just do it. Or do I have to work it out myself?'

Rose got up, went to the window, and saw that a grey mechanical dove was perched on the sill outside. At once she operated the mechanisms that opened the panes. Max leaned out and grabbed hold of the bird. It was a crude thing – clockwork – but it had done its job. A note was concealed in a compartment on its breast.

Max took the note and dropped the bird to the floor, where it lay kicking feebly, expending the last of its temporary power.

'What is it?' Rose asked, trying to look over Max's shoulder. 'What does it say?'

Wordlessly, he passed the scrap of paper to her. 'Bergun's Foundry? Where's that? I've never heard of it.'

'An inn in the free zones,' Max said.

Rose turned the paper over, shook her head. 'Who sent this?'

'The person who wishes me to go there,' he said.

'You or me, though? It came to my home.'

'It's for me. The people I know use these devices regularly.'

'But no one knows about this place. How did they find you here? It must be a trick. Coffin has many informers and spies in the free zones. This is terrible. If he's learned of my connection with you, plus the location of my hiding place . . .'

'Stop worrying,' Max interrupted. 'This is nothing to do with Coffin.'

'Then who is it to do with?'

Max pressed the fingers of one hand against his eyes. 'I don't know, but I have to go. Perhaps the free zones are the safest place for me now, seeing as Coffin is flooding the sewers with Irregulars. He won't think I'd go back to my old haunts so blatantly.'

'That's a big risk to take, Max.'

He smiled wearily. 'I have to take it.'

'I'll get changed,' Rose said. 'It won't do for you to go anywhere without your new accomplice.' She walked briskly to her bedroom.

'My new accomplice?' Max called after her.

'Yes,' she called back. 'The Gold guards took note of me last night. Coffin believes me to be a youth, so I'd better dress like one, hadn't I?'

Chapter Five

The Lady of Ladies

Going back to the free zones, Max felt as if he hadn't trodden their worn streets for years. But it really was a homecoming. He felt he could be invisible here, even if his companion commanded more than a little attention. She did not look like a boy but nonetheless possessed a certain androgynous quality. Her garb was that of a thief, close-fitting for agility. No one knew her there, though, so they were curious. 'You are like a beacon,' Max hissed to her. 'You'd have been more sensible to dress down in plain women's clothing like a dowdy seamstress or something.'

'You didn't say that back at my eyrie.'

Max didn't respond. He detected the flirtatious undertone to the lightly spoken remark. His instinct was to reply in kind but he forced himself to keep a distance. Part of him still found it difficult to trust Lady Rose. In the early days of his reintroduction to Clan Silver, he had wanted to trust and like his newfound relatives, but he'd quickly discovered they looked down upon him, especially the younger ones.

They found the inn quickly and apart from having to slip past a few ridiculously obvious Irregular spies, met with no obstacles. Max could tell Rose was quietly surprised that no one recognized him, but this was familiar territory. He didn't need spells or trickery to blend in with the surroundings. They were part of him.

As they passed nearby to the entrance to the Well of the Heart, Max noticed it was strongly guarded by both Irregulars and Battle Boys. Clearly, following Max's assault on the water worker Coffin had realized that the wells could be used to enter the sewers. The next time he went to Shriltasi he wouldn't be able to use any of the well routes.

Max realized that whoever had sent the note must know him well enough to suggest a neutral meeting place. Bergun's Foundry was not a hostelry he had frequented with Menni. He ordered a jug of ale for himself and Rose at the bar and then indicated they should sit down at a corner table, where they could watch the other patrons in comparative privacy. At that time of day there were few other customers.

'Do you see anyone you recognize?' Rose murmured, taking a sip from her tankard and then smothering her reaction of disgust.

Max shook his head. 'No, but that means nothing. The Ashen have accomplices in the free zones. I'm hoping the message came from them.'

They had nearly finished the jug of ale, and Rose – despite her initial distaste for the brew – was clearly beginning to have a taste for it, but still no one had made themselves known to them. Max was beginning to wonder whether they were wasting their time. The note had given no specific time. Had they to wait here all day? Max shifted in his seat impatiently. Time was something they had little of. Then, almost as if conjured by his anxious thoughts, an urchin child came up to their table, a girl dressed in clothes too big for her.

'Be off,' said Max, feeling that the last thing he needed was a beggar whining round him.

The girl held out a piece of paper to them solemnly. Rose took it quickly. '"Lady of ladies, the ancient lady",' she read aloud, then frowned up at Max. 'It's a flyer of some kind.'

Max took it from her and uttered an amused snort. '"Come hear her wondrous words".' He put the flyer down and took a sip of ale. 'I'll tell you what that is – a vaguely disguised reference to a fortune-teller. They're everywhere in the free zones nowadays.'

'A fortune-teller!' Rose picked up the flyer once more. 'I'm curious.'

'Don't be,' said Max. 'They're all fakes.' He stared coldly at the child who was still lurking by their table. 'Clear off, you hear.'

The girl did not move.

'Give her a coin,' said Rose.

Sighing, Max withdrew his purse. But the girl took a step backwards, frowning. 'Lady of ladies,' she said in a strange sly lisp. 'You see her, hear her. Good.'

'Take the money and go,' Max said. 'We haven't got time for this.'

The girl shook her head. 'No, you must. Things to see, to hear. Good.'

Max waved a dismissive hand at the child and deliberately turned his back on her.

Rose looked contemplative. 'Don't be so hasty. I think we should pay this lady a visit.'

Max studied her for a moment, then glanced back at the child. Was this a message for them, after all? 'Perhaps you're right,' he said, pushing his chair back from the table.

'Good, good,' said the girl, her face still solemn.

They followed her out of the inn and up a dark, dismal alley, where rubbish steamed beneath shattered windows. The child skipped ahead of them, jumped over the skeletal remains of a dead dog. Overhead, banners of grimy laundry hung motionless. 'This is depressing,' Rose said.

'Not a part of the city you'll have visited often,' Max remarked.

The urchin had come to a halt before a dark doorway, which was shuttered inadequately with a rusting sheet of corrugated iron. The building itself seemed weary to the point of crumbling and sagged heavily upon a number of rust-streaked buttresses. All the windows were covered in sacking. 'Hardly a salubrious location for business,' Rose said.

'Only the desperate come to places of this kind,' Max replied. He squeezed through the flaking portal and saw the child standing spectrally in the shadowy corridor beyond. She hopped impatiently from one foot to the other. Once Rose and Max were inside, she walked up the corridor, pausing before a doorway, where a ragged scarlet curtain hung down. 'Here,' she said, holding up the curtain.

Max walked past her into the room beyond. It was filled with the smoke of an acrid resin that burned in a bowl on the cluttered table that dominated the chamber. Behind it sat a veiled figure, presumably the Lady of Ladies. Ancient gnarled hands rested upon the table top, loosely laced together. They were elegant hands, despite their raised veins and knobbly knuckles. Rose came into the room behind him. 'Do you know who we are?' she said.

Max winced. The power of the Iron was in Rose's voice, the tone of authority, of familiarity with being obeyed. 'We received your flyer,' Max said in a slightly apologetic tone. 'We were persuaded to sample your skills.'

The old woman lifted her veil. Even in great age, her face was very beautiful, dignified. As a young woman, she must have been exceptional. Her hair, of purest white, gleamed like platinum in the light of the candles that lit the room. 'Maximilian,' she said softly, in a low throaty voice.

'Forgive me, madam,' Max said, 'but have we met before?'

The old woman nodded. 'Oh yes, but you won't remember. You were very young.' She made a graceful gesture with one hand. 'Please, both of you, be seated.' She smiled at the urchin who still hovered by the door. 'Good girl, Kitty. Bring our guests some tea.' The woman turned her smile on Rose. 'I promise you the beverage will be neither poisonous nor foul. Don't be misled by the filthy appearance of this building's frontage.'

Max could see that the room, despite its clutter, was clean. 'My companion is in a state of shock,' he said. 'You will have to be patient with her.'

'I commend you being here at all, Lady Rose,' said the woman.

'You know me,' Rose said.

The woman closed her eyes briefly and inclined her head. 'I do. Don't you know me?'

Rose frowned, peering at the woman intently. 'Should I?'

'In your dreams, Rose. In your dreams.'

'You?' Rose shook her head. Her face had flushed a little. 'Who are you, for the Jewel's sake?'

The woman's smile did not falter. 'I am Serenia, the honourable Serenia Silverskin, though few think me, or any of my relatives, honourable nowadays.'

'Silverskin!' Max snapped. 'What do you want with me?'

'I want nothing of you. I have summoned you here for your benefit, not mine.'

'I want nothing of you,' Max said. A hot anger had ignited within him. Part of him was aware this reaction was extreme. 'Silverskin turned their backs on me as much as Clan Silver did.'

'You are bitter,' said Serenia. 'Understandably so. But you must appreciate your family walks along a narrow blade. We have to employ caution in every aspect of our lives. Had we interfered in your life, it would have brought you no benefits – not until now, that is.'

Max made to stand up, but Rose grabbed hold of his arm and pulled him down. 'Say what you have to say,' she said to Serenia. 'I also want to know what interest you have in me.'

The lady inclined her head gratefully. 'This will become apparent. You are aware by now, Max, of the legacy of your blood. The witch mark burns upon you.'

'It was put there,' Max said. 'Were you responsible?'

'Allow me to speak,' Serenia said, unruffled. 'At this point in time, you no doubt feel as if you have no control. All is in flux. Knowledge and crucial information lie beyond your grasp, but the wheel of fate is turning slowly. All will come together. You must not fear.'

'Must not fear? They tell me I am dying.'

'And who is not? Death is not a thing to be feared, Max. Human suffering is worse. We are under the illusion that this life is the most precious thing, all there is. But that is not so. We are all part of the life-force of the multiverse. We are beings of energy, housed in flesh. Our own life-force cannot be destroyed, merely changed. Life is the school of the soul and should be enjoyed for what it is, along with its sensual pleasures. But you should not be afraid of what lies beyond it. Still I did not bring you here to lecture you on this.' She delved into a pile of books on the table and withdrew a small thick volume, which she pushed across to Max with her fingertips. 'This is for you.'

Max heard Rose draw in her breath and utter a smothered sound of excitement. 'What is this?' he asked.

'A grimoire of the Silverskins,' Serenia said. 'Not only does it contain information about the forbidden knowledge scorned by the Metal, but also much of the true history of Karadur-Shriltasi. It is only right that you should have it. It is time now. It belonged to your mother.'

Max picked up the book. Its cover was of scuffed leather, its pages tissue-thin, filled with cramped spidery handwriting. 'She wrote this?'

'Not all of it. Many of your female ancestors have inscribed those pages. No man has ever owned it before.'

'This is what we need,' breathed Rose. She looked up at Serenia. 'I can't believe you have something like this. It's priceless.'

'Indeed.' She paused. 'Max, you may use some of the rubric in this text in conjunction with the spellstone given to you by the Ashen.'

'You know a lot about my recent movements.'

'We have always known your movements. We have shadowed you, Max, all your life. You will be our salvation.'

Max put down the book. 'Aha – we come to the crux of the matter.'

Serenia shook her head. 'Do not make assumptions. The Silverskins are the only living remnant of what existed before the Reformation. We are relics, Max. And you are precious. It is why the Ashen respect you. The Lords of the Metal, in their fear, chose the way of the mechanist. They cut from them all aspects of mysticism, believing it to be a portal for weakness. The Ashen and their kind below perhaps went too far the other way. The Silverskins were always functional – combining mechanism with mysticism. That is the true way – the middle path. Extremes of any kind are to be avoided. We are the bridge, and if Karadur-Shriltasi is to survive and perform its eternal purpose, that bridge must be firm.' Serenia got to her feet, unfolding like a serpent until she stood tall behind the table. She began to pace slowly around the room. 'For millennia, the Silverskins have laid low, waiting, always waiting for the time that would come, for the one who would come. But we are not entirely mystics, as I said. We realized that the time had to be *made*, as did the one. We made the time. We made you. Your mother made you.'

'It was one of you, then, in Gragonatt,' Max said. 'You put the mark on me. You cursed me.'

'Yes,' said Serenia. Her cool grey eyes glittered with an almost youthful brightness. 'It is your purpose, Max. What you were born for.'

'I had no choice in that and, as a human, I am now a creature of choice. What if I choose now to deny the purpose you chose for me?'

Serenia regarded him stonily. 'You are speaking of free will, of course. Traditionally, the manipulation of *barishi* must not compromise the free will of the individual, but your purpose is certainly preordained. It is an unfortunate paradox. We can make you, but we cannot give you a conscience, nor a sense of duty. It would have been easier for us if you'd been brought up in our family stronghold, with these things instilled into you since birth.'

'Then why didn't that happen?'

'It wasn't what we wanted for you. A cloistered childhood would not have produced the person you are now. Menni Vane, the sojourn with Clan Silver, the life of an outlaw, all were essential components of your development.'

'You are monstrous,' said Rose, her tone tinged with a disgusted awe.

'Perhaps we are,' Serenia said amiably. 'Max, you took your mother's name. It meant something to you. Put aside your pique and pride now. Take hold of your destiny. I believe that in your heart you've always known it.' She glanced at Rose. 'She knows. One day, if this city survives, she will rule it. Her instincts tell her you are an important part of Karadur's future. It is why she is here with you now. It is why I have spoken to her through her dreams. She is valuable, Max. You should feel some of what she feels. Your continued reluctance and resistance seem merely like posturing.'

Max was silent for a moment, while Serenia stood over him, her hands folded at her breast. Rose was unusually silent, her face pale. Max put his fingers on the soft cover of his mother's grimoire. 'The lost artefacts,' he said. 'How important are they?'

'Very,' said Serenia. 'You will recover them.'

'Things have not been progressing smoothly in that area.'

Serenia waved a hand in the air. 'Minor setbacks. Once you are committed, you will find your path easier.' She took the grimoire from beneath Max's hand. 'Jenny Ash is economical with what knowledge of *barishi* she gives you. The spellstone has many uses. The information in the grimoire will give you access to these uses. It lists a host of *barishic* symbols.'

'He already knows,' Rose said in a quiet voice. 'I've seen him use *barishi* – creatively.'

Max shook his head. 'I've been lucky. Essentially, my so-called abilities are untried and erratic.'

Serenia nodded. 'You are new to them and they to you. But the more you use them, the more skilled you will become, and very quickly. You relieved Clan Gold of the Dragon Mirror last night, I believe?'

Max nodded. 'Rose said it was part of Clan Iron's icon.'

'That is correct. You will find a conjuration in the grimoire that will enable you to control the Mirror. One of its functions is the creation of powerful illusions. For instance, you can make a person look into it and see their greatest fear looking out at them.'

'And its other functions?'

Serenia shrugged. 'Several. As a weapon, it can direct concentrated beams of *barishic* force that can blind and burn. That same force can be used for good, as a revitalizing beam. This, you will find, can help you restore your friend, the unfortunate Master Vane. The mirror is also a portal, through which elemental entities may be summoned. It reflects the ultimate truth and the ultimate lie. No one has used it for any of these purposes for millennia.' She opened the book, indicated a page. 'I will show you which symbols in the grimoire will aid you. Just use the stone as normal with them, and direct its energy towards the mirror. It is really quite simple for someone with the relevant ability.'

Max stared at her for a moment. 'I appreciate your help, though it would have been more useful earlier.' He paused, then asked accusingly, 'What happened to my parents?'

Serenia peered at him through hooded eyes. 'They suffered,' she said. 'It was a noble sacrifice.'

Max uttered a sound of disbelief and disgust. 'Is that all you have to say?'

Serenia inclined her head. 'For now. At present, I think there are more important things to discuss. We should reconsider all that you know and have learned.'

Kitty entered the room bearing grimy mugs of tea, which she set before them. Serenia waited until the child had departed once more before she spoke again. 'The entire city is decaying – but why? Is it merely through age or because the people have lost their way? But something far worse is also happening.' Serenia splayed her hands upon the table. 'The density of the ice is becoming thicker. In ages past, secretaries of the Iron Lord kept a record of the ice's movement. This practice ceased during the Reformation, as it was felt everything had been brought to order. A sad oversight. It was quite by chance that one of our people noticed that the markers whereby the ancients measured the thickness of the ice, have been consumed by it. It claws at the very walls of the city, sucking out its warmth. Don't you see what this means? We face complete extinction.'

Max shuddered, remembering when he'd found himself out there in that desolate waste. 'Are you sure of this?'

Serenia nodded. 'There is no doubt. We are prisoners of fear, Max. I believe the life-force of the city – even the heat of its living inhabitants – has kept the ice at bay. If Karadur fails, then it will be engulfed. We could do nothing to stop it. Do you know what the ancient scriptures have to say about this?'

Max shook his head. 'How could I? They were outlawed millennia before I was born.'

'It is said that should Karaldur-Shriltasi fall to the ice it would herald the demise of the entire multiverse. This site of this city is the heart of creation. What stood here before – countless millennia before – was the cauldron of life, from whence it dispersed to seed countless other worlds. If Karadur dies, then death – true nothingness – would prevail everywhere. It would move outwards like a deadly disease. All human striving, throughout existence, will have been for nothing.'

Max was silent for a moment. 'These are only legends,' he said at last.

Serenia smiled, without warmth. 'Even legends are founded on facts, no matter how ornately they are wrapped in words. The multiverse revolves in great cycles. We are trapped here, in our little part of it, ignorant of what happens beyond our limited perceptions. This is the age of great decay, but only human endeavour can change it. Our ancestors possessed more wisdom than we do, more awareness. The decay has affected not just our environment, but our very being. Can't you see this? Can't you feel it in your bones?'

Max shifted uncomfortably. 'You speak beyond my sphere of experience,' he said. 'The world I have recently been introduced to is perplexing, to say the least. How can I say whether your beliefs are true or not? My gut instinct is this: perhaps we *are* part of a grand scheme – I don't have the knowledge to tell – but, if so, we are small components in it and therefore can only act in small yet significant ways. I have been shown a path, which I may or may not follow. All I know for certain is that I want the father of my heart restored to me.'

'But Max,' Rose said, 'there is so much more to it than that. What Serenia has told us makes perfect sense. It is our purpose – yours and mine both – to do something now.'

Max shook his head. 'You're leaping ahead. Only yesterday, we talked simply of recovering lost artefacts. Now you want us to act like gods.'

Rose shook her head, her mouth set in a thin line. 'I know how I must sound, but I feel it.'

Max ignored her and addressed Serenia. 'What of the Ashen? Surely they are a part of this, and in many ways more equipped to deal with the situation.'

Rose interrupted before Serenia could speak. 'No, they are too different. You know they are. We are human, with human hearts.'

Max turned on her. 'Why believe that humanity is the epitome of creation? I think you have too much of your father's ideology within you. The Ashen are not inferior to us. In many ways, I would say the opposite is true.'

'Lady Rose does have a point,' Serenia said smoothly. 'The Ashen are amoral creatures, but this is not the reason they cannot act now. Humanity is different, because it has a responsibility. I believe we are the guardians of the multiverse, but flawed nonetheless. And those of us whose eyes are unscaled, who have the awareness to see truly, have a duty to act.'

Max sighed. 'I find it hard to think in such grand terms.'

'You must get used to it quickly,' Serenia said. 'When you have reunited

all the artefacts, something unimaginable will happen. Have no doubt of it.'
She sipped at her tea.

There was a silence. Then Rose said abruptly, 'I don't want you in my
dreams. It's an intrusion.'

Max glanced at her in surprise. She did not seem herself.

Lady Serenia regarded her thoughtfully. 'You invited me in,' she said.
'You were hungry for knowledge and I heard your call. Your voice is a
shout upon the ether.' She narrowed her eyes slightly. 'I know your heart,
Rose. It was that which spoke to me first.'

Rose and Max returned to her eyrie in silence. Rose sensed that Max was
angry: with her, with himself, with his family, with the world. She hardly
dared speak to him, aware that the wrong words might conjure a swift
retaliation. He perhaps resented the fact that Serenia had included her –
a daughter of Iron – so definitely in his future plans. She would have to
explain, tell him about the strange dreams. It still seemed inconceivable to
her that Serenia was responsible for them.

Soon after they'd entered Rose's retreat, she said, 'You said you were
tired earlier – too tired to use *barishi*. Do you think you'll still be able to
shrink the mirror, like you said?'

Max shrugged irritably. 'I don't know.'

'Perhaps I can help . . . ?'

He frowned at her. 'How?'

'Well, last night, I certainly felt the effects of *barishi*. Perhaps you could
use my energy to augment your own.'

He considered for a moment, with undisguised poor grace. 'All right.'

Rose was annoyed with herself for behaving in such a placatory manner.
Max was being petulant and there was no time for that. If she was in his
position, she'd act very differently. Still, she wasn't, and at least she had
some influence over him now. She was also itching to examine the book
Serenia had given him but sensed she must bide her time.

They stood before the mirror in the main room, and Max pulled out the
spellstone. He described the appropriate symbol in the air and took hold of
Rose's hand. She wasn't sure what she should do, but instinctively relaxed

and imagined that her life-energy was flowing into him, strengthening him. This was, she realized, very painful on an emotional level. It was so intimate, and yet not. She and Max had been through some hair-raising experiences together but she could tell he was still holding her at arm's length in many ways. He was so different from the man she had met in the market only a few days before. Then, he'd wanted to woo her. Now, he seemed to be reverting increasingly to the sulky youth he'd once been. She couldn't see into his mind, couldn't possibly understand how he must feel, but still couldn't help feeling wistfully disappointed.

The fact that their joint effort was successful seemed almost incidental. The mirror lay small between them. Max picked it up and put it into a pocket of his coat.

'Don't you want to know what Serenia meant when she mentioned visiting my dreams?' Rose asked, with false carelessness.

Max glanced at her. 'It's up to you.'

'She pointed me towards the Dragon Mirror. Perhaps she knows where all the other artefacts are.'

'Somebody does,' Max said glumly, 'perhaps everybody except us – or except me.'

'I don't know anything more than you do. I feel used – as you do. But, in a strange way, what we've learned gives me hope. It's an elaborate game, but it seems clear certain people are guiding you towards a definite outcome. Perhaps we have no choice but to play the game. We can be angry about it, or we can use it as an opportunity to learn. That too is our choice.'

Max grimaced. 'That is easy for you to say. You don't have a silver heart threatening to take your life.'

'I know.' She paused, then said firmly, 'I'm coming to Shriltasi with you.' She braced herself for an argument.

Max only shrugged. 'If you want to.'

Down in the sewers, the dark tunnels seemed to reverberate with the rhythm of distant running feet, shod in heavy boots. Max and Rose entered through a cramped, stinking duct and made their way to Watersmeet. With scarves tied over their faces, they crept along a narrow path, bent almost double.

Rose, who had eavesdropped for several minutes on her father's earlier conversation with Coffin, had told Max how the Irregulars had most likely begun their search at Watersmeet and fanned outwards. She and Max would just have to get there as quickly as they could and trust that if they met any opposition they could use *barishi* to help them. The sewers were a complex labyrinth of tunnels and chambers, and they expected that the last place someone would look for a fugitive would be in one of the more open thoroughfares.

After what seemed like hours, they emerged from a dank tunnel into an area lit by hissing gas lamps – one of the purifying stations. From here it would be easy to follow one of the great canals to Watersmeet. Now they progressed more cautiously. Occasionally they heard hoarse, loud voices, echoing out from somewhere up ahead. The roar of Watersmeet itself gradually increased in volume as they approached it.

Only a hundred yards or so from the great cascade, they heard a loud commotion. Before they had time to act, or even think, a cloaked figure came running towards them, pursued by a troop of Irregulars. Some of the Irregulars held aloft flaming brands that cast leaping shadows on the wall. Without pause, the fleeing figure pushed roughly past Rose and Max, effectively bringing the Irregulars down upon them.

Max drew his weapons instinctively, noting that at least Coffin wasn't with the troop. They were led by the captain's deputy, Sergeant Rawkis, who recognized Max instantly and expelled a bellow of sadistic delight.

'Use the spellstone,' Rose said behind him. He heard her draw her swords – perhaps she didn't have as much faith in *barishi* as she liked to believe. 'The shrinking spell. Make manikins of them.'

Max took out the stone and was about to describe the appropriate symbol in the air when an instinct made him pause.

'Max!' Rose hissed. The Irregulars were almost upon them.

Max delved in his coat pocket for the shrunken Dragon Mirror. He held it up in one hand, gleaming surface outwards. In his mind, he could see the symbol that Serenia had pointed out in the grimoire. The symbol of the dragon. He no longer had to draw the symbols – just visualizing them strongly was enough. Even as a blade sliced the air in front of him, Max directed all his will and intention towards the mirror. At once beams of red–gold light shot out of it, which he directed into the eyes of the Irregulars. It seemed they were caught in stasis. He could see the steam of their breath, still upon the air, the pores of their rough skin, the individual hairs on their jowls. Then a gout of fire burst from the mirror. It sprang from Max's hand, unfolding itself to its proper size. It was real and solid, hanging in the air, yet also weirdly spectral. Max could not see the surface of the mirror, but could visualize the image of the Irregulars' reflection. The men had paused in their approach, eyes wide in astonishment.

Send their hatred back to them! Max thought. *Send it to them in the form they fear most.*

One of the group lifted a hand to point at the artefact. He cried out in a guttural voice. 'Aiee, she comes! Sekmet! Sekmet!'

Most of the Irregulars fell to their knees before the mirror. Others backed away, swords scraping along the ground.

'She is angry in her resurrection!' Max cried. He was unsure of where the words came from, but they seemed the most appropriate. Red and gold light flared brighter from the mirror.

All of the Irregulars now abased themselves upon the ground, some actually in the water of the canal itself. Max watched with a kind of fascinated horror, but then Rose touched his arm. 'We should go.'

He nodded and quickly limned the symbol to shrink the mirror once more. Even when this was done, the air still glowed red and gold. Rawkis was upon his knees, hands clasped in prayer before him, eyes screwed tight. His body rocked, his mouth worked soundlessly. The rest of the Irregulars moaned like frightened hounds.

Without another word, Max and Rose ran past them.

Chapter Six

Sharp Edge of Steel

The Upper Council of the Metal sat in their traditional chairs around the image of the Camera Obscura. Lord Iron noticed that there was more of a *frisson* of excitement about them. Hardly a surprise. One of their own had been summoned to the Council. They wanted him to explain why he had recently been found scuttling about in the sewers, where he'd been apprehended by a group of Coffin's Irregulars.

Coffin himself stood to attention just beyond the ring of chairs. He had already told the assembly of how his men had caught sight of an unknown person acting suspiciously and had pursued them. He had also related how, in the process of this pursuit, the group had encountered the criminal Silverskin, and that the actions of the person unknown had obstructed the outlaw's arrest. In the confusion, Silverskin had employed some kind of conjuring trick to befuddle the Irregulars and had escaped. The unknown person had continued to flee, but shortly thereafter had been apprehended by another group of Irregulars. The individual had then been revealed to be none other than Sir Clovis Pewter.

Now Pewter's face burned red as he sat among the Council. His clothes were still sodden and a definite sewer whiff drifted from them as they dried in the warmth of the Camera. 'I tell you again, Lord Iron,' he said, 'I find it a great affront to be treated like a common criminal. I am a gentleman of the Metal. Surely it should be Coffin and his brutes who are called to account here!'

Lord Iron suppressed a sigh. He had his own suspicions why Pewter might have been lurking in the sewers – his strange appetites were rather more than rumours. 'This is only a formality, Sir Clovis. I'm sure you understand these are delicate times. All we need to know is what you were doing down there, and why you attempted to flee Captain Coffin's men.'

Pewter attempted to muster some dignity, which was difficult owing to his bedraggled condition and less than sweet perfume. 'I was down there for the same reason they were! Coffin has spent long enough hunting for Silverskin and failing miserably. I decided to take matters into my own hands and conduct my own search.' He paused. 'I sought only to please you, my lord.'

Lord Iron nodded. The rest of the council sat silently, perhaps curious as to how he would deal with this situation. Carinthia Steel smiled softly, as if waiting for Iron to make a mistake. Lord Tin's face was grey, while his fragile Silver wife looked close to tears. The Golds and Silvers were grim. Only Fabiana Copper looked upon Iron with supportive warmth.

'I am pleased to hear your motives were noble,' Lord Iron said dryly. 'However, your words still do not explain why you fled the Irregulars. Surely you needed only to make yourself known to them to avoid the unpleasant fracas that ensued?'

Pewter's colour was now nearly that of the metal for which he was named, so deep was his furious blush. 'They . . . they surprised me, that's all. I know I shouldn't have run from them but I wasn't expecting a great tromping drove of thugs to descend upon me. I admit I saw Silverskin with a companion. It was a chance to take them into custody, but I knew I wasn't strong enough to succeed on my own. I assumed if I led the Irregulars to them, they would be seized. Instead, Silverskin used some magic—'

'What?' Lord Iron raised a disapproving eyebrow.

'Some illusion, my lord . . .' Sir Clovis shrugged helplessly, glancing at Captain Coffin as if for support. 'Something he used to confuse the Irregulars.'

Lord Iron gestured with one hand. 'Well, we have yet to hear the full evidence of what exactly occurred. But, despite that, to a cynical person it might seem that far from capturing the outlaws, rather you helped them evade the Captain's men.'

Pewter lowered his eyes modestly. 'If that is so, it was inadvertently, my lord.' He displayed his palms and addressed the entire company. 'My lords and ladies, do any of you really believe I was down there for some nefarious purpose?'

There was no reply, although Iron was sure one or two were on the verge of speaking, Lady Copper in particular.

Pewter, now finding higher moral ground, risked a smile. 'The Irregulars were happy to pursue me – for no reason – and now that same troop of thugs, by their own admission, failed to capture Silverskin.'

'Yes,' interrupted Captain Coffin, clearly unable to contain himself any longer. 'At the very moment you were shoving past him in your escape.'

There was a silence. 'It was very confusing. The dim light down there . . .' Pewter shook his head as pitifully as he could. Then he looked directly at Coffin. 'Anyway, it is I who should be casting aspersions about here. Those damned brutes of yours robbed me!'

Captain Coffin's eyebrows rose. He glanced at Lord Iron.

'What exactly do you mean, Sir Clovis?' Iron asked.

'A valuable object was taken from me,' Pewter said. 'A ring. I wasn't wearing it on my hand, because it's far too valuable, but I keep it in a purse around my neck. Silverskin didn't have the chance to nab it, and the only other people I encountered in the sewers were Coffin's men. I believe the theft occurred when I ran into a second group of Irregulars who were coming towards me. These were, of course, the idiot individuals who saw fit to take me into custody. They stole from me.'

'Is this possible, Coffin?' Lord Iron directed his gaze upon the captain. 'Have your men turned to petty crime as well?'

Coffin shook his head emphatically. 'Certainly not. They are incorruptible and obey me to the letter. The accusation is risible. Sir Clovis no doubt lost his property while wading about in the sewers.'

'I must agree that seems the most likely explanation,' Lord Iron said. He glanced sternly at Pewter. 'I suggest you stay away from insalubrious areas in future, Sir Clovis. They are hardly a place for a gentleman of your status to frequent.'

Pewter bowed. 'Very well, my lord. I am sorry to have caused this inconvenience, but I still insist I was merely trying to do my public duty.'

'Then you are to be congratulated for your spirit, if not for your common sense.' Iron raised a hand. 'You may leave us now, Sir Clovis. You are clearly in need of a change of clothes and a bath.'

Pewter remained hesitantly where he was.

'Is there something further to wish to say?' Lord Iron enquired.

'My property,' Pewter said. 'It was stolen from me. I am anxious to have it restored.'

Captain Coffin raised a hand, glancing at Lord Iron for permission to speak. Lord Iron inclined his head and Coffin said, 'I'll have my men search the area carefully where you encountered them.'

'That seems reasonable,' Lord Iron said. 'Remember my warning, Sir Clovis. Now go.'

With a bow, Pewter left the chamber. His mother, Lady Silver, looked pleadingly at Lord Iron, who nodded. She too got up and left the room to hurry after her son.

Lord Tin shook his head heavily. 'These are indeed strange times,' he said. 'Who would have thought we'd see a day when one of our own was held to account? My own son . . .'

'This must be difficult for you,' Lady Copper murmured, leaning forward in her seat, her face creased into a sympathetic expression.

'It is difficult for all of us,' Lord Iron said sternly. He cleared his throat. 'Now, we have other business to address. Captain Coffin, would you care to give your report?'

The captain came forward. 'It has a direct connection with the illusion Silverskin created to evade capture. As you all know, there have long been rumours of secret cults in our city – among the common people, naturally. However, during my investigations in the free zones, more information concerning this subject came to light. It appears incontrovertible that some ancient cult has been revived among the Foundrymen – perhaps only a fear of it.'

'A secret cult?' Lady Copper said. She laughed sweetly. 'Surely that's the sort of talk that should remain confined to the markets and the warrens of the free zones.' She glanced at Lord Iron. 'You do not, of course, take this seriously.'

'We should at least hear the evidence,' Lord Iron said.

Lady Steel uttered a contemptuous snort and flicked the fingers of one hand towards Coffin. 'You place too much faith in this man,' she said. 'When I attempted to alert you about untoward happenings in the city, I was shoved aside with a sneer.'

'For which you lost no time in reprimanding me,' Iron said. 'You at least, Lady Steel, will want to hear of this, I'm sure. It confirms your own theories, does it not?'

Lady Steel, uncharacteristically, said nothing but remained rigid in her seat, her face set into an expression wholly derived from the qualities of her family metal.

Coffin coughed, his fist to his mouth, then resumed. 'Intelligence reports suggest that certain gullible members of the Metal have also become involved in this cult.'

'Do you have names?' Lady Gold asked.

Coffin shook his head. 'Regrettably, no. My informers spoke only of high-ranking individuals being associated with the cult. It revolves around an ancient goddess named Sekmet, whose worship derives from before the Reformation. As you are no doubt aware, my lady, the ancestors of your noble Clan were involved in it.'

Lady Gold made a careless gesture. 'It was millennia ago. I hope you're not suggesting that members of my Clan are involved in it *now*.'

'As yet, I do not know who is involved,' Coffin said.

'How reliable are your informers?' Lord Gold enquired. 'This is a very serious allegation.'

'Reliable enough,' Coffin answered. 'Naturally, I will continue to investigate the matter myself and find hard evidence. I would not expect any of you to act upon information from free-zone spies alone.'

'So what evidence have your "loose-lips" given you?' Lady Steel asked coldly.

'Simply that the cult exists. Meeting places change, and I have not yet been able to infiltrate the group. I'm sure it's no coincidence that when Silverskin employed an illusion to confuse my men he created an image of Sekmet. As you are aware, the Irregulars are drawn mainly from the ranks of the Foundrymen. Some of my men have told me of their suspicions that ancient practices have been revived. They are not of your calibre as people, so these things upset them. Superstition still lies close below the surface in the common man.'

'It seems to me,' Lord Iron said gravely, 'that this is merely another symptom of what ails our city. Stringent action must be taken. We need to rid our streets of these ridiculous rumours and fears. If indeed any foolish people are indulging in forbidden practices, they must be rooted out and rehabilitated, whether they are of common blood or not.'

'Surely you do not believe members of the Metal are involved, Prometheus,' Lady Copper said.

'It has been impressed upon me from more than one quarter,' Lord Iron said, casting a meaningful glance at Lady Steel, 'that I should be more open-minded. It grieves me even to contemplate that our people are in danger of sinking back to barbaric ways, but turning a blind eye is folly. We must not give this cult − if it exists − any credence by believing it to be based on anything but primitive delusion. But we should equally accept that some of our people might be seduced by it.'

'Indeed,' said Lord Gold. 'Karadur is in turmoil. People might be turning to such things out of fear.'

'Seeking certainty,' added Lady Copper.

'Yes,' said Lord Iron. 'We know from history that all religions and cults are based on the fear of what humanity does not understand. Our people are frightened by the upheaval in the city and in their ignorance turn to these ancient systems for relief. Callous individuals can take advantage of such a situation to gain control, power and perhaps even riches for themselves. I am sure this is what we are dealing with.'

'We are not dealing with it,' Lady Steel said laconically. 'We're merely talking about it. These are not times for debate but for decisive action.'

'We cannot act in ignorance,' Lord Iron said. 'Until we have names, dates, places, we can do nothing. It is up to Captain Coffin to supply the information we need.'

Lady Steel narrowed her eyes a little. 'We should rely more upon our own abilities and position. Perhaps the reins of power lie too heavily in your hands, Prometheus.'

Lord Iron sensed the collective intake of breath around the chamber. Everyone was looking at Lady Steel in surprise. But were any of those expressions feigned? He spoke smoothly. 'Every time we meet this subject seems to arise. You are ambitious for your Clan, my lady, and make no secret of your belief that the Council should be led by a Steel, undoubtedly yourself.'

'I do not deny it. The Council has too long been run by the cabal of Gold, Iron, Copper and Silver. There are many other Clans in Karadur, kept low by an outmoded tradition. The Upper Council should be expanded.' She turned in her seat to address others in the chamber. 'What of Clan Platinum, Mercury and Lead, to name but three? Those indulged with a seat on the Lesser Council are expected to feel privileged and grateful. Other Clans are not even represented in the Councils at all, but have to have their own little ineffective, voiceless committees . . .'

'That's enough,' said Lord Iron. 'The system has worked efficiently for millennia. The other Clans are given their chance to speak when we meet with the Lesser Council. It would be unwieldy and impractical to have everyone crammed into this chamber. The Lesser Council has as much a voice as it needs.'

'Are we really here to discuss this?' Lady Copper said. 'It is a different issue entirely to the pressing matters that assail us.'

'I don't think it is,' said Lady Steel resolutely.

'No one is denying the seniority and capability of your clan, Carinthia,' said Lord Iron. 'But may I remind you that I was elected to this position – by members of both greater and lesser Clans.'

'I know that,' said Lady Steel, 'but fresh issues have arisen since then, urgent issues.'

'Well, if the Metal considers me ill-equipped to deal with them, no doubt I shall be voted out of office at the next election,' Iron said.

Lady Steel made a sound of derision. 'In three years' time? I doubt we have that much left to us.'

Lord Iron smiled without humour. The truth was that he had the same fears himself, though he couldn't bear to admit it in front of Lady Steel. 'For the Jewel's sake, listen to yourself!' he said. 'Whatever problems we face at this moment, Karadur will endure forever.'

'I pray you are right,' Carinthia said.

Lord Iron waved a dismissive hand. 'Anyway, as Lady Copper pointed out, elections and leadership are not matters for discussion now.' He glanced at each of the Councillors in turn. 'May I suggest we all do some careful investigation of our own among our Clans, just to make sure there is no truth in Captain Coffin's suspicions?'

'Melodia and I will give it our attention immediately,' said Lord Gold, his wife nodding her head furiously beside him. 'Of all the Clans, we will be under the most suspicion, given our ancient heritage. I am most anxious to clear Clan Gold's name as soon as possible.'

'The same goes for my own Clan,' said Lord Iron. 'The Foundrymen are equally culpable in this respect.' He paused, then said, 'Are we in accord?'

The assembly muttered 'Aye' and began to rise from their seats.

'Continue your investigations, Captain,' Iron said to Coffin, 'and do not let the matter of Silverskin's capture be sidetracked by the issue of the cult. It may be a rumour forged deliberately in order to divert you from your task. Question people throughout Karadur. Leave no dark corner unexplored.'

Coffin bowed. 'It will be done, my lord.'

Chapter Seven

Domain of the Slug King

When Max and Rose reached Shriltasi they made their way directly to the Stone Grove.

'Slow down,' Rose said, as she fought her way through a tangle of dusty brambles behind Max. 'From what you've told me, Master Vane won't be going anywhere.'

Max did not reply. He intended to use the mirror to restore Menni, as Serenia had suggested, but something inside him insisted on urgency. He felt uneasy.

They passed through the tall hedges that surrounded the garden and found a group of Ashen waiting there. A couple were sitting on the ground, while three more were leaning on the statues. It appeared that they had been waiting for something. Max was alert at once. He looked immediately to where Menni's statue had stood – and he uttered an outraged cry. Although a host of pale green statues still populated the silent garden, Menni's was not amongst them.

Max leaped forward to the nearest Ashen and seized him by the arm. He shook him furiously. 'What have you done with him? Where's Menni?'

Another Ashen stepped forward, clearly a person of rank, denoted by the gold embroidery of curling dragons upon her tunic and her air of authority. With surprising strength, she peeled Max's fingers from the arm of her companion who dropped away, rubbing his bruises. 'We have done nothing with your friend,' said the high-ranking Ashen. 'Calm yourself, Sir Fox. We must speak at once. We have rather more of a problem than the disappearance of Master Vane on our hands.'

Max folded his arms belligerently. 'What problems?' he enquired in an icy tone. 'All I care about it what's happened to Menni.'

The Ashen had clustered into a defensive group opposite him. Their leader raised her hands in a conciliatory gesture. 'I will explain,' she said. 'I am Rowan, bow-mistress to King Jack.'

'I don't care who you are,' Max began. But Rose put a hand on his arm.

'Do you know what's happened to Master Vane?' she asked carefully.

Rowan nodded. 'To some degree. What concerns us more is the disappearance of Jack and Jenny.'

'What do you mean?' Max asked.

'The Porporrum are becoming ever bolder,' Rowan said. 'We can only assume they have a stronger force to lead them. Normally they fear this place, but only a few hours ago they led an incursion into our territory. Their objective was clearly the abduction of Jack, Jenny and Master Vane. We were taken by surprise. They succeeded.'

'Where have they taken them?' Max snapped.

'Presumably to the Thorn Hive, their own territory,' Rowan said.

'And have you done nothing to secure their release?'

'We took many casualties,' Rowan said coldly. 'We need to form a strategy. Nothing would be gained from blundering into Porporrum territory. They outnumber us and would have the advantage in any case. Foolish as it may seem to you, we were awaiting your return anxiously. We believed you would help us. Jack and Jenny have faith in you.'

Rose frowned. 'You said you thought the Porporrum were led by a stronger force. What did you mean by that?'

Rowan cocked her head upwards. 'Someone from up there,' she said. 'Everything is changing. You must use the power of the witch mark, Sir Fox, to bring the Ashen king and his sister back to us.'

'They may be dead already,' Max said.

Rowan closed her eyes and shook her head. 'I don't believe so. I can't believe so. Will you help us?'

Max considered. 'It seems I have little choice.'

'It will be a trap, of course,' Rose said.

Max glanced at her.

'Well, it's obvious. Who would kidnap Menni Vane, and why? To get at you, certainly. They'll be expecting you to go after him.'

'You have the advantage,' Rowan said. 'You are who you are, stronger than the Porporrum, for they are essentially primitive beings. At the very least, you need to discover the power behind them.'

'I will do what I can,' Max said, 'but will need your cooperation. You know Shriltasi better than I do. Some of your people must come with me.'

Rowan hesitated. 'You don't know what you're asking. But if any of us have to face the Thorn Hive, I will. I can ask no other.'

'Just you? What are you so afraid of?'

'The Porporrum have ever been responsible for the welfare of the creatures of this realm. They have an empathy with them. The creature that guards their territory is the most terrible – Gorpax, the slug king.'

'Slug king,' said Max, smiling. 'What kind of beast is that? Couldn't it be vanquished with a barrel of salt?'

'Max!' said Rose reprovingly.

'Well,' Max replied. 'It sounds absurd.'

'"Absurd" is one word,' said Rowan, '"hideous" another, and "fierce", and "indestructible".'

'No ordinary slug, then,' Max said. 'Is that the worst foe we'll have to face?'

'Yes,' said Rowan stonily. 'And when you do face it, you'll see why there could be none worse.'

Rowan led the way into the humid forest of Shriltasi. Rose had been determined to accompany them and Max had not tried to dissuade her. He'd already learned how helpful she could be in a crisis, although some suspicious part of him couldn't help thinking she might be involved in a greater conspiracy. She seemed genuine and sincere, but she was still Lord Iron's daughter, a great lady of the Metal. Serenia Silverskin had an interest in her and clearly respected her. If anything, Rose seemed too good to be true and that was what informed Max's fears about her. He felt torn, but resolved to go along with her for now, while keeping his senses vigilant and alert.

Rowan took them into an area where the foliage was very dense, its leaves covered in a waxy dust. A menacing atmosphere pervaded everything. Sound was muted, but Max could perceive almost inaudible rustlings in the undergrowth around them. Were the Porporrum already near them, creeping along unseen, waiting to spring an ambush? The wan, diffuse light of Shriltasi became ever dimmer. The air smelled musty like old hay, very similar to how the graffy run had smelled. Max's body was tense, waiting for a thousand small pricklings: Porporrum darts cast from the shadows.

Rowan signalled for them to stop moving. She stood motionless, stooped, as if listening intently. The forest seemed to breathe around them, exhaling a sour breath.

'Are we being watched?' Max murmured to the Ashen.

She glanced back at him. 'Undoubtedly. But I'm not sure by what. Creatures other than the Porporrum inhabit these groves. They will be curious about us.'

'Don't you ever venture here?' Rose asked.

'Lines were drawn,' Rowan answered shortly. 'We respect them. Once the Porporrum did, also.' She began to creep forward once more.

Max noticed that the branches around them were woven together now in some places, again similar to what he'd seen in the graffy run. They were venturing through an untidy tunnel of dusty foliage.

Rose gasped and her companions turned round. 'A face,' she hissed, pointing. 'There. It's gone now.'

'Keep moving,' said Rowan.

After some minutes the Ashen came to a halt. They had come to the edge of a clearing, surrounded by lofty grey-trunked trees. At the centre of the clearing was a tumble of immense rocks, as if a giant had dropped them there. The rocks were covered in a network of clinging vines whose thick stems adhered firmly to the stone. Rowan hissed through her teeth.

'What?' Max whispered. 'Are we there?'

The Ashen shook her head, touched Max's shoulder and gestured wordlessly at the rocks. With Rose pushing up alongside him to see,

Max peered in the direction Rowan pointed. He could see something moving feebly in the net of vines, a pale green limb, a swatch of auburn hair. 'It's Jenny Ash,' he murmured. 'Can you see her, Rose? They've imprisoned her there.' He addressed the Ashen. 'She seems to be alone. Are we expected, do you think?'

Rowan again shook her head, but uncertainly. 'Impossible to tell. I chose to take this route because it's not the direct path to the Thorn Hive. But perhaps they anticipated our movements.' She took her bow from her shoulder, an arrow from her quiver. 'Whatever the risk, we must free her quickly. The vines are eating into her body.'

Max drew in his breath. 'There doesn't seem to be anyone around. If you cover me, I'll get over there.'

Rowan nodded. 'It will be done.'

Rose made to accompany Max, but he stopped her with a gesture of one hand. 'You wait here. We have to see if this is a trap. We can't risk both of us being ambushed.'

'I have no doubt we're expected,' Rose said dryly. 'Take care.'

Max paused for a few moments at the edge of the clearing, then moved forward cautiously, glancing around him. The forest was silent – perhaps too silent. Nothing moved. It was as if the great motionless canopy above absorbed every noise. Even his own footfalls were soundless against the short turf.

When he was halfway to the rocks, Jenny saw him. She shook her head in agitation, uttered a strange, whistling hiss. Max put a finger to his lips but Jenny seemed delirious. He could not silence her. As he approached, he could see that her clothes were torn, her limbs scratched, oozing strange green ichor. The tenacious vines were pressing hard against her body. A mesh of thin pale rootlets burrowed into her flesh. Jenny threshed within her bonds, writhing and hissing, less human than Max had ever seen her. Even her face seemed animal, her lips drawn back from sharp milky-green teeth, her eyes mere glittering black slits in her face. The moment was unreal. He found himself wondering why he wanted to free her. She was alien to him, an impossible contradiction of all he'd ever known. An instinctive revulsion shivered through him. He realized she was speaking a word – the name she called him – Fox – the last consonant drawn out into a sibilant wheeze.

Max had grabbed hold of one of the vines to begin climbing the rocks when Jenny uttered a louder cry. A sharp burning pain went through his thigh. He looked round and saw that a group of Porporrum had crept from the forest around him, their gargoyle faces set into frozen snarls. They were small creatures, but there were a lot of them, and they were fully armed with primitive weapons: blowpipes, clubs and knives. At once Max scrambled up the rock face, coming to a halt on the ledge where Jenny was entwined.

'Use *barishi*, Jenny!' he cried. 'Protect yourself.'

Jenny moaned, her head rolling from side to side. 'I have none,' she whispered hoarsely, through lips that it appeared she had bitten through with pain. 'This ground is cursed. *Barishi* cannot flow well here. Powerless . . . hurt . . .' Her words degraded into an agonised burble.

Max glanced across the clearing and saw Rowan's anxious face peering back at him from the narrow gap in the foliage. As yet, the Porporrum didn't appear to have noticed her. But if she fired an arrow they'd be upon her.

The little people, uttering triumphant squeals and chittering cries, began to clamber up the rock. Max drew his sword. He had the advantage of position, but already a rain of small darts was falling upon him. They pricked his scalp, his face. If one took him in the eye, he'd be defenceless.

He heard a screeching roar, looked across the clearing and saw Rose run forward recklessly, both of her swords brandished. At the same time, Rowan released an arrow. The Porporrom froze in surprise for a moment. Then most of them dropped off the rock and scampered over to where Rose stood waiting for them. Using this brief respite, Max drew his dagger and began hacking at the vines around Jenny. He tore the rootlets from her flesh, conjuring a hundred small wounds.

'Gorpax will devour me,' Jenny murmured, head hanging. 'I am their sacrifice. Poor Jack . . .' She seemed on the verge of unconsciousness.

'Hold on,' Max urged her. 'Stay awake, Jenny. Help me help you.'

Feebly, Jenny pulled at the bonds around her. The vines were beginning to snap, releasing her, but their grip was relentless. This would not be a quick job. Max sawed at the fibrous stalks, focusing himself on the task. A

Porporrum leaped onto the rock and dived at Max's leg. He paused to slash at it with the dagger. The creature fell away, whimpering, bouncing off the rock onto a group of outraged comrades below. One of Jenny's arms was free completely now. She reached out with it, brushed trembling fingers against Max's face. He ducked away. 'Help me, will you?'

Jenny pulled at the vines, shaking her head as if to clear it. More Porporrum had reached the rock. Max was forced to abandon his task in order to fend them off with his sword. The creatures really were quite stupid. They were little match for him. He could see Rose battling valiantly in the clearing below, Rowan firing arrows from the edge of the forest. But more Porporrum were scuttling through the trees. He needed to free Jenny quickly and make an escape.

Then, strangely, the Porporrum began to retreat. They did not appear frightened or defeated. With dread, Max realized that reinforcements must be nearby.

He heard it before he saw it: a slapping, sucking sound. It was accompanied by a repellent sighing and shrilling that sounded somehow wet. The trees were cracking, buckling to the left of the clearing. Something immense was approaching swiftly.

'Gorpax,' said Jenny, her voice dull with despair.

The trees peeled to the side and what at first seemed to be a gigantic grey-green rock appeared between them. Then it opened its fleshy maw and Max realized he was looking at an immense gastropod. The toothless mouth dripped slime and its glistening body emitted an overpowering acrid stench, which bought an involuntary flood of mucus into Max's mouth. He could taste gall, bitterness. He retched uncontrollably.

'The slug king,' Jenny said. 'Come to devour us.' She had freed both her arms and now hugged Max to her, her face buried against his shoulder.

'Jenny Ash, have courage,' he said, pulling away. 'Free your legs. Quick as you can.'

'No point,' Jenny said. 'Gorpax is here.'

'And I am the one to save you, remember?' Max said. 'Where's your faith?'

The shadow of Gorpax hung over them now and a foul, glutinous rain of slime fell upon them. The creature wheezed and then shuddered abruptly. Max saw one of Rowan's arrows sticking out from its undulating pale underbelly. Gorpax flexed its muscular body and the arrow popped out again, leaving no wound. Max could understand why the Ashen feared this creature.

Jenny had finally clawed free of her bonds and Max grabbed her hand. He dragged her to the edge of the ledge and cried, 'Jump!' But before they could do so, darkness descended. The great body of the slug king fell down upon them.

It was like being drowned in rotten flesh. Max breathed in sticky tendrils of the stuff, taking it into his lungs and throat. It was the most bitter taste imaginable. The heavy bulk of Gorpax pushed against his bones. He could feel his ribs cracking. His whole body would be crushed, then absorbed into this loathsome mass. Vomit rose in his throat but he could not expel it. It burned there until he somehow managed to swallow it. Yet he did not feel afraid. His mind was detached, calm.

Use the witch mark . . .

Feel it there, he told himself. *Feel its power in this cursed place. Feel its fire. It burns into you, eats into you. It is stronger than this foul horror. Silver fire. If you have to die, take this abomination with you.*

A great heat started up in his chest. He could not breathe, his lungs were full of glutinous liquid, yet strength coursed through him. He could gather it, push it out. He couldn't scream, but his whole head reverberated with a silent cry. Through sheer force of will, he summoned the power of the silver heart to scour the slug king from him.

At once, Gorpax's bulk shook to a great, trembling cry. It reared up, dragging Max and the senseless Jenny with it in a caul of malodorous slime. In moments, Max, heavier than the Ashen, fell free, back onto the rock. He retched, coughed out a gout of foulness, then sucked in a lungful of air. His chest felt as if it was about to explode, but he had no time to think, only to act. Jenny was hanging in the slime above him. He grabbed hold of her arms and pulled her free. Almost blind, he leaped off the rock.

An eternity passed. He fell into a void. Then his body hit the ground, jarred by an immense shock. He felt hands upon him, pulling him, dragging him. Spokes of silver light wheeled before his eyes. His flesh was on fire.

Afterwards, Max had little recollection of the flight back to Asholm. He came to his senses on a bed of soft golden leaves that enfolded his body in a rustling blanket. The light was a dim golden emerald and the gentle sound of crystal wind-chimes made music around him. Rowan was leaning over him, a dripping sponge of damp dark moss in her hand. When she realized he was conscious, she carefully dabbed his face with the moss, which released a pungent herby aroma. He swallowed and found his throat was raw.

'Do not try to speak yet,' Rowan said.

Max blinked, shook his head. 'Rose . . . Jenny . . .' he croaked.

'They are safe,' Rowan answered. 'Lady Rose has a few dart pinpricks and shallow knife wounds, but few of the Porporrum got that near to her. She fights like a gibboldess.'

Max nodded painfully. He felt as if he'd survived a strangling. A sharp burning in his chest prompted him to rub the flesh there. His fingers encountered metal. Astonished, he raised his head and saw that the mark over his heart had changed. It was now a hard silvery disc, embedded in his body.

Rowan gently pushed him back down to his pillow of leaves. 'Yes, the witch mark is fully active now. It saved you. When the slug king enveloped you, Lady Rose and I thought you were lost, but then the silver fire came and Gorpax released you. The fire hurt it, and it retreated. We realized what had happened once you jumped down to us. The heart was glowing still. We were afraid to look upon it.'

'We cannot deny the truth now, Max.' Rose's voice. He saw her standing just behind Rowan. She was dressed in a long gauzy gown of Ashen silk, decorated with intricate patterns of leaves.

Max merely stared at her. He felt he had no strength. He was useless. Jack could heal him a little, but Jack was not here, and Jenny was injured.

Rowan smiled, which at first Max thought was rather inappropriate. 'I have very good news,' she said. 'You will find your strength again.' She clicked her fingers and a small Ashen girl glided forward, carrying a box of

woven twigs in her hands. 'Behold,' said Rowan. She gestured for the girl
to open the box.

Max raised himself slowly onto his elbows and peered into the proffered
container. 'The ring!' he said, and looked up at Rose. 'The owl ring.' It
lay in a nest of soft green cloth.

Rose looked into the box. 'Where did you find it, Mistress Rowan?'

'In the half-world,' she said, 'where the waters run.'

'The sewers of Karadur?' Max asked.

Rowan nodded. 'Yes. Our trackers keep a thorough watch of the secret
paths, seeking to deter anyone who might find the entrance to Shriltasi.
They found this ring in the waters of one of the great canals. Whoever
took it from you, Sir Fox, surely lost it there.'

'A fortunate coincidence,' said Max, with some scepticism.

'It is indeed,' Rowan replied, apparently oblivious of any irony. 'Take
it and awaken it. The talons of the owl will assuage your pain, give you
strength.'

Max took the ring from its box and its bearer glided backwards, disappearing into the shadows of the chamber once more. 'When I first awakened
the owl, the parts of the ring were separated. Their union somehow invoked
the totem creature.' He held the ring up, turned it in his hand.

'You can awaken it,' Rowan said. 'Use the spellstone Jenny gave you.
The stone is attuned to the owl. This occurred when its parts were first
united in the presence of the stone. Merely put your intention into the
symbol on the stone and direct it towards the ring. It will activate the
required frequency of *barishi*.'

Max held the stone and the ring before his face. At first he thought he
didn't have the stamina or clear-headedness even to try and accomplish what
Rowan suggested. But the moment he directed the merest hint of intention
towards the artefacts, he felt them grow slightly warm in his grip. He could
feel the potential of *barishi* pulsing around him. It was in him now, part of
him, as easy to manipulate as the muscles of his own body.

'Max,' Rose breathed softly

He did not look at her, feeling the intensity of power building up between
his hands. The ring glowed, but not with a radiance he could perceive with

his physical eyes. He sensed it there, and perhaps Rose did too. In his head, he heard a distant cry: that of a bird of prey. He sensed movement in the air around him, like the beating of wings. The beats were slow, measured, but with each one, something manifested more strongly before him. He sensed a strange ether steaming out of the ring. Gradually, the shadowy shape of the owl took on form above the artefact. He could see the wings now, flashing shards of copper. Their movement was a scintillating blur.

'By the great Jewel!' Rose said, louder this time. He sensed her take a step backwards in surprise. In fact, he was quite aware of many of her thoughts: surprise, a little fear, wonder.

The owl had manifested fully now and alighted on the leafy covering over his chest. 'Give me your strength,' Max said – and, with a precise, delicate movement, the owl extended one barbed foot and placed the wicked claws gently upon the disc over his heart. At once, Max was suffused with an unbearable heat. His body arched. He cried out. The owl had to beat her wings to keep her balance. The silver heart flexed in his flesh, as if fighting the influence of the owl's talons. Then, abruptly, the heat turned to soothing coolness; waves of energy pulsed through him.

Max lay gasping upon his bed, feeling as if he'd just swum across an endless ocean. His limbs tingled as after some great exertion, and his breath came hard. But he could not deny the surge of energy that was still coursing through him. He laughed aloud.

Rose came forward, eyeing the owl warily. 'Max, are you all right?'

Max nodded. He put out a hand to the owl, who was now regarding him with her surprised round stare, wings folded along her back. She allowed him to run his fingers over the beautifully worked feathers, then hopped to the side of him so he could sit up.

When Max looked at Rose, he saw she had tears in her eyes. Her fingers were pressed to her lips. 'I have never seen anything . . .' She broke off, shaking her head.

'This is the War Owl of Clan Copper,' Max said. 'One of the lost icons.'

'It is the most incredible thing,' Rose said, pulling a rueful face to indicate how inadequate her words seemed to her.

Max got out of bed and realized he was dressed in one of the Ashen robes. He could feel every shred of its delicate fibres against his skin. It was as if the garment caressed him. The owl lifted from the bed and landed lightly upon Max's shoulder. It was incredible how little she weighed. Each part of her must have been so intricately crafted, from the thinnest sheets of metal. Yet she was strong too. Perhaps a strange alloy had been used in her construction. 'I want to see Jenny,' Max said. 'Perhaps the owl can help her too.'

Rowan smiled. 'She does not need its touch. Our own people have worked upon her. She is just a little tired, but completely healed. I will take you to her.'

Rowan led Max and Rose to Jenny's rooms. Far from the grand throne chamber where Max had first conversed with Jenny and her brother, her own apartments were modest and homely. She sat propped up on silken pillows in a bed of leaves. Golden branches arched over her head and shimmering transparent curtains of pale green fabric hung down from them, held back against the walls. A single servant was in attendance. There were dark viridian shadows above Jenny's cheeks, and her face was drawn, but her eyes were still bright. She did not raise herself from her pillows as Max and Rose approached her bed, but smiled widely and held out a hand. Max took it.

'Sir Fox, you are my gallant hero,' she said. 'I am most grateful. And you have your owl back.'

'She is not mine, exactly,' Max said. The owl lifted from his shoulder and flew up to the branches of the canopy over Jenny's bed.

'Sit down,' Jenny said, patting the leafy coverlet beside her. She looked at Rose. 'Both of you.'

She did not relinquish Max's hand, but squeezed it with her narrow fingers. Her skin felt dry and hot. 'The owl is yours,' she said. 'The *barishi* within you gives her life. She is loyal to you, for you are the one she knew would come, as the Ashen have known. Your personal *barishi* united the three parts of the owl into one. Aeons ago, the Lords of the Metal divided her into pieces. Now she is whole and will serve you as long as your purpose is pure.'

Max smiled wryly. 'I have never been called pure before.' He returned the pressure upon Jenny's hand. 'Tell me, Jenny, where is Menni? What happened? What of your brother?'

Jenny turned her head away, troubled. 'The Porporrum came – a horde. They were driven creatures, far more organized than we would normally expect of them. It happened very soon after you left us. Jack and I were in the Stone Grove. We heard a commotion as our guards noticed the presence of intruders and tried to repel them, but they were outnumbered. Many were injured in the struggle and three died. The Porporrum came straight for us, fearless as gibbolds. They didn't even look at the other stone-forms in the garden. They cast about us nets fashioned from the stems of a plant that hampers the flow of *barishi*. We could not fight back. We were knocked senseless. The next thing I knew I was on that terrible rock and a crowd of Porporrum were dancing around me, chanting the name of Gorpax. That's when I knew they intended to sacrifice me to him. I was in despair. I couldn't feel Jack's presence in my mind, but that was probably because of the ground I was on. I hope so, at least.' She sighed. 'They called to the vines to bind me and left me alone. I have never experienced anything so terrible. I could feel the vines crawling up me, hooking roots into my flesh. Perhaps the Porporrum intended to break down my body, make me more digestible for their hideous slug king.' She closed her eyes briefly. 'Then you were there, and I felt the light come back to me. You were the most beautiful creature I'd ever seen. I'll not forget it.'

Max felt Rose shift uneasily on the bed behind him. 'Menni,' he prompted gently.

Jenny shook her head, her face screwed up with grief. 'I don't know where your friend is, nor Jack. I only pray my brother is more use to them alive than dead, and that your friend hasn't been broken into pieces. You must find them, Sir Fox. You're the only hope they have. If Jack is dead, I have to know. Whether he lives or not, bring him back to me, Fox. Bring him back.' Tears glittered on her cheeks and her slim body shuddered beneath the coverlet.

Max could feel her pain like a physical force beating against him. He fought to shield himself from it before it swamped him. 'Who leads the

Porporrum now, Jenny? Do you know? Rowan thinks that someone from Karadur is influencing them.'

'I don't know,' she said. 'I saw no one but the Porporrum. But someone is leading them. They have never dared to infiltrate our territory before.'

'What of renegade Ashen? Last time we spoke, you suggested to me that not all of your people fled Ash Haven with you.'

'It's possible, I suppose,' she answered. 'But I don't feel that's the explanation. It's a darker force than that, and very powerful. Few things can sever the link I have with Jack or conceal him from me.'

'He could be dead,' Rose said, perhaps a little too harshly.

'If that were the case, I believe his spirit would come to me. But how can I tell? If this unknown force is so powerful, it could trap his essence as easily as his body.'

'Do you think Jack and Menni might be in the Thorn Hive?' Max asked.

'It would be a good place to start looking.'

'But difficult,' said Rose.

'Not any more,' Max said, placing a hand over his heart.

Rose raised an eyebrow. 'I feel you should guard against overconfidence. These arcane skills you have acquired are still fairly untested, and we don't know yet what we're up against.'

'The owl is yours to command,' Jenny said. 'She will obey your will. She is a powerful weapon.'

Max released Jenny's hand and stood up. 'I shall leave at once.' He glanced at Rose. 'You do not have to accompany me.'

'No, I don't,' Rose said, also rising from the bed. 'But I intend to.'

'And I too,' Rowan said. 'I go for my lord.'

Max raised his left hand, where the owl ring reposed on his second finger. At his unspoken command, the owl lifted from her perch above the bed and flew down towards him, changing into smoky ether as she did so. But this essence did not flow back into the ring, as Max expected, but directly into the spellstone at his neck.

'It seems you have become quite an adept,' Rose said.

'I told you,' Jenny said quietly. 'She is with you always now.'

Book Three

The Value of Antiques

Chapter One

The Thorn Hive

Clovis Pewter stood before his cult statue, his fists clenched tight at his sides. He felt breathless, almost light-headed. Control was slipping through his fingers like sand. There were too many hidden factors. He shouldn't have listened to Lady Sekmet, his priestess. What had they done?

She had sent a messenger to him the day before, a nondescript free-zone ruffian, who had carried a note demanding a meeting, in a neutral area, deep within the free zones. Pewter had never met with Lady Sekmet in Karadur. He had wondered whether he'd get to see her face this time. She could hardly wear the mask of a gibboldess in the city, not even in the free zones where unusual appearances were common.

The meeting had taken place in the workshop of a clockmaker, a room deep in shadow annexed to the cramped shop where a multitude of timepieces filled the air with the sound of life ticking away, moment by moment. Pewter had had no idea whether the Lady knew the clockmaker or not. The old man had simply shown him into the curtained room behind the shop as soon as he arrived. Pewter's heart had beat fast as he'd tried to focus his eyes in the gloom. Large clocks had held sway there, stern sentinels of time's passing. Lady Sekmet had been veiled like a corpse, swathes of thin creamy gauze wrapped around her face and upper body. There had been no hint of her features, not even the glint of an eye.

'I do you the honour of revealing my identity,' Pewter had said, without greeting. 'Lady, please extend me the same courtesy.'

She had made no move, as motionless as the shrouded body she resembled, propped up in a chair. Then a sound had come from her, a simple exhalation. 'Sit down,' she'd said, her voice strained, as if she sought to disguise it.

I must know her, Pewter had thought, and his mind had chased evanescent memories, seeking clues from the nuance of her speech, the shape she made in space and time, her movements. But though a vague familiarity had tugged at his mind, he could not pin it down. It was like trying to remember a song when only one nagging phrase of the tune repeats itself endlessly in the mind's ear. He'd sat down anyway, intrigued and bemused. 'Why am I here?'

The lady had remained upright and motionless, like an animated doll in her chair. 'We must free ourselves from Jack Ash,' she'd said, plainly and simply.

Pewter had expected small talk, a build up to the point of the meeting. He was unprepared. He laughed. 'Why?'

There had been a short pause, then she had murmured, 'He has a hold over you. It is dangerous. It is folly. We put ourselves in jeopardy at his hands. He will betray us.'

Pewter had frowned. 'I can't see that. He has given us so much. He didn't have to.'

'Gives, but holds back,' the lady had whispered. 'He knows more than he says about the sacred artefacts. He plays with us. I feel this in my blood.' She had bowed her head. 'Sekmet has taught me this much.'

Pewter had felt uncomfortable then. It was as if, merely by mentioning the goddess's name, she had been invoked into the room. This woman before him had taken on the goddess's mantle. In ritual, she *was* Sekmet. He had shifted nervously in his seat. 'You have spoken plainly so far. Please go on. What do you think we should do?'

'Jack Ash must be forced to reveal the whereabouts of the artefacts to us. I am quite sure he has several more of them in his possession. He thinks he is clever, far more so than we are, but he is wrong. We must use the force of the goddess to aid us. Are you in accord with me?'

Now Pewter wondered whether he had been glamorized by Lady Sekmet in the same way that Jack Ash was able to glamorize him. Her words had seemed profound, so true. She had been an icon of power herself in that tiny room: a dark, smouldering power. It had felt as if the goddess herself had spoken to him. How could he deny her desires? And yet he still found it difficult to relinquish entirely his awe and admiration of the Ashen king. It hadn't felt right, what she'd told him to do, but he'd gone along with it regardless, all the while fighting unease.

Lady Sekmet had dominion over the strange Porporrum: Pewter couldn't stand being near them. Really, she had not needed him at all, for it had been she who'd ordered the little people to invade the Ashen territory and kidnap Jack and Jenny. Pewter and the lady had watched from a safe distance, she using magnifying eyeglasses that occasionally she would allow her companion to look through. Pewter had pointed out the statue of Silverskin's erstwhile comrade, Menevek Vane. What was a statue of him doing in this place? The Porporrum had provided an answer. Lady Sekmet, sensing another tool at her disposal, had ordered the Porporrum to take the statue as well. They had resisted fiercely at first, in sheer terror, until the lady had told them the statue was that of a consort of Sekmet herself, stolen by the Ashen, deprived of its proper worship and position. Eventually they had caved in to this dubious persuasion.

All had gone according to plan, so Pewter could not understand why he felt so anxious and uneasy now. Jack Ash and his sister were in bonds, perhaps soon to die, but even if they lived they would be no threat. The native folk of Shriltasi were drawn in increasing numbers to the worship of Sekmet, seemingly willing to accept Pewter and the Lady as their spiritual leaders. If anything, it all seemed too easy. What was the hidden factor?

But you know already, a voice seemed to whisper in his ear. *It is Max Silverskin. You have danced at the edge of his world, but now you have stepped through the veil and walked right into it. He is dangerous and you poke at him with a sharp stick. One day, he will retaliate.*

Pewter shuddered. It had taken all his nerve to enter the Stone Grove and strike Max Silverskin senseless in order to retrieve the ring. Jack Ash had told him what to do. He was clearly no ally of Silverskin's, and yet . . . And yet what? The ring was lost again, and Pewter had barely escaped with his skin in the sewers. Coffin was on to him, he was sure. Tomorrow, Lady Sekmet had assured him, all would be put right. The artefacts would be in their hands. They would vanquish their enemies. He wished he could have her confidence.

Max, Rose and Rowan avoided the glade of the slug king, creeping furtively through the hissing forest towards the Porporrum settlement. Occasionally, Max would smell a faint bitter scent in the air that made his throat convulse in recollection. The slug king might have slithered through these ancient trees at some point but had left nothing more than its scent behind. The forest was alive with twitterings and rustlings but whatever moved around them remained unseen. Once or twice, Rose drew in her breath and told the others she'd seen faces in the foliage, but Rowan insisted they press on. They had equipped themselves with ropes and grapples from Asholm. Rowan had already explained they might have some climbing to do.

A great booming sound pulsed through the branches ahead of them, as if an alarm horn had been blown. Rowan said this was not so. The horns of the hive had a spiritual significance, which the Porporrum kept to themselves. Presently another sound insinuated itself through the thick foliage: a buzzing, rumbling rhythm, as of a host of gigantic insects.

'That is the music of the hive,' Rowan whispered. 'The Porporrum talking together.'

'How many live there?' Max asked.

Rowan shrugged. 'Legion,' she said.

'And the delightful slug king?' Max said. 'Can we expect another encounter with His Majesty?'

'After periods of activity Gorpax must rest,' Rowan said.

'Still, the word you used to describe the Porporrum numbers was "legion" . . .'

Rowan flashed a smile at Max. 'But we have an advantage.'

Max frowned at her.

'The owl. She has the sight. She will show us the safest routes.' Rowan squatted down and pointed through the leaves. 'Look through here. You will see it.'

Rose and Max hunched forward. Through gaps in the foliage they saw an incredible construction, rearing up in a wide clearing. 'That's the Hive?' Rose murmured.

Rowan nodded. 'Yes.'

It was conical in shape, rising in gallery upon gallery of woven thorns until its apex merged with the forest canopy overhead. The thorns were ash-coloured, spiked and vicious, yet it was clear the Hive was not constructed of dead branches. It was a living organism, blooming with small curled leaves and delicate purple and white roses. It was an extraordinary patchwork of vibrant colour against the softer greens, pale browns and greys of the forest.

There was a main entrance just above ground level, reached by a wide ladder fashioned of polished branches tied together with hairy vines. Further up were small round entrances, where birds flew in and out. Porporrum were busy in the clearing where a stream had been dammed to create a pool of clear water and certain crops were husbanded. Max and his companions observed the Porporrum's activities for a while. 'I can't see us being able to enter the place without being seen,' Rose said.

'Send in the owl,' Rowan suggested. 'Tell her to find your friend and Jack, if they are within.'

It was easy now, almost second nature, for Max to summon the owl. She seemed to know there was a need for secrecy, for her manifestation was silent and swift. She hung before him in the cramped confines of their hiding place, her wide eyes burning with a strange intelligence. In his mind Max formed his desires, which the owl appeared to intuit at once. She slipped through a hole in the foliage and swept on soundless wings up to the apex of the Hive. Wan light coming down through the forest canopy conjured gleams in her metallic feathers. She was a marvel. *What have we come to*, Max thought, *that we deny such creations as this? What was Karadur like when* barishi *was used there? What wonders were constructed in the workshops of the clans? Could that time ever come again?* Emotion surged through him. Did he have the chance to try and make that happen?

After some minutes the owl returned to them. Without waiting for a command from Max, she settled upon his shoulder and directed a beam of light from her eyes onto the packed dirt beneath them. The owl showed them moving pictures of her journey through the Hive. Many kinds of birds roosted in the upper storeys, so her presence was not noticed, despite her rather unusual appearance. She had kept to the shadows, flitting from hidden perch to hidden perch. The Hive was a warren of cramped passages and chambers where strange small beings Max had not glimpsed before were intent upon their daily business. Similar to the follets who served the Ashen, these were imp-like creatures, so slender they seemed to have been fashioned from bundles of twigs.

'They are spriggans,' Rowan explained. 'Lesser forest creatures used as servants by the Porporrum.'

Some of the spriggans farmed large insects from which they extracted a milky substance, presumably a foodstuff of some kind. Others wove cloth in darkened rooms, their twiggy hands flying over primitive looms. The owl flew towards what seemed to be the centre of the Hive, to a chamber clearly above ground level. It was larger than any other the owl had shown them, a circular vaulted room, surrounded by pillars fashioned from the trunks of trees and carved with curling symbols. In the centre of the room was a raised dais upon which stood what appeared to be some kind of religious statue. Pale light from a hole at the apex of the Hive shone down upon it. It was only when the owl flew in closer that Max caught his breath. The statue was Menni. He had been draped with necklaces and ruffs of woven grasses and vines, his body hung with ropes of flowers. The marble he had become glistened, as if it had been rubbed with oil.

'What is this?' Max murmured, almost overcome with relief that Menni was still intact.

'Strange,' Rowan replied, shaking her head. 'Why would they venerate your friend in this way?'

'Are you sure it's veneration?' Rose whispered.

'Oh yes, the centre of the Hive is their temple.'

'What do they normally worship? The slug king?'

Again, Rowan shook her head. 'No, they worship no living thing, nor any gods. In this place, they celebrate the force of *barishi* itself and petition its avatars, certain wood spirits. To my knowledge, they have never used physical representations in their practices before.' She looked up at Max and Rose. 'Again, this speaks of outside influences.'

'At least they haven't damaged him,' Max said.

The owl had come to the end of her journey now and ceased to project the image.

'She found your friend, but not Jack Ash,' Rowan said, with disappointment. 'I dare not think what this means.'

'We'll take one thing at a time,' Max said. 'How do you propose we enter the Hive?'

'I think we should climb up it and enter through the open crown,' Rowan replied. 'Then we can drop directly into the temple.'

Rose uttered a derisive snort. 'How do we do that, exactly? We can't just squirm out of here and saunter across the glade. There are dozens of Porporrum out there.'

'We need a diversion, of course,' Rowan said. 'It won't be that difficult. Few Porporrum in the Hive will be awake, and most of the rest of them will be out foraging in the forest. Once we're inside their domain, we should be fairly safe for a time. The spriggans won't pay attention to us. They'll only make a fuss if approached directly or threatened.'

'No problem,' said Max. He reached up and stroked the owl's shining breast. 'Well, my lady, can you wreak a little havoc out there for us?'

The owl regarded him inscrutably for a moment, as if considering his words, then lifted from his shoulder and flew out into the glade once more.

'We'll have to act quickly,' Rowan said, moving forward.

The owl was hovering about twenty feet above the ground and had begun to emit piercing shrieks. All the Porporrum ceased their activities and looked up at her. But if Max and the others emerged from their hiding place now the Porporrum would be sure to notice.

'That is not much of a diversion,' Rose said.

Max glanced at her irritably. 'Wait,' he said.

The owl continued to call out and presently other winged shapes emerged from the forest around her. A host of owls.

'Feather sisters,' Rowan said in wonder. 'She has summoned them.'

The Porporrum had now begun to jump up and down, gesturing above them. The owls were a soft, whispering mass overhead. At another shriek from the War Owl, they attacked.

'Now,' Rowan urged.

While the Porporrum fought the owls, chittering and gibbering in rage, Rowan led Max and Rose round the edge of the glade towards the rear of the Hive. Once in its shadow, they began to climb. The tightly woven thorn-wall exuded a strange moist heat and seemed to writhe beneath them. The familiar scent of musty hay rose around them, blended with the sweet scent of roses. They used the great curved thorns as handholds and footholds, hauling themselves upwards. The living branches, heavy with swags of roses, created a camouflage around them, even though the smaller, younger thorns growing there snatched at their clothes and hair. Eventually, with the distant sound of the Porporrum's battle with the owls still echoing below them, they reached the summit. The canopy was very close overhead. Max felt he could reach up through the dusty leaves and touch the false sky of Shriltasi.

Now they fastened the grappling hooks to the apex of the hive and peered down into the gloom of the temple below. 'Doesn't seem to be anyone about,' Rose whispered.

'There may be attendants,' Rowan said. 'We'll have to deal with that situation if and when it arises.' She dropped a silken Ashen rope down into the darkness and smiled at Max. 'Ready, Sir Fox?'

Max positioned himself on the edge of the hole, his legs dangling inside. 'Completely,' he said and, grabbing hold of his rope, dropped into the Hive.

They each landed in silence, while around them the temple buzzed as if constructed of a mass of bees. Max was reminded of the episode in the graffy run. Did the Porporrum keep bees in here? The air was thick with the scent of a bitter-sweet incense: pine and honey.

Max went directly to Menni and began to strip off the garlands that covered him.

'No time for that,' Rowan said. 'Let's get him out of here. We'll have to lift him out through the roof.'

'I could use the spellstone to shrink him,' Max said. 'Then I could carry him in my pocket.'

'The spell won't work against this stone,' Rowan said. 'Believe me, we've tried it. It is immune to the effects of *barishi*.' She ran forward with Rose and the pair of them began attaching ropes to Menni's limbs. Then Rowan swarmed back up to the hole above and urged Max and Rose to throw the ropes around Menni up to her.

'We'll never manage this,' Rose murmured to Max. 'He'll be too heavy.'

Max gave her a caustic glance. 'The Ashen are stronger than they look.'

'I bet they are!'

Max ignored this remark and tossed a rope up to Rowan. She missed it and the rope fell back onto Max's head. Rose smirked. He had to throw again and this time Rowan caught it. Rose threw another rope upwards.

Eventually, Rowan had the six ropes attached to Menni in her hand. Max began to climb out and Rose stood with her hand upon one of Menni's arms, ready to guide him once the others started to lift him – if they had the strength. Max reckoned Rose would be proved right about the weight. It would need the three of them to get Menni to the top.

Max and Rowan began to haul on the ropes. Max felt Menni shift. They could do it. He was sure they could.

Then Rose uttered a cry of alarm. Max glanced over the edge of the hole. It was difficult to see what was going on but he heard activity. He glanced at Rowan. 'Porporrum!'

Without a word, Rowan dropped Menni's ropes and launched herself over the side of the hole, Max following. Once in the temple, they saw Rose surrounded by a half-dozen or so Porporrum, all wearing flapping robes and tall conical headdresses adorned with crowns of thorns. They carried long curling knives, which they brandished in the air before them.

'They are shamans,' Rowan said, running forward. 'Not fighters. We'll make short work of these.'

The noise these non-fighters were making, however, was bound to alert others. Max saw a group of black spriggans at the door, all bobbing up and down and waving their long-fingered hands about, mewing like startled kittens.

Rose dispatched one of the Porporrum and his body fell back with a grunt. His companions paused in their habitual frozen pose of shock, then uttered higher shrieks and renewed their attack. Rose's legs were running with blood from several cuts. Rowan leapt up and soared through the air like a bird. She landed at Rose's side, a long knife held ready.

Max felt almost superfluous. It was clear his companions needed no help from him. Rowan's blade flashed in a blur and several Porporrum flew back, spouting brownish ichor from mortal wounds. Then Max noticed a furtive shape lurking near what appeared to be an altar of some kind at the back of the room, between two tall wooden pillars. It was a Porporrum and now it was pulling out panels of the altar, delving inside. Max ran forward just as the little creature took something out of the hole. He saw a flash of gold but without pausing to examine what the Porporrum held struck at its face with his sword. The creature fell, hacking at the air with the object it held in his hand. Max was momentarily blinded by a flash of light, then all was quiet.

He glanced round. Rose stooped, panting, her hands upon her thighs, her face streaked with Porporrum blood. Rowan looked fierce, almost insane, her green eyes wide, teeth bared. All the Porporrum were dead, but there was an unmistakable roar of others approaching at speed. The spriggans must have hurried to alert their masters.

'There will be hundreds of them,' Max said. He glanced up at the roof. If they wanted to survive, surely they'd have to abandon Menni and make a swift escape? He looked down at the dead Porporrum at his feet. It still had the golden object in its hand. Max reached down and took it. It was a clawed baton, perhaps a ceremonial object. Quickly, he glanced inside the altar, but there was nothing more of interest within.

Rose came over to him, pushing damp, sticky hair from her face. 'We have to go, Max. I'm sorry.'

Behind them Rowan uttered a snarl. The doorway was filled with outraged Porporrum. They stopped there, gesturing and shrieking, but Max knew they would only pause for a moment. Rose ran for the ropes and this provoked the Porporrum into rushing into the temple. There seemed to be a sea of them. Darts were already flying through the air.

'Rowan!' Max called.

The Ashen seemed delirious, ready to fight, to take on the entire Porporrum nation. Max ran to grab hold of her. When he touched her arm, she turned on him with a snarl. A Porporrum leaped forward and stabbed at her with a wooden spear. Rowan jerked backwards into Max. In desperation, Max flailed out with the baton.

At once, the Porporrum uttered a synchronous wail and fell to their faces. It was as if they had been felled with a single blow. But they weren't dead. They were abasing themselves.

Stunned, Max knew he hadn't touched a single one of them. He looked at the baton in his hand. 'What *is* this thing?'

Rowan pulled away from him, one hand pressed to her side. 'Holy relic,' she gasped. 'Must be! They're afraid of it.'

'Max!' Rose called desperately from above. 'Come on!'

The Porporrum were still abased upon the floor, uttering frightened cries. Had the creature who'd tried to get to the altar been trying to find himself a weapon or had he been intent on removing this relic from the vicinity of the fighting? Max stepped forward to the nearest quivering Porporrum and touched it on its bony head with the baton. The little creature screamed in horror and emptied its bowels over the Porporrum behind it.

'We have nothing to fear,' Max said. He called up to Rose. 'Come down. It's all right.'

'Are you sure?' Rowan asked. She looked weak, dazed.

Max nodded. 'I am. In my heart.' He looked around the temple and saw, propped up beside the altar, a wide wooden sled. The Porporrum must have used it to drag Menni into the Hive. 'Can you fetch that?' he asked Rowan, gesturing. 'I'll stay here to keep this little lot in order.'

Rowan nodded once and, joined by Rose, went to fetch the sled.

Experimenting with his new-found power, Max gently kicked the Porporrum before him. 'You. On your feet.'

The creature squeaked and shuddered.

'Do they understand our language?' Max called to Rowan.

'They do,' she replied. She and Rose were already hauling the sled back across the room.

'Then you heard me,' Max said to the creature at his feet. 'Get up and put the statue on the sled. Hurry, or I'll take out your brains with this thing.' He made a pass through the air above the Porporrum's head with the baton.

At once the small being scrambled to its feet and chittered at some of its companions, who also leaped up. While the rest of the Porporrum remained trembling, lying flat on their faces, Max's reluctant helpers began to manoeuvre Menni onto the sled.

'What is that thing you have there?' Rose asked. 'Why are they so afraid of it?'

'Maybe it's not the relic itself they fear,' Rowan said, 'but who wields it. The combination of the two.'

'Are you all right?' Max asked her.

She nodded. 'A small wound, but with a burn in it. Nothing serious, just painful.'

'Another artefact for our collection,' Rose said. She frowned. 'Shouldn't you summon the owl?'

Max closed his eyes briefly. He could sense the owl, still battling furiously with her forest allies against the Porporrum. 'She is still occupied outside. We need to get there quickly and help her.' He growled at the Porporrum around him. 'Hurry up.'

Once Menni was on the sled and secured there with ropes, Max directed the Porporrum to drag him out of the Hive. They went down through the spiralling sloping corridors, meeting many other Porporrum on the way. At first they cried out in anger, ready to attack, but all Max had to do was show them the baton and they cringed away from him.

Once outside, they saw that the owls were still skirmishing with a large group of Porporrum. The birds swooped and soared, lashing out with beaks and claws, while the Porporrum fought back with darts and arrows. The air swirled with a snow of bloody feathers. Many ragged bundles of feathers upon the ground indicated how many casualties the owls had taken. Max paused on the top of the ladder by the entrance and uttered a roar. The effect was instantaneous, magical. The Porporrum all froze in horror and the owls fled back into the forest. Only the War Owl remained, flying to Max's shoulder and alighting there.

Max was filled with an immense sense of power. He felt like laughing. He held up the baton for all to see. Feathers still drifted down onto the motionless scene. 'I have your relic!' he cried. 'Know that you cannot take liberties with me or the Ashen any longer. Take these tidings to your masters, whoever they are. Tell them to tremble. Tell them I will seek them out and destroy them!'

'Steady on, Max,' Rose murmured behind him. 'Don't overdo it.'

'You are Iron,' he hissed at her, suddenly filled with an inexplicable resentment.

'I am Rose,' she said. 'Get down the ladder, Max. Let's get Menni out of here.'

Max jumped to the ground and the Porporrum in the glade fell to their faces. He felt filled with a great golden strength. It had become part of him, fierce and implacable. He could feel the silver heart burning in his chest, but it did not pain him.

The Porporrum had begun to drag Menni towards the forest, the path that led back to Asholm.

'We should take captives,' Rowan said. 'Perhaps the gang who're dragging the sled. They can be interrogated once we get home.'

Max nodded. Her words seemed to come from far away, through a buzzing roar in his head.

Chapter Two

From Stone into Flesh

A cringing, craven group of Porporrum stood clustered together in the great hall of Asholm. Jenny sat upon her brother's throne, swathed in a silvery-green robe, her auburn hair plaited loosely and hanging down over her breast. She gazed upon the little creatures sternly.

'You were once our allies,' she said, shaking her head. 'How has it come to this?'

The Porporrum seemed mindless with fear.

Jenny rose gracefully from the throne and approached the quivering group. 'You must tell us who leads you now,' she said. 'If you cooperate, no harm shall befall you.'

The Porporrum all began chittering at once.

'Silence!' Jenny commanded and pointed to one of the creatures. 'You. Speak to me.'

'Paw, paw,' it said. 'Porporrum have paw. No more. No more. Shines for him now.' It pointed at Max.

Jenny glanced at Max. 'Give me that,' she said, gesturing at the baton he still held in his hand.

'We must restore Menni at once,' he said, oddly reluctant to relinquish the object. 'We can interrogate these imps later.'

'Max, give me that,' Jenny repeated, softly and firmly.

Max handed her the baton. She turned it in her hands. 'Where did you get this?' she asked the Porporrum.

'Gibbold lady,' it answered. 'Her paw.'

'This gibbold lady,' Jenny said. 'Does she lead you?'

'Shining,' answered the Porporrum urgently. 'Makes the golden one come.'

'Does she lead you?'

'Bow our heads,' said the Porporrum. 'When she comes. Gives us light, she does. Great goddess come to us.'

Jenny began to prowl around the group, who followed the baton with their eyes. 'Is she from above, this lady?'

'She came,' answered the Porporrum. 'We bow. Is all. Powerful. Make us kings of all.'

Jenny sighed and tapped the baton against the palm of her hand. 'We'll get little useful information from them.' She paused, her face becoming both harder and more sorrowful. 'King Jaxinther. Where is he?'

'Gibbold lady,' said the Porporrum. 'Jack's hers.'

Jenny snarled and instinctively raised the baton to strike the creature who fell to the floor, whimpering.

Rowan stepped forward to place a restraining hand on Jenny's wrist. 'At least he's alive, my lady.'

Jenny blinked at her, as if blind.

Rowan shook her slightly. 'Think. He's alive, isn't he? We have information now. All is not lost.'

'Menni,' Max said. 'Remember Menni.'

Jenny recovered her composure and carelessly handed the baton to Rowan. 'Yes,' she said. 'Your friend, I know.' She frowned. 'What ails you, Fox?'

He shook his head. 'Nothing.'

'You were rubbing your chest. Does it pain you?'

Max hadn't even realized he was doing it. 'No. Just conscious of the heart, that's all. I can feel it all the time.'

Jenny considered. 'The baton affected you, didn't it? I see it now. Since I took it from you, you look different.'

Rose uttered a choked laugh. 'You could say that.'

'What do you mean, Lady Rose?' Jenny asked.

'I mean you're right. When Max held the baton, he became – shall we say – more than himself. I half expected him to tell the Porporrum to crown him king!'

Max looked at her sourly. 'Easy for you to cast aspersions, Lady Iron. Are you envious?'

'Don't be ridiculous!'

'Enough!' Jenny said, raising her hands. 'We will consider this matter later. Now, Sir Fox. Let us address the business closest to your heart. Master Vane.'

The Ashen had installed Menni in a chamber off the throne room. Here muted light came in through windows draped in diaphanous emerald fabric. The Dragon Mirror, restored to full size, had been erected on a wooden framework opposite the statue. Menni looked peaceful in the diffused light despite the rather grotesque ruff of grasses at his neck, which had survived his journey from the Hive.

Jenny went up to him, extended a hand, but did not touch the cold marble. 'Well, Master Vane, your imprisonment will soon be over.' She looked at Max. 'Sir Fox, you must now summon *barishi* into the Dragon Mirror, let it do its work. You must also bring forth the War Owl.'

'Gladly,' Max said. He went to stand before the mirror, and for a moment was acutely conscious of Rose's attention upon him. When he glanced at her, he saw sorrow in her eyes – and something more. He could not contemplate it. Menni was the only thing that mattered.

All Max had to do now was think of *barishi* and a heat started up in his body. The more he used it, the more freely it seemed to flow through him. Instinctively, he closed his eyes and raised his hands, palms outwards, towards the mirror. In his mind, he could see a golden stream of *barishi* flowing from his hands towards the polished surface. He could feel the heat of it building up within him. After some moments, he felt a hand on his arm and Jenny's voice murmured softly, 'Stand aside now.'

Max opened his eyes. The surface of the mirror shone like quicksilver. It seemed liquid, moved by a tide of *barishi*. Max stepped away from it, so the strange rays emanating from the artefact could fall upon Menni.

'Now the owl,' Jenny said. 'Direct her to help restore Master Vane.'

Max summoned her from the stone and she perched upon the frame of the mirror, complementing its rays with a *barishi* stream of her own. The energy of the two artefacts combined, creating a single beam of radiance that emitted a low tone.

Menni was bathed in a strange metallic light that seethed over his body. It was so bright Max could not at first discern what effect it was having. But then he saw his friend's arms jerk. Menni uttered a great cry of alarm and fear and leaped forwards, only to fall to his knees. He hunched there, shaking his head wildly.

'Menni,' Max said, hunching down beside him. 'It's me. Speak.'

Menni raised his head, blinking. He stared at Max without recognition. Max looked up at Jenny. 'He doesn't know me.'

'He will need time to recover,' she said. 'Have no fear, Sir Fox. Your friend is restored to you. My people will care for him.'

'Are you sure there will be no permanent damage?'

'Permanent *effects*, maybe, but not damage.' Jenny clapped her hands and a group of Ashen males came to assist Menni from the room. He went with them meekly, barely able to use his limbs.

Max was suffused with a sense of disappointment. He didn't know what he'd expected. A tearful reunion? Menni's undying gratitude? After everything they'd been through, his friend's restoration seemed an anticlimax.

Jenny appeared to sense his thoughts. 'You mustn't worry, Sir Fox. Once he has rested and received healing treatment, he will know you again.'

Max shook his head, unconsciously rubbing his chest. 'It doesn't seem real.'

'But it is.' Jenny reached out to touch his arm with light fingers. 'And we know Jack is alive. We can do something now.'

'I know what I have to do!' Rose announced.

Everyone turned to look at her.

'It's pointless going out on these little sorties, trying to solve the problems ourselves. It's time my father was forced to accept what is happening. In a way, it is his responsibility. Hidden knowledge won't remain hidden. It's pushing up from its grave. I will go and speak to my father. The Council must be made aware of all that is happening.'

'You're insane!' Max snapped. 'Iron won't listen to you. He's so hide-bound by the tradition he fears, he's more likely to throw you into Gragonatt than sit and listen to your words.'

'I have to agree,' Jenny said. 'We know what to do. The lost artefacts must be recovered and then the Fox can use them to . . .'

Rose uttered a contemptuous snort. 'Oh, for the Jewel's sake, shut up! Artefacts, legends. It's all very well, and only a few days ago I felt that way myself. If we had all the time in the world, we could continue our questing. But Max doesn't have that time. I'm convinced of that now. Look at him. That thing is alive in his body. It's eating him. I can see it.' She turned away. 'We need help. Strong help. If any of the artefacts remain in the Clan vaults, my father must force the families concerned to relinquish them. If someone from Karadur has influence over the people of Shriltasi, the Council must root them out, bring them to justice. Much as I detest Captain Coffin, I can't help feeling he and a horde of his Irregulars would be of more help to Jack Ash than Max, Rowan and myself. Let the Porporrum stand against them.'

No,' Max said. 'You're deluding yourself, Rose. You can't bring the Irregulars down here. It would be a disaster. Your father would no doubt order them to butcher everyone they found, to make sure Shriltasi becomes as non-existent as he wants it to be.'

'You don't know my father,' Rose said coldly. 'Despite his conformity, he is a fair man. If I can only make him face what he finds distasteful, if I can only make him accept this is a time for change, he will help us. I know it.'

'You're a fool,' Max said. He narrowed his eyes. 'Or has it been your plan all along to bring the forces of the Metal into Shriltasi?'

'Don't be ridiculous,' Rose snapped. 'If that was so, I'd have brought the Irregulars down here before now, wouldn't I?'

'You mustn't argue,' Jenny said, staring directly at Rose with cold eyes. 'We should all be in accord at this time.'

'It is impossible,' Max said. 'We have different agendas.'

'We do not!' Rose cried desperately. 'Oh, you're as blind as my father is!' She began to march out of the room.

Max hurried after her, grabbed her arm and swung her round to face him. 'You're not leaving. I'll not let you reveal everything to the Metal.'

'I am leaving,' Rose said. 'Will you strike me to stop me?'

Max hesitated. 'The Ashen will stop you.'

Rose pulled away from his grasp. 'I want to say "Trust me", but I know you don't. All I can tell you is that I'd never do anything to harm you, Max. Never.'

Max had to glance away from the intensity in her eyes. How could he doubt her? Yet something within him wanted to taunt and goad her, punish her for the blood that ran in her veins. 'Go, then,' he said. 'But know that I see it as betrayal.'

Rose said nothing, holding his gaze for a few moments longer. Tears welled unspent behind her eyes. Then she walked away from him.

Lord Iron strode through the smoking halls of the great foundry, followed by Captain Coffin and watched by his expressionless, glistening foundrymen, who had paused in their work to see what the commotion was. Iron's anger was echoed by the turmoil around him. Gigantic buckets of molten metal swung overhead on cranes, vast rivers of white-hot steel surged back and forth across the floor. Crimson sparks vomited from the furnaces and everywhere was oily smoke and gouting steam.

'Were is she?' Iron demanded, his voice echoing through the lofty galleries. 'Where is my daughter, Coffin?'

Only an hour before, Lord Iron had been due to meet with Rose for dinner again. But she had not kept the appointment. This was most unlike her, so Iron had sent his valet to fetch her. But Rose's apartments in the family manse were empty. It was clear she had not been there for some time. It was, the valet cautiously advised his master, as if they were not lived in at all. At these words, Iron had been filled with a leaden river of dread. He knew that he had stumbled upon a secret, and he disliked secrets intensely. People only kept them because they were doing wrong. Rose was his precious, his closest confidante. Where was she?

'I'm sure you should not worry, my lord,' Coffin said, striding to keep up with his employer who seemed incapable of remaining still.

'She must have been kidnapped. Yes, that's it.' Lord Iron came to a halt and wheeled around so that Coffin nearly bumped into him. 'Silverskin could have her.'

Coffin raised his hands in a placatory gesture. 'I am sure that is not so, my lord. We would have heard some whisper about it. I don't believe there's any need to worry. My instincts tell me Lady Rose will show up safe and sound very soon.'

Lord Iron eyed the Captain narrowly. 'I pray that you are correct. But I wouldn't have to worry about Silverskin at all, would I, if he was in custody? Why isn't he? Why have you failed me so miserably?'

Muscles in Coffin's cheeks convulsed. Iron knew it infuriated the man to be humiliated in this way in front of the foundrymen. They were, after all, only a shade removed from his own Irregulars. Authority and appearance meant a lot to Cornelius Coffin. He would take this as a personal affront.

'My lord, I understand your concerns,' Coffin said clearly, through gritted teeth. 'And I have done all in my power to investigate the matter. The only conclusion I can draw is that Silverskin has allies . . . important and influential allies.'

'Meaning?'

'Allies among the Metal, perhaps from the same ranks as those who have turned from tradition.'

Lord Iron raised his brows. 'What? You dare to make such an accusation? You have failed in your duties, and now have the temerity to blame those who employ you for your incompetence?'

'Not all, my lord. You know that I love and serve the Iron unquestionably. But I do not speak of your own noble Clan, or indeed any of the other pure-blood Metal families. I was thinking of certain amalgams, perhaps Bronzes, Brasses . . . or even Pewters.' He paused for effect. 'Remember what is being said among the common people. Talk of the cult. I'm sure there is a connection between all that irks us.'

Lord Iron regarded Coffin speculatively. 'I see,' he said coldly, but now without anger. 'You suspect Sir Clovis, don't you? But that is absurd. He patently loathes Silverskin and is a complete sop. I cannot envisage him as the mastermind behind any plan effective enough to inconvenience us.' He uttered a scornful laugh. 'The fool can't even keep hold of his own property, remember.'

'It is still something of a mystery what he was doing in the sewers,' Coffin said carefully, 'and he gave us no specific details concerning this item of value he lost. He could easily have been there specifically to meet with Silverskin. Pewter hampered my Irregulars, so that Silverskin escaped me yet again. Silverskin always escapes, and on two occasions Clovis Pewter was present. I find it difficult to look upon this as coincidence.'

Lord Iron nodded slowly, recalling how Clan Gold had also recently been reluctant to describe property stolen from them. 'I see your point, but I have known Sir Clovis all his life. He is an effete dandy, yes, but I would never call him a potential criminal. His father is a very wise and decent man.'

'I would not dispute that, my lord,' Coffin said. 'I too respect Lord Tin beyond measure. But think of the mother's side of the family. Perhaps Sir Clovis is not such a fool as he likes us to think he is.'

'You are casting aspersions upon Clan Silver? Think what you're saying, Captain.'

'I am not casting aspersions, my lord. I merely suggest matters for your consideration. You have allies among the Metal who are loyal to you, but there are others who are not.'

'Steel,' spat Lord Iron, eyes glittering. For a moment, he was silent. 'No, I cannot even contemplate Carinthia being a secret traitor. She is outspoken and ambitious, but speaks all too plainly to be a creature of intrigue. Surely, if she was, she'd keep to the shadows, beyond suspicion.'

Captain Coffin shrugged. 'I am making no judgements. In my mind, I juggle possibilities. One of them shines more brightly than the others, and that is that Pewter and Silverskin are related. If there is any truth at all in the rumours surrounding our Fox of Akra, he would make a useful ally for someone of his Clan who is manoeuvring for control.'

'The idea is outrageous! Captain, I appreciate your creative thoughts on the matter, for it seems we need an inspired idea to help solve our dilemmas. But I feel you're allowing failure and self-pity to cloud your judgement. Max Silverskin is as mortal as you or I.'

'I was not suggesting otherwise, but he could have . . . access to forbidden arts.'

Lord Iron stared at Coffin for several long moments. In his heart, he knew that the Captain was right to discuss this matter, but he couldn't bring himself to concur openly with the man. 'I will concede there is a slight possibility Silverskin could have a friend or two amongst the Metal. These are strange times, and those of weak heart will turn to ridiculous means to assuage their fears. If this is so, the traitors will be discovered and punished. But for all that, Silverskin is one ordinary man, and we command all the power of Karadur. He should not be able to hide from us.'

'Apart from that one occasion when he was sighted in the sewers, my men found no other evidence down there, my lord.'

A soft voice sounded behind them. 'Perhaps you weren't looking deep enough, Captain.'

Lord Iron looked up and with a surge of relief saw his daughter standing there in a gash of crimson light. 'Rose, where have you been? I've been out of my mind with worry. So many untoward things are occurring at the moment. I was afraid to think what might have happened to you.'

Rose came to stand beside her father. 'You mustn't worry. I'm perfectly capable of looking after myself.'

'Good evening, Lady Rose,' Captain Coffin said unctuously, removing his wide-brimmed black hat. He bowed with ostentatious reverence.

Rose's mouth twitched. She spoke briskly. 'I'm glad to find you here, Captain.'

Coffin actually blushed. Iron wanted to strike the man.

'No one could be as happy as I to find you here, my lady.'

Rose dismissed him from her attention. 'I'm sorry I missed our appointment, father. I've been involved in pressing business.'

Captain Coffin raised his brows. 'My lady, you speak with gravity. What is this matter?'

'One that concerns us all, which is why I'm pleased you're here. I suggest we go somewhere less public to discuss it.' She cast a significant glance at the foundrymen who were all clearly listening to the exchange.

★   ★   ★

Lord Iron took them to his private office, which was situated far above the foundry floor. Here a hungry fire burned in a narrow cast-iron hearth, and leather-bound ledgers filled the floor-to-ceiling bookcases that lined the room. Lord Iron sat down behind an enormous desk and beckoned for his daughter and Coffin to take seats opposite him. 'So what's this all about, Rose? Do you have information concerning the renegade?'

Rose tapped her fingers against her crossed thighs. 'In a manner, yes.'

'How did you come by this information?'

'At the moment, I cannot reveal my source. I beg you with all my heart to listen to what I have to say, without judgement or comment. Will you do that?'

Lord Iron raised his hands. 'Speak.'

Rose drew a breath. 'Very well. Captain Coffin has had great difficulty in taking Max Silverskin into custody. He has scoured the city in its entirety, and found nothing. Silverskin flits into visibility and disappears again, almost as if by magic.' She raised a hand to stem the outburst on her father's lips. 'Please listen. You said you would. I'm not saying Silverskin can disappear at will, like a wizard out of an old tale, but that he has a better hiding place than any could imagine. No one, especially you, Captain, would look for him there.'

Lord Iron frowned. Already a discomfort had come into his flesh. 'What do you mean, my dear?'

Rose paused for a moment, staring him in the eye. He could see the child she'd once been looking out at him, desperate for him to approve of her. 'Father, what if there was a world below the sewers?'

There was a complete silence, but for the crackling of the fire. Lord Iron could feel Coffin's eyes upon him, but would not honour him with a glance. Eventually he said, 'Below the sewers?' He put a warning into his tone, an imperative for his beloved daughter not to say any more. She could know nothing. She'd heard rumours. A daughter of his blood couldn't know anything of Shriltasi. A day would come when he'd have to burden her with the ancient knowledge, for that would be part of her responsibility as leader of her Clan, but until she heard the truth from him she could only pick up fictions and lies.

Rose nodded. 'Yes. There are old stories that tell of a place as large and complex as Karadur but which lies far beneath the surface.' She hesitated. 'You must have heard those stories, father?'

Lord Iron nodded. 'Yes, yes, I have.' He sighed. 'I don't relish hearing them fall from your lips, Rose. They are dangerous stories, relics of a time best forgotten.'

'I know their history,' Rose said quietly.

Lord Iron glanced at Captain Coffin, who had assumed a bland expression. He wouldn't know what they were talking about. Iron didn't want him to know. 'The legends do not apply in this situation. I know we are all confounded as to how Silverskin has managed to avoid capture, but our Captain here has mooted a new theory. He believes that Clovis Pewter may be offering the renegade sanctuary, perhaps in the Moonmetal Manse itself or even Sawhollow House. Both domains are large and sprawling enough to provide a hiding place.'

Rose couldn't contain a smile. She flicked a glance at Coffin. 'Really? The least I can say is "far-fetched".'

'I know how it sounds,' Coffin said. 'But, forgive me, my lady, my theory is no less wild than yours.'

Rose cocked her head to one side. 'You think so? Believe me, Captain, there is so much you don't know.'

'Rose,' Lord Iron said sternly, 'I will not countenance this nonsense.'

'It is *not* nonsense, and you know it,' Rose said hotly. 'It's about time you faced up to . . . certain things.'

'Captain,' said Lord Iron, 'I feel you should leave us now.'

'No!' Rose got to her feet. 'He needs to know, father.' She turned on the Captain. 'There was a time, before the Reformation, when Karadur existed above and below ground.'

'Rose!' Lord Iron also got to his feet.

'No, I will have my say! Shriltasi was the subterranean land, conceived and constructed by our ancestors and other races who once dwelled upon the surface, when all was fertile and green. These people used *barishi*, magic. For a very long time, the two realms were in perfect accord. Then, during the great Clan Wars, people witnessed the devastating effects of *barishi* used wrongly, and the Council of the Metal decreed it should never be used again. They made it law that all human contact was severed with those for whom *barishi* was a facet of life. Shriltasi exists, Captain, and my father knows it to be true. Magic still lives there, but the land is dying. As Karadur is dying.'

Lord Iron stared with wild eyes at his daughter, speechless.

Captain Coffin cleared his throat, with manifest embarrassment. 'And you think that Silverskin hides in this . . . place.'

'Not just that,' Rose said. 'I'm quite certain that members of the Clans are once again going into Shriltasi and using, for their own benefit, the powers of *barishi*.'

'Rose, that's quite enough!' Iron roared. 'Have you lost your mind? Do you realize what you're doing to yourself? If anyone in the Council should get to hear that you've spoken in this way, you will never inherit from me. You'd be lucky to escape Gragonatt!'

'Because they're afraid, aren't they?' Rose cried. 'Bury what you're afraid of. That's the best way, isn't it?' She thumped her father's desk with bunched fists. 'But it won't *stay* buried. You are a fool to deny this, father. Because others don't, and that gives them the advantage over you – over us!'

'I don't deny people want to believe in these old tales – certain people,' Iron said, in a calmer tone. 'But Rose, for the Jewel's sake, don't be seduced by them yourself.'

'I'm not,' Rose said. 'Don't take me for a fool. I know Shriltasi still exists.'

'How, my lady?' Coffin asked.

She expelled a choked laugh. 'How do you think? I've been there!'

For just a moment, Lord Iron felt his heart fall still in his breast. He looked upon his daughter, saw the earnest zeal in her eyes. She was not a bad girl. She was his jewel. Yet, somehow, she had become tainted. Her rooms had looked as though they'd not been lived in. Where had she been living? He dared not conjecture, could not bear to ask, because he knew she'd tell him the truth. He wasn't ready for it now, perhaps never could be. Whatever his beloved daughter had involved herself in, her good sense was affected. It was worse than if she'd died before his eyes. 'Rose, you cannot have been there . . .'

'I have,' she said. 'And so have others from Karadur. Why do you deny it? Why? What are you so afraid of?'

Lord Iron sat down heavily, his head sunk upon his chest. 'All that was terrible was buried there, all that was evil and corrupting. It was sealed for eternity.'

'You knew, you've always known,' Rose said softly. 'Who else in the Council is aware?'

Lord Iron sighed. 'This is knowledge that would have come to you when you were near to taking my place as head of our Clan. But it seems you have found things out for yourself. This is not the way, Rose. You have acted unwisely, recklessly.'

'Who else?' Rose asked.

'It is the burden of Gold, Silver, Copper and Iron to be the guardians of this knowledge. The head of each Clan knows the truth, but no one else.'

'Lady Copper, then?'

'Yes. As you've no doubt concluded, she spoke vaguely of this subject the other night.' He looked at Coffin. 'I hope you realize the gravity of what you're hearing now, Captain. It must never, under any circumstances, be repeated. You have been drawn into a secret that few people know. Respect that secret.'

Coffin bowed his head. 'Be assured you can trust me.'

Iron shook his head. 'I hoped this day would never come, but of course the knowledge would not be passed on if there wasn't some risk the past might return. If people have somehow found a way back to that abominable realm, they must be touched by its evil. It has a song, that place, and the song seduces the gullible.'

'Then in your eyes I am both gullible and stupid,' Rose said with dignity.

Iron glanced at her briefly, then gazed down at his desk, unable to answer. It was still too difficult to believe that Rose had discovered Shriltasi's existence, never mind been there herself. The implications were terrible.

'What is evil to you?' Rose demanded. 'That which you do not know, that which you cannot see with your own eyes, touch with your own hands?

You fear *barishi*.' She leaned forward. 'I know why our ancestors did what they did. The Clan Wars were terrible and *barishi* was used wrongly to cause suffering and destruction. I know that power corrupts, but we cannot deny what is. Ignorance is no defence. Millennia ago, the Clans buried half of what they were and have been afraid ever since of that corpse coming back from the dead to haunt them. It's what our stringent traditions and laws are all about. Well, it has come back, because some people have overcome their fears and practised a little necromancy.' She sat back down again, clearly well pleased with her analogy.

Lord Iron looked at her and it seemed she was a long distance away, a tiny stranger. He felt feverish, hot. If Carinthia should get to know about this, he would be finished. Rose would be finished. Jewel knew what they'd do to her.

A cool voice broke into his fever. 'I will go there, my lady. Show me the way.'

Coffin.

Lord Iron raised his head. 'Do you understand what you're suggesting, Captain? If you set foot in that accursed place, you will break the law far more than any criminal you've apprehended, even if I ordered you there myself. Would you risk everything you've worked for so assiduously?'

Coffin contemplated these words for a moment, then said, 'I will do anything to take Silverskin back to Gragonatt. I would risk my very soul to keep you and your family safe. You need have no fear of what has been said within this room going any further. I swear upon my life to keep it secret. You may also trust my men.' He stood. 'My lord, give me permission to go to this place. Should trouble derive from my actions, the responsibility will be mine alone. If citizens of Karadur are visiting this place, I will find them. They will not speak of it to anyone, I promise you that.'

Rose turned in her seat. 'I thank you, Captain. But you must promise me one thing.'

'Anything, my lady.'

'If I show you the way to Shriltasi, you must not harm any inhabitant of that realm, not even those who would appear to be enemies. The Ashen of Shriltasi are in conflict with another race there, the Porporrum. This is because someone – or some people – from Karadur is influencing the Porporrum. They should be contained, but your Irregulars should certainly not slaughter them. As for captives, take only Karadurians, if you find any. Will you give me your word on this?'

Coffin bowed his head. 'Of course. I swear it.'

'Rose, what do you know of these people, the Ashen and so on?' Lord Iron said. 'Why should you have concern for them? If they still exist, they are little more than animals.'

'I have friends in the underworld,' she answered stiffly. 'Friends who care about the fate of Karadur-Shriltasi as keenly as you or I. They might not be human, but they are not animals. We are not that different. We should be working together now, for Shriltasi's problems are ours.'

Lord Iron knew he could forbid it. He could chastise his daughter sternly and have her locked in the family manse until she came to her senses. He could bribe Coffin never to reveal what he'd heard that day. What greater bribe than Rose herself? *No, don't even think that.* He rose slowly from his chair and went to a narrow window that looked down into the hellish processes of the foundry floor. It seemed to him that a hideous apparition hung in the smoky crimson air, a monstrous goddess dragged up from the reeking past. The goddess of the foundry: Sekmet. The events of the last few days had been leading to this moment. The signs had been there all along, but most of them he'd tried to dismiss.

He turned to Coffin. 'Do it,' he said.

'Father.' Rose got to her feet again, came towards him, smiling, hands outstretched.

He winced away. 'No, not now, Rose. Leave me.'

'Father . . .' Her hands dropped. He heard the sorrow in her voice.

'You have brought me great despair, my daughter,' he said. 'You have failed your Clan.'

'Failed? But how? You've told Coffin to go to Shriltasi. You've . . .'

'I don't expect you to understand,' Iron interrupted. 'I know I am facing an inevitable circumstance, but I'm still disappointed you are involved in it. Very disappointed. Sometime soon you will explain to me how you came by your information, and also certain details about your recent living arrangements, but for now I don't want to hear it.'

'This makes no sense,' Rose said. 'You can't just dismiss me. We have other vital matters to discuss. The whereabouts of the lost icons for one thing. I believe we need them now.'

'No,' Lord Iron said. 'We have nothing further to discuss. Enough damage has been done already.'

'Some of the Clans might still have the icons in hiding,' Rose persisted. 'You should call a meeting of the Council and force them to relinquish them.'

'Rose!' Lord Iron snapped. 'You have said quite enough. I can see the sense of venturing into forbidden territory to pursue dangerous criminals, but I will not countenance any further nonsense than that. I wish you to go. I will talk to you tomorrow.'

'Father . . .'

Coffin touched her arm and said quietly. 'My lady, we should leave.'

He led her, bewildered, from the room.

After Rose and Coffin had left, Lord Iron continued to stare down into the foundry. His vision was blurred and it seemed as if the whole fabric of the building was falling apart. Filth. Rust. Soot. Corruption had crept like a dank steam through the Metal itself, spreading corrosion in its path. Iron had no choice now but to accept that Clan members might be involved in unlawful practices. But who were those traitors? Steel? Pewter? Had Carinthia been seduced by the exotic allure of forbidden arts? And Pewter. A weak man, who was perhaps searching for strength down imprudent paths. Then there was Rose. Lord Iron sighed deeply. She saw herself as a herald of the future, bravely venturing into dangerous territory, seeking truth and answers for the people of Karadur. He should have been more alert. He'd neglected her inquiring mind. He hadn't imparted the correct education. All those months she'd been visiting Clan Silver's library, she had clearly been delving into hidden aspects of history. People had commented on the frequency of her visits to the place – even Carinthia Steel who, it seemed, shared similar interests. And now Rose had actually trodden the cursed soil of Shriltasi. How would that have affected her? What must he do to draw her back to rightful behaviour? Whatever he'd said to her, he didn't believe she was evil. She was immature, obviously, and her uninformed youthful ideals had led her off the path.

Again Lord Iron sighed, feeling as if the weight of the world oppressed his lungs. The Metal had become lax. The ancient books in Silver's library were now regarded as no more than amusing curios of a less enlightened age. At one time, no one but the inner cabal of the Upper Council would have been allowed to peruse them. *Danger slips in so slyly*, Iron thought. *We have become complacent and must now pay the price.* But how could he root out the traitors within the Metal? Who could he trust? Should he call an emergency meeting of the inner cabal and reveal what he knew? But what if one or more of the members were part of the conspiracy? He had to take action, and quickly. And what could he do about Rose? *Last night, Fabiana came to you*, he thought. *She has suspicions of her own.*

Lord Iron rang a bell to summon his secretary from an adjoining cubby. The man came swiftly to his employer's summons. 'Take a letter, Strood,' Lord Iron said. 'When it is done, I wish you to convey it personally to Verdigris House.'

Chapter Three

The Comfort of Copper

Rose would not weep in front of Coffin. Once beyond her father's office, she deftly removed her arm from the Captain's grip and pattered down the ringing stairs to the foundry floor. He followed her. Of course he did. She was torn between wanting to speak to him further and dismissing him with a curt word.

There was so much more she should have said to her father. It had all come out in the wrong order. She'd alienated him before she'd said some of the most important things. Rose sensed a severance in the air around her. She knew Lord Iron was horrified by her revelations and that some part of their relationship had changed for ever. Why was he so stubborn? A shred of unease needled through her. Was it because he was right and she was wrong? She turned to Coffin. 'Perhaps we could speak further, Captain. Will you accompany me to the manse?'

He bowed. 'Nothing would please me more.'

Rose shuddered, not in revulsion but presentiment.

She took him to the room that had once been her mother's parlour, where as a child Rose had sat before the fire while her mother worked at her embroidery or else read aloud from books. To Rose, it was the warmest room in the manse, the cosiest. Coffin would feel ill at ease there because it was so plainly a woman's room. *Perhaps I should come here more often*, Rose thought. There was no fire in the grate and a faint sense of desolation hung in the stale air, but it wasn't cold. Rose sat down in a plump-cushioned chair beside the scoured hearth and, legs outstretched, rested her feet on her mother's footstool. She bade the captain sit opposite her.

'I hope I haven't shocked you,' she said.

Coffin shook his head. 'Not at all. I was intrigued by what you said. How did you learn it?'

'It doesn't matter. All that does is that Shriltasi exists and that Karadurians are visiting it, causing trouble.'

'It would explain why we've been unable to locate the meeting place of the cult of Sekmet,' Coffin said.

Rose frowned. 'What is this?'

Coffin explained all he knew on the subject.

Rose nodded, her lower lip stuck out. 'It's likely they are meeting in Shriltasi.'

'Indeed. I have grave suspicions concerning Clovis Pewter, too. What you've revealed to me today has tied some loose ends. I believe Pewter may one of those visiting this underworld.' He told Rose about Pewter being apprehended in the sewers, and also of how her father wasn't convinced of his involvement.

'Pewter.' Rose smiled coldly. 'If your suspicions are correct, it almost makes him interesting. Still, as you said, it would explain . . . certain things.' She paused. 'What are your feelings concerning Max Silverskin, Captain?'

He blinked. 'My feelings? They don't come into it. He is a criminal, a troublemaker. That's all there is to it.'

'You resent him because he always bests you, don't you?'

'I hardly relish being made to look a fool, no, but I am somewhat relieved to learn he may have help from within the Metal. I am not incompetent, my lady, merely perplexed. I feel sure now that I will soon have the wretch in custody.'

'But is that the way to go?'

Coffin frowned. 'What other way is there? Are you suggesting I kill him?'

She laughed. 'Certainly not! As the Heir-in-Waiting to Iron, I could hardly revert to barbaric practices, could I?'

'Your father might say you already have.'

That stung. 'You are impertinent, Captain.'

'I don't mean to be. You have to admit your ideas are . . . unconventional.'

'It's necessary. Tradition is a blindfold. The world crumbles around us, while we see only what we want to see, the "reality" we imagine in the darkness before our eyes.'

Coffin hesitated, then said, 'In some ways, I agree with you. The Metal has become too soft. Wayward influences do as they please. Gragonatt is not enough of a deterrent.'

'You would like to see a return of execution and torture, then?'

He stared at her, his thoughts almost visible in his expression. She could tell that he was wondering how much he could confide in her. She leaned forward in her chair and spoke coaxingly. 'Come now, Cornelius, you've heard some of my secrets. Tell me yours. I know you have ambition.'

'Does it please you?' he said sharply.

Rose put her head to one side. 'That depends. We should be frank with one another.'

'I think that rebellions should be put down firmly. I think that Silverskin should be publicly executed as an example. His followers should be rounded up and burned. That would put an end to all the nonsense going on, in Karadur and this other place below as well.'

Rose felt the heat creep up her neck and forced a laugh. 'We need allies, Cornelius. My father may well hang onto his seat on the Council at the next election, but he will not live for ever. When he dies, I will be at my most vulnerable. Steel will come down on me like a hawk, and their own allies will make themselves known at this time.'

'Iron has allies,' Coffin said. 'You shouldn't worry.'

'I'd like stronger allies,' she said. 'Perhaps more unusual ones.'

'The people you met below . . .'

She nodded. 'Of course, but . . .' She looked Coffin in the eye. How much did he care for her? How far would he go? 'I'd like Max Silverskin on my side.'

Coffin actually laughed.

Rose drew away from him abruptly. 'Why is this so amusing?' she snapped.

He shook his head. 'I'm not the only one who would laugh, my lady. Forgive me, but can you really imagine the Clan leader of Iron employing the likes of Silverskin? It would do nothing to promote your aims and much to destroy them. You would be throwing your enemies a reeking carcass, which they'd tear to pieces with great delight.'

'I don't just want allies among the Metal,' Rose said earnestly. 'I want the people of this city to trust me. I want to help them. The Metal can think what they want of me. They hide in their manses, playing at lords and ladies. You come from the streets, Cornelius. I know you know what I'm talking about. Or is your only aspiration to become like the Lords, effete and useless, throwing endless parties while the world dies?'

He sobered. 'No. Like you, I see the Metal returning to true power, all weakness cut away. But the method you suggest would not facilitate this. Even the people of Karadur would laugh at you, my lady. They'd see any attempt to ally with Silverskin as an act of defeat and desperation. Not all the common people are criminals, you know. Only a minority support Silverskin's kind.'

Perhaps there was some truth in that, but what would it matter? In just a couple of days' time, Max would have made a difference to reality or he would not. There really was no point to this aspect of their conversation. 'Thank you for speaking so plainly to me,' she said, injecting her habitual reserve into her voice. 'Now, we must discuss your visit to Shriltasi. It's essential you discover who from Karadur is playing games there.'

'I will do all in my power to do as you desire,' he said. 'I hope that in the future I may be of even more use to you.'

I've been too open, Rose thought. *He's seen this interview as something more than it is.*

But didn't you exploit that? another voice whispered inside her. *You encouraged him.*

'I'm confident you'll serve me as well as you serve my father,' she said.

'Your confidence is well placed, my lady.' He paused. 'I desire only to be all you would want of me.'

'You are that already,' she said, floundering.

He stared at her through narrow eyes, smiling. He thought she needed him. He thought he had a hold over her. Max should kill him for his effrontery. A hollow, dismal laugh echoed within her mind. Max would not care. Coffin clearly loved her. Max didn't. *But this will not make me bitter,* she thought.

I mustn't let that happen. 'We will go to Shriltasi soon,' she said. 'I'll take you there.'

'I'll find Silverskin as well, if he's skulking there,' Coffin said. 'You must put all thoughts of him from your mind. I'll find him and his new lackey, Velvet Mask. Let's strip the boy of his disguise and see what pretty meat Silverskin is dallying with since old Vane disappeared.'

'Velvet Mask,' Rose said. 'Is that what you call him?'

'Almost a girl,' Coffin said contemptuously. 'It's plain to see what's going on there.'

'Things are never plain,' Rose said. 'You can rely on that.'

Coffin was silent for a moment, then said, 'There is one other matter you should be aware of.'

She raised her eyebrows. 'Which is?'

'When you were late for dinner with your father, he sent someone to your rooms. The messenger reported it appeared that you never lived there. As you can imagine, this caused your father some concern.'

Rose sighed, rubbed her face. 'I do not live beyond the Forge, Captain. There is nothing sinister in this. I find the Tower oppressive, that's all, and have found for myself more congenial surroundings in the vicinity. I need privacy. I need peace. That's all there is to it.'

'You should tell your father this, perhaps.'

Rose stared at him for a moment, then inclined her head. 'Thank you. I'm grateful you told me this.'

'I am your ally,' Coffin said. 'You need never doubt that.'

After Coffin had left, Sword, the steward of the Iron Tower, knocked on the parlour door and came into the room. Rose was still sitting by the empty hearth, staring moodily at the soot-blackened bricks of the chimney.

'My lady,' said Sword, bowing from his great height. 'Two letters came for you.' He held out a pale cream envelope and another, which had a silvery-grey sheen.

Rose sat up straight and took them from him. The cream envelope bore the seal of Clan Copper, while the other was marked with the device of Clan Steel.

'Shall I have a fire lit for you in here?' Sword enquired.

Rose shook her head, frowning at the letters. 'No, no. Thank you, Sword.'

The steward departed.

Rose opened the envelope from Verdigris House. The letter within exuded a subtle flowery perfume and was inscribed in Fabiana's delicate graceful hand. Gently, she chided Rose for not having visited her immediately. 'If you are free, please drop in on me this evening. I want merely an hour of your time.' Rose put the letter down and opened the envelope from Steel. No perfume there. The letter within was crisp and white, the writing angular and strong. Rose almost laughed. Carinthia was also inviting her to visit, but the letter gave no indication as to why. *Suddenly I am so popular*, Rose thought cynically. But what could Carinthia want with her? *They approach me because father is so unmovable*, she thought. *They think I am more easily manipulated.* Perhaps she should let these two powerful women continue in their belief.

Rose wanted to return to Shriltasi and report to Max about what had happened with her father, but shrank from his scorn. He had been so cold earlier, almost hostile. Perhaps her evening would be put to better use if she did visit Fabiana. Rose had no female confidantes, and had never yearned for them, but told herself she was intrigued to discover what Fabiana might think of Carinthia's invitation.

Rose sent no prior word to Lady Copper that she'd accepted the invitation but merely turned up at Verdigris House, late in the afternoon. Truffle showed the visitor into the lady's parlour. Like all the rooms in the manse, it was decorated in rich autumnal shades. Couches were strewn with crushed-velvet cushions adorned with tassels and the carpet was thick underfoot, like a forest lawn. The wallpaper was of an ornate design of bronze-coloured vines that dizzied the eye as they crawled up the walls. The room reminded Rose of what an artist's impression of Asholm might be like.

Fabiana was sitting in the midst of a whispering group of young female relatives, who were engaged in the genteel pastime of needlepoint. All looked up in surprise at Rose's arrival and a silence fell upon the room. Motionless needles glinted in the firelight.

'My dear,' crooned Fabiana. She put down her sewing and rose from her chair. 'Thank you for accepting my invitation, though I confess I did not expect to see you this soon.'

'I hope I haven't inconvenienced you,' said Rose.

'Not at all. You must stay for tea, of course.' Fabiana smiled upon her relatives. 'Shoo now, darlings. Lady Rose and I have news to catch up on.'

In a rustle of silks and satins and with many curious if not piqued glances, the girls left the room.

Now she was actually in the manse, Rose was unsure whether the visit was wise. Back at the Iron Tower, she'd told herself she'd wanted to talk with Fabiana about Carinthia, but she realized that this was not her sole reason for coming here. She had a need to unburden herself, to speak of the argument with her father, but of course that was impossible. The only person she could confide in was Max. Fabiana was no substitute, but it seemed the woman's acute senses had already divined that something was amiss. She embraced Rose warmly, if briefly, then drew away, her hands still upon her guest's shoulders. 'Rose, you look a trifle out of sorts. You have come here early because of urgency, haven't you?'

Rose looked away. 'Impulse, maybe.'

Fabiana indicated for Rose to take a seat and sank back into her own chair. 'Well, has this anything to do with your father? I must tell you he has sent me a message that he wishes to see me tonight. This, and your presence here, are unprecedented. I can only assume I impressed you both last night.'

Rose was surprised about Lord Iron's message. 'Did my father say why he wanted to see you?'

Fabiana shook her head. 'Only that he wanted to continue our discussion.'

Rose clamped her lips into a line. 'We have quarrelled,' she said.

'May I ask what about?'

Rose rubbed her fingers over the plush arms of her chair. She was silent for a few moments, gazing at her hostess's face. Fabiana's expression was one of puzzled enquiry. Rose sighed. 'He thinks my views, like yours, are inappropriate, I suppose.'

Fabiana put her head to one side. 'What views are these?'

Rose felt as if she was being torn apart inside. There was a possibility, seeing that Fabiana was part of the Council's inner cabal, that Lord Iron would tell her everything. Surely it would be better to come clean now and deal with consequences? But what if her father had no intention of such honesty? It was a dilemma.

'Your silence speaks most eloquently,' murmured Fabiana. She leaned forward, hands clasped upon her knees. 'Rose, I can only tell you that you can speak your mind to me. I will treat our conversation with the utmost confidence. Also you should know that, whatever you say to me, I will not be shocked.'

'You cannot say that,' Rose said.

Fabiana leaned back against her cushions. 'What a sad state we have come to. No one trusts anyone. If we are to move forward, Rose, someone has to break this ice of silence. Do you fear the cold waters beneath?'

'I do not fear what lies beneath,' Rose said carefully, 'but feel I am alone in that. It is the crux of my dilemma.'

'Ah, beneath,' said Fabiana. 'Secrets buried for millennia. They intrigue you, don't they? All your life, you've sensed they're there. They've plagued your dreams and haunted your waking moments. You have been driven to scour dusty libraries, trying to satisfy your hunger. How do I know this? Because I used to feel the same. The only difference is that I learned the truth from my mother before she died. Times are different now. Urgency surrounds us. It is as if countless ghosts are shouting in our ears, trying to get our attention but not being heard. You are sensitive to this. It is hardly surprising. You are the daughter of a great Clan, and the secrets are your heritage.'

Rose swallowed past the lump that was rising in her throat. To hear Fabiana's words was a great relief. So much so that she felt like weeping. 'You know me,' she said.

Fabiana rose from her chair and came to crouch by Rose's side. Her warm smooth hands gripped one of Rose's own. 'My dear, you are not alone. It is a great tragedy that your mother died when you were so young. She should be here for you now. I do not wish to sound importunate, but I am happy to fulfil that role for you.'

Rose put her free hand to her eyes. She could not stop the tears. The image of Max filled her mind, surrounded by a swirl of other images: Shriltasi, the artefacts, the Ashen, the angry face of her father.

'Laferrine was not like your father,' Fabiana said, reaching out to stroke Rose's hair. 'She would know that now is not the time for silence, and that the rigid rules should be bent. You cannot help feeling the way you do, and in my eyes it is unfair, if not cruel, to keep you in the dark. Your ancestors are calling to you desperately.' She withdrew a scented handkerchief from her sleeve and pressed it into Rose's hand.

Rose wiped her eyes, blinked and sniffed. 'I wouldn't . . . I wouldn't have put it like that.'

Fabiana smiled. 'I do not mean literally, of course. Just that we are in danger of making grave errors and that if our ancestors were alive, they'd be boxing our ears.'

'Yes,' said Rose. I think we are making mistakes.' Fresh tears welled from her eyes. 'I may have done a terrible thing.'

'You?' Fabiana laughed gently. 'I hardly think so. What is so terrible?'

Rose shook her head. 'I can't tell you. Not yet. In a few days, I will.'

Fabiana squeezed Rose's hand. 'You can trust me. Speak now. Speak your heart.'

Rose felt as if a great shadow was seeping out of the fire, filling the room. It loomed around her, sapping her strength. Absurd. She felt cornered, vulnerable, as if her secrets had a life of their own and might come spilling from her lips, beyond her control. She had never felt like this before and hadn't broken down in front of anyone since she'd been a child. She had always coped with everything. Perhaps it had all become too much to bear and she was not as strong as she liked to believe. 'Carinthia,' she blurted, desperate to divert the conversation.

'Carinthia?' said Fabiana. 'What of her?'

'She wishes to see me. She sent a letter, as you did.'

'Did she indeed?' An uncharacteristic coldness had come into Fabiana's voice. 'I feel you must be careful of her.'

'She could be part of something . . . something dangerous. Coffin has heard rumours of it.'

'Ah yes,' said Fabiana. 'I have heard Coffin's rumours. Do you really give them credence?'

'I would not disbelieve anything I heard at present. Too many strange things are happening.'

Fabiana nodded. 'Hmm. However, I think we should guard against giving Carinthia more credit than she deserves.'

'She is ambitious and makes no secret of it. I think she'd do anything to acquire power.'

'True. And, as I said, you should be wary of her. But her schemes are all – shall we say – concerned with the immediate. Does not make a monster of her, Rose. I believe that despite Carinthia's outward appearance of unorthodoxy, at heart she wishes only to rule the Metal in your father's place, in exactly the same way he does. With a steel fist, rather than an iron one.' Fabiana paused. 'If anything, she would benefit from thinking more like you do.'

'I think she does,' Rose said, then shook her head. 'I mean, I think she has looked in the same places I have, searching for answers.'

'All knowledge is open to interpretation,' Fabiana said. 'I very much doubt Carinthia reaches the same conclusions you do. She does not want to make an ally of you, but only seeks to pick your brains. Do not give her the satisfaction.' Fabiana rose and returned to her chair. 'You should decline the invitation.'

Rose's head was swimming. She felt almost obliged to agree with Fabiana's suggestion. Was this what it was like to have a strong mother-figure in your life? If Laferrine were alive, would she feel this same desire to comply? Rose strove to regain some control. 'I had thought to visit her in order to gain information, to hear what she had to say.'

'You would get nothing. She'd merely badger you into confiding in her.' Fabiana laughed, and the sound was not at all like her usual expression of joy. 'Believe me, the woman is adept at turning on the charm when she needs to. Do not fall prey to it. The best way would be to avoid the possibility at all costs.'

Rose considered. 'You tell me not to make a monster of her, yet you say attempts to convince me otherwise.' She cleared her throat. 'Despite appearances now, I am not a fool, Fay, nor weak.'

'I know,' Fabiana said. 'You are tired and confused, and I am flattered you feel comfortable enough here to display your emotions. I cannot stop you visiting Carinthia, but can only advise you to caution.'

'I appreciate that.'

'So,' said Fabiana, 'what of the other things that worry you? Carinthia is not your greatest concern at the moment, is she?' Fabiana smiled. 'If I didn't know better, Lady Rose, I'd say you have the look of a woman in love.'

Rose could not prevent the heat that rose to her face. 'That is the least of my problems. The fate of Karadur is my prime concern.'

Fabiana stared at her for a few moments. 'Perhaps the two are linked.'

'No.' Rose stood up, craving physical movement. She didn't want to talk about this.

'You will have to have a husband one day, Rose. A strong man, who is your equal.'

'There is no such man,' Rose said.

'Is there not?' said Fabiana.

Rose stared at her, speechless. Fabiana could know nothing. She was guessing, and yet it was as if she knew the contents of Rose's heart already.

'Very well, I respect your reticence,' Fabiana said. 'But follow your instincts, Rose. In a woman, that is generally the right way to go, and not just in matters of the heart. I have no desire to bully you into confiding in me when you are clearly in a quandary over what to say. Know only that my door is ever open to you.' She smiled. 'And I shall remember what you said about telling me everything in a few days' time. I will keep you to it.'

'Thank you,' Rose said.

'Sit down again. I will order my servants to bring us a meal. We will enjoy good food together and talk of inconsequential things. Such pastimes are balm for the troubled heart, and you should indulge in them more often. I presume you will not want to be present when your father arrives.'

'I am sure he would not be happy to find me here.'

'Don't worry. I shall speak to him later and try to make him see sense about you. I'm tempted to tell you everything myself but realize this would not really be appropriate. Prometheus would never forgive me, and I have to say that I do value your father's favour, which it seems I am winning slowly. All I can do is convince him to confide in you.'

Rose nodded. 'Again, thank you.'

'It is my pleasure,' Fabiana said.

Rose left Verdigris House long before her father was due to arrive there, and returned to her private eyrie. Her heart felt made of iron, too heavy to beat. She went to the great curved windows and looked down upon the city. Lights had dimmed. The hour was late and most people were sleeping. Rose opened the window and stepped out onto the balcony, looking down on the distant streets. She could not weep now. She could barely think. What had she done this day? Had it been right? Images swirled in her mind like molten silver. She had opened the way into Shriltasi for Coffin and the Irregulars, she had angered her father and then gone running for advice to a woman she barely knew. On top of all this, she was in love with a man effectively sentenced to death, who clearly did not return her affections. Fabiana had perhaps intuited Rose's feelings, but she would be appalled if she knew in which direction they lay. Max was a criminal. Even if the prophecy of the silverheart came true, so that he was redeemed in the eyes of the Metal, Rose couldn't imagine him ever wanting to be part of her world. But she could love no one else.

Max sat at a table in Jenny Ash's chamber, picking disheartenedly at a meal. His chest felt tight, the metal disc hot against his flesh. He was uneasy about the harsh words he'd exchanged with Rose. He'd been too hard on her. Something about the artefact they'd found earlier that day had affected him, conjured deeper suspicion and resentment within him.

Jenny was staring at him speculatively, stirring her dinner with a wooden fork. 'Why so sad, Sir Fox?' she asked, head to one side. 'You mustn't worry about Master Vane.'

Max shook his head. 'It's not that. I'm just conscious of time running out. What's going to happen to me, Jenny?' He tapped his chest. 'When this thing meets my heart will I just die? Why was it put into me?'

'The silver heart gives you power, but there is a price. You might lose yourself.' She put down her fork. 'For now, you must not brood upon it. This has never happened before, so how can we know how it will end? Come now, show me the book your Silverskin relative gave to you.'

Max lifted his coat from the floor, took the book from one of the pockets and handed it to her. Jenny turned the pages for a while, saying nothing. Occasionally, she'd gasp in pleasure. 'This is a priceless thing,' she said at last, looking up. 'You were lucky to get it.'

He shrugged, bit into a woodfowl's leg. The meat was gamy. 'I've not had a chance to examine it.'

'But it says so much about the artefacts,' Jenny said, tapping the pages with one finger. 'And some of it is written in Ashen – clearly a code the Silverskin women used. We need this knowledge. At the Reformation, we too lost wisdom from the past. ' She got up from her place opposite him and took a seat beside him, the book in her hands. 'Look.' She turned back a few pages, indicated a picture. 'This is the Dragon Mirror.'

'We know that already. We know it conjures illusions.'

Jenny shook her head. 'But it's so much more than that. I don't know why I didn't realize. The Mirror is an aspect of a totem beast.'

Max looked at the book with more interest. 'What kind of beast?'

'The obvious,' Jenny said. 'A dragon. You must conjure it forth as you did with the owl.'

'The owl conjured herself once the parts of the artefact were brought together,' Max said. 'Are there more parts to the mirror?'

'Yes.' She read a few lines. 'The mirror is its eye.'

'What are its other parts?'

Jenny read for a few moments. 'Its skin . . .' She frowned. 'Its skull. The book was written long after the artefacts were lost. There is scant information on the other parts of the dragon. The Silverskins don't know what happened to them. Perhaps Clan Iron has them.'

'Do you think Rose knows that? Is she keeping information back?'

Jenny shook her head. 'I don't think so. Lady Rose does tend rather to show her heart in her eyes. I believe her to be ambitious, but not duplicitous.'

'I wish I could share that conviction,' Max said dryly. 'What does the book say about the other artefacts? There are four altogether, aren't there?'

Jenny nodded, leafing through the book. 'Some of this ancient script is difficult even for me to read.' She stopped at one of the pages. 'Ah! This is what we want. Look, Fox, look. What have we here?'

Max looked down at the book and saw a picture, delicately drawn in brown ink. 'By the Jewel, that's the baton I found!'

Jenny nodded. 'It's as the Porporrum told us – a paw. It's the paw of Sekmet, the gibbold goddess.' She looked up at Max. 'Totem of Clan

Gold.' She frowned. 'It's so mixed up. Sekmet was a goddess venerated by the foundrymen of Clan Iron.' She was silent for a while as she scanned the page next to the drawing, then read aloud. '"This great force, she of the red stare, is one of the four, they who were invoked during the Clan Wars. The dragon, the deva, the owl and the gibbold, they who were worshipped above all, by those of the land and below the land".' She fell silent, squinting at the cramped text. 'I think I see,' she said.

'Tell me,' Max said.

'Before the Wars, the Four were venerated equally by all. When the conflict started, each Clan called upon the archetypal power of one of the forces. Sometimes, two clans might choose the same force. For example, Gold petitioned the fiery force of Sekmet, but so did the foundrymen. Different aspects of the same *barishic* frequency were drawn into conflict. No wonder chaos ensued. No wonder the Lords of the Metal were anxious to put all that from them for ever. It must have been insane.'

'What makes the rest of the Gold artefact?'

Jenny turned a page, read in silence for a moment. 'The tail and the tooth,' she said.

'And where will they be? In the Hive, do you think?'

Jenny frowned. 'If they were, they'd have been in the temple. Did you check the hiding place before you left?'

'Yes. It was empty but for a few wooden bowls and some foul-smelling incense. The other parts could be in Karadur, of course.'

Jenny considered for a moment. 'They might, but I think there's a more likely place . . .'

'Where?'

'Well, if the Porporrum had the paw, it's possible they have the other parts as well. I think the shaman you killed was trying to take the paw to safety. Sekmet was once a mighty force in Shriltasi. Her own creatures roamed here in their thousands. There is a place, now shunned by all in the way the Porporrum shun the Stone Grove. It is a temple on an island, once sacred to Sekmet. During the unrest, when the Clan Wars raged above us, terrible things happened there. Sacrifices were made, hideous sacrifices. Priests and priestesses would daub themselves with the entrails of their victims to see the future. It would be an ideal place to hide the artefacts.' She shook her head. 'There has been activity in this location for some time. Our spies believed that some of our estranged people have revived the worship of Sekmet. No malign *barishic* influence has yet touched us from it, so we have paid it little attention.'

'If the cult of Sekmet has been revived, this is an obvious location for its headquarters,' Max said.

'Yes. We will go to the temple tomorrow.'

Max sighed heavily. 'Even if we find the rest of the gibbold icon there, what about the remaining parts of the dragon, and this other one, the deva? What form does that take?'

Jenny wrinkled her nose. 'The book reveals little on that score. Not even the Silverskin adepts knew everything about the icons. One thing's clear to me, however. You must carry the mirror with you always. There's no doubt that *barishi* flows strongly enough within you for you to keep it in a diminished state for lengthy periods.'

Max nodded. 'In case I come across the other parts. That makes sense.' He yawned and stretched. 'We have only two days left, Jenny. What will happen if we haven't found all the icons at the end of this time?'

Jenny regarded him for a few moments. 'I don't know. That's the truth. We must simply carry on and trust that you are meant to find them.' She reached out and clasped his hands. 'Whatever happens, I will be with you. Have no fear.'

Before Max retired for the night, he went to visit Menni. He found his old friend propped up in bed with a young Ashen girl sitting beside him, her hands upon his chest, apparently concentrating on healing him. Menni's eyes were closed, but he was smiling.

When she saw Max standing in the doorway, the Ashen girl got up and left the room on silent feet. Max approached the bed. 'Menni?'

The older man opened his eyes and Max almost winced away. Physically, there seemed nothing different, but when that gaze first fell upon him, he thought that a stranger looked out from Menni's eyes.

'How are you feeling?' Max asked.

'With greater ease than before, lad.'

Max smiled. 'It's good to have you back.' He sat down in a chair of woven branches by the bed. 'Can you remember anything of what happened?'

Menni frowned. 'A dream,' he said and then shook his head. 'A woman came to me earlier and told me a strange story. It was about you, this place. Is it true?'

'Probably,' Max replied. 'A lot has happened recently.'

'Tell me about it,' Menni said. 'I'll trust it more from your mouth.'

Max related all that had occurred since Menni had been transformed.

Afterwards Menni said, 'Irons, Silverskins, hidden lands. It's hard to believe. I wonder whether I'm dreaming this.'

'You're not,' Max said. 'I wish you were. Here is the evidence.' He unlaced his shirt and showed Menni the silver disc set into his flesh.

Menni regarded it with distaste. 'This is evil work,' he said. 'Wrong. You should try to get it removed.'

'It can't be,' Max said. 'Menni, we have to accept the unacceptable. We need to know who's behind the Porporrum now. Can you really remember nothing of the last couple of days?'

Menni screwed up his eyes. 'I remember . . . cold, distant sounds. Like being in Gragonatt, only the walls were myself.' He sighed. 'My perceptions were limited. I wasn't aware of movement, even though you and that green-skinned woman have both told me I was taken to a temple.' He raised himself and grabbed one of Max's arms. 'You have to understand, lad, I wasn't there. I wasn't there.' Menni released Max and fell back on the pillows, blinking. 'I wasn't there.'

Max shuddered. He spoke quietly. 'Jenny has assured me the effects of your ordeal will disappear in time. Just rest, my friend.'

He left the room, disquieted. All these years he'd relied on Menni's presence, almost as though it was a lucky talisman, yet over the past couple of days he'd been forced to survive without him. Now his friend and mentor was an invalid, his mind tormented. *I am alone*, Max thought. *Despite Jenny, despite Rose, I am alone.*

Chapter Four

Power of the Gibbold

In the morning Jenny's attendant presented herself at Max's door and informed him that Jenny had invited him to share breakfast with her. When he went to Jenny's chambers, he was surprised to find Rose Iron sitting at the table. His first response was relief, perhaps pleasure, but a harder feeling of suspicion eclipsed it. 'Good day to you, madam. Have you returned to continue our quarrel?'

Rose remained sanguine. 'I returned out of courtesy, to inform you of developments. I must tell you of the interview with my father and our dear friend Captain Coffin.'

Max listened with mounting disbelief and disapproval as Rose related what had transpired the previous night. At the end of her narrative, Jenny spoke first. 'I hope you were wise in your decision, Lady Rose.'

Max detected this was an understatement of Jenny's feelings.

'I feel Coffin's behaviour is dictated solely by his affection for me,' Rose replied.

Max laughed coldly. 'How confident you are in that. You're on dangerous ground, playing with the feelings of a man like that.'

'I do what is necessary,' Rose said. 'I can deal with the consequences.' She made a dismissive gesture. 'Anyway, it seems likely that Clovis Pewter is visiting Shriltasi, and perhaps Carinthia Steel.'

At the end of it, Max grimaced. 'Pewter? Surely not. Steel, maybe. Pewter hasn't got the wit to be part of this cult.'

'A sentiment you share with my father,' Rose said. 'How ironic. Coffin, however, is quite convinced. As I said, he believes Pewter is an ally of yours.'

'Which perhaps signifies how accurate his other assumptions are.'

Rose shrugged. 'It hardly matters. My father has admitted he knows Shriltasi exists. He cannot go back on that.'

'I doubt he will,' Jenny said. 'But I also wonder how he will deal with the situation. He could send Coffin's Irregulars down here to destroy what's left of our realm. Then he'd never have to worry about it again. Nobody would, because it would mean death for both our worlds.'

'I'm sure my father is aware of the dangers of that as much as you are,' Rose said stiffly. 'He is no fool, Jenny Ash.'

'Yes, he is,' Jenny said. 'If he wasn't, he wouldn't perpetuate the ridiculous traditions his ancestors dreamed up.'

'You have no right to speak ill of him,' Rose snapped. 'He cannot help the way he was brought up or what he was taught to believe.'

'He's sick,' Jenny said. 'You all are. Karadur is poisoned. You can't sense it, because you're used to it, but the very air you breathe and the water you drink are foul. Your city will not sustain any of you for much longer. And while your mighty Lords deny the existence of Shriltasi, you will never save yourselves.'

'My father does not deny it. The mere fact he spoke as much as he did on the subject shows how good a man he is at heart.'

'You were wrong to confide in him at this time,' Jenny said. 'I don't dispute that your father is an intelligent man, but intelligence does not necessarily bestow awareness. You should have left the Fox and I to solve the dilemma. At the proper time, the power of the silverheart will force everyone in Karadur to open their eyes. We do not need your help.'

'But it's not just your problem,' Rose said. 'I have as much right as you to be involved here. If you say otherwise, you're as short-sighted and hidebound as you accuse my father of being.'

'So the argument continues,' Max said with exaggerated weariness. 'It's done now, whether for ill or good. We can't waste time with it. We have work to do.'

'What work?' Rose asked sharply.

'You just concentrate on your little theory about Pewter,' Max replied.

'You don't believe me, do you?' Rose sighed. 'We should work together, Max.'

Max glanced at her and divined from her expression that what she really meant was 'We humans should work together'. The blood of her ancestors was strong in her veins. He thought she considered herself superior to the Ashen, in every sense.

'When are you bringing Coffin down here?' he asked. 'And what exactly do you hope to achieve by that?'

'I'll bring or direct him here today. He is good at what he does. If Karadurians have infiltrated Shriltasi, he'll find them. His snuffers will track them down.'

'Snuffers, Irregulars.' Max laughed scornfully. 'They will tear this place apart.'

'They will not,' Rose said firmly. 'Coffin will do as I ask, for he expects to reap great rewards from co-operating.'

'I think you are naive to trust him so readily. He'll be down here looking for me.'

'I'll not lead him to you, if that's what you fear. I'll keep him well away from Asholm.'

'Presuming I'll remain here.'

'Where are you going?'

Max said nothing and Rose raised her eyebrows.

'I can't trust you,' he said at last. 'I can't trust the cruel, ambitious Iron.'

'You did,' Rose said shortly. 'Who changed your mind?' She glanced pointedly at Jenny.

'You seek power,' Jenny said. 'If you ally with us, it is to further your own cause.'

'You too have changed your song,' Rose said. 'At one time you were eager to make alliance with the Iron. Do you believe you no longer need me?'

'We never needed you,' Jenny said. 'We were curious, that's all – Jack especially. But he is not here now. You are a clever creature, Lady Rose. Do what you do best. Seek power in the upper world, and when the

Fox of Akra is victorious, rule wisely in your father's place to make change.'

'You cannot dismiss me,' Rose said. 'Don't think you can.'

'But don't you have an appointment with your lovesick paramour?' Max said.

Rose stared at him unflinchingly. 'Don't be misled,' she said. 'The Ashen care nothing for your welfare, only for their own survival.'

Jenny laughed. 'Oh, hear the lady speak. It is me you talk of, or yourself?'

Rose got up and addressed her remarks to Max alone. 'I came to tell you all I know. It was the act of a friend. I hope, when you've thought about this, you'll realize that – for yourself.'

'No one influences my opinions,' Max said. 'Not Jenny, not you. I have my own mind.'

Rose stared at him for a few moments and looked as if she wanted to say more, but then uttered a sound of frustration and walked out.

Jenny made a sneering sound. 'Her title means nothing in Shriltasi. She forgets that.'

Max was still staring at the door. 'Yet you were the one who suggested I go to her for help a couple of days ago. What's changed your mind about her?'

'She's performed her function,' Jenny answered shortly, then stood up. 'We should get ready to leave now. Time is short. Bring the gibbold paw with you.'

'Now you sound like Rose,' Max said. 'Don't bludgeon me with orders, Princess Jenniver.'

Jenny smiled. 'You remembered my full name. How sweet.'

'Let's go,' said Max.

It was an area that looked as if some great fire-breathing beast had sighed upon it. The sward was crisp and brown and swept down to the edge of a wide lake whose motionless surface gleamed like lead. A ring of tall trees surrounded the water, their foliage russet and rustling although there was no breeze. Wizened spears of reeds and squat willows with yellowing leaves rimmed the lake itself. In its centre was an island of high rock covered in shrivelled bushes and twisted poplars. At its summit, a glimpse of stone could be seen. A desolate place. It looked cursed.

An oily-plumed water fowl lifted from the reeds with an eerie cry and the War Owl, perched on Max's shoulder, uttered a soft mew. 'This place has seen horror,' Max murmured.

Jenny, who was crouched beside him in a thicket of dead bracken, nodded slowly. 'Have no doubt of it, Sir Fox. Once this was a vibrant, holy place, but at the time of the Reformation, its energies changed. Sekmet breathed upon her own sanctuary, and took its life.'

'Is that the temple at the top of the island?'

Jenny nodded. 'It's been little more than a ruin since the Reformation, permeated by a dark *barishi* current.'

Max noticed a couple of ancient punts tied to a jetty at the water's edge. He gestured at them. 'We can use one of these to cross over.'

'Wait a while,' Jenny said. 'In the old world, the time would be approaching noon. A significant time for the worshippers of the goddess. If this place is still used, a ceremony is no doubt about to take place. I suggest we find a better hiding place.' She indicated an old and distorted oak tree nearby. Max thought the limbs, though wide, looked desiccated and frail, but Jenny started climbing it without a thought. She looked down and patted the pleated bark of the tree. 'Come on, Sir Fox. This old man is sturdier than he looks.'

'I weigh considerably more than you do.'

Jenny rolled her eyes. 'Fox. Climb.'

Max tested the branches and then gingerly hauled himself aloft, until he reached Jenny's perch on a huge wide limb.

'Only the darkest of Sekmet's rituals were performed at night,' she said. 'When her followers lived in the world above, before the ice, she was a personification of the sun's fire. Her fierce heat could take life, but could also sustain it. As with so many things, her worship has become polluted, warped.'

'If Sekmet's a goddess of fire,' Max said, 'how come her temple was built surrounded by water?'

'This island represents the primal mound of creation,' Jenny answered, 'from where all gods came.'

'I wonder how her cult became revived in Karadur,' Max said. 'Clearly, people other than Rose have been delving into the old libraries.'

Jenny smiled tightly. 'Don't be deceived, Sir Fox. I think many practices continued above that the Lords thought they'd abolished. Not everyone will have agreed that the use of *barishi* should cease.'

'That is a thought,' Max said.

'You should have thought more of it before. What about your mother's family?'

He nodded. 'I'd heard the tales, of course, but, like everyone else I knew, thought they were just rumours.' He touched his chest. 'I'd never felt *barishi* within me.'

'What do you think animates the Jewel of All Time?'

Max stared at her. 'I'd always believed it was the light of the Ruby Moon.'

'Light? Just that?' Jenny laughed softly. 'Your people are sleepwalkers.'

Further conversation was curtailed by movement and sound below. Max and Jenny froze upon their perch. Looking down, they saw figures emerging from the trees around the lake. All wore concealing cloaks. Some were large and burly in build, suggesting they were foundrymen, while others were more slight. Karadurians? Ashen? They climbed into the punts and poled across the lake to the island. The punts had to make several trips, with some of the larger individuals acting as boatmen. Eventually, no more came from the trees and the last figures had crossed to the island.

Max made to start climbing down, but Jenny stayed his arm. 'Wait,' she said.

'Why?' Max asked. 'They've all gone over.'

Jenny shook her head. They remained where they were for several minutes, until Max was beginning to wonder whether Jenny was being too cautious. Then the Ashen drew in her breath. Two furtive shapes had emerged from the trees to the right of the lake. Like those who had passed before, they were swathed in hooded capes. After making a swift examination of their surroundings, they hurried towards the water's edge.

'How did you know?' Max whispered, though it was unlikely the individuals below could have heard them speak.

'The high priest and priestess,' she breathed. 'They would not travel with the others.'

The two figures walked cautiously along the sagging jetty to where the last punt was tethered to the slats – clearly a man and a woman. With suspicious, jerky movements, the male figure then untied the punt while the woman climbed into it. Presently, they were poling the vessel across the water, cleaving the scales of rotten lily pads, the boatman hunched over, intent on his labour.

Once the priest and priestess had disembarked and disappeared into the greenery on the island, Max and Jenny climbed down the tree and approached the jetty. Max put his hands on his hips and examined the island. There were no more punts available, so they'd have to bring one back to them. He took a coiled Ashen rope from his belt and placed it in the beak of the War Owl, murmuring a soft command. At once the copper bird swept into the air and headed for the island.

After a few minutes, the owl returned to them. In her beak she still had the end of the cord, which she dropped at Max's feet. Max picked it up and began to pull. The slack was taken up and then a punt was gliding back towards them, tied to the cord.

'Are you ready for this?' Max asked. 'There will be quite a lot of them over there.'

Jenny nodded. 'I am confident of your protective powers.' She grinned. 'Also, we are wearing cloaks ourselves. I'm thinking the celebrants will be so intent on their ritual that they won't notice two extra bodies.'

They climbed into the punt and steered a careful course through the mass of lily pads and weeds. A rotten stench rose from the water and occasionally its surface would be broken by slick-backed creatures that could have been fish or amphibians. Max was aware of a heaviness in the atmosphere, which seemed to drain the energy from him. He hoped Jenny was correct to be confident in his powers. This place was more cursed than the Slug King's glade. It oppressed him, as if the spirits of thousands of tortured souls shouted soundlessly in his ears.

Once at the island, they pulled the punt ashore on a beach of black shingle, then followed an upward trail, made difficult by tangled broken grasses and torn bushes, towards the island's summit. The only sound was the occasional mournful cry of a water fowl, and a strange high-pitched buzzing, which Max suspected existed only in his head.

At the top of the island, the bushes had been hacked away to make entrance to the temple easier. The building was a truncated pyramid with a single entrance portal at the front. It was far larger than Max had expected. A carving that represented the gaping jaws of a gibbold surrounded the doorway. The image was worn now, the cruel fangs blunted by the passing years. But the shape of them, the intention that had once been worked into them and that still haunted them, spoke of barbarity and cruelty. Max extended a hand but could not bring himself to touch the stone. He was sure that, if he did so, he would be swamped with terrible impressions from the past.

'Listen,' Jenny hissed, raising a hand.

Max could hear it: a faint, rhythmic chanting. Many voices. Low and fierce. 'It seems the ritual has started,' Max said. 'We must not be late.' He summoned the owl to conceal herself in the spellstone once more and stepped into the darkness beyond the portal.

Beyond, a corridor branched to both left and right. The right path was partially blocked by fallen rubble so Max and Jenny were forced to turn left. They advanced carefully, alert for the sound of footsteps, but all they could hear was the gradually increasing din of the chanting. Max heard hunger in it, and greed, and lust for blood. Sweat broke out on his upper lip and beneath his arms. He felt that if he continued forward he would be contaminated, soiled. But perhaps that was part of some protective enchantment that guarded the place.

Eventually they saw light ahead, issuing from a doorway in the right side of the corridor. Max peered round it. The pyramid must be hollow for they stood at the edge of a square arena, with banks of stone seats rearing up towards the summit. The arena floor was mostly filled with celebrants, as were about a third of the seats, but no one was sitting down. The gathering was clearly excited about the ceremony to come.

Max examined the celebrants with interest. Many of the worshippers were clearly foundrymen or Irregulars, having the characteristic heavily muscled bodies and massive heads. That made sense, for the worship of Sekmet had once been common to these people. But others present were far slighter in build, almost as small as Jenny Ash. Some still wore their concealing cloaks but others were almost naked, clad in strips of furry hide. The entire congregation had their attention riveted upon whatever was happening in the middle of the arena.

Max and Jenny pulled their own hoods over their heads and began to climb the seats in order to get a better view. No one paid them any attention. They didn't venture far beyond the crowd for fear of becoming noticeable, halting a few rows behind the worshippers. From there they could see at the centre of the arena a cage in which half a dozen men and women prowled and growled. They wore the skins of gibbolds and seemed to be trying to act like them too. 'Sacrifices?' Max murmured.

Jenny shook her head. 'I don't think so.'

In their cage the pseudo-gibbolds licked their lips as if in anticipation, sniffing at the air and roaring with an unspeakable hunger.

Jenny tensed. 'Look – what's going on over there?'

Beyond the cage, a group of burly foundrymen was tying a writhing body between two tall stone pillars, which were crowned with the snarling heads of gibbolds. After a moment, Jenny uttered a muted curse and gripped Max's arm. He realized why. The bound figure was Jack Ash, still draped in his silvery snake-leather cloak. This was perhaps more than they could have hoped for.

Jack's pale hair was smeared with blood and feathers, but from the moment the foundrymen stepped away from him, it was clear he was still fighting against his captivity. He threshed in his bonds, howling like an enraged beast. Small he might be, but Max sensed that if Jack were loose now he'd take more than a couple of the foundrymen with him before he died.

Now the crowd fell silent but for the snuffling grunts of the people in the cage. A man stepped from a doorway below the ranks of seats opposite: clearly the high priest. He wore the skin of a gibbold over golden priestly robes and upon his head reposed an elaborate ceremonial helmet, fashioned from what appeared to be the skull of a great reptile. He walked forward and those in the arena stepped aside to grant him passage. The priest carried himself with great regality and solemnity. For this reason it took Max some moments to realise he was looking at Clovis Pewter. 'By the Jewel, Rose was right,' he said. 'That's Pewter down there, no doubt about it.' He couldn't help chuckling. 'Well, well, cousin, what dark secrets you have hidden from your family.'

'We must save Jack,' Jenny said. 'Use the owl, Fox. Use *barishi*. Save him now.'

'Hush!' Max said, putting a hand on her arm to stop the Ashen from stampeding down the steps into the crowd. 'We must observe a while. There'll be some ceremony, won't there? If they're going to do anything to him, it won't be immediately.'

Jenny rubbed her face. 'This is terrible. I can't sense him in my mind. They've done something to him.'

'Keep calm,' Max said. 'It's the only way to help him.'

A woman now emerged from another doorway, clearly the officiating priestess. She was dressed in splendid robes of gold and scarlet, the shoulders draped with tassels of gibbold tails. Over her head she wore a huge mask fashioned into the face of a snarling gibboldess. Was this a Lady of the Metal, perhaps even Carinthia Steel? The priestess walked slowly into the arena to stand before the bound Jack Ash. Here she raised her arms and when she spoke her voice, though slightly muffled by the mask, rang out across the arena. The acoustics of the place were so well designed, Max was sure that even the back row could have heard the faintest whisper in the arena below.

'Jack Ash, do you know why you are here?' cried the priestess.

Jack stared at her sullenly, his lips curled into a snarl.

'You have angered Sekmet, Ashen,' the priestess shouted. 'Now you must pay the price!' She turned to the crowd. 'My sisters and brothers, come, show your faces to the sun, Sekmet's holy fire.'

At once, all those who wore hoods in the congregation threw them back to reveal their heads, even though the light in Shriltasi was anything but sunlight. Max drew in his breath. He could see that many of them were noblewomen of Karadur. Some even wore the symbols of their clans on their brows and breasts. Others were, as he'd suspected, foundrymen, perhaps even rogue Irregulars. How had they forged an alliance with the genteel ladies of the Metal? Yet more had the green skins of Shriltasi natives. Max gestured towards them, an enquiring expression on his face.

'Ashen renegades,' Jenny hissed in contempt. 'How can they countenance this being done to one of their kind? Whatever divides them from their king, their loyalties should lie with him, not with upworlders.'

Max did not comment.

The High Priest now stepped forward. He emitted a ghastly scream, perhaps what he considered to be the call of the gibbold. Several of the worshippers began to dance around him, ducking and hissing, striking out at unseen assailants with clawed hands.

'In your folly, you sought to deceive the mighty Sekmet,' Pewter roared. 'You sought to use us for your own ends. You are an abomination, Jack Ash. You deserve to die. You have stolen our Holy Objects. You sought to deceive the Metal. You took Sekmet's name for your own purposes . . .'

Jack Ash lifted his head and laughed raggedly. When he spoke, his voice was cool and measured, ringing out through the arena. 'You are fools, playing childish upside games. You turn upon me now, yet without me you would not be here. Whatever you hoped to achieve, all I've seen is that you've degenerated to the level of beasts. You have become slaves to superstition and fear. I showed you the way to make gold of yourselves, but you have remained like clay.'

He continued to speak but Max could not hear the words, because Jenny murmured urgently in his ear. 'What is he saying, Fox? What does he mean?'

'I'm not sure,' Max said dryly, 'but I'd like to find out.'

'I'd have known about this,' Jenny said. 'I would have. This doesn't make sense.'

'Hush,' Max whispered. 'Listen.'

'You betrayed us!' cried the High Priestess below. 'Our movements have been anticipated. Our revolution is threatened. You have allied yourself with the renegade Max Silverskin who has stolen an artefact sacred to us. Where are our objects of power?'

'Where they belong!' Jack snarled.

'Surrender their whereabouts to us now and die with dignity.'

Jack shook his head wildly. 'You can kill me, but if you do you will bring disaster upon your own heads.'

His threats clearly did not disturb the priestess. 'You will be sacrificed to avenge Sekmet's honour!' she hissed. 'Disaster will only fall upon us if you do not die!'

'Your sister undoubtedly has the Paw Ororo,' said Clovis Pewter, more calmly. 'But where are the Tooth and the Tail?'

'Where they belong,' Jack said.

'That's no answer.'

'It's all you'll get.'

'You told us you shared our common goals. You wished to bring Sekmet back among us so that she can rule in place of the Lords of the Metal. Blood is needed to revive the whole of Karaldur-Shriltasi. You swore to help us!'

'Did I? The memory escapes me. All I can recall is that I told you the truth and helped you wake up to reality. I made no promises.'

'Where's the Tooth, Jack Ash?' Pewter cried in a ringing tone, wheeling around to indicate the expectant crowd. 'Tell these people now. Where is the Tail? If you speak, your death will be less painful.'

Jack Ash closed his eyes and threw back his head. He said nothing. It looked as if he was trying to summon *barishi*.

Jenny growled through her teeth. 'Now, Fox. Do something!'

Max still did not feel the moment was right. What, in fact, could they do? *Barishi* might be strong, as was the War Owl, but there were too many people present. The foundrymen would envelop them before they even reached Jack's side. Still, he did not feel all was lost. An instinct told him to wait and watch. Jenny's senses were clouded by emotion. He must curb her desire to throw herself into the arena in a pointless attempt to save her brother.

Clovis Pewter and the High Priestess stood before Jack Ash and raised their arms, crying, 'We call upon thee, Oh Sekmet. Come unto us. Give us your power and your fire.'

The crowd echoed their words, a cacophony of sound. Max's skin prickled. He could not make the mistake of holding these people in contempt. They were not without their own power. He could feel it rising around him, charging the air.

Below, Pewter roared and shuddered as if possessed. He began to run through the crowd, lashing out with his hands, which were gloved with gibbold paws. People moaned and fell if he touched them, writhing upon the ground in some kind of religious ecstasy. Max was sickened by what he saw.

'Beasts,' Jenny hissed. 'Foul beasts!'

Pewter pounced upon Jack Ash and, with the gibbold claws, sliced through the Ashen's voluminous silken shirt to the flesh beneath. Jack's body jerked and greenish ichor sprang from the wounds. The cloth of his shirt had been gored away, revealing his pale chest and also an object that hung from a cord around his neck. A large pouch. Pewter uttered a howl of triumph. Max sensed instinctively that Pewter knew exactly what he was doing. This whole performance was contrived, preordained.

Pewter reached for the pouch and tore it from Jack's body. He held it aloft for all to see, his paws stained by Jack's viridian blood. It was as if he'd ripped the Ashen king's heart from his body. Then Pewter flung the pouch to the High Priestess, who caught it deftly. She opened it and took out two objects: a slender curved ivory knife and a short length of tasselled rope. 'The Tooth and the Tail,' she cried, holding the artefacts above her head. The crowd bayed in triumph.

Between the pillars Jack moaned, his body slumping from the ropes that held him.

The priestess signalled for the crowd to be silent, then addressed Jack Ash. 'You thought to use the power of these artefacts to save yourself, but we are not as stupid as you think. You should have acted sooner. We knew you had them, Jack Ash, and it was our wish for you to surrender them to us in Sekmet's presence. We could have taken them from you at any time. You must know that.' She laughed. 'Now who is the fool?'

'Blood!' cried one of the female worshippers, who wore the emblem of Clan Brass on her brow. 'Give us his blood!'

Jenny leaped forward and had clawed her way through the rear ranks of the crowd before Max managed to grab hold of her and constrain her in his arms. 'Jenny, no!' he hissed in her ear. She writhed in his hold, as inhuman and fierce as he'd seen her in the Slug King's glade.

'Release the zealots!' the priestess cried, and a brace of foundrymen began to march towards the cage, where the inmates were howling and threshing and fighting among themselves. They no longer looked human but were debased, mindless creatures.

'My blood will only offend Sekmet,' Jack gasped. 'Don't you understand that? It is not the blood of red meat.'

'The zealots must feed,' said the priestess. 'And if your whey-thin sap is all they'll drink, then let it be a symbol of a richer substance.'

The crowd roared in hunger and began to dance, ripping at their faces and chests with their fingernails.

'Silence!' commanded the priestess. 'You'll have your share. But first the zealots must feed.'

The foundrymen were unlocking the cage and it seemed that Jack would very soon be torn apart by the maddened zealots. Now immersed in the crowd, Max and Jenny were jostled by the people around them. Max wondered if the moment had come to act, when a booming voice rang out from behind him.

'Your reverence, forgive my interruption, but fresh meat is here. Your captive is now nothing more than a side dish.'

Max and Jenny both turned. Above them they saw the grinning face of Sergeant Rawkis, Coffin's right-hand man. 'Behold, my brothers and sisters,' he yelled. 'Max Silverskin himself and the sap boy's sister!'

Rawkis carried a monstrous flensing cleaver in each massive fist. With an almost insouciant air, he began to descend the few steps between them.

Max acted without thinking. He visualized the sign of the owl in his mind and with quicksilver speed she manifested before them and flew at Rawkis's face.

Instinctively Jenny fled one way and Max the other, while Rawkis, uttering furious growls, attempted to hack at the owl with his cleavers.

The bird was too quick for him, and every time Rawkis missed her she slashed his face with her claws.

The worshippers of Sekmet seethed towards Max and Jenny. At the centre of the arena, Clovis Pewter cried out encouragement to the foundrymen in a voice half human, half animal roar. The foundrymen were all unarmed, but this clearly had little relevance. Their flexing fists, their heat-hardened hides were weapons and shields enough.

Max had drawn his sword. He did not feel afraid. The power of *barishi* pulsed through the silverheart, a pain that was almost pleasure. He heard Jenny's voice from far away and turned to see her almost engulfed by a crowd of worshippers. 'Fox, you have the power of the gibbold. Use it! Use it!'

She must mean the gibbold paw. He remembered the effect it had had upon the Porporrum but doubted it would be quite so effective against foundrymen. Still, he drew it from his pocket and brandished it in his left hand. The foundrymen clearly recognized it, for they began to bay and strike at the air with their fists, advancing more quickly.

'Fox!' cried Jenny. 'Call upon her name. Call upon Lady Sekmet. Claim the Power of the Beast. Make the sign!'

Max's head was muzzy. He tried to remember the symbol they'd seen in his mother's spellbook. Then it was before his mind's eye, glowing as if hanging in the air before him. 'I call upon thee, Oh Sekmet!' he cried, as he'd heard the priestess do. 'Come unto me! Give me your power and your fire!'

The baton grew hot in his grip, so much so that he nearly dropped it. Simultaneously, the silverheart convulsed in a tide of *barishic* power. The foundrymen paused in their advance. Max knew their first instinct was to abase themselves, as the Porporrum had done, but these were fiercer creatures than the little forest people. They looked to their priestess for instructions.

'Seize him!' she cried, pointing at Max with a rigid arm. 'He is a heretic, unworthy of the lady's power. He employs illusion to protect himself.'

'No illusion, madam!' Max cried. He spun round, holding the baton at arm's length, and golden sparks flew off it. When they touched the skin of the foundrymen, their flesh sizzled and burned. The foundrymen backed off, shaking their great heads in confusion.

The arena had gone strangely still. Even the zealots, clutching the bars of their cage, eyes rolling madly, had fallen quiet.

'Release Jack Ash,' Max said.

He imagined that, behind the mask, the face of the priestess would be convulsed with rage and frustration. She stood erect, hands clenched by her sides, seemingly wordless with fury.

'Silverskin, see sense,' said Clovis Pewter.

Max glanced at him. 'Release Jack Ash,' he repeated, 'or I'll burn you all.'

Pewter laughed nervously. 'This is a wonderful show. Just what we need. Come now, cousin, let's put aside misunderstandings. We all want the same thing.'

'You want my brother dead!' Jenny cried. She pushed through the crowd and began to untie Jack's bonds. Nobody moved to stop her. They seemed entranced by the drama being enacted before them.

'Don't insult me with your lies,' Max said. 'Our aims will never be in accord.'

'But they are,' Pewter insisted. 'Much as it may distress you. We both want to see an end to the rule of the Council, its outmoded, unwittingly destructive ways. This is the true way, cousin, that of power and of glory. We should never have been enemies.'

'Don't listen to him,' Jenny cried. 'Use the paw, Fox. Kill him.' Now free of his bonds, Jack tumbled down into his sister's arms.

Again Pewter laughed, pointing at Jenny and her brother. 'These people – these Ashen – were the slaves of Karadur, back in the Golden Age. Some of their erstwhile subjects, who you see here in this congregation, have seen the light and know the old ways must be restored. But these . . .' Again he gestured at Jenny and Jack. 'They seek to rise above their station. Their own people have turned against them. It is time for us to take up once more the reins of power. Jack Ash had to be chastised, Max. You must see that. Given the chance, he and his followers would raze Karadur and put all our people to the sword.'

'Liar!' Jenny cried. 'We are not the killers. We never have been. If we had, we would not have been driven from Ash Haven and Queen Mag would still be alive.'

'You will account to the Metal,' Max said. 'Let the Lords know the truth. If you wish to seek change, then it should be done openly, in debate, not in secret with abominable rituals and lust.'

Pewter shook his head. 'Our rituals are not abominable. You've felt the gibbold's power. It is ours to wield. We have become over-civilized, impoverished because of our denial of it. If you say otherwise, you are a hypocrite.'

Pewter took a few steps towards him. 'Many people stand with me,' he said. 'You would be wise to join them. Even Coffin's trusted aide has pledged allegiance to me.'

Max glanced at Rawkis, who stood rather defeatedly on the arena steps, his gored cheeks dripping blood. The War Owl hovered over him, keeping him in check. 'This is not the way,' Max said. 'You know it. It is simply greed.'

'Not at all,' Pewter said, unruffled. 'I know your destiny, cousin. I admit to the folly of believing I could gather and wield the artefacts myself, but now I realize the true destiny of Karadur is for us to work together . . .'

He might have said more, but the High Priestess lunged forward with a ragged scream. She held the cord she called the tail in one hand, twirling it round her head. In the other, she brandished the tooth knife. This she threw directly at Max, and it struck him on the heart. Gold and silver fire erupted before his eyes and he dropped his weapons. He fell to his knees, a metallic scream reverberating through his head. The fire seemed to condense in his heart, but the knife had not harmed him. Quite the opposite. The priestess had no idea what she'd done.

Max felt himself lifted to his feet by an unseen agency. *Barishi* coursed strongly throughout his body. He leaped forward and grabbed hold of the priestess's arm, noticing Jenny as a green blur hurrying past him to pick up the baton and his sword. 'Show us your face!' he cried, and made to rip off the priestess's mask. With a snarl, she slapped him across the eyes with the tail, and Max was momentarily blinded. His fingers scraped against the hard mask, and then he had her other arm in his grasp. He pulled the tail from her fingers, but with a final shove at his chest the woman slithered out of his grasp and sprang away. Max shook his head to clear his vision. Pewter had used the moment of disorientation to urge the foundrymen forward once more.

Jenny skidded to Max's side, pressing the paw, the tooth and the tail into his hands. 'The sign, Fox. Make it now.'

Everything was chaos around them, converging bodies, howling cries. Max made the sign in his mind and felt the flex of *barishic* power in his hands, in his eyes, in his heart. The foundrymen staggered backwards, their eyes wide. For a moment a strange muttering sound emanated from the women around them. Then one of them uttered a wail and others followed her lead. The arena filled with the echo of their cries, thrown back from the high tiers of seats. Clovis Pewter had backed away, his face distorted with fury and terror. The priestess appeared to have vanished.

Max looked down at the artefacts in his hands. They had indeed become one. The tail had wrapped round the paw and the tooth, and together the parts formed an unusual double-ended weapon. The heat emanating from it was too much to bear. Max had to place the object at his feet. Before his eyes, he could see a shape manifesting from the conjoined artefacts, just as had happened when he'd united the parts of the War Owl. But this was something far stronger, something more terrifying. A red steam was pouring from the artefact, rising up, enveloping his body. He felt it probing its way into his nose and throat, searing his eyes, pushing against the pores of his skin.

Max opened his mouth to cry out and a mighty roar erupted from his throat. It echoed around him, paining his ears. What had happened to him at the Thorn Hive had been but a faint indication of the true power of the gibbold. He felt it possessing him, curling up in his heart and mind, kneading him with needle-sharp claws. His consciousness shot out of his body, until he was hanging high above the arena. Below, his body had transformed. He had become a metal gibbold-headed creature, rustling with thousands of tiny slivers of steel and gold, his golden face burning with a savage light. Part feline, part man, this beast stood looking down on its enemies who seemed to have shrunk to a quarter of their natural size and were fleeing in all directions. The creature expelled another gusting roar, loud and commanding enough to wake the ancient dead.

Some of the supplicants fell flat on their faces, squealing and begging for mercy. Their movements seemed blurred. There were Jack and Jenny, hugging one another, crouched upon the ground, gazing up at the monstrous being Max had become.

But it is not me, he wanted to tell them. *It is Sekmet, her power. I am here, invisible, high above.*

The gibbold creature ignored the worshippers who lay terrified before him. He began to stalk forward, crushing limbs in ignorance beneath his powerful paws, but he had no interest in slaughtering for its own sake. He marched through the temple, the great stones shaking to the thunder of his tread, and prowled down the twisting path outside. A bodiless consciousness, Max followed, until the beast came to stand at the edge of the lake, staring out towards the opposite shore. Here he threw back his head and emitted another mighty roar. For a moment, Max's awareness was dragged back into the great form. He could feel the power of Sekmet coursing through him. He was possessed by the energy of the gibbold, flaming with the life-force of *barishi.* It was mindless power, yet somehow despairing. He could do anything with it: explode the temple, crush the false worshippers, flee this realm, fly through Karadur, then up and up into the void among the stars, lost to this place forever. It would be so easy. Intention would do it: nothing more. The gibbold snarled softly and raised his arms, flexing his claws towards the false sky.

Then Jack Ash's voice pierced his mind. 'Not yet, Max. Not yet. Come back to us.'

Max looked down and saw a small, slender creature rushing towards him. At first he could not recognize it as Ashen, never mind as Jack himself. Max's first instinct was to lash out and knock the irritation away. But Jack was too quick. Despite his wounds, he jumped up and touched Max lightly on the heart with the flat of his hand. A cooler *barishic* current flowed through Max's body. He could feel it expelling the influence of the gibbold icon. For several excruciating moments of disorientation, Max reeled on the spot, his vision boiling with golden motes of light. He fought the expulsion, but then reality see-sawed to stability and he was himself again. The power had not fled completely, however. Beside him stood the manifestation of an immense golden gibboldess, her shoulders almost level with his chest. Her eyes were flame, but she looked upon Max with benign understanding. The gibboldess, who was the lost icon of Clan Gold.

Jenny Ash had also come out of the temple with her brother. 'This creature is yours, Sir Fox,' she said, 'in the way that the owl is yours.' She was holding Max's sword, which she now held out to him. In her other hand she held the gibbold artefact.

Max could not contest her words, as he knew them instinctively to be right. The owl was still within the temple, guarding Rawkis as he'd instructed her. Now, in his mind, he summoned her to return to him. She flew out of the temple and swooped towards him. For a brief moment, she hovered before his chest and placed her claws gently against the silverheart through his shirt. She had the power to soothe him, to quiet the heart. How could these two magnificent creatures be real? Max began to shiver. He felt light-headed now, dizzy. Almost tenderly, Jack Ash put his snakeskin cloak around Max's shoulders and Jenny handed him the gibbold artefact.

'You have some explaining to do,' Jenny said sternly to Jack.

Jack opened his mouth to speak, but his sister interrupted him. 'But not now. We must leave, get the Fox out of here. Get into one of the punts.'

Max shook his head. 'We don't have to. There's a far more efficient mode of transport at our disposal.'

'Is there?'

Max nodded and lifted Jenny bodily in his arms. She uttered a squeak of delight and surprise. 'Will you carry me across the water, Fox?'

He smiled and placed her upon the back of the gibboldess, who stood serenely before them. Jenny laughed nervously and ran her hands through the thick fur. 'She is purrs rather than claws at the moment.'

'Jack, get on,' Max said. 'She can carry us all.'

Once both Ashen were mounted upon the beast, Max climbed up behind them. He could feel the great power of the gibboldess beneath them, an energy thrumming to be used. With a brief command, he urged the War

Owl to merge once more with the spellstone at his neck, then focused his mind to direct the gibboldess to bear them back to Asholm.

Before she could move, however, Max heard shouting voices behind them. He turned and saw Clovis Pewter running from the temple, leading a group of foundrymen.

'Go, Sir Fox!' Jenny urged.

Max laughed quietly. 'In a moment or so.' He had no fear. Clovis Pewter appeared to him as a pathetic dreg of humanity and although the foundrymen were following him, there was no mistaking the awe, fear and reverence in their eyes as they beheld the gibboldess. Max waited until Pewter halted a few yards away. 'Haven't you had enough, cousin?' he asked.

'If you leave here, you do so as my enemy,' Pewter said. 'Consider the wisdom of this.'

Brave words, Max considered silently, which unfortunately were undermined by the pallor in Pewter's cheek and the fact that he was virtually hopping from foot to foot in agitation.

'I have never been anything but your enemy,' Max said. 'You and your kind have always made this clear to me.'

Pewter shook his head. 'You are blind, duped by the Ashen. It is a fool's path. You will be destroyed – you and your repulsive comrades.'

'It is *you* who will be destroyed!' Jenny cried. 'Your own people will do so. Make the most of your pathetic ceremony. It will be your last!'

Pewter stared at her in cold hatred. 'You cannot frighten me with lies, you weed of a creature.'

'It is true,' Jenny said. 'Soon you will see for yourself. Perhaps some of your own followers aren't as faithful to your cause as you believe.'

'Believe it, cousin,' Max said. 'Coffin is on his way to Shriltasi, fully equipped to hunt you down. Good luck.' Dismissing Pewter from his attention, he sent a mental command to the gibboldess. At once, she sprang from the shingled shore towards the water. Pewter uttered an outraged howl behind them, but Max did not look back.

Perhaps the lake was in reality very shallow, but to Max it seemed as if the great creature skimmed over the water's surface. He felt new energy flow through him, Jack's serpent cloak flying behind him. Two of the icons were now in his possession. He dared to think he might recover the others before it was too late.

Once they reached Asholm, Max jumped down from the gibboldess's back and lay on the grass outside the palace, panting. He felt exhausted, depleted. The gibboldess stood over him, as if waiting for a further command.

'You must put her into the stone,' Jenny said, 'as you did with the owl.'

Max nodded and sat up. He took the stone in his hand and formed the symbol in his head. The gibboldess turned to scarlet steam and flowed into the stone. Now a golden sign, that of the gibbold, was set into one of the quarters.

'Only two more.' Max said. The silverheart flexed in his flesh and he winced.

Jenny smiled at him tightly. 'Yes . . .'

Max turned to Jack. 'So what was all that about at the temple? Will you explain it to us now?'

'Jack, were you really working with those people?' Jenny asked.

Jack sighed. 'It is a long story,' he said. 'I would like to refresh myself, if you don't mind. Then we will talk.'

'You can have a few minutes,' Jenny said coldly. 'I need to know, Jack. Now.'

Chapter Five

Deceptions and Lies

Tired and saddened, Rose summoned Captain Coffin to her father's office in the family manse. Lord Iron wasn't there. She knew he would avoid her. The morning was cold, as if the ice was creeping into Karadur, lulling it into a frozen sleep. Rose flicked through the mail on the desk and found another letter addressed to her from Carinthia Steel. The woman was most persistent. She'd barely given Rose time to reply to yesterday's missive. Fabiana was no doubt right about Steel. Rose threw down the card impatiently. There were more important things to worry about. What, for example, had happened to the intimacy she'd shared with Max Silverskin? They had almost been friends, hadn't they? It had all gone wrong. No doubt Jenny Ash had something to do with that. Rose smothered a spurt of anger and jealousy. This would do no good. She must remain focused.

Rose knew that Coffin had been waiting in the ante-room for nearly an hour. But she still made him wait a further few minutes before she bade her father's assistant show him in.

'Good morning, my lady,' Coffin said, bowing in an exaggerated fashion. 'I hope all is well with you. You are somewhat late for our appointment.'

'Unavoidable,' Rose said. 'I trust you are ready to descend to Shriltasi.'

'Ready and eager,' Coffin said. 'I confess to maintaining a slight degree of scepticism and am eager to witness this underworld wonder for myself.'

'You remember what you promised? Leave the native people alone and concentrate only on arresting any Karadurians you find.'

'I remember,' Coffin said. 'It makes sense. When you come into your own in Karadur, these underworld people will also be your people. You want their respect. I understand.'

She stood up. 'Then we must leave at once. It is rather a cramped journey, for we'll have to use thoroughfares through the sewers.'

Coffin hesitated. 'My lady, when this is over . . .'

Rose fixed him with a stern eye. *Don't speak*, she urged in her mind. *Please don't.*

Coffin cleared his throat. 'I just want you to know I do this for you. I would risk my life . . .'

'Be assured I know this,' Rose interrupted in the most imperious voice she could muster. 'My father and I commend your loyalty. Now, time is short.' She gestured towards the door. Coffin continued to stare at her for some moments, but then clearly thought better of saying more. As he turned his back, Rose's shoulders slumped in relief.

Just outside, she found one of her father's servants waiting for her. 'You have a visitor, my lady.'

'Who?' Rose demanded. 'I am about to go out.'

'Lady Steel,' the servant replied.

Coffin, ahead of Rose, turned round. 'What does she want with you?'

'I have no idea,' Rose replied. 'Go to your carriage, Captain. I will join you shortly.' She gestured at the servant. 'Bring her here.'

Back in her father's office, Rose calmed her racing heart. She had nothing to be afraid of. Steel knew nothing. But she was clearly desperate to see Rose.

Carinthia billowed into the room in a soft cloud of white fur cloak, trailing a miasma of strong jasmine perfume. Her face was a powdered mask, the eyebrows finely drawn in arches of surprise above her ophidian hooded eyes.

'Carinthia,' Rose said, standing up behind the desk. 'This is an unprecedented circumstance. Do sit down. What can I do for you?'

Lady Steel put her head to one side as she arranged the voluminous folds of her cloak around her in a chair. 'I was in the area. Thought I'd call in.'

This unlikely response alerted Rose at once. She sat down again. 'Forgive me, but this is most unusual. I find myself inundated with invitations from you, now this.'

'You have not responded to my invitations.'

'You've barely given me time! If you have something to say to me, please say it.'

Carinthia Steel examined Rose with unblinking eyes. 'Never one for social graces, are you?' she said. 'But I like that in you. I like the way you have no time for trivialities.' She leaned forward. 'Of all the women of the Metal, I see you and me as a cut above the rest. This is a changing time. I have pondered the matter and see no reason for us to be enemies.'

'No? I thought you were manoeuvring to remove my family from its position as Head of the Council.'

Carinthia shrugged expressively. 'Your father, for all his good works, is getting too old for the job, that's all. And I do think some of the other clans should be more prominent in the government of Karadur.' She paused, then said, 'Something strange is going on in the city. I know you know about it, Rose. You have been visiting the libraries, as have I. Are you prepared to speak about your discoveries?'

'No,' Rose said, 'simply because there is nothing to tell. I merely have an interest in old literature.'

Carinthia uttered an exasperated snort. 'Oh, don't come that with me. I know very well what you're looking for. Perhaps I am looking for the same thing.' Again a pause. 'Perhaps we should be looking together.'

One thought shot through Rose's brain: the women of the Metal who were rumoured to be part of the cult of Sekmet. Was Carinthia one of them? Was she, in fact, seeking converts? Rose managed a laugh. 'I'm flattered you consider me to be a potential library partner, but I really don't think we're looking for the same thing.'

'You don't trust me, do you?' Carinthia said. 'I can hardly blame you. Still, I hope you will think on this matter and, if you change your mind, come and see me.' She stood up. 'We should be allies, Rose. There is too much ignorance among the Metal. We are like two gibboldesses, sizing each other up. We should forget about our territorial instincts and realize that together we will be of more use to our city.'

The gibbold metaphor was not lost on Rose. Was that a secret signal from Carinthia? Rose inclined her head. 'I shall indeed think about what you said. Support from you at Council meetings might be more persuasive than secretive hints about the libraries, however.'

'I merely do my job as I see fit,' Carinthia replied. 'I will support you, Rose, but not hidebound clichés from your father. I see the spirit of the future in you, and that is something Karadur sorely needs.'

Rose shuddered. Hadn't Fabiana said something very similar? 'You have given me much to think about.'

Carinthia stared at Rose for a moment, then gathered up her cloak. 'I hope so. Good day to you, Lady Iron. I hope you will overcome your aversion and visit me soon.'

'I am not averse to you,' Rose said. 'Simply very busy. Good day to you, Lady Steel.'

After Carinthia had gone, Rose went out to the courtyard, where Coffin was waiting impatiently beside his steam carriage. 'You look thoughtful,' Coffin said. 'What had Lady Steel to say?'

Rose climbed into the carriage ahead of him. 'Do you think Carinthia Steel could be one of the Sekmet worshippers you spoke of?'

Coffin sat down on the bench opposite her. 'Now there's a thought!' He shook his head in amusement.

'I'm serious,' Rose said.

'Did she say as much?'

'I don't know,' Rose replied, frowning. 'I really don't know.'

Jack Ash sprawled on a leaf-strewn couch in his chambers, looking haggard. His sister sat beside him, while Max stood rigidly by the door, arms folded.

'Jack, you are a fool,' Jenny said, shaking her head. 'What did you hope to gain?'

Not for one minute did Max think Jack Ash was a fool. He was probably something far more dangerous than that. Jenny had dragged Jack's story from him, although Max suspected that some details were still absent. It transpired that some years ago, when Jack and Jenny had first begun their forays into Karadur, Jack had visited the city without his sister. He and a group of Ashen had performed a play, similar to the one Max had seen in the Market. That day, Jack had caught the eye of a nobleman, who had offered to buy him a meal and a drink after the performance. That nobleman had been Clovis Pewter.

'I couldn't resist it,' Jack said. 'In conversation with this man, I realized that the Metal had weak spots – chinks in its armour, if you like. Pewter craved power. He felt he was a lesser being among the Lords, his potential ignored. All I did was simply tell him how he could achieve power for himself.'

'Through Sekmet? Jenny asked coldly.

'Eventually.' Jack glanced at Max. 'Pewter is no Silverskin. *Barishi* is weak in him. He needed a focus and the old foundry goddess was the perfect example. It appealed to him. And to many others. The women of Karadur, in particular, sensed that all was not right with their world. It was easy for Pewter to find recruits.'

'But why?' Jenny said. 'He wasn't The One Who Would Come. You didn't believe he was, did you?'

Jack hesitated for a moment. 'Back then, the One had not materialized. I had to accept that he or she might never come. Therefore I decided to create my own.' He sighed, with what Max perceived was exaggerated weariness. 'Then the Fox of Akra came to us. I realized I'd been wrong. I had to change my plans. Pewter already knew about Shriltasi, for I had brought him here and shown him the temple. It was too late to go back on that, so I decided he should merely be used as a disruptive force in Karadur. Once we found Silverskin, I put my loyalty behind him. You must believe that.'

'Perhaps you underestimated Pewter,' Max said stonily. 'I presume it was he who arranged for the Porporrum to take you, Jenny and Menni into captivity?'

'Not him alone. His priestess has a greater influence.'

'Who is she?'

Jack's gaze slipped away from Max's scrutiny. 'That, she keeps to herself. I've never seen her without the mask. But she must be high-ranking. She guards her privacy with a gibbold's zeal.'

Max wished that Rose were present. She had a greater knowledge of the Metal and could perhaps suggest candidates for the priestess's role.

'The priestess wanted the artefacts of the gibbold for herself,' Jack said. 'She knew that Silverskin had come to Shriltasi and that he was trying to collect the lost icons. She decided to take matters into her own hands.'

'And you had the artefacts all along,' Jenny said, sadly. 'How could you do that? You knew the Fox needed them.'

'They were safe in my keeping,' Jack said. 'I would have given them to Silverskin at the appropriate time.'

'When did you find them?' Max asked. 'Where and how?'

'At the time of the Reformation, when the artefacts were separated, the Council of the Metal wanted them destroyed. Fortunately, others thought differently and hid the objects, sometimes in Clan vaults, as with the mirror, some with the Ashen, such as the Copper bead.'

'That's odd,' Max interrupted. 'Why would the Lords entrust any of their artefacts to the Ashen, especially at the time when the two realms were sundered?'

'Not all the alchemists of the Metal agreed with the new laws,' Jack explained. 'You must remember that these men and women were magi, working with *barishi* constantly. You can imagine how they must have felt to be told their craft was now illegal. The innermost cabals of all the Clans knew a time would come when the icons would have to be restored. They secreted them in the most appropriate places. Several other artefacts were hidden in Shriltasi. There is a labyrinth below the temple of Sekmet. Some time ago I took a group of foundrymen there. They conveniently sprang many of the protective traps ahead of me. The artefacts were housed in a chamber far below the island. One of them I gave to Pewter's group, the paw, which the Fox found in the Thorn Hive. The others I kept to myself, as insurance.'

Jenny was frowning, her face a deep viridian hue. 'The loss of Ash Haven,' she said, in a small voice. 'Jack, did that happen after you allied with Pewter? Please tell me Karadurians weren't responsible.'

He shook his head. 'No. Don't think that. Our enemies at court initiated that. I didn't meet Pewter until some time after we'd left Ash Haven.'

Jenny's shoulders slumped in what Max could tell was both relief and sadness. 'You should have told me all this before,' she said. 'Jack, I lost touch with you. That was deliberate, wasn't it? The Karadurians didn't cause it, nor the Porporrum. You cut yourself off from me so I wouldn't discover the truth.'

'You found the gibbold artefacts,' Max said. 'What of the others? I have a feeling you know more than you've said.'

Jack closed his eyes briefly, then stared up at the ceiling of woven withes. 'Perhaps now is the time,' he said. 'Fox, I knew your destiny was to reunite the artefacts, but I'd been working on that task myself for some time. I had been successful. But would it have interfered with your destiny simply to hand these artefacts over to you? It seemed too easy. You had to learn for yourself, recognize them for yourself. As you have done.'

'With Jenny's help,' Max said, 'as well as Rose Iron's. You, on the other hand, would appear to have been far from helpful.'

'I had no choice,' Jack said. He turned his gaze to Max. 'How do you feel at this moment?'

Max exhaled in annoyance. 'There is no time for that. We were discussing the artefacts.'

'It is pertinent,' Jack said. 'Reflect for a moment. How do you feel?'

Max closed his eyes, opened himself up to inner sensation. A shudder went through him. 'Enclosed,' he said, opening his eyes again. 'That's the only word for it. Strange.'

Jack nodded. 'That cloak you wear. Concentrate on that.'

Max touched the shimmering snake leather. 'This . . . ?' It was alive on him, a second skin against his back. He removed it and held it before him. 'What is this?'

Jenny uttered a wordless exclamation. 'The skin of the dragon!' She turned to her brother. 'Is it, Jack?'

'Yes,' Jack said. 'It is the second of the dragon artefacts.'

'Where did you get it?' Max demanded, turning the cloak in his hands. He could feel the *barishi* within it now, a slippery current.

'In Karadur. I quested for it, using psychic vision. It was hidden in a chest in the Foundry of Clan Iron. Forgotten, wrapped in rotten cloth. Not even Rose Iron or her father knew it was there.'

'You knew where they all were, didn't you?' Max said. 'I knew it! All along, you've been playing with us.'

'No!' Jack snapped. 'You don't understand. The path is as important as the destination.'

'Then you should have replaced the cloak where you found it,' Max said. 'Perhaps Rose and I would have discovered it for ourselves.'

'Where is the other dragon artefact?' Jenny asked in a tight voice.

Max felt sympathy for her. Jack had disappointed her greatly.

'Pewter has one other,' Jack said reluctantly. 'It is the helmet he wore in the temple today.'

'Jack!' Jenny cried in anger. 'How could you do that, hand precious objects to that . . . that thing?'

'He can't use them effectively,' Jack said. 'He can do no harm with it.'

'That is hardly the point,' Jenny said with anguish. She shook her head and pressed her hands briefly against her eyes. 'By the Jewel, my bead . . .' She looked up at her brother. 'When Pewter took it . . . Jack, you'd told him about it, hadn't you? You sent me to the Moonmetal Manse. It was no coincidence Pewter caught me there!'

Jack turned his face to the wall and Jenny stood up. 'You have betrayed me,' she said. 'I cannot believe it.'

'I did what I thought was right,' Jack answered. 'The Metal has to embrace Shriltasi once more. It seemed the only way. Pewter is easily led.'

'But his priestess isn't,' Max said softly. 'You didn't plan for that, did you? How did he find her?'

'*I* found her,' Jack said.

'How?'

'The same way I found Pewter. She came to me after a performance in one of the taverns. She was disguised even then, a thick veil wrapped around her face. Her instincts were sharp. She knew something was afoot in Karadur. She could smell it. She wanted to be part of it. When she saw me, she recognized a gateway. Right from the start, she knew what I was. I admired that in her.'

'We must discover her identity,' Max said, then smiled wryly. 'Perhaps Coffin will do it for us.' He frowned. 'I wish I could get word to Rose. We were harsh on her, Jenny.'

Jenny pursed her lips. 'Perhaps. I still can't condone her telling Cornelius Coffin the way to Shriltasi. We cannot guess the consequences of that.'

'Well, one thing is certain,' Max said. 'In the absence of Rose's help, we must get to Pewter before Coffin does and retrieve the last dragon artefact.'

Jenny nodded. 'Our trackers will be able to help us. I have posted lookouts at all the main entry portals to observe Coffin's actions.'

Without another word to her brother, she walked past Max and out of the room. Max directed one last glance at Jack, who shrugged. 'I had no choice,' he said.

'The last artefact,' Max said. 'That of Clan Silver. Where is it?'

'Beyond my reach,' Jack replied.

'Where is it?'

Jack stared at him, unblinking. 'Only you can find it.'

Max exhaled through his nose in exasperation and followed Jenny into the passage outside.

'We should leave at once,' Jenny said. Her expression was closed in. It was clear she did not want to discuss her brother's actions.

'I'd like to see Menni first,' Max said. 'How is he?'

'Enjoying the attentions of his healers,' Jenny said with a tight smile. 'He will be fine, Fox. You really shouldn't worry.'

'I think he'd prefer to be at home.' Max shook his head. 'It's too risky to move him now. You must do it tomorrow, Jenny.'

She hesitated. 'I will, but I hope that you will . . .'

'Just promise,' Max said.

Jenny sighed heavily. 'You have my word.'

Before they even reached Menni's chamber, one of the Ashen healers came hurrying towards them, her face flushed a deep hue. She bowed hurriedly to Jenny. 'My lady, Master Vane has gone.'

'*What?*' Max demanded. He ran past the girl into the room and found the bed empty. Jenny entered soon after, accompanied by the healer.

'Where has he gone?' Max demanded. 'More to the point, how? Weren't you people watching him?'

'He slipped away,' the girl said awkwardly. 'Asked for food. I went to fetch it and when I returned I found him gone.'

'He's trying to get home,' Max said, scraping his fingers through his hair. 'By the Jewel, what if he runs into Coffin?'

'We will deal with it,' Jenny said firmly. 'Master Vane does not know our territory. My trackers will find him.' She turned to the embarrassed healer. 'See to it at once.'

The girl bowed low. 'I will, my lady.'

Before they left Asholm, Jenny met with Rowan in the main hall of the palace. The bow mistress had much to report. 'Clovis Pewter has rallied the Porporrum,' she said, 'and they are on the move towards the Well of the Heart. It is clear they seek to escape by overwhelming the Irregulars through sheer numbers. Foundrymen from Karadur have been directed to all other well portals. Also, the Porporrum have sung their battle songs to Gorpax. He has heard them and moves to the summons.'

Jenny nodded thoughtfully. 'This is all in our favour. In the mêlée we may be able to isolate Pewter and retrieve the helmet.'

'He will avoid the mêlée,' Max said, 'you can be sure of that. Pewter is no fighter, although he is adept at ordering others to fight for him. My bet is that he'll flee to the sewers and escape, leaving the Porporrum and his religious followers to deal with the Irregulars.'

'I will, of course, come with you,' Rowan said, bowing to Jenny.

'No,' Jenny replied. 'You must remain here. If anything should happen to me, I want you to assume control.'

Rowan frowned. 'But King Jack . . .'

Jenny removed a seal ring from her right hand. 'This is my authority.' She took one of Rowan's hands and pressed the ring into its palm, closing the fingers over it. 'Use it.'

Rowan stared at the ring in confusion. 'As you wish, my lady.'

Rose's first thought when Coffin's company emerged into Shriltasi was that Max had betrayed her. Just beyond the entrance, a large group of foundrymen appeared to have been waiting for the Irregulars to arrive. They were armed and ready. Coffin had no time to marvel at his surroundings, but Rose could tell he was almost pleased to find enemies so quickly.

'It seems you were right,' Coffin said to her. 'On every count. I suggest

you return to Karadur now, my lady. This will not be a sight for your eyes.'
He gave a command for his men to attack.

Rose did not stay to watch the fight. Coffin was concentrating wholly on
directing his men. He did not even notice that Rose slipped away into the
forest rather than returning to the portal. She had to see Max now, sure that
if she didn't the sixth day would pass and she'd never see him again. She
would be resolute, refuse to be pushed away, even if she had to fight Jenny
Ash to do it.

She ran fast, so desperate to reach Asholm she was sure she'd lose her way.
The garden of Shriltasi was silent, watchful. She had no doubt many Ashen
observed her progress, but none challenged her.

At Asholm she found Rowan in the main hall, addressing a group of her
bowmen. Rowan seemed surprised to see her.

'Where's Max?' Rose demanded without greeting.

Rowan bridled a little at the abrupt question. 'He has recently left with
Jenny. Something important has occurred here, I think, but Jenny did not
tell me about it. They left in a hurry.'

'Where were they going?'

Rowan shrugged. 'They intended to pursue Clovis Pewter into the
between world. He is making for the Well of the Heart.'

'Right. Thanks.' Rose turned to leave, but a barked command stilled
her feet.

'Wait! Rose Iron, wait!'

Rose turned and saw that Jack Ash had come into the hall. A strange
atmosphere came with him. Rose got the impression Rowan was uneasy
in Jack's presence. Something had definitely occurred here, as Rowan had
put it. Had Max rescued Jack from the Porporrum or had he escaped by
himself? He looked ill, dark green shadows beneath his eyes.

'If you're going after the Fox, I'll come with you,' he said.

'You don't look up to it. What happened?'

'It is a long story. I'll explain as we go.

'You should stay here, my lord,' Rowan said, with clear unease. 'If anyone
accompanies Lady Iron, it should be some of our trackers.'

'Whatever my sister has told you, I am still your king, in every sense,' Jack said coldly. 'Find Lady Rose a suitable Ashen disguise, especially a mask. It would not look well if Coffin or any other Karadurian sees her in Silverskin's company.'

Rowan inclined her head. 'As you wish, my lord.'

Once away from Asholm, Jack told Rose what had happened at Sekmet's temple. This narrative prompted Rose to ask questions. Primarily, she was curious about Jack's alliance with Pewter. Reluctantly, he gave her the story. Rose suspected there was rather more to what had happened than Jack's version of events but realized it would be pointless to press him to reveal more.

'So you were found out,' she said. 'By everyone. Such is the reward for allying with the likes of Pewter. I am amazed at you!' In fact, she wasn't amazed at all. Rose felt that nothing Jack did could surprise her. She simply expected the unexpected from him.

'I did not ally with him, exactly,' Jack said. 'He was a means to an end, that's all.'

'But all your plans were sent awry, regardless!'

Jack did not appear amused. 'My plans are as they always were. I just didn't expect the high priestess to step above herself in that way.'

'Mmm,' Rose murmured. 'The more I hear about this, the more I suspect that Carinthia Steel is involved. She could be the high priestess. But would she have had time to leave Shriltasi and then visit me at home? It is a puzzle.'

Further speculation was curtailed by the sound of voices up ahead. Both Rose and Jack drew their weapons, for it seemed the voices were raised in argument. Perhaps a group of Coffin's Irregulars had run into some of their comrades who'd become part of the Sekmet cult. But as they stepped through the trees into a small clearing, they realized they had come across Max and Jenny instead. It seemed they had taken a prisoner of their own. Max had Clovis Pewter pinned up against an oak trunk. Pewter was making most of the noise. He looked ridiculous, clad in torn robes, his head adorned with an ornate helmet that had been knocked askew and now tilted over one eye.

'Max!' Rose called, lifting the Ashen mask she wore from her face.

Max turned and released his hold on Pewter, who stumbled away from him, righting his helmet. 'Lady Rose!' Pewter cried. 'I am so glad to see you. This ruffian . . .'

'Be quiet,' Rose said. She went directly to Max. 'Are you all right?'

Max nodded. 'Fine.' He cast a furious glance at Pewter.

'Everyone is friends,' Pewter said in a cracked voice. 'It's as it should be. All friends. I was seeking Max Silverskin. We should all make amends.' He glanced fearfully at Jack Ash, who merely shrugged. 'She made me help her, Jack. I never wanted to do . . .'

'Be quiet,' Jack said. Rose sensed that he wanted to maintain a certain distance from the proceedings.

'Pewter is frightened,' Jenny said. 'He wants a shelter to hide behind and knows Coffin's the least likely candidate.'

'What of your high priestess?' Rose asked him. 'Where is she now?'

'I have no idea,' Pewter said. 'She is mad, in any case. I intend to make a full report to the Council.'

'I'm sure you do,' Rose said sarcastically. 'You clearly have a great desire to end your days in Gragonatt.'

'But *you* are here,' Pewter said to her. 'You must be acting for the Iron, so I presume your father has sent you to Shriltasi.'

Rose said nothing but Pewter correctly interpreted her silence. 'I see. Like me, you are here in secret.' He glanced at Max. 'And with unusual friends.'

Rose dismissed him from her attention. 'Max, what are you planning to do now? The sewers are full of Irregulars. It is dangerous for you even to be out in the open here in Shriltasi.'

'I intend to return to Karadur,' Max said. 'I have acquired the gibbold icon of Clan Gold, and now Pewter has kindly delivered the last dragon artefact to us.'

'What is it?'

'This,' Max said. He took the helmet from Pewter's head. Clovis cringed away.

'The last dragon artefact?'

Max stroked the silvery-grey cloak he wore. 'This is the skin of the dragon.'

'Then you must unite them.'

'Soon,' Max said. 'I have a compulsion to reach Karadur first.'

'Is that wise?' Rose asked.

'I feel it is what I have to do.'

Rose fought an urge to embrace him. He looked strangely vulnerable, his face pale with pain. 'Then I will be at your side. Say nothing! I am with you. That is all.'

'I too!' Pewter said.

'Side with those who are strongest,' Jack said coldly.

'As you do,' Pewter spat back.

'We may run across Coffin,' Rose said. 'If that happens, I feel I should speak to him.'

'You shouldn't,' Max replied.

'Why not? I have influence over him.'

'Because he's a man, he has feelings for you, and I hardly think he'll welcome news of your alliance with me and the Ashen – whatever influence you think you may have.'

'Coffin is a man of principle. He is loyal to the Iron.'

Max merely pulled a wry face. 'You have much to learn of the nature of men, Lady Rose. If Coffin catches one glance of my face, his desire for blood will take over, loyal or not.'

'Perhaps you are right,' Rose said. 'But what is there to gain from maintaining old enmities? If there was ever a time for truce, it is now. Maybe you should be the one to make that overture.'

Max shook his head and sighed. 'I wish your view of the world – and of people – was valid, Rose. But, sadly, I suspect it is not.' He glanced around the company. 'Suspicion, hostility, fear – these are the ties to bind us. Does this bode well for tomorrow? No. Still, we must carry on.'

'We are ready,' Jenny said.

How can we be? Rose thought. *We have no idea what we're facing, no idea of what tomorrow will bring.*

Book Four

The Time of the Crucible

Chapter One

The Fight at Watersmeet

Events were not proceeding as Cornelius Coffin had hoped. He'd expected to find a small group of Karadurians who could easily have been taken into custody. Instead, he'd been faced with a fighting force of determined men – foundrymen, even some of his own Irregulars. Coffin prided himself on his intelligence network, as well as on his natural instincts. Therefore it had turned his blood cold to recognize his own sergeant, Rawkis, in the makeshift army that opposed them. He thought himself a good judge of character, adept at sniffing out deceit. Yet here was someone whom he'd trusted above all others – and who had secretly been an enemy.

There had been little time for his senses to take in the astounding reality of Shriltasi. During the fight, many cloaked Karadurians, under cover of the foundrymen's assault, had attempted to flee back to the upper city. Coffin directed some of his Irregulars to go after them, snuffers scrabbling ahead.

Coffin had gone in pursuit of the treacherous Rawkis who was leading what appeared to be a group of women from the scene. The Irregulars chased Rawkis as far as Watersmeet. Coffin, through some kind of foreboding instinct, had left men stationed at the four great entrances to the central well. He anticipated Rawkis would be trapped there. But as he emerged from one of the arterial tunnels, so did another company, and it was not that of Sergeant Rawkis. Coffin gripped the rails of the walkway and stared across the boiling water.

Max Silverskin led the company, at his side his new accomplice masked in green velvet. He had no army with him, only the boy and a small couple, male and female, who looked scarcely human – no doubt denizens of the subterranean world. Coffin laughed softly. This was the end for the Fox of Akra. He no longer cared whether Rawkis escaped or not. This was the real prize of the day. Coffin was already imagining the praise he'd receive from the Council for his efficiency.

Silverskin really had gone native. He was dressed like an historic barbarian, swathed in a cloak of strange iridescent leather, his head adorned with an antique helmet fashioned into the semblance of a reptile. He carried a peculiar sword and his neck was draped with a crude talisman. The effect was savage, but it was only an effect. The Irregulars could dispose of Silverskin's meagre company quickly and capture the thief alive. What a triumphant day. Not only had Coffin exposed the secret cult, most of whose members would soon be in custody, but he'd finally cornered the Fox of Akra. He would prove himself this day, prove himself a fitting suitor for Lady Rose Iron.

Silverskin gazed across the water with an unreadable expression on his face. What was he here for? Why didn't he try to escape? Coffin exhaled a mutter of irritation. What did it matter? He gestured for a group of his men to split up and approach Silverskin from both sides along the curved walkway. Still the wretch did not move. *Stay where you are, pretty boy,* Coffin thought. *You are a potential treasury, that is all, which will soon be safely deposited in my bank.* Oh, Rose would look upon him with greater favour once he was a rich man. She could be a haughty woman, but he imagined her icy reserve would melt at the prospect of marrying a million platinum mirrors.

Coffin followed his Irregulars round the walkway. They had come to a halt some feet from Silverskin's company who had made no effort either to flee or attack. Coffin had the uncomfortable feeling that the Fox of Akra actually wanted to talk. This didn't fit into his plans, because it provoked needling memories of certain things Lady Rose had mentioned concerning Max Silverskin.

'Good day to you, Sir Fox,' said Coffin, bending low from the waist and sweeping his right arm across in an elaborate bow. 'How gratified I am you have come to meet me. It almost seems as if you are willing to surrender yourself willingly.' The rushing water distorted his voice, so that the air was filled with uncanny echoes.

Silverskin's expression did not change. 'Drop the performance,' he said. 'We have serious business to discuss, a common foe. I come to . . .'

Coffin laughed. 'Save your pleasantries. I do not want to hear them.' He gestured to his men. 'Take them.'

Even before the Irregulars had taken a step forward, there was an abrupt movement in the tunnel behind Silverskin's company. A figure pushed through them, wearing soaked, filthy robes. It took Coffin a few moments to recognize Clovis Pewter. The man was wild-eyed and looked insane.

'Coffin, thank the Jewel you are here!' he cried. 'Arrest these people at once!'

Coffin could not help but relish the moment. He spoke with care. 'I was in the process of doing so, Sir Pewter. You hardly need to encourage me. However, it is most timely you should come bursting forth in this manner. I should inform you that you too are under arrest.'

Pewter stared at him madly. '*Me*? This is *outrageous*! Why?'

'I think the official charge will be treason, but I'm sure there are several others.'

'How *dare* you!' Pewter said. 'I am a scion of the Metal, involved in clandestine work to help our city. You have neither the power nor the authority to arrest me.'

'Unfortunately, you are in error,' Coffin said. 'I have been watching you for some time, and have discovered that you are a member of an unlawful organization. I have no power to *sentence* you, true, but I *do* have the power to take you into custody so that you can explain yourself to the Council. I think you'll find they'll be very interested to learn about your practices.'

Pewter straightened up. 'I have done nothing unlawful. If love for my city and my people are sins, then I will gladly stand to defend myself before my peers.' He pointed at Silverskin. 'Here is the real criminal. A thief. He has stolen valuable property from me, property that, in truth, belongs to the whole of Karadur.'

Silverskin laughed. 'Who is the thief, cousin? Didn't you steal from Jenny once? Your alliance with me was amusingly short-lived. And now, it seems, you have miscalculated yet again.'

Pewter glared wildly around him. 'They all plot against us, Coffin, believe me.' He pointed at Silverskin's masked accomplice. 'And she – she's the worst.'

'*She*?' Coffin laughed. 'A fetching misunderstanding, but I think you'll find you're wrong.'

'Am I? See the evidence for yourself.' Pewter lunged towards Silverskin's accomplice and tore the velvet mask away, along with the black hood that had concealed the head. A spill of auburn hair tumbled forward.

Coffin felt as it he'd been turned to stone. The beautiful Rose Iron. She stood there before him, defiant.

'See!' cried Pewter, gesturing in triumph. 'See! She is Silverskin's doxy. All the time masquerading as a loyal daughter of the Iron, while she lives out her fantasies in his bed.'

Coffin reeled back. He could not speak. The object of all his finest feelings, his noblest aspirations and most selfless devotion was the consort of a common thief? No wonder she had spoken of Silverskin in the way she had. The shock was too much to bear. How many of those he had trusted led secret lives and plotted against him?

'Cornelius,' Rose began, hands extended. 'Pewter speaks in that manner only to inflame you. Politically, Max and I are in accord, and I would have liked to have been honest with you about it, but . . .'

Coffin raised a hand and turned away from her. For just a moment, the turbulent waters below looked almost inviting. He saw a million platinum mirrors falling down around him, to be swallowed by the foam. His future. His dreams. Falling. Useless.

Ephemeral despair was overtaken swiftly by white-hot rage. He was consumed by the desire to destroy everything that had ever tasted a moment's pleasure. And the primary object of his hatred was no longer the Fox of Akra.

With a snarl – careless of whether Silverskin lived or died – Coffin spat a command at his Irregulars. 'Take them all. If they fight, kill them, but save Lady Iron, even if you maim her. She must be taken to her father in chains.' He shook his finger towards her. 'This is a sad and shameful day for your clan, my lady.'

'Don't make us fight you,' Rose said. She drew her sword from its scabbard with a silvery hiss.

'Then surrender,' Coffin said.

'I cannot,' Rose said miserably.

Suddenly, Pewter jumped in front of Rose, knocked her to one side and flung himself at Silverskin, tearing the strange helmet from his head. Then he leaped away.

The green-skinned woman at Rose's side cried, 'Jack, the helmet!' Her companion lunged forward and grabbed for Clovis Pewter, who ran backwards onto one of the walkways that crossed the waters below. Simultaneously, the Irregulars surged forward and attacked Silverskin and his company in the mouth of the tunnel.

Coffin stood clutching the walkway rail, numb with sorrow and shock. The movements of the fight around him seemed blurred. He felt disconnected, almost intoxicated. *Rose, why?* He could see her now, red hair threshing, as she nimbly held her attackers at bay. At that moment Coffin loved her more than he'd ever done. He wanted to see her dead.

He turned away and, as he did so, the sounds of ringing steel, panting breath and hoarse grunts faded away. He looked out across the tumult of Watersmeet, staring blindly at the two figures, now shadowy, who fought on the narrow walkway. Shadows were moving everywhere, closing in, threatening to engulf him. Was this grief? Shadows were roiling in the water. No, more than that. Dark, sinuous shapes.

Coffin came to his senses and gripped the rail more firmly as he gazed down into the water. What, by the Jewel, was down there? Even as he watched, Clovis Pewter got the better of his assailant and pushed the green-skinned man back over the rail, bending his spine to what looked like a very painful extent. 'You are dead, Jack Ash!' he cried.

Pewter's enemy growled and lashed out with his free hand, ripping the helmet from Pewter's head. Pewter howled, grabbed to retrieve the object and failed.

The one he'd called Jack Ash somersaulted backwards over the rail. He was falling towards the water. It seemed he fell too slowly, his limbs flailing as if in a sinuous dance. Abruptly, time seemed to accelerate and Jack hit the water with a mighty splash.

Pewter leaned over the rail above, shouting imprecations. Then he looked up and yelled over to Coffin. 'Get your men to retrieve the artefact. It is vital!'

Before he could utter a word, Coffin heard a cry and saw the green-skinned woman rush forward, heedless of the Irregulars, clearly mindless and unstoppable in her desire to save her companion. By the Jewel, these strange green-skinned people had courage. Even as two Irregulars tried to take hold of the woman, Coffin found himself pondering whether there'd ever be a time he could commission a new army – of people from Shriltasi. The woman snarled and lashed out at her attackers, moving with great precision. It was clear the Irregulars were wary of approaching her, perhaps nervous of her alien appearance. She made use of their hesitation by throwing a shining, silken rope down to the water. Her companion groped for it, the helmet still held in one hand. Then the waters surged apart to reveal a creature Coffin had only seen in history books.

A huge body reared up, cascades of water crashing from its great flanks. Immense taloned fins, like sails, sprouted from behind its fishlike head. Its mouth was filled with several rows of scimitar teeth, while great tusks curved upwards from its lower jaw to frame its skull. It exhaled and water spumed from a blowhole on its back, while a wide crest of long spines and webbed skin opened out in a shimmering banner around its head. As well as fins, it had flippers that were armed with long black claws. The flippers flexed on the air like hands. It was a velpi, a beast of scintillating colours, of gleaming scales and immense soulless eyes. But surely this was impossible. Velpis were extinct – or perhaps had never existed except in legend.

Jack Ash had managed to climb halfway up the side of Watersmeet but the velpi did not seem to be interested in him. It leaped from the water, butting the ancient walkway with its gigantic head, goring at it with its tusks. Clovis Pewter staggered as the metal screamed and buckled. He tried to run back towards the edge of Watersmeet. But the velpi lunged upwards again, striking the rusting metal with its heavy head.

'Jack!' Pewter cried.

Why should he expect help from that quarter? Coffin wondered. Pewter was a fool, always had been. The walkway broke in the middle and both sides swung down with an agonized squeal. Pewter tried to keep his footing and haul himself upwards.

Coffin yelled for his men to throw ropes. But it was too late. The water was alive with dark threshing forms, and Pewter, clawing at the broken struts of the walkway, slid down inexorably towards their waiting jaws. Again he called upon the green-skinned man. 'Jack, help me. Only you . . . Forgive . . .' His words were broken up by the crashing tumult of violent water.

The greatest of the creatures surged once more from the depths, fluid cataracting from its blowhole. It fell down upon Pewter who, in his last moments, seemed to give himself up in resignation to his monstrous executioner.

The Irregulars had all gathered around the rail. Some had even thrown ropes they had brought with them for the descent to Shriltasi. Now they hurled their weapons at the creatures below, clearly revolted by what they'd seen. The waters were a soup of blood.

Only Coffin, still disorientated by the revelation of Rose's secret, noticed that Silverskin's party had dragged Jack Ash to safety.

Coffin ran after them. He ran with all his strength, as if his feet were winged. He came to a halt in front of Rose Iron on the narrow walkway. 'I'll not let you flit away,' he said.

Rose stared at him, her eyes wide, her mouth a bloodless line. But there was more than fury in her expression. Regret? Sorrow? Coffin had no time to ponder it. She brandished her bloody sword at him. Even her hands were stained with gore.

Behind them, the Irregulars struggled valiantly to fight off the velpis. The creatures soared up from the water on wing-like fins, snapping at the men with their razor teeth, dragging bodies down to the churning foam.

Coffin feinted at Rose. He felt exhilarated and wanted to draw blood. *Her* blood.

She jumped backwards. 'This is an unusual courtship, Captain,' she said.

'There is no courtship,' he answered coldly. 'Believe me, madam, there's few honest men would want to marry a thief's whore.' He lunged again, and Rose deflected the blow.

'Whore, is it? You should watch your tongue, Captain. You are in danger of offending me. Only hours ago you were swearing fealty to me.'

'Hours ago I was a duped fool,' Coffin snapped. 'I don't take kindly to being used.' He ????????? his attack.

Rose began to fight him in earnest, and Coffin realized then just how proficient a swordswoman she was. On many occasions she almost broke though his guard, but he managed to keep her at bay. He could see that Silverskin was behind her on the causeway but, because of the lack of room, the renegade was unable to come to her assistance. Silverskin, with that white-gold hair, that well-boned face with its hint of noble blood. His looks had cast a glamour over the woman. She was no different from any other silly female of the Metal. Coffin's only gratification was that Silverskin was forced to watch while his doxy fought for her life. No matter how accomplished she was, eventually she'd tire – long before Coffin did.

Max flinched every time Rose parried one of Coffin's thrusts but she appeared to be in total control. Her body moved with grace and ease. Why should she need him? She'd looked after herself all her life. He glanced beyond them at the walkways across the water and realized that the maddened water creatures had all but wiped out the Irregulars. Any who survived lay motionless. If they had any sense, they'd be faking death. Max felt compelled to walk towards the gangway that spanned the water, for a moment forgetting utterly the woman who fought behind him. He gazed down into the churning depths, dazzled by the iridescent hides of the rolling beasts. What had invoked them? Velpis, creatures of myth and dream. As if his thoughts had attracted their attention, the leader of the shoal now reared up from the foam and turned a frenzied eye upon him. It lunged up and, for some seconds, towered over Max, its claws dripping with the diluted blood of its victims, its fangs clashing in its weirdly beautiful head. Then it fell back into the water, drenching the entire area with bloody foam.

The cold wave brought Max back to his senses. Once again he became aware of movement, the clash of blades. Behind him he saw the Ashen hovering uncertainly by the tunnel's entrance. They had not fled. Not even Jack, whose loyalty was in doubt.

'Jenny,' Max called. 'You and Jack go into the tunnel. Now. Get away from here.'

Jenny blinked at him but did not move. She had her arms around Jack who appeared to be on the point of collapse.

On the main walkway that circled Watersmeet, Rose had managed to divest Coffin of his sword, but he'd picked up one of the heavy flensers dropped by an Irregular. It was clear he had little aptitude with this weapon but he still swung at Rose madly, as if trying to cut her in half or at least take off a limb. With sheer mindless force, he was forcing her back towards the tributary tunnel. Max knew he must go to her now. There would be more room in the canal passage for him to help Rose. But before he'd taken a single step, the velpi reared up beside him once more. It reached out with a leathery flipper and, with a delicate manoeuvre, flicked away his sword and picked him up.

In his mind Max heard the War Owl scream, as if to remind him of his power, but he felt no urge to call on her. He was hanging over the water, held lightly in the velpi's claws. It examined him curiously with a glistening eye. Max was sure it was aware he was different from the others. Had the presence of the artefacts, humming with *barishi*, summoned it from some lightless pit below Watersmeet? He felt he was being judged.

Instinctively, Max struggled to pull the Gibbold Mace from his belt. Once it was free, he made the sign of the gibboldess in the air with it.

Immediately, *barishi* began to flow through him. His consciousness was again expelled from his body and he was looking down upon himself. His hair formed a glowing golden mane, blazing around him like fire. A male gibbold's mane. His eyes burned with an orange flame. His hands were paws, armed with sharp steel claws.

The velpi uttered a great scream – whether of approval or fear Max could not tell – and then threw Max away from it. His body hit the walkway by the tunnel with a bone-jolting crash and, as it did so, his consciousness streamed back into his. Dazed, he scrambled to his feet. Already the power was leaving him. Weakness stole through his flesh. The witch mark burned, but not in the way it had before. This was aggressive, destructive. The velpi still hung in the water, examining him. Max felt that, at any moment, he'd feel its thoughts in his mind. It knew him.

Then a great and terrible sound echoed around the mighty columns of Watersmeet. It was the sound of a stagnant lake, thick with slime, crashing through a dam. It was the cry of the spawn of a starless void, a slapping, guttural roar. Max looked up and saw the massive bulk of Gorpax, the Slug King, squeezing itself from the tunnel opposite. The ancient metal walkway groaned and buckled beneath its bulk. It was followed by a troop of Porporrum who all jumped up and down on the walkway, brandishing their weapons and hooting wildly.

The Slug King oozed forward and flopped down the gushing tributary into the water, eye stalks erect, huge maw open. Whatever the Porporrum had intended, it was clear Gorpax was aware of only one thing: the chief velpi. Gorpax lunged towards the water beast as if at a familiar enemy. The velpi reared from the water, all its fins and spines outstretched like marvellous wings. It was the most beautiful creature, almost the complete antithesis of the abomination called Gorpax. *How can I help it?* Max thought and was about to summon the Owl, hoping she might lend her strength to the fight. But then the velpi reached out with its flippers and took the Slug King into its embrace. At once a terrible hissing filled the air and a noxious steam erupted from the Slug King's body. A terrible acrid stench made Max's eyes water. Gorpax threshed in the velpi's grasp, uttering hideous shrieks. Slime dripped down from its body as it started to melt and shrivel.

Salt water, Max thought. *I smelled it here once. The velpi must have come from salt water. Its touch is lethal to the slug.*

The velpi uttered a cry of triumph, which rang like the clangour of immense bells around the columns of Watersmeet. For just a moment, it looked once more upon Max and then fell back into the water with a mighty splash. It had all happened so quickly but there was no time to think about it. Rose was still holding off Coffin, while the Porporrum were streaming round the walkway, enraged and maddened – presumably by the loss of their Slug King.

Rose was now a few feet into the tunnel, with Jenny and Jack close behind her. Jenny held the helmet in her hands and, when she saw Max approaching at speed, threw it towards him. It arced high into the air and Max leaped up to catch it, almost falling over the rail into the water.

'Make the sign of the Dragon!' cried Jenny desperately. 'Make it, Fox. Bring the last three together!'

Max frowned at her. 'What sign?'

Jenny bunched her fists and yelled. 'You know it in your heart. Trust your instincts. Ride the *barishi* within you! Unite the artefacts, Fox. Now!'

The Porporrum were almost upon him. Quickly, Max placed the helm upon the floor before him and took out from his pocket the diminished mirror, which he put beside it. He held up the spellstone and restored the mirror to its original size. Then he took off Jack's shimmering cloak and placed it beside the other two artefacts.

He felt utterly calm, as if time had slowed around him. Carefully he drew a sign upon the air. He did not know whether it was the right sign. Perhaps, at this stage, that did not matter. He swayed upon his feet, looking down at the artefacts. As he watched, a steely grey smoke emanated from them. They writhed upon the metal walkway like liquid metal, melding into one another. In moments they had combined. At Max's feet lay a suit of chain mail of the finest weave. He bent down to touch it, rubbed it between his fingers. It was as light and slippery as silk, yet he knew it would also be of the most durable fabric. A hiss made him draw back. The totem beast was manifesting before him, rising as steam from the armour at his feet. It was sinuously serpentine, but with multiple legs. Its gleaming flanks were adorned with small wings. It was clear the nomonon had been designed with this beast in mind.

The dragon wagged its head from side to side, as if seeking the one who had brought it to life. Its skin was the snake-leather cloak. Its head was the reptile helm. Its eyes were the mirror, reflecting only truth. A black forked tongue darted forth from its lipless mouth and, with an expression of unfathomable intelligence, it looked directly into Max's eyes. He was physically jolted by a sense of recognition. A voice echoed in his mind: *You have brought me back.*

With a long, shuddering hiss, the elegant creature reared up and lunged towards the approaching Porporrum, who all stopped dead in their tracks. The dragon prowled forward, low on its belly, like a cat. After only a moment, the Porporrum began to piss themselves in terror. Uttering squeaks, and shaking their weapons uselessly, they moved back in a simultaneous surge towards the tunnel behind them, heading for the comparative safety of Shriltasi.

Max had no desire to hurt the Poporrum. He summoned the dragon back to him. The creature bent its long snout towards the ground at his feet. Without a command, it began to coil up before him. It grew smaller and smaller until it transformed once more into a silvery steam, which curled towards the spellstone and was absorbed by it. There it reposed as a glowing symbol, along with the Owl and the Gibbold. The *barishic* armour still lay at Max's feet.

Max leaned, panting, against the wall. He willed strength to come to him. He needed it to help Rose, she who had always helped him. He could see it now. But Rose did not need his help. Blinking, he watched her, as if through a film of blood. Coffin was retreating up the tunnel and Rose had his flenser in her hands. She threw it after him and it clanged upon the path. Then all was still.

Max dragged himself upright as Rose came towards him. He managed a weak smile. She halted a few feet from him, hands on hips, her eyes filled with uncertainty.

Max stretched out a shaking hand.

Rose looked at it for some moments, then crossed the final space between them and took it. Max squeezed her fingers. 'Forgive me,' he said.

Chapter Two

The Laying of Ghosts

Once Rose and her companions emerged from the sewers, they found the city in turmoil. Rose had never seen anything like it. Irregulars and Battle Boys surged everywhere, as if in a panic, but they did not seem to notice her or her companions. The city pulsed beneath a pall of fear. The past was coming back, rising from the drains. Everyone could feel it.

With comparative ease, Rose led the group to her eyrie. It was fortunate she'd not revealed the location of this place to Coffin. Where else was safe for her now? She wondered whether Coffin had yet reported to her father. It would perhaps have been far better to return to Shriltasi but Max had insisted they go to Karadur. Rose was worried by his condition. Only a day remained, and from the pallor in his face, the slight tremor of his limbs, it was clear that the witch mark was affecting him more strongly. She could do nothing. Only hope and pray. But pray to what?

Yet her exhaustion and sorrow fought with an undeniable sense of exhilaration. Despite her fears for Max, Rose could not help but take pleasure in the way she'd fought off Coffin and won Max's confidence. She glanced across at him, where he sprawled in one of her sagging chairs. He had the spellstone in his hands, turning it over and over, inspecting the symbols. Her heart ached to see him like this. She knew he was trying to gain some understanding of the power he commanded and perhaps use it to save himself. He looked nauseous, diminished, as if he was becoming insubstantial like a ghost. Rose could not bear to think that these might be the last hours she could gaze upon this man.

Jenny Ash was striding about the room, inspecting Rose's belongings, apparently oblivious to Max's distress. Jack lay on the sofa, looking dazed. His shirt hung open, and Rose could see the wounds Pewter had inflicted on his chest. He really should have returned to Shriltasi where he could have been healed in Asholm. Jack had gambled with all of them, and Rose was still not sure who was the winner. One thing was clear, however. They could not stay here for ever. Her father might send Battle Boys to search the entire area, looking for her hiding place. Perhaps, subconsciously, that was why she had agreed with Max they should all come here – for a final confrontation. Let her father face the reality of the Ashen.

'We should not just be hiding here!' Jenny announced, almost as if she could hear Rose's thoughts and dreaded an encounter with the Lord of the Iron.

'You cannot return to Shriltasi just yet,' Rose replied smoothly. 'Max wanted us to come here. We should trust his instincts at this time.'

Jenny exhaled heavily and nodded. 'I suppose so.' She cast a glance at Jack, said nothing, then went to Max's chair and kneeled beside him. The suit of chain mail, the dragon artefact, was slung over the back of the chair. It looked like a discarded silk wrap. Jenny put a hand over the witch mark, shook her head. 'Poor Fox. How the heart eats at you.' She gave Rose a challenging glance. 'I will try to help him.'

'Summon the owl,' Rose said to Max. 'She might be able to help you.'

Max frowned and batted Jenny's hand away. He did not summon the War Owl. 'I was thinking,' he said. 'The fourth artefact, that of the Silver. Perhaps I should go the Silverskins, ask to speak with Serenia. She might have more to tell me. Someone has to.'

'Surely that would be too dangerous,' Rose said, 'for the Silverskins more than for yourself. You're in no state to use *barishi*.'

'But I have to know . . . I have to . . .' Max pressed his hands against his face.

'The wisdom of the Dragon,' Jenny said softly, 'the vision of the Owl and the power of the Gibbold. Nine into three makes one.'

'You've said this before,' Max said, lowering his hands. His eyes were reddened with exhaustion and pain. 'I remember a rhyme you told me. But there are more than nine, aren't there? What about the fourth icon?'

Rose went to stand on the other side of the chair. She felt that, like her brother, Jenny knew more than she was prepared to tell. For some reason she kept her silence, and Rose was convinced no amount of questioning would get her to open up. 'What rhyme is this?' she asked Max.

'I can't remember it properly,' he replied. 'Tell her, Jenny.'

Jenny closed her eyes and chanted softly: 'Nine things make three things. Three things bring a fourth thing, four things make one thing, one thing makes everything.'

Rose leaned down and put a hand on Max's shoulder. 'I know this rhyme. I heard it in a dream. Serenia spoke it to me.'

Max reached up and briefly touched her hand. 'What help is it to us, though?'

Rose considered. 'Well, isn't the meaning obvious?'

Max grimaced and shrugged. 'It seems to suggest the three icons somehow bring about the fourth.'

'Exactly!' Rose said. 'Perhaps the three have to be combined somehow. Is that possible? Did you study your mother's book? Surely, the answer is in there.'

'It's not,' Jenny said.

'I have no reason to believe anything you say,' Rose said coldly. 'Max, do you still have the book?'

'It's in Shriltasi,' he said.

'Oh, for the Jewel's sake!' Rose cried. 'You should keep it on you.'

'I have enough trouble carrying the other artefacts,' Max said. 'I'm a walking museum.'

'The book cannot help him further,' Jenny said. 'I've examined it thoroughly.'

'We can't just wait here!' Rose cried. 'Tomorrow . . . Oh, how can we tell what will happen tomorrow? But one thing I don't want is for us to just sit around here, watching Max . . .' She could not say the word.

'We must sleep,' Jack said.

'Sleep?' Rose laughed raggedly. 'That's the last thing I'm capable of.'

Jack fixed her with an unwavering stare. She shuddered, remembering the times he had come to her in the library of Clan Silver, late at night, while the world slept. *Listen to your dreams* . . . The words were in her head – not Jack's voice, a woman's. Rose felt herself flush. She tore her gaze away from Jack's stare. In her dreams. Serenia. She glanced back at Jack. 'Then help me sleep. I know you can.'

He closed his eyes briefly, nodded. 'I will come with you.'

'What?'

'This time you must be in control. I'll help you.'

'You know nothing of my dreams,' Rose said bitterly.

Jack said nothing.

There was a silence, then Jenny stood up. 'Trust him, Lady Rose. I think he's right.'

'Trust him?' Rose laughed again, shook her head. 'You're asking the impossible.'

'I know,' Jenny said. 'None of us trust one another. Yet here we are, at the end of the world, and all we have is ourselves.'

'We don't know it's the end of the world,' Rose said, knowing she was trying to be difficult.

'It's the end of your world,' Jenny said. She gestured towards Max. 'Look at him.'

Max was clearly unaware of their conversation, his gaze fixed upon the spellstone. It seemed his mind was going.

'Do it,' Jenny said. 'There's been no love between us, Lady Rose, but we've reached a time when we must move beyond our feelings. My brother has betrayed us all and it hurts no one more than it hurts me. But we should give him this chance.'

Rose glanced back at Jack, who shrugged. 'You have nothing to lose.'

Rose sighed. 'Very well. Come to my boudoir, then, trickster.'

She gestured for Jack to follow her into her bedroom and there lay down upon the bed. The red light of evening filled the room. 'Just make me sleep,' she said awkwardly. 'Use *barishi*. I'm wide awake.'

Jack stood over her, bracing himself with one hand against the wall. 'It will be more than sleep,' he said. 'Prepare yourself for it, Rose. I will plunge you straight into the realm of dreams. It may be uncomfortable.'

'Get on with it,' Rose said. Her jaw was tight. There was a pain behind her eyes.

Jack sat down beside her and placed his hands over her face. Every time she took a breath it was as if she breathed him into her. His alien scent was so strong. Heat built up in his palms, intense heat. Then a bolt of white fire burst out of Jack's flesh. Rose cried out, but the sound seemed to bounce off Jack's hands and be pushed back inside her. Her head whirled with pain and a myriad swirling colours. She could no longer feel the bed beneath her. She was dropping down into a void, sick with vertigo.

'Relax,' Jack's voice murmured. 'Don't fight it.'

In the darkness, Rose flailed her limbs. She could feel them moving, but could see nothing. Perhaps she had no body in this place.

'Take control,' Jack said. 'Create your world around you. There is ground beneath your feet. Feel it.'

At first, Rose could not focus herself enough to concentrate. She was immersed in the sea of primal nothingness, the ocean of thought before thought is born.

'Feel it,' Jack murmured.

There is ground, Rose told herself. *I must believe it.*

Her feet flexed against a solid surface. Now the blackness around her began to pulse with blots of blue and green light. The colours spun round her, faster and faster, making her dizzy. 'Jack!' she called. Her mind was frozen by an instinctive terror, the fear of the unknown.

'Control it!' Jack said. 'I will be with you shortly.'

'Where are you?'

There was no reply. Rose closed her eyes, denying the chaotic blur of light around her. *When I open my eyes, I will be in a room*, she told herself. *It will be the ballroom of the Moonmetal Manse.*

For a moment, she dared not open her eyes. But when she did so, she found herself in the place she'd willed to form around her. It was empty, strangely dark. All the silver and crystal decorations in the room barely caught the light. They were like lead, mercury. Rose turned round slowly. She could hear her own breath echoing from wall to wall.

Behind her stood Jack Ash, arms folded, head cocked to one side. In this realm, he had no wounds and did not appear in any way tired or ill. 'Well done,' he said.

'It started here once,' Rose said. 'I was dancing . . .'

'Call Serenia Silverskin to you.'

Rose frowned. 'How?'

Jack smiled. 'She is adept at calling you to her. Turn the tables. Call her.'

'But she might not be asleep.'

'That is irrelevant. In this place, there is no time. You can call into the past, present or future.'

Rose sighed. 'Well, I'll try.' She composed herself in the centre of the room and called aloud, 'Serenia, Serenia Silverskin. Come to me. It is I, Rose Iron, who calls you.'

The echo of her words bounced around the vast chamber. Rose glanced at Jack. 'Is she coming?'

Jack shrugged. 'Wait and see.'

'Perhaps I should call again . . .'

Jack said nothing. The silence around them was absolute, impenetrable.

Then Rose heard footsteps, from very far away. Quick, light steps. It sounded like a woman walking briskly along a stone-floored corridor.

'Is that her?' Rose murmured.

Jack again remained silent but he turned round. Behind him, one of the darkened entrances into the room had become illumined with a soft, white light. It was like a tunnel into infinity. The footsteps gradually became louder and eventually a billowing silhouette could be seen against the light: a woman in a flowing gown.

Rose had no idea how Serenia would feel about this summons. But when the Silverskin matriarch emerged into the hall her expression was benign. She halted a few feet from Rose and bowed slightly. 'My lady, you called upon me, your humble subject.'

Rose detected irony in this statement. 'I did not mean to be importunate, madam. I have urgent need to speak with you. Using the proper channels might put your family in jeopardy.'

'I would hope you would not summon me for anything less than crucial. This is a critical time and I am very busy.'

Rose nodded. 'I appreciate that, but I would like to tell you all that has transpired since we met. Then I would like to ask you questions. Are you agreeable to this?'

Serenia inclined her head, smiling gently.

Rose wondered how much Serenia already knew of what she said, but the woman did not interrupt her story. At the end of it, Rose said, 'So you see, we have reached an impasse, and time is short. Do you know what we must do next?'

Serenia paused for a moment, then said, 'I will tell you the ultimate step, which must be taken once all others have been taken. It is neither my place nor yours to take those steps. They are Maximilian's responsibility alone, and he must quest for the knowledge he needs to accomplish them. All I will tell you is this: Maximilian must restore the Jewel of All Time to its proper setting.'

Rose fixed her with a stare. 'That might be difficult. I think you know that the Jewel is . . . missing.'

Again, Serenia inclined her head. 'It is not in its accustomed place,' she said. 'But neither is it beyond reach. It has had to disappear into the underworld of the soul for a time, for only through that can it be reborn. And it *will* be reborn, Lady Rose. That is beyond our control. You do not even need faith to believe it. It will simply happen at the right point in time.'

'And when it does, Max must replace it?'

'Not within the Grand Market. The Jewel has not been in its proper setting since before the Reformation. Its true home is at the apex of the Guild Tower, where metal hands wait empty to be refilled. At the time of the Reformation, the Lords took the Jewel from its setting, which the Clan magi had constructed. In doing so, the Lords diminished the artefact's power. They sought to contain it within the Tower, for they feared its force. The Jewel controls Time, which is the greatest power in the multiverse. Maximilian must restore the Jewel to its correct function and place.'

Rose sighed, shook her head. 'This is not enough, Serenia. Max is failing quickly. We do not have the Jewel and lack the fourth artefact. Tomorrow, if the prophecy is correct, the silverheart will kill him. I have no reason to doubt that prophecy now. I only have to look at him to see how true it is.' She held out her hands in appeal. 'I know we want the same things, but Max and those who support him are floundering in the dark. Please help us. I know you can.'

'I am doing what I must,' Serenia answered. 'No more and no less.' She took a few steps forward and cupped Rose's face with long, cool hands. 'My dear, this is the dark night of the soul, the longest night, when those who love the valiant hero must keep the vigil for him through the cold, lonely hours. The fear and sorrow in your heart are a necessary part of what must be. Hope can only be born from the absence of hope.'

Rose could not stop the tears that flooded her eyes. They fell down onto Serenia's hands. She felt it then: the complete absence of hope, the abyss of despair, the everlasting night, when light and warmth have fled.

'Live through this night,' Serenia murmured. 'Live through it with your heart and soul. Be cleansed by it. Let your tears wash away all the shadows of the past. In the morning, you must emerge into the light raw and fresh, for it is the day of revelation, of trial and of struggle.'

Jack Ash stepped forward. 'Leave her alone,' he said in a smooth, reasonable voice. 'It is you who create this darkness around her. You are making her part of your dream.'

Serenia's hands dropped slowly from Rose's face. Rose could do nothing but stand there, weeping silently. Her very soul ached with desolation.

The Silverskin matriarch turned to face Jack Ash. 'And what is it you want of me, Jaxinther? You want me to absolve you?'

Jack laughed. 'I am not here for myself. Take your curse from Rose.'

'It is you who carry a curse. The ghost that haunts you stands at your shoulder.'

Rose's vision was blurred by tears but, as Serenia spoke, she thought she could see a shadow just behind Jack. She blinked and then uttered a cry of revulsion, stepping away from the apparition revealed to her. It was Clovis Pewter, his skin a hideous bloated green, rent with deep wounds, bleached by the waters of the velpi's realm. His face was barely recognizable: one eye socket empty, half his scalp torn away. He looked upon Jack with malevolence, hunger and sorrow.

At Rose's cry, Jack turned, then leaped away. 'You have summoned this fetch!' he cried to Serenia.

The Silverskin matriarch shook her head. 'Indeed not. He is your fetch, Ashen king. But for you, this pathetic soul would be as he was, an inconsequential lordling of the Metal with a head full of dreams. You dragged him from his blissful sleep, gave him the promise of power. You showed him wonders, opened his eyes, then cut away the lids with your sweet words so he could never sleep again. Now his body rots in the silt beneath Watersmeet and his soul follows the light of yours, as he followed you in life. It is all he knows. You are ridden by it, Jaxinther.'

Rose thought Jack would react angrily to these words, and was therefore surprised when he bowed his head. 'I would be rid of it, Dame Serenia.'

'Then rid yourself of guilt. It is the only tie. What is done is done, and cannot be undone.'

Jack raised his head and for some moments appeared to force himself to face the spectre. Pewter stared back through his single remaining eye. Dank water pooled on the floor around him. Eventually, Jack said, 'Clovis, hear me. You were responsible for your actions, as I was for mine. I did not wish ill upon you.'

'Betrayal,' wheezed Pewter.

'I did not betray you,' Jack said. 'I could not save you from the velpi.'

'I betrayed . . .' Pewter murmured sorrowfully.

'And paid with your life. There is no debt between us.'

Pewter held out his arms, rags of flesh and weed hanging down. His limbs trembled.

Jack glanced at Serenia, but her face was expressionless.

'Forgive,' said Pewter.

Jack closed his eyes briefly, then reached out to embrace the hideous apparition. 'I forgive you,' he said.

Rose felt bile rise in her throat. How could Jack touch that dreadful thing? But, as she watched, Pewter's appearance changed as Jack held him. When the Ashen king stepped away, Pewter appeared as he had in life, free of wounds, dressed in the clothes of a Clan gentleman. He was smiling. His body was surrounded by a halo of white light, which grew increasingly brighter until the image of Pewter could no longer be seen within it. Then, with a mighty crash, the light exploded and a million sparkling particles shot out into the room. Rose felt them pass through her flesh, and their sizzling passage filled her with joy, renewed her hope.

Jack stood motionless, arms hanging limply down, his expression dazed.

Serenia went to his side. 'Walk forward from this point with new knowledge, Jaxinther' she said. 'What you have learned has changed you, as all lessons change the soul.'

She raised her hands. 'I will leave you now. There is nothing more to say.'

At once, Rose was awake and her own room in the eyrie swam into focus before her startled eyes. Jack Ash lay beside her, his brow creased into a frown. Then he gave a start, hit at the air and sat upright, breathing heavily.

Rose regarded him. 'You feel guilt. Now there's a revelation I did not expect.'

Jack looked down at her. 'She pushed us out. By the Jewel, that woman owns power.'

'Guilt, Jack?' Rose couldn't help smiling, even though the initial sight of Pewter's shade had been disgusting and the fact of his death so pathetic and sad. But it heartened her to know the Ashen might have finer feelings after all.

Jack grimaced. 'Pewter was a lost soul, misguided and naive. I did not intend for him to die.'

'I'm sure you didn't. But I'm surprised that you care he did.'

'If he'd remained true to me, he'd be alive. It is the woman who is responsible.' Jack got up from the bed. 'Serenia did not mention her. Perhaps we should have asked questions about this mysterious high priestess. She is a danger to us all, self-obsessed and hungry for power. I think she has attracted some malevolent force to her. She will have to be dealt with, Rose.'

'Deal with your own feelings first,' Rose said. She yawned. 'I'm tired now.'

'Don't go back to sleep,' Jack said. 'Remember what Serenia told us. We must keep the vigil.' He went towards the door.

For a moment, Rose lay motionless upon the bed, bathing in the last ruddy rays of the dying sun. She could feel the immensity of the multiverse all around her, stretching out into infinity on all sides. She was just a small thing, a mote upon the web of reality, as was Max. But all things were upon the web, and if one strand vibrated, all others must feel it. If it vibrated strongly enough, the web might break. She stood up, stretched and glanced up at the skylight where the sky was purple, glinting with a million stars. 'Give me strength,' she murmured.

Chapter Three

A Recipe for the Fabulous

Max was aware of shadows around him: Rose handing hot drinks to the Ashen; Jenny crouched by his feet; Jack standing behind his chair, his hands upon Max's shoulders. The heat of *barishi* flowed from the Ashen but it was not strong enough to drag Max back to full consciousness, nor could it assuage the pain in his body. He was only partly in this world now. The beat of his heart was thunder in his ears: slow, fitful. He could feel the roar of the silverheart. His bones ached with its power. Silver tendrils hung poised above the pulsing muscle of his living heart. They were waiting to strike. How many hours left to him? Was this the beginning of the end? When dawn came, he might simply die.

For now, he could not retain hold of conscious awareness. He was being sucked down into a pit of grey feathers. Nothing seemed more inviting. Nothing mattered there.

Max woke with a start to find himself in a completely strange environment. For some moments of utter disorientation, he could not remember where he'd fallen asleep or any of the events leading up to it. Then he realized he felt totally alert, healthy and vital. His hands flew to his chest, where the witch mark burned and glittered. But it did not pain him. He felt at one with it. Max laughed aloud in incredulity and relief. What had happened? Another miraculous escape like that from Gragonatt? He looked around himself. There was no sign of Rose or the others.

He was in what appeared to be a man-made cavern, lit by dim greenish globes of light that were stuck into the walls like living gems. The walls themselves were damp, glistening with veins of silvery ore. He could hear running water nearby, a cold, clear sound. The air smelled faintly metallic. Max had no weapons with him but he reached for the spellstone at his neck and found it still in place. He shivered. The air was bitterly cold and he had no coat. His breath steamed before his face.

Several dim-lit tunnels led off the cavern and, hugging himself against the chill, Max chose one at random to investigate. He walked for what seemed like hours and then found himself in another cavern, which looked suspiciously like the one he had left behind. Perhaps this was a maze.

He chose another tunnel and had just ventured into it when a blaze of light bloomed up ahead. It shot towards him like a ball of fire. Max turned and ran back to the cavern, only for the light to overtake him. It brought with it a fierce, hot wind, which knocked him to the floor. The light was so intense, he was blinded by it, filled with it. He breathed it in, feeling it sear his lungs. Was this the legacy of the witch mark? Was this his death on the sixth day?

He rolled onto his back, eyes screwed tightly shut. His lungs laboured for breath. The silverheart felt like a thousand white-hot needles, pressing into his flesh.

'Maximilian.'

A woman's voice.

Max opened his eyes to find the white light had vanished. The shadowy figure of a woman stood over him. She was dressed in a soft grey robe, over which was flung a woollen cloak of darker grey. Her hair was silver-white, in two plaits over her chest, yet her appearance was young. Her face was his own: softer, more feminine, but she could have been his twin.

'Who are you?' he asked, getting to his feet.

The woman regarded him for a few moments, her expression filled with tenderness, curiosity and some sadness. 'Do you not know me?'

He shook his head. 'I feel I should.'

'I am your mother, Maximilian.'

'You can't be.' Impulsively, he reached out and grabbed the fabric of her cloak in his fingers. It felt warm and soft to the touch.

'I am Sophelia Silverskin.' She smiled. 'Don't you know that all things are possible in dreams?'

'I'm dreaming . . .' He should have realized. It would have been too good to be true if he'd escaped the ravages of the silverheart.

Sophelia nodded. 'It was time for me to come to you again, Max. It is only possible in this manner.'

'Are you dead?'

'There is no death, only transformation. I chose a path in life that led me away from the flesh. I sacrificed physical gratification to gain understanding. You must listen to me now, for there is much for you to learn. Let us go to a place where we may converse in comfort.'

Sophelia made no movement or sound but in an instant the surroundings changed. Max found himself in a chamber, which again seemed sub-terranean. But this room was furnished with heavy wooden chairs and sofas, and there were thick animal hides upon the floor. In one wall was set a hearth, where a fire burned high. Sophelia was reclining on one of the sofas and no longer wore her cloak. Before her, on a low table, a flagon steamed. She gestured for Max to take a seat and reached out to pour them hot drinks from the flagon into earthenware cups. 'I doubt that this seems strange to you by now,' she said. 'You will have lived through many bizarre experiences.'

'You could say that.' Max accepted a drink and sipped from it. His mouth filled with a herby perfume and he sensed the fluid would calm him. None of this felt like a dream. The physical sensations were too real. 'Can you tell me what I need to know?'

Sophelia inclined her head. 'As a mother, I can advise my son on his path through life, but it is only advice. You have free will.'

He smiled ruefully. 'You are only a figment of my dream. You do not exist.'

'It is a mistake to think that mundane reality is the only one,' Sophelia said. She leaned back against the cushions. 'I will tell you my story, which one day you should be able to verify. Then you will learn about reality. I will tell you one thing: it is impossible to make anything up. In the multiverse, everything already exists. Everything you could possibly think of. Learn to control your dreams, and you learn to control your mundane reality. But you are not here to learn about that.'

Sophelia looked away from Max into the leaping flames of the fire. 'I was born to a destiny, as were you. The portents that surrounded my birth advised our family that I had a purpose in life. That purpose was to conceive a child with a scion of the Metal — of the Silvers, to be precise. Augustus never knew my purpose. He never knew I selected him and seduced him with this in mind. He was a good man, Max, whatever you might think of Clan people now. He should not have suffered in the way he did. If Clan Silver had accepted our relationship and allowed me to be his wife, all of our lives would have been so much easier. But perhaps that would not have been the right way. We are all like blades, forged in the fire, strengthened by it, and the fire is experience, endurance.' She looked back at Max and smiled. 'Sad though it seems, I cannot imagine you would be who you are if you'd grown up as a pampered son of the Metal, even though I would have indoctrinated you carefully with the Silverskin beliefs.' She laughed. 'A witch in their midst. In some ways, that would have been delicious.'

'I would have wanted it that way,' Max said. 'I never knew you, or my father. Haven't you ever considered I might have deserved the life that was denied me?'

Sophelia nodded. 'Of course. But I am proud of you, Max. I have watched over you from the moment I left you. You have never disappointed me.'

'Why did you leave — or how?'

'Augustus was cast out by his family for loving me. Things have never been easy for the Silverskins, and it was made clear there'd be trouble if they took us in. Serenia would still have done so, but your father and I decided against it. Augustus was a romantic. He believed he could learn to live a new life in the free zones. He would learn a trade, provide for his wife and son. A boy's dream. But it was not to be.' She sighed sorrowfully. 'He wasn't murdered or assassinated, Max. He died of a fever. The life he'd led made him ill-prepared to live among those for whom disease was a common hazard. Not even I could save him. Ultimately, he gave up. He blamed himself for ruining my life, when in fact he had only ruined his own.'

'Were any of the stories true?' Max asked. 'Did you venture out onto the ice, find lost cities?'

She shook her head. 'No. I have seen the cities, Max, but not with living eyes. If you can ever return to me, I will tell you about them, but this is not the time.

'After your father died, I took you to the Silverskin temple, which is hidden deep underground. Serenia breathed in the smoke that comes from the world's core there, and divined your future for you. We learned that to be the One Who Would Come you had to live apart from us and learn your heritage for yourself. You needed to be forged in the fire, Max. We could have brought you up as a Silverskin adept, skilled in *barishic* arts from the earliest age. But then you would not have been a man of pleasure, of sensation and adventure – all those human things that the ascetic abhors. Don't think I accepted this judgement easily. I argued with Serenia and all the other elders of our tribe, both in this world and the etheric realms. I wanted to snatch you and run back to the free zones, but ultimately I knew I could not hide you. I had stepped upon the path and there was no going back. Serenia told me I could not help you in this world. I had to let you go. But I was not without my own power. I entered the smoke myself and the multiverse told me that there was a way I could still be part of your destiny. I took poison to accomplish it. Beyond the flesh, I could be instrumental in your development. I could put the witch mark upon you.'

'You?' Max pressed a hand against his eyes. 'It was you in Gragonatt?'

Sophelia nodded. 'Yes. From being a discarnate spectator of your life, I could now have a physical effect upon you.' She leaned towards him. 'I know you have suffered. I have felt your bewilderment. But now, before the dawn of the last day, I am permitted to give a mother's gift to you.'

'The last icon,' Max said, staring her in the eye. 'Is it that?'

'Listen to me. The icons must be brought together in the crucible, where male, female and androgyne are united, where the elements are united, where the moral humours are united – where all things are united and made whole. From this you will gain the greatest of liberties: control of your own immortal soul. This is the legend of the great Reconciliation, when all peoples, all nature, all that is good and all that is alive, shall come together in harmony. Only then can the Cosmic Balance achieve perfect resolution.'

'But I don't have all the icons,' Max said. 'If you truly want to help me, give me knowledge of the fourth.'

'You will have the knowledge you need, but there are other things you need to know first. Some forces deny the Reconciliation and work to prevent it happening. You have felt their influence already and before the end of tomorrow must confront and defeat them. They work through humanity, as do the other forces of the multiverse. Your destiny is to harmonize these forces. If you fail, the multiverse will plunge into an infinity of chaos.' She drew away from him. 'And if that should happen, angels become men, men become beasts and beasts return to the mud.'

'Do I have a choice in this matter?'

'Of course. You could choose simply to die, never wake up from this sleep you are in now. You could choose to let fate take its own course. But once free of the flesh, you would see the terrible wrongness of that, and then it would be too late.' She drew a symbol on the air. The sign hung there, glowing golden-green. 'Look, Max, how Karadur shudders and crumbles.'

A hypnotic spell seemed to flow from her fingers. Max was a disembodied spirit flying through the streets of Karadur. Against the dark horizon, crimson flame gushed from chimneys whose smoke turned the air black. Each building, bound or supported by great metal bands and girders, groaned and trembled. He looked upon the Guild Tower, which was patched with rivets. Even as he watched, slivers of metal fell from it and crashed into the market square below. He saw, at the apex of the tower, four sets of cupped hands, each fashioned from one of the primary metals of Karadur. He'd never noticed them before. They seemed to be reaching for something.

'Death,' Sophelia murmured, and the sound of her voice dragged Max's mind back into his body. 'Only you can change it. In the crucible.'

'The crucible? Where is that?'

'In the Old Forge.'

'You're saying I should throw the artefacts in there?'

'Yes. The crucible once belonged in the alchemist's tower in Shinlech fief. It is more than it seems, for men put their intentions into it for millennia.'

'What about the fourth icon?'

Sophelia put her head to one side. 'Max, is it still such a mystery to you? Don't you know what the fourth artefact is?'

He shook his head, simultaneously conscious of a sense of rising dread. It was as if he knew the answer before she spoke.

'You are, my son.'

Deep below Filgree House, the sons and daughters of the Silverskins gathered in the family temple. The black walls were covered in carvings: ancient gods and demons, frozen in a ceaseless journey. Incense filled the air with smoke and perfume, writhing between the tall scarlet columns that supported the roof. The only light came from bowls of burning oil that cast shadows upon the walls, making the carvings appear to move. Voices rose and fell in an ululating chant.

Serenia stood before the fissure in the floor, where a coil of yellow steam rose upwards from the ground. Her eyes were red and streaming as the hot steam scalded them. Her throat was raw as if she'd been shouting aloud for hours. Her mind was far from the realm of flesh.

Serenia travelled the glittering web of the multiverse. She saw before her a tumbling brightness, a condensed ball of etheric essence. It had always tumbled this way, in and out of multiple realities. It existed in all places at all times. But, for a while, it had been absent from Karadur.

Now, Serenia cried out in her mind. *Return to us, radiant one. We are ready for you once more. We take upon ourselves the destiny of the Jewel. We are ready.*

The Jewel of All Time. Its absence from Karadur had brought darkness and uncertainty, but these were necessary for transformation to begin. It was like the dark of the moon, or the eclipse of the sun, but far greater than either. This was spiritual darkness, when, for a time, the world had become estranged from the multiverse, a lightless node upon the web. The Jewel had tumbled from Menni Vane's hands into infinity and only Serenia could call it back. She knew it heard the call.

It spun and tumbled faster now, approaching at speed. In Karadur, it was a jewel the size of a man's head, but its true being was the size of a sun. Serenia braced herself for the impact. All her life, she had prepared herself for this moment.

The jewel crashed into her, through her, filling her being with searing light. She could feel the life being burned from her, but still she reached out and clasped that power to her, uttering a wordless shriek of pain.

In the temple, the Silverskins stood around their fallen matriarch, hands joined in a circle, willing their strength and purpose into her. Serenia was curled into a ball, holding something tightly to her belly. She coughed and droplets of blood sprayed out across the floor. It was done. The jewel had been born once more into the world.

Chapter Four

Keeper of the Jewel

Never once in all the millennia of its existence had The Old Forge ceased production. Standing in the Camera Obscura, Lord Iron observed the image of his mighty foundry. He looked upon the chimneys and smoke, the blackened bricks and sparking skies, and tried to find certainty in them. In a way, his grief and sorrow over his daughter had purged him. He felt weirdly insubstantial, estranged from the terror that possessed his city, as if he had become no more than a form of raw suffering. Even before he'd come here to meet Cornelius Coffin, he'd sensed that something terrible had happened, an experience he'd never had before. As he'd climbed the stairs to the Camera, he'd heard the cacophony coming from the city streets: people shouting, their voices laced with hysteria. He'd heard the crash of buildings falling to the ground. All was crumbling. He'd tried repeatedly to contact Fabiana over the last twenty-four hours, but she'd been too busy with crises in her own domain to see him. Now, he suspected, there was a possibility he'd never see her again.

When he'd visited Verdigris House, Fabiana had comforted him about Rose. He'd liked the way he hadn't had to speak openly: Lady Copper hadn't demanded facts from him. She'd intuited what troubled him and had told him not to worry. He'd felt that, in some way, Fabiana had consented to shoulder the burden of responsibility for Rose. She'd wanted to become a surrogate mother. The other implications of that relationship were not lost on Iron. He liked Fabiana. He admired her strength and also the endearing streak of vulnerability within her. At times during their meeting, it was as if she'd been asking him to help her but in what way she had not disclosed.

He liked that too, the way she managed to be open and forward yet at the same time reticent and cautious. She'd made it clear she looked to him for strength, and that she wanted to be a part of both his and Rose's life. No doubt she'd think differently if she heard about Rose's latest escapade. Not even the tolerant Lady Copper could possibly condone such actions.

Behind him, Iron heard Captain Coffin clear his throat. The man was uncomfortable with the silence that had followed his report.

Lord Iron did not turn round. 'Are you absolutely sure my daughter was with him?' His voice was as cold as the frozen waste beyond the city.

Coffin spoke humbly. 'Regrettably, my lord.'

'And she admitted to conducting some kind of relationship with the criminal?'

'Virtually, my lord . . .'

A vast groan shook the city outside and seemed to echo in Lord Iron's heart. He was held in the steely grip of emotions he could barely comprehend. 'If you lie, Coffin, for your own disgustingly meagre advantage, I shall destroy you.'

Coffin came to Lord Iron's side so he could not avoid looking at him. 'I swear to you that Lady Rose is part of Silverskin's band, my lord. She fought with him and against me.'

Lord Iron clasped his cold hands together and spoke more to himself than to the Captain. 'She never embraced authority. She never understood its importance. This explains her absences and that outlaw's ability to evade capture.' He felt as if his whole body wanted to shake. But if he allowed it to the shaking would not stop and he would shatter to pieces. He was part of the city, its leader. He crumbled within as Karadur crumbled. Perhaps this revelation was inevitable. 'Coffin, where is she?'

'I think she must still be in the sewers, my lord. We have sealed every entrance we know of. Every inch of Karadur will be searched, and . . . the place below. I would like to search her apartments now.'

'Search my daughter's private apartments!' Lord Iron wheeled round to him and Coffin took a step back. 'You forget your place. If anyone should make such a search, it will be me.'

'First we have to find them,' Coffin said, unperturbed.

The captain had changed, Iron realized. Here was a man who believed himself cuckolded. *My last ally, lost,* he thought. The grim black smoke from the foundries seeped through Lord Iron's heart. He felt weary now. *Rose, how could you?* 'Whatever unwise activities Lady Rose is involved in, she is still of the Metal. She is still my Heir-in-Waiting, and I have faith that she will come to understand her destiny. Make no mistake, Coffin. Silverskin has seduced her, blinded her. She is young, impetuous, romantic. She must be made to see reason.'

Coffin shifted uncomfortably. 'But if I come across her, then surely I must take her into custody? We must learn from her the nature of Silverskin's abilities.'

'You will do your duty by apprehending outlaws – and whoever chooses to keep their company. But you will do no more than your duty. I grow tired of your follies and obsessions.'

'My lord, you must face up to the facts. Silverskin and his allies control such powers!'

'Tricks and illusions!'

'No, they are supernatural powers, my lord. It must be said! I have seen the creatures they can summon. We must face up to reality, because it is the only defence we have. I haven't slept since last night. I have pondered everything that has happened, until my mind reeled with it. I saw what Silverskin did yesterday. I was blinded by fury at the time, but in the small hours of the night it came back to me. I believe he could have destroyed my men and me with a single word. He did not. There was something different about him.'

'He stole the woman you loved,' Iron snapped cruelly. 'Are you so easily seduced?'

Iron flushed. 'I make no secret of my feelings for your daughter. She abused me, yes, because I know she was aware of how I felt. That sounds importunate to you, I know, yet it is the truth. Lady Rose has made a point of cultivating my cooperation, using my feelings against me. Yesterday I hated her for it. But if I am to be all that I aspire to be, I must be greater than that. Silverskin and Lady Rose must be captured, because they have transgressed the law, but they know something – something vital.'

Iron made a sound of scornful irritation, but Coffin pressed on. 'In all honesty, I now doubt whether their seizure is possible by any normal means. That is why Lady Rose's private chambers should be searched. We may learn something there. At present I have no information on how to trap them. The usual methods are clearly ineffective.'

Lord Iron was gratified to see Coffin wince beneath his disapproving gaze. 'I have heard quite enough of this! Your dented pride has forced you to seek unlikely causes for your failures. Desperation makes you babble lunacy! Take control of yourself. Go about your business, man. Search the city. Do your duty. But do not bring me tales of demons and ghosts. Otherwise your next visit to the Gragonatt Fortress could be permanent.'

Coffin hesitated, then bowed his head. 'Yes, my lord.'

Lord Iron knew the man who left the Camera was a troubled, puzzled creature. If Coffin's resolve was crumbling, all must be indeed lost. Iron returned to his contemplation of the image of gouting stacks. Tears gathered in his eyes. The blood-red light was too intense out there, too fierce. He turned away from it. Despite what he'd said to Coffin, he knew the man was right. The past had come back, with all its gibbering horrors. He'd been a fool and perhaps should have heeded others' words before this had happened. Steel had warned him, and Rose, and even Fabiana. If he'd dared to open up the old thoroughfares and investigate Shriltasi weeks ago, would it have made any difference? Rose had asked him to meet with Silverskin, and now he could understand why. She must have been intimate with him for months. How could she keep such a secret? Why hadn't he seen her duplicity in her eyes? *But Rose is no fool*, he told himself. *Think about it. She tried to tell you, but you wouldn't listen. Perhaps you should have gone along with her suggestion. No avenue of investigation should have been left unexplored. Perhaps Silverskin might have had something useful to say.*

But it was too late now. Rose was estranged from him, and the city was dying around them. He remembered Max as he'd seen him in Gragonatt a year before: defeated, despairing, certainly incapable of escape. Something had happened to Silverskin then. It was clear now that no human hands had aided his breakout. The signs had been there all along, but fear had ensured that no one had talked about them when they should have done. Common people in the streets had more sense than the Council. They'd guessed it, seen something in Silverskin that made him different. But what was his part in the drama now?

Lord Iron swivelled the mirrors of the Camera until the decaying city spun around him in a dizzying kaleidoscope of colour and broken images. 'Rose, where are you?' he said aloud. 'Come back to me.'

Serenia Silverskin contemplated the man before her. He looked old now, poor thing. Knowledge had made him old. Menevek Vane had played his role well through the years, but he'd never been meant to get this close to the fire. Now he was burned by it, changed irrevocably. He sat in her parlour, lost in his thoughts, drawn there because there was nowhere else to go. Serenia had reached out to him, led his weary feet from Shriltasi. Perhaps that was cruel, but at this time Serenia had to ignore feelings of pity and compassion. Menni didn't want explanations. He merely wanted to forget, to be absolved of his responsibilities. The room was silent but for the crackle of burning logs in the hearth.

Serenia sipped from a porcelain cup and said softly, 'Menni, your tea is getting cold. You should drink it. Tea is a great restorative. Why, some of the greatest men in Karadur come to drink my tea.'

Menni glanced up at her and hastily took a drink from his cooling cup. 'Things are not well with me, my lady. Things are not well.'

Serenia smiled at him. There were herbs in the tea that would help soothe his mind and bring a little joy where there was none. 'I know, Menni. Drink up.'

She remembered the day he had first come to her, a man in his prime. He'd been a flirt in those days, brash and full of bravado. But she'd always known he was the right choice. She'd told him back then, 'You needn't play the game with me, young man. Never forget that I can see into your heart, and what I see is good. So stop posturing and trying to appear otherwise.'

It had been easy to subdue him, although she doubted anyone other than she could affect him that strongly. 'You are going to have a baby,' she'd told him.

He'd laughed, of course. She'd let his laughter run its course and by the time it had petered out he'd seen the steel in her eyes and had known she spoke literally. There had been excuses: his lifestyle, his income, his notoriety. Serenia, who knew all of this already, listened patiently and then rang a bell by the hearth. A girl had come in, carrying Maximilian in her arms. Sophelia had been dead for only a day.

'This is no ordinary child,' Serenia had said, 'and when you have taken him from this place, you might as well forget you ever came here. He is yours now. You are his father.'

Menni grimaced and the child was put before him. He had twitched aside the swaddling and looked within. Serenia had known that the moment Menni saw the child, he would be ensorcelled. The shine had been strong in Max, even then.

Menni had returned to Serenia's house only once and that had been to discuss with her the possibility of Max being restored to the Metal. Serenia had known the experience for Max would be dreadful, but also that it was necessary. She had let Menni think he'd dreamed up the idea himself. She had argued with him a little.

Menni had never really questioned why the Silverskins should want to give one of their own to him. He clearly did not believe in the tales of sorcery and magic. He had simply believed he'd been chosen because Max was rather an embarrassment to both families and they needed a good foster parent for the boy. Menni had been convinced he was a fine specimen of humanity, the best. And, in essence, that had been the reason he'd been chosen anyway. But Serenia had also wanted danger for Max, the grittiness of life on the edge. She had wanted to immerse him in the warrens of criminality so that he could discover morals and ethics for himself. 'If you are a jewel,' she had told the child before Menni had taken him, 'then your shine must eventually show through.'

It seemed as if all that had happened only moments ago, but in fact it had been twenty-five years. The arrogant dandy of the streets was now an ailing man in his fifties, old before his time. And Max . . . *Ah, Max. No one yet knows what you are, or will become.*

'Menni, I have one last task for you,' Serenia said.

Menni looked up at her. He'd been staring into the fire. She saw the fear in his eyes: fear of what she might ask, and fear of herself, because he knew he wouldn't be able to refuse.

'It is not that great a task,' she said gently. 'If anything, it's the completion of something you've already begun.'

He shrugged and said nothing.

Serenia got up and went to a cupboard. From this she removed an object wrapped in silvery-grey silk. It rested in her hands like the severed head of a man. She sat down again and unwrapped the object in her lap.

Menni drew in his breath. She heard his teacup rattle against the saucer and looked up. 'You recognize this?'

His eyes were round. 'You know I do,' he said. 'I should have known it would be in your keeping.'

'Hardly that,' Serenia said. She put her hands upon the Jewel of All Time and her fingers became silhouettes against its light. 'When you dislodged the Jewel from its plinth, you released it from a kind of imprisonment. The Lords have contained its power for millennia, for they feared it. For a while, it left this world and fell through the layers of the multiverse, affecting other realities in its passage. The necessary transformation in Karadur could only begin to occur once the stabilizing influence of the Shren Diamond was absent.'

Serenia could tell that Menni hardly heard her words. He did not want to hear them. 'I summoned the Jewel back to us. And now you must give it to Max.'

Menni frowned. 'I don't know where he is.'

'I can tell you where to find him. It is quite essential that you – as the nearest he has to a father – help him fulfil his destiny. Will you do this?'

Menni nodded slowly, his eyes never leaving the Jewel. 'Once it blinded me.'

Serenia laughed. 'No, Menni, no, it didn't. Quite the opposite.'

Chapter Five

Birth of the Deva

Max awoke in the pale light of dawn, which came as orange flame through the windows of Rose's eyrie. His companions were grouped around him, awake but tired. When he opened his eyes, they became alert. Their voices were a babble around him. For some minutes he could not understand their language but he could tell that they were relieved he had come back to them. *So close, yet so far.* Knowledge hung heavily within him.

Rose had made breakfast and then told Max about her dream. 'We need to find the Jewel today,' she said. 'I'm sure we can.'

There was no doubt of it in Max's mind. After hearing Rose's words he knew he couldn't avoid the Jewel, even if he'd wanted to. He only hoped he'd have enough strength to replace it in its proper setting. If not, Rose must do it.

'How do you feel?' Jack Ash asked.

Max wasn't sure. He was alive, that was all he knew. The silverheart was a fire beneath his ribs, but it hadn't taken his life. He knew now that it never would. That would have been the easy way. He didn't answer Jack's question but Jack reacted as if he had. He simply looked into Max's eyes, turned to his sister and said, 'He's still with us.'

'Did you dream, Max?' Rose asked. She kneeled before him, her hands curled around his, which lay limply upon his thighs.

He nodded.

She closed her eyes, drew in her breath. 'Do you know what you have to do?'

Again, a nod.

'Can you tell us?'

He did have a voice but it didn't seem to be his own. He could hear it but it was outside of him. 'The Old Forge, the crucible.'

Rose thrust her hands between her knees, her back rigid. 'You intend to unite the artefacts there?'

'Yes. It is the place. The heart of The Old Forge.'

A great booming crash came from outside. It sounded as if an iron-clad building had just tumbled to the ground. So little time. The city was breaking up.

'Today, we will walk the streets of Karadur unseen,' said Jack Ash. His voice rang with the certainty of a prophet's.

Outside, it seemed to Max as if the entire city reflected his own condition. As they walked through the streets, the buildings corroded around them. But perhaps that was only in his head. Girders and buttresses creaked and splintered, and ancient brick crumbled to dust. The air was full of it: an acrid powder mingled with ash and smoke.

Max could hear the voice of Karadur. Day by day it had become louder. The creak of machinery, the bleat of human cries, the tumble of stone: this was the lament of the city as she mourned the approach of death. People were running wild-eyed through the streets, aimlessly, panicking. Routine had foundered and the hell-light of Sekmet rained down upon all. A madness had come upon the city. And those who were not mad could slip invisibly among those who were.

Max wore the dragon chain mail, bore the owl ring on his right hand and carried the gibbold weapon at his belt. The mail covered his head and hung to below his knees. It was so light, he could barely feel it. He led his companions through the open iron portal of The Old Forge. They were greeted by immense leaping shadows, jets of fire, smoke and steam. The main crucible presided over all, an ancient deity, a cauldron of creation. White-hot metal bubbled in its depths, tended by the sweating foundrymen whose great muscles rippled like living red metal. They toiled on, as if oblivious of the lunacy that gripped the city outside. Perhaps they didn't notice that the creeping decrepitude that assailed Karadur had even found a way into the eternal foundry. Rust pocked the walls, the stairs and walkways. Some of the swinging buckets of boiling metal had cracked, so that molten iron dribbled to the black floor. Occasionally, a flaming splash might fall upon the hide of a foundryman. They would not always notice that they burned. Their backs bent and straightened, bent and straightened, as they worked blindly on, slaves to the metal they served.

Max went directly to the main crucible and stood beneath it. It was a monstrous pot-bellied vessel, constructed of an exotic alloy known only to the foundrymen. It glowed with gold and crimson streaks of light, which streamed over its surface of steely blue-grey. The rivets that held it together were surrounded by a strange green iridescence. Occasionally, the crucible appeared to bulge, as if alive. From its vast mouth poured a constant flow of molten metal. Below it, roaring furnaces gave it life. On gantries above it, foundrymen with skin the colour of old terracotta worked constantly to sustain the crucible, to offer it the scrap metal on which it fed.

Max took out the spellstone and made three signs upon the air.

Within moments, the foundrymen ceased their labours and began to drop their tools. They straightened up, faces aflame with wonder and terror. Max knew they could see Sekmet stalking down the main aisle of the foundry. She purred to them, their goddess.

She came to a halt behind Max at the crucible. Hovering over her was the copper Owl, while the Dragon writhed at her feet.

The foundrymen began to chant in a single wailing voice. Their arms made sacred gestures. They beat their chests. The foundry filled with the cacophony.

Inevitably, it lured Lord Iron from his office. He stood upon the platform high above the foundry floor.

'The first of them,' Max said.

'Father,' Rose murmured.

'First of who?' Jenny asked.

'The witnesses, the players,' Max replied.

Above them, Lord Iron gripped the rail of the platform and stared down upon his workers. Max knew the man could see the legendary beasts. Such was his astonishment that he did not notice who else was present.

'Back to work!' he yelled. 'Pay no heed to these illusions.'

The foundrymen turned to stare up at him, moving like a single unit.

'The foundry cannot fail,' Iron cried in a hoarse voice. 'We must maintain the city. Make the metal to sustain it. Back to work!' His words were tinged with madness.

Max could see into Lord Iron's mind. He saw the terror there, the grief, the feeling of having lost control. It was like being trapped in a nightmare, aware of it yet unable to wake.

A few of the foundrymen obeyed their master's command and picked up their fallen tools, but most of them were still entranced by the sight of the golden gibboldess. Max knew that to them, she was no illusion, and no one could persuade them otherwise. She was the resolution of all their forgotten dreams.

'Must I summon the Battle Boys to make you obey?' Lord Iron roared.

Still the foundrymen were unmoved by his words.

'Father!' Rose cried.

Lord Iron froze. Then, with unnatural slowness, he turned to look down upon his daughter. His expression was unreadable.

Rose ran towards the steps that led to the office. But another voice cried out, 'Halt! In the name of the Metal, halt!' The words echoed round the vault of the foundry.

Rose turned, drawing her sword instinctively. It was the voice of Cornelius Coffin. Max looked round and saw Coffin silhouetted at the portal, with a group of Irregulars behind him.

'The second,' said Max.

'Throw the artefacts into the crucible,' Jenny urged. 'Hurry, Sir Fox.'

Max did not move. He waited for another presence, unsure of who it might be. But he felt it before it came. He felt it slinking through the streets, smelled the burning stench of its concentrated purpose. It lived in a human body, but it was not human. It was foul matter, the dark flotsam of the multiverse, antagonistic to all living things, to expansion, creation and elevated expressions of feeling. This was what Sophelia had talked about: the forces that opposed his destiny.

'Come, then,' Max said in his mind.

Coffin and his Irregulars came marching down the main aisle, Coffin's eyes fixed on Rose. He didn't seem to notice the fabulous beasts or even Max himself. Max could see the man's pain, the shards of shattered dreams that pierced his heart.

'Coffin, arrest them!' Lord Iron called.

'Father, no!' Rose cried.

Lord Iron called desperately to his daughter. 'Rose, I know you have acted in ignorance, not from evil. With you beside me, reunited, we shall resume our authority, our great responsibility. You will uphold all the traditions of the Metal. You, Rose, will sustain us. Come back to me, Rose . . .'

Rose began to sprint once more towards the stairs. Max knew it wasn't that she wanted to rejoin her father in the way he planned. Max couldn't call her back. He caught Jack Ash's eye and saw that he also sensed what must come. That was only natural. Jack was familiar with this force. Max could see it so clearly now. Jack was an expression of the cosmic joker, random chance, which was the glue that sustained the many levels of reality. Without chaos, there could not be order, and vice versa. They existed within each other. Balance must be restored.

Rose had almost reached the platform.

'Fox, the icons!' Jenny cried, taking hold of Max's arm and shaking him. 'Come back to us. Do what has to be done.'

He heard it. A hiss.

Rose was reaching for her father with desperate arms. Lord Iron stood rigidly, held in the grip of battling emotions. He wanted to break down and fall into his daughter's arms. He wanted to strike her. He wanted to die. A shadow hung over him, a foul, boiling shadow. Then it assumed a physical shape, manifesting from the darkness of the narrow walkway that ran down the side of Lord Iron's office. A woman in a long dark cloak, her arms raised. It was she who had assumed the role of Sekmet's high priestess. For a moment, she appeared to Max as a hideous spider-woman. Her arms were stiff and contorted, held over her head. Her movements were a furtive scuttling. She had crawled up the side of the foundry that way, dropping down silently through a grimy skylight hidden among the great rafters overhead. A poisonous spider. Then she was human again, her face hidden by a cowl, one arm raised. Metal glinted in the red-shot darkness. She held a knife.

Max could tell that Rose thought the woman was attacking her father. She did not realize she herself was under attack. The dark one would be attracted to destroy anyone of whom Max was fond. And he was fond of Rose, he knew that now.

Rose lunged forward, uttering a cry of warning. Lord Iron wheeled round and staggered away from the woman who came swooping towards him.

Jenny Ash uttered a cry of revulsion and pushed past her brother to go to Rose's aid. Max knew she could smell the essence of the dark one, the rottenness that ate at her soul. She embodied the opposite of *barishi*.

Coffin advanced more quickly now, shouting orders to his Irregulars who began to run, some towards the crucible, others towards Lord Iron's office.

The icon beasts were quiescent, awaiting Max's command. He would not even think it. The gibboldess did not respond to the woman who wanted to wield her power. Max knew that in these final moments the beast was not even aware of her.

Jack Ash stared at Max, as if trying to burrow with his sight through to Max's mind. He was like the beasts, waiting.

Not yet.

On the platform outside Lord Iron's office, the priestess grabbed hold of Lord Iron around the throat. Her blade glittered. Rose hesitated and, in that moment, the priestess leaped from the platform, taking Lord Iron with her.

In slow motion, they fell to the foundry floor, the priestess's robes billowing about them. Rose practically flew to the platform rail and looked over, her face distorted with terror and shock. Jenny, on the stairs, began to run back down them.

Lord Iron's body hit the floor with a sickening thud. The priestess landed on top of him, covering him with her robes. Then, with slow, stretching movements, the priestess uncurled herself and stood up. Lord Iron did not move. The priestess's hood had been flung back in the descent. Now she threw back her head and uttered an inhuman guttural roar. Her hair threshed around her wildly. A Lady of the Metal. A great Lady.

'Fabiana!' Rose cried.

'Lady Copper,' murmured Jack Ash in wonderment. 'I suspected Steel.'

Fabiana twisted her head round to an unnatural degree on her neck and hissed up at Rose. 'Little fool,' she snarled. 'You should have been with me. I would have been lenient with you. The Copper woman cares for you.'

The priestess prowled towards the crucible, her eyes glowing with crimson light. Jenny Ash hurled herself at the woman with serpent speed but the priestess merely knocked the Ashen aside with a careless hand. Jenny's body flew through the air and landed with a crash in a pile of scrap metal. The priestess's sights were set on Max. He could sense that her whole being was concentrated on destroying him. Her hands were hooked claws, ready to tear the silverheart from his breast.

Irregulars had surrounded Max and Jack but made no move to lay hands on them. Others had reached Lady Copper and tried to restrain her but she shoved them aside even more easily than she'd disposed of Jenny. When she struck out at them, blood flew from the wounds. Her hands alone were greater weapons than the sharpest blade. She had brought with her into the foundry the essence of primal fear. It made the air damp and cold. It froze human hearts with recognition of their greatest terror. Not even the dour Irregulars could be unaffected. Coffin stood some feet behind his men, unable to move.

Max knew that this was not Fabiana Copper. She no longer existed; she had died that morning. The transformation would have been slow, creeping through the unsuspecting victim like a deadly disease. This was an incarnation of anti-life, contained within a human form but as large and formless as the multiverse itself. He could not fight it. The priestess hissed and stamped her feet against the ground, making the whole building shake. Spars of metal crashed down from the ceiling. Fabiana's spine was bent, her hands flexing upon the air.

Max turned to Coffin. 'This is the true enemy of Karadur,' he said. 'Not me, nor anyone of the free zones. If Karadur had remained true to its purpose, this force would have found no entry portal here. The Metal could not overcome their human failings. They became greedy, aggressive. The Clan Wars were the greatest rituals to invoke this dark force. It has held sway here for millennia. I was born to dispel it.'

The priestess laughed, a low bestial grunt. 'You! Small fleshly thing. You are nothing.' She scuttled forward, arms hooked and raised.

To Max's surprise, Coffin uttered a hoarse wordless cry and sprang forward. But Max did not let the man intervene. He opened his arms and took the priestess into his embrace. At once she twisted and writhed in his grasp, tearing and biting. He felt her teeth sink into his cheek, rip away the flesh. Her feet kicked at his shins. He felt the bones splinter. The silverheart raged within him, its tendrils fastening about his natural heart.

Max drew in his breath. 'Of the nine three are made. Of the three must the fourth be made. Of the four, let one be made. Mighty powers of the multiverse, I call upon ye. Aid me. Hear my petition.'

These words invoked the priestess to greater fury. Max knew that very presently, even though she was partly constrained by his grip, she would shred him to pieces. It was time.

In his mind he sent out a beacon call to the icon beasts. The spellstone at his neck grew hot. The three creatures came to him and lifted both him and the priestess in their paws and claws. They flew towards the crucible.

In the last moments, with the raging heat searing up to eclipse even the burn of the silverheart, Max saw the face of Rose Iron looking down upon him. He saw the love in her eyes, the greatest love. She would throw herself into the crucible instead, if it would save him.

'Max, no!'

He sent a command to the icon beasts. *Now*. They released their burden and Max and Fabiana fell.

The white-hot metal consumed them.

Rose screamed. She could not help it. It was the scream of the grief of the world, low and despairing. She could not believe such a sound could come from a human body. It was like vomiting grief. She wanted to expel it until her throat bled. Was this how it was supposed to end? Serenia had given no hint. What about the Jewel? Max had not fulfilled his task.

The foundry was utterly silent. No one moved. Even the sounds of madness from outside had ceased. Karadur was held in stasis. Rose could feel that everyone present at the crucible, from the Ashen to the dumbest Irregular, was affected by Max's sacrifice. Even if they did not understand it, or the reason for it, it moved them.

Rose's eyes filled with tears. The dark night of the soul had not passed, it seemed. She was still there in the cold, filled with hopelessness. Briefly, she rested her forehead against the rail around the platform, pressing her flesh into it, conjuring pain.

'Rose.'

Jack's voice.

She looked up and saw, above the crucible, an image of the spellstone talisman hanging in the air. A fourth symbol glowed upon it now: the Heart of Silver. The fourth icon.

'It was the silverheart all the time,' Jack called. 'It was Max himself. Even I did not realize that.'

Rose walked numbly down the stairs to the foundry floor, where Jenny had picked herself up and was now rubbing at her bruised limbs. Rose went at once to her father, who was being examined by Captain Coffin. It was strange to be close to Coffin now. It seemed all their reasons to be enemies had vanished. 'Is he alive?' Rose asked.

Coffin nodded. 'Barely.'

'Jack!' Rose called. 'Help me.'

While Rose cradled her father's head, Jack Ash ran his hands over Lord Iron's body. Everyone felt numb, Rose knew. No one could take in what had happened.

'Can he be saved?' Rose asked.

Jack drew in his breath. 'There is life within him, and the injuries are not beyond my scope, but . . .' He looked into Rose's eyes. 'He is a broken man in more than one way. He wants to leave this world.'

'Father,' Rose said desperately, pressing her fingers against his cheeks. 'Don't leave me. I have to tell you so much.' She bent her head so that her forehead touched her father's. She could not lose both of them. It was too much to bear.

Lord Iron coughed feebly and a few spots of blood dribbled out over his lips. He tried to raise a shaking hand and Rose caught hold of it, gripped it hard. It felt frail and slender in her own hand. The fingers were so cold. 'I love you,' she said. 'Father, believe me when I say I have done nothing wrong. Karadur is my life, my soul. All my actions have been in the name of our city. Max has sacrificed himself that Karadur might live.'

Lord Iron opened his eyes very slightly. Just damp slivers could be seen glinting between his papery eyelids. 'Child,' he whispered. 'The secret is that we were once a great civilization of two cities. One lay above, the other beneath. They were sundered . . .' He stopped, coughing more blood.

'I know,' Rose said. 'You don't have to tell me. I know my heritage, and I shall use the knowledge wisely. You must not doubt that.'

'Fabiania will teach you,' Lord Iron said. 'She has promised.'

'Yes,' Rose murmured. 'I know. Don't try to talk, father.'

Lord Iron closed his eyes.

Coffin put out a hand and gripped Rose's shoulder. 'We must carry him home,' he said in a low voice. 'Summon the family physicians.'

Rose shook her head. 'No, he wouldn't survive it. Send your Irregulars to bring someone here.' It would only be a formality. Rose knew in her heart her father would die. She could not find the strength to shake the captain off and realized she didn't want to. Coffin, in his own way, had cared for her father too. Whatever set them apart, whatever misconceptions Coffin might have about so many things, he had always acted in the manner he thought best and right. He was not an enemy, just ignorant.

A couple of Coffin's men left the building to find physicians. All around the foundry, the foundrymen began a low lament, joined by the voices of the Irregulars who instinctively felt the song. This was the lament for the passing of the Lord, for Prometheus Iron, but also for Max. Jenny came limping to Rose's other side and curled an arm around her shoulder. She pressed her face into Rose's hair. Rose could hear her low sobs, feel the heat of her tears. This was so right. Those who had opposed her now joined her in grief. They were in accord.

Jack began to murmur softly, in a tongue Rose did not know. It was a prayer, she could tell that.

'Where's Max?'

The voice was low, querulous. Rose looked up, blinked away tears. A man stood before them, an old man. She recognized him from her first meeting with Max in the market. Menni Vane. He held an object wrapped in cloth.

'Gone,' she said.

Menni's face crumpled into a perplexed frown. 'But I have to give him this. Lady Serenia sent me.'

He unwrapped the object. Rays of light spilled from it. The Jewel of All Time.

Fresh tears fell from Rose's eyes. *Too late. Too late.*

The lament of the foundrymen grew louder and the sound seemed to conjure power within the jewel. It glowed brightly in Menni's hands, radiating rays of every hue. It seemed to change the song of the mourners so that it sounded like the chorus of a million human voices raised in joy, not sorrow. It was a song to celebrate the triumphant mastery of the immortal soul.

Up above, the great crucible shuddered. All eyes turned towards it. It swung upon its mighty chains, coughing out gouts of white smoke. There were shapes in the smoke, writhing and turning. Were these the totem beasts reborn?

The crucible began to rock more rapidly. Gobbets of molten metal flew from it.

Then, with a mighty cry that could penetrate the furthest reaches of the multiverse, something erupted from the crucible. It soared up into the air, human in form, yet with clashing copper wings, blazing dragon eyes, and a skin of tawny, gibbold gold.

It was an angel, whose heart blazed silver on its chest.

A deva with the face of Maximilian Silverskin.

The foundrymen all fell to their knees. The deva, the fourth icon of the Clans, hung above the crucible, shaking its wings. It flung back its great golden head and flexed its steel fists. A laugh of pure joy and freedom echoed around the foundry.

The deva turned its monstrous, beautiful face towards Rose and her companions. For a moment Rose feared it would turn upon them. Its teeth glittered sharply behind its fierce smile.

Then, raising its magnificent head, it roared with lust and fury in celebration of life restored. Its feathers glowed with vitality, its eyes burned with inner fire. With a crack of its wings, amber eyes blazing and ivory teeth clashing, the deva flexed its muscles. It roared again and swooped down towards them.

Max was aware within the skin of the deva. It was the same as when he'd been possessed by the gibbold power, only so much stronger now because he comprised all four icons. He'd lost consciousness until he'd risen like a phoenix from the boiling crucible. There was no pain now.

He flew down towards the Jewel and plucked it from Menni's hands, registering only briefly the way Rose and the others cringed away from him. Then he flew high towards the foundry roof. There, amid the sluggish coils of black smoke and dancing cinders, he roared a song of rapture. It was his gift to those below. He knew it could not fail to touch their hearts, their souls.

Max burst through a filth-streaked skylight, surrounded by flying splinters of glass. He swooped out into the cold, clear air above the city. He looked down upon a vast complex of ruins and decaying monuments, of buildings scarcely able to keep their shape. Chaos had already touched the physical reality of Karadur. Grimy smoke covered all, with occasional glimmers of dim yellow light guttering through.

Max flew down into the streets, towards the Grand Market. His powerful wings carried him through the outer gates, past the astonished guards and over the outdoor market, where the few stall-holders who'd bothered to open their businesses stared up in awe.

His wordless song harmonized with a high, sweet sound, which emanated from the Jewel he carried. The echoes of this song rang through the entire multiverse. Every living ear could hear it. It reverberated throughout the vast eternity of matter, possibility upon possibility, world upon world.

Now Max flew up through up the outer struts and buttresses of the Guild Tower. He could see the faces of the Council members looking from the windows of the Hall of Justice. They had no doubt gathered in panic, seeking Lord Iron who, despite their criticisms, was still their rock, their tower. Now they stared out in shock at the wondrous being that flew past them. They had no choice but to confront their prejudices and self-delusions. They looked upon the end of their rigid authority, the shattering of their fearful traditions. Only one face seemed free of terror, and in that face, Max saw fierce wonder, the realization that dreams can come true. It was the face of Carinthia Steel.

Rose had considered Carinthia a threat, Max knew, but now he could see into Lady Steel's heart. She had been judged for her outspoken character, condemned as the enemy, when in reality that entity had been hidden behind the mild façade of Fabiana Copper. Like Rose, she'd been looking for answers, resentful that knowledge had been kept from her. She was not without fault, but if she had been Head of the Council, as she'd desired, events might have progressed rather differently over these last days. Her time, however, was yet to come. Max knew that, in the future, Rose Iron would have an ally in Lady Steel. It would never be an easy alliance, because Carinthia liked to be in control, but Max was confident Rose would be capable of handling her. She would channel Lady Steel's talents to their best use and educate her in areas where her knowledge was lacking or her opinions biased. Carinthia would comply because she respected strength and innovation. She was an example of the new face of the Metal, its potential.

Max wheeled up above the Guild Tower, higher still into the clear cold air. At its summit four cupped hands – of gold, silver, iron and copper – reached beseechingly to the sky. They seemed to yearn for what they had once held. Max could see the past now, as a spectral image overlaying the present. He could see the Shren Diamond lying radiant amid the hands, its life-giving rays falling throughout Karadur. He could see within the tower, where the magi of the Clans channelled the power of the diamond for acts of creation. A golden age, yet within that gold a darker element had emerged. What had caused it? A petty squabble among the alchemists, an aching resentment that had bloomed in silence and darkness? Perhaps it would never be known, but a chink in the fabric of reality had unleashed the force that had animated the Clan Wars and created the Reformation. That force had been banished now.

Max flew through the ornate metalwork of the tower's crown and, hovering above the summit, gently placed the Shren Diamond into those waiting hands.

The unearthly music around him shrieked to a great crescendo, as if all the metal in creation had a living voice. A vast blossoming of rainbow light poured from the Jewel – countless beams of radiance that spread throughout the multiverse, bringing life, hope and the chance of a new beginning to all the creatures that dwelled there.

Max tumbled backwards. It seemed as if he fell through space, witness to the limitless variety of the multiverse, that rich, fantastic balance of Law and Chaos that spread to infinity. Layers of reality flashed before his eyes. He could see the great web of energy that comprised creation. Everything was within his reach. Everything. His mother had told him: you cannot make anything up. It already exists. Take control of your dreams. They have already happened.

My dream is that Karadur-Shriltasi is restored, Max thought, and knew that he could will it so. For just a few brief moments, he was the essence of creation, forged in the heat of the crucible.

He flexed his great wings and swooped down over the city. He knew that it was not his task to will the crumbling buildings back to their original states. They would be rebuilt by human hands. It was his task to restore the hearts and souls of the inhabitants. Through his own unbelievable existence, he would rip the sleep from their eyes. He could feel all the faces looking up at him, feel their shock, terror and wonder. But he could also feel the hope within them. They had mourned their magic, without knowing what they mourned. Now it flew, resurrected, above them.

Max soared to the walls of the city and saw that beyond them the ice had begun to melt. It would not disappear immediately, but change had begun. Where once poisonous smoke had belched from fissures in the ice, lazy steam now coiled up into the air. Life would spread out from the city, from above and below. In ages to come, farms and villages would exist here, and oceans and field and forests. It would be everything the Karadurian hearts had yearned for, yet had not dared to imagine.

Max wheeled back to the city and flew as straight as an arrow down through the Well of the Heart. He had to see Shriltasi. It must be made lush once more. As he flew over the forests, the lakes and the fields, he could see that harmony had seeped back into the underworld. The synthetic sunlight seemed brighter, conjuring more vivid colours in the foliage. The Ashen danced through the fields, clearly aware of the great change. When they saw him soaring overhead, they did not fall silent in shock, as the Karadurians had done, but called and waved to him.

Karadur-Shriltasi and her people had been denied for too long. Now everything that his mother had ever seen or dreamed of was possible, all that her ancestors had known and tried to communicate. It had been folly to focus only upon one aspect of reality. The Lords had tyrannized the citizens' minds. Ignorance had been made a virtue. It had led to decay and to death.

But now the Reconciliation had come. It was a time to celebrate.

Max turned back to Karadur-Shriltasi, the city at the centre of the multiverse. A city whose slender towers of ivory, gold, bronze and ebony would one day rise afresh against the bright horizon.

At The Old Forge, Rose and the others had emerged into the daylight. Jack Ash and Cornelius Coffin carried Lord Iron between them, accompanied by a pair of physicians. Menni was supported by Jenny Ash. He looked confused and dazed. *But not for long, old friend*, Max thought. *In the light of this new day, you will be healed of your hurts.*

Max landed lightly before the group and they shrank back. He raised his wings over Lord Iron and placed his steely hand over the old ruler's heart. He could feel the faint flutter of life, the stronger flutter of a soul seeking escape from the flesh. He spoke without words, directly to Lord Iron's mind. 'It is done. Karadur is restored. You may leave in peace, go to the shining place that awaits you.'

Max. Lord Iron's voice was a tiny whisper inside Max's head. *I can see you. What you are. I was wrong . . .*

'You did only what you had to do, played your part,' Max said. 'It was necessary.'

Care for her, Lord Iron said.

'With all my heart,' Max replied.

He withdrew his awareness from the dying Lord's mind and opened his eyes. The first person he saw was Rose, her face. Even in grief and suffering she was beautiful, and it was not simply a surface beauty. 'Do not fear for your father,' Max said. 'He is at peace.'

Rose stared at him, mute, her face pale.

'Do not fear me, either,' Max said. 'What you see before you has a short life this day. But the man I am within it will live on. We will live on.'

He gathered Rose to his breast, enfurling her in his copper feathers. He could feel her living warmth, smell the strength of her spirit. Holding her in his arms, he opened his wings, which beat upon the air. 'Let us enjoy this while we can.' He bore her high above the reborn city.

They flew on magical wings, sure in the knowledge that the world was new and innocent below.

They flew to the highest point, where the Jewel of All Time spilled its life-giving rays over all the city.

They flew in joy and in love.

To fulfil their fabulous destiny.